The Council of Shadows

S. M. STIRLING

The Council of Shadows

A Novel of
THE SHADOWSPAWN

A ROC BOOK

ROC
Published by New American Library, a division of
Penguin Group (USA) Inc., 375 Hudson Street,
New York, New York 10014, USA
Penguin Group (Canada), 90 Eglinton Avenue East, Suite 700, Toronto,
Ontario M4P 2Y3, Canada (a division of Pearson Penguin Canada Inc.)
Penguin Books Ltd., 80 Strand, London WC2R 0RL, England
Penguin Ireland, 25 St. Stephen's Green, Dublin 2,
Ireland (a division of Penguin Books Ltd.)
Penguin Group (Australia), 250 Camberwell Road, Camberwell, Victoria 3124,
Australia (a division of Pearson Australia Group Pty. Ltd.)
Penguin Books India Pvt. Ltd., 11 Community Centre, Panchsheel Park,
New Delhi - 110 017, India
Penguin Group (NZ), 67 Apollo Drive, Rosedale, North Shore 0632,
New Zealand (a division of Pearson New Zealand Ltd.)
Penguin Books (South Africa) (Pty.) Ltd., 24 Sturdee Avenue,
Rosebank, Johannesburg 2196, South Africa

Penguin Books Ltd., Registered Offices:
80 Strand, London WC2R 0RL, England

First published by Roc, an imprint of New American Library,
a division of Penguin Group (USA) Inc.

First Printing, May 2011
10 9 8 7 6 5 4 3 2 1

Copyright © Steven M. Stirling, 2010
All rights reserved

LIBRARY OF CONGRESS CATALOGING-IN-PUBLICATION DATA:

Stirling, S. M.
The council of shadows/S. M. Stirling.
p. cm.—(Shadowspawn; 2)
ISBN 978-0-451-46393-7
I. Title.
PS3569.T543C68 2011
813'.54—dc22   2010052285

Set in Adobe Garamond
Designed by Ginger Legato

Printed in the United States of America

Acknowledgments

Thanks to Richard Foss, for help with the fine details of food, wine, and restaurants, and invaluable hints about Paris and other locations.

To Kier Salmon, for *all sorts* of help throughout construction!

To Marino Panzanelli and Marco Pertoni for help with Italian, and also the other members of the Stirling Listserv.

To Melinda Snodgrass, Emily Mah, George R. R. Martin, Walter Jon Williams, Vic Milan, John J. Miller, Jan Stirling, and Ian Tregellis of Critical Mass, for constant help and advice as the book was under construction.

To Jack Williamson, Fred Pohl, Sprague de Camp, and other Golden Agers for inspiration; and Roger Zelazny and Fred Saberhagen.

To Joe's Diner, which makes the best Greek salad in Santa Fe, and to Roland and Sheila Richter, proprietors, who put up with the weird guy in the far booth cackling and talking to himself as he typed. And to Lisa, favorite waitress.

The Council of Shadows

CHAPTER ONE

Ellen Tarnowski ran through the darkness, darkness so thick that the jungle was merely shapes of a deeper black.

Branches flogged at her naked body, ripping and stinging, stinging again as sweat ran down her body in the hot, airless night. Rocks cut at her feet, and mud clung. Breath rasped in and out through a mouth gone dry as old leather, though she struggled to keep it even, as years of cross-country running had taught her. Fear made her heart thunder between her ribs, and her hands were outstretched to keep her from running into a tree trunk. They did nothing when a foot came down on emptiness. With a scream she pitched forward and tumbled down the slope, clutching at bushes that cut her hands and wrenched loose strands of her long yellow hair.

Behind her came a high, racking snarl that built up into a great squalling feline screech. There was the rage of hunger in it, and killing-lust, and an appalling hint of laughter.

The tumble ended with a thump that knocked the breath out of her, in a little clearing of waist-high grass and flowers that showed like pale trumpets in the night. Clouds parted above, and great strange-colored stars shone like jewels around a pale moon. Ellen pushed herself backwards with hands and heels, her eyes going wider.

A tiger flowed down the slope and slunk into the open. It was nightshade itself, striped in black-on-black, its eyes pools of molten sulfur yellow. It snarled like an ivory-fanged saw as it came forward, placing its paws with slow precision. As the teeth showed a voice sounded in Ellen's mind, hatefully familiar, soft-toned and musical.

Hallo, chérie. *'Allo, my sweet tasty curvy little blond wonton dumpling of delight! Let's* play *now, shall we? Play-play-play!*

It came closer, taunting in its sleek fluid grace. Then its muscles rippled beneath the midnight coat as it crouched to spring.

Now, how about a nice cozy scream? Fear first, mousy-girl. Then the agony. Then the blood, your lovely blood . . .

Ellen did scream as it leapt. Then another streak came through the darkness. The arcs met in midair, and the two huge cats went tumbling over in a blur of striking paws tipped with claws like knives, gleaming fangs and blazing yellow eyes. The newcomer was more massively built, as much like a bear as a cat, tawny colored, with heavy hulking forelimbs and seven-inch fangs that jutted saberlike below its jaws. The tumble ended with both rearing and hammering at each other in a blurring frenzy of paw strokes.

Ellen screamed again, this time in rage. A sword lay near her on the ground, its silvery curved blade marked with glyphs that blazed back the moonlight. She snatched it up, darted in and struck a long lashing blow with both hands on the hilt, as if it were a backhand smash in a game of tennis. The black hide of the tiger parted and blood spilled, the red nearly black itself in the night. She struck again and again and again, lost in the hate that possessed her—

And woke.

"Uhhh. Uhhhh. Uhhhh."

She gasped for breath, feeling her sweat soaking the sheet and suddenly turning cold and gelid, eyes blinking in the light of the bedside lamp. Adrian's hand closed on her arm, careful not to make her feel constrained as a hug might.

"You're awake, darling. You're awake. I'm here."

She grabbed him with a sudden convulsive movement, burrowing into the strength and warmth as his arms closed around her gently. The big room had the still darkness that comes an hour before dawn, and she could smell the sea and cool scents of dew and rock through the balcony windows. After a few moments she began to shiver in reaction, her skin turning to goose bumps. Adrian wrapped her in a blanket and pulled her back against him, rocking her slightly as her dry sobs wound down.

"That was a bad one," she said. "Adrian, was that sabertooth you?"

He nodded, his chin moving against her head. "Yes. I walked into that part of the dream."

Ellen felt dizzy with exhaustion. "Why didn't you kill her?"

"Too risky, my sweet one. That wasn't Adrienne. Adrienne is dead; what you saw in your dream was a memory, a projection, part of your own psyche. Only you could kill it safely. As you killed Adrienne herself. You were very brave, then and now."

Ellen sighed wearily. "I wish killing the memories were as easy," she said. "I just got around my childhood and then I get more trauma dumped on me. Dad goes, Adrienne steps into the all-powerful-nightmare-abuser slot."

"I am so sorry, my darling," Adrian said softly.

She thumped her fist against his back in weak anger. "Not your fault! *You* didn't do it!"

Then she was too tired to speak, but too shivering-taut to sleep. Adrian laid her down, stripped off the sopping sheets, and began kneading the muscles along her spine with strong, expert fingers. There were muted clicks as things adjusted and relaxed; then he covered her again and brought a glass.

"Drink," he said. "You need to hydrate and get your blood sugar up."

It was sweet lemonade; the landlady of the *pensione* kept a carafe of it in their rooms, squeezed each day from the grove that surrounded the building. She drank it gratefully and lay back in his embrace, cocooned in the blankets.

"Sleep, darling, sleep. I will watch over you."

"Urrgggh," she said.

Ellen knuckled at her eyes. Adrian waited until she'd blinked them clear before sitting down on the edge of the bed. Bright sunlight spilled through the louvers of the bedroom window, falling over the hatched tile floor and cream-colored stucco of the walls and the tumbled linen of the bedding. She sighed and leaned her head against the flat muscle of his shoulder, like hard living rubber under the soft fine-grained olive skin.

"I'm sorry," she said.

"I am sorry that you have the dreams," he said. "I'm glad that I can help."

"Oh, brother, do you ever!" she said, and sighed. "It can't be much fun, being on a honeymoon with someone who wakes up screaming every five or six days, and . . . well, you know, freezes up sometimes."

He chuckled. "Anyone else would be catatonic, or dead, or mad beyond help after six months as my sister's prisoner. You are a very strong person, my love."

Ellen laughed too, ruefully, stretching, aware that she smelled a little of stale fear-sweat.

"I'm sort of a *stinky* person right now. I'll go shower."

"And I will see to breakfast," he said.

God, he's tactful, she thought—right now she wasn't in the mood for a shower *à deux*, something they often enjoyed.

But then again, he's telepathic. Men keep saying women expect *them to read their minds. It's a little odd being married to one who really* can *do it.*

Adrian was usually fairly tactful about reading her actual *thoughts*, but apparently he couldn't help picking up her feelings. The really important thing was that he *cared* about them, too, but actually knowing for a fact what they were made him feel marvelously sensitive to her.

The hot water leached tension out of her muscles; she let it cascade over her face and sighed.

A new life, she thought. *After a near-death experience . . . I don't really miss my old one. In the old one, I didn't have Adrian. But I do miss being* normal, *the way I was back in Santa Fe. Funky-artsy normal, at least. I wonder what's happening back there? Have they forgotten me already? How did they react when I just . . . vanished?*

The Santa Fe Fire Department was turning off their hoses; dank steam rose into the night, and chilly water dripped from the buildings to either side where they'd sprayed to keep the flames from spreading; there was a blank wall across the street. It was high-desert winter, cold, dry, moonlight visible on the white peaks of the Sangres floating off to the north. No city stink, which he liked; there were only sixty thousand people in what passed for New Mexico's capital city.

Capital large town, maybe, Eric Salvador thought.

"So what made it burn down, hey?" he asked the investigator from the fire marshal's office.

"Arson," she said to the detective. "And it burned *up.*"

"Yeah, arson. Some specifics would be nice, Alice," he said.

"That's the thing. I can't find any reason it *should* have burned. None of the usual indicators. It just did."

"Very much."

He ducked under the yellow police tape, a stocky man of thirty or so with a mustache and a blue jowl who'd put on a few pounds lately, not many, not enough to hide his hard outlines, with his coarse black hair still in a high-and-tight. There was a deep scar across one olive cheek, and he rubbed at it with a thumb; it hurt a little sometimes, where the flying metal of the IED had cracked the bone. The scar ran down under his mustache, giving a bit of a quirk to his mouth.

"One thing I can tell you," the investigator said. "This thing burned *hot.*"

"Heavy accelerants? I can't smell anything."

"Right, gasoline or diesel you usually can. But damned if I can prove it yet, maybe with the lab work . . . I'd say yes, though. I've never seen anything like it. It's as if it *wanted* to burn."

"Alice . . ."

"You know I'm not superstitious. But there's no sign it started in one place and spread. Everything capable of combining with oxygen just went up all at once, *whoosh*. The *cutlery* melted, and that's a lot hotter than your typical house fire."

The building had been a little two-story apartment house, one up and one down. This wasn't far off Canyon Road and the strip of galleries, and close to the Acequia Madre, the ancient irrigation canal, which meant it had been fairly expensive. But not close enough to be real adobe, which in Santa Fe meant *old* and *pricey*. Brown stucco pseudo-pueblo-Spanish style built over frame, like nearly everything in town that stayed on the right side of the building code.

Alice had worked with him before. She was a bit older than he—mid-thirties—and always looked tired, her blond hair short and disorderly. He liked the way she never let a detail slip by, no matter how hard she had to work at it.

" 'Santa Fe, where prestige is a mud house on a dirt road,' " she said, quoting a local saying. "So it's not likely an insurance torch. Not enough money here."

"Yeah. I couldn't afford *this* place either. When it was still here. You're right, it must have gone up like a match head."

There wasn't enough left to tell any more details. There *was* a heavy wet-ash smell where bits and blackened pieces rested on the scorched concrete pad of the foundation. He blinked again. That smell, and the way the bullets had chewed at the mud brick below the window flecking bits of adobe into his face. The way his armor had chafed, the fear as he made himself jerk up over the sill and aim the M-4, laying the red dot, the instant when the mouj had stared at him wide-eyed just before the burst tracked across his body in a row of black-red dots and made him dance like a jointed doll . . .

"Eric?" Alice said, jarring him out of the memory.

"Sorry," he said. "Deep thought."

She spared him any offensive sympathy and he nodded to her in silent gratitude, still feeling a little shaky. *Got to get over this. I can have flashbacks later.*

"Let me have the workup when you can," he said.

Of course, when I was on the rock pile I said I'd deal with it later, when it wouldn't screw the mission. This is later, I suppose.

"I'll zap it to your notepad," Alice said. "I've got to get some more samples now."

He turned away. Cesar Martinez was talking to the Lopez family, minus the three children who were with some neighbor or relative; the couple was sitting in one of the emergency vans, and someone had given them Styrofoam cups of coffee. His own nose twitched at the smell, though what he really wanted was a drink. Or a cigarette. He suppressed both urges and listened to his partner's gentle voice, calm and sympathetic. He was a hotshot, he'd go far, he was *good* at making people want to help him, soothing them, never stepping on what they had to say.

"I was going to go back in. They were gone, and I was going to go back in and then—" the husband said.

Cesar made a sympathetic noise. "You were having dinner when the man forced you out of the house?"

"Take-out Chinese, from Chow's," the wife said. Her husband took up the thread:

"And this man came in. He had a gun . . . a gun like a shotgun, but smaller, like a pistol," Anthony Lopez said. "It still looked pretty damn big. So was he."

He chuckled, and Salvador's opinion of him went up. It was never easy for civilians when reality crashed into what they thought had been their lives.

"How could you tell it was a shotgun?"

"Two barrels. Looked like tunnels."

"And the man?"

"He was older than me—fifty, sixty, gray hair cut short, but he was moving fast. He had blue eyes, fair, sort of tanned skin, but you could tell he was pink underneath?"

"Anglo, but weathered?"

"Right. And he was dressed all in black, black leather. And he shouted at us, just, 'Go, go, go, get out, run, keep running.' We did."

"Exactly the right thing to do," Cesar said.

"But I was going to go back. Then it burned . . ." he whispered. "If I had—"

You'd be dead, Salvador thought. *On the other hand, if the guy hadn't run you all out, you'd all be dead. There's something screwy here. Arsonists don't care who gets hurt and they* certainly *don't risk getting made to warn people.*

Mrs. Lopez spoke again. "There was a younger man outside, when we ran out. He didn't do anything. He just *stood* there, with his hands in the air, almost like he was high or something. And there was a, a van or a truck over there."

She pointed to the wall of the compound across the street from what had been her house. Salvador made a note to see if they could get tire tracks.

"When we were across the street the younger man sort of, oh, collapsed. The older man with the gun, the one in black, helped him over to the van, not carrying him but nearly, sort of dragging him and putting him in the backseat. Then they drove off."

Cesar tapped at his notepad and called up the face-sketch program.

"The younger man looked like this?" he began, and patiently ran them through the process of adjustment.

Salvador stared, fascinated as always, watching the image shift, slowly morphing and changing and then switching into something that only an expert could tell from a photograph of a living person. He knew that in the old days you'd had to use a sketch artist for this, but now it was automatic. It would even check the final result against the databases with a face-recognition subsystem. When they'd given all the help they could Cesar went on:

"Thank you, thank you both. We may have to talk to you again later."

He blew out a sigh as the couple left and turned and leaned back against the end of the van, looking at the notepad in his hand. Salvador prompted him:

"Their stories were consistent?"

"Yeah, *jefe*. Right from the start, it wasn't just listening to each other and editing the memory."

He touched the screen. "Okay, sequence: When Mrs. Lopez got home with the kids, around five, Ellen Tarnowski's car, she's the upper-floor tenant, was there. Mr. Lopez, the husband, got home a little later and noticed it too. Because she's usually not back from work by then."

"They friends with her?"

"They know her to talk to, just in passing. Said she was nice, but they didn't have much in common."

The senior detective grunted and looked at *his* notepad, tapping for information; Mr. and Mrs. Lopez were a midlevel state government functionary and a dental hygienist, respectively. Ellen Tarnowski . . .

Works at Hans & Demarcio Galleries. Okay, artsy. God knows we've got enough of them around here.

There were three hundred–odd galleries in Santa Fe, plus every other diner and taco joint had original artwork on the walls and on sale. Half the waiters and checkout clerks in town were aspiring artists of one sort or another, too, like the would-be actors in LA. She looked out at him, a picture from some Web site or maybe the DMV: blond, mid-twenties, full red lips, short straight nose, high cheekbones, wide blue eyes. Something in those eyes too, an odd look. Kind of haunted. The figure below . . .

"Jesus."

"Just what *I* said. Anyway, she comes downstairs just after Mr. Lopez arrives. Mrs. Lopez looks out the kitchen window and notices her because she's wearing—"

He checked his notes again.

"—a white silk sheath dress and a wrap. She knew it was Tarnowski's best fancy-occasion dress from a chat they'd had months ago. Another woman was with her. About Tarnowski's age, but shorter, slim, olive complexion or a tan, long dark hair, dark eyes . . ."

"Really going to stand out in *this* town."

"*Sí,* though if she's going around with *la Tarnowski* she will! I got a composite on her too, but it's not as definite. Mrs. Lopez said her clothes looked really expensive, and she was wearing a tanzanite necklace."

"What the fuck's tanzanite?"

The other thing we have hundreds of is jewelry stores.

"Like sapphire, but *expensive*. Here's what she looked like."

He showed a picture. The face was triangular, smiling slightly, framed by long straight black hair. Attractive too, but . . .

Reminds me of that mink I handled once when I was young and stupid

11

and trying to impress. Pretty, and it bit like a bastard. Took three stitches and a tetanus shot and the girl laughed every time she saw me—remembered me hopping around screaming.

"I don't think she's Latina, somehow," he said aloud, as his fingers caressed the slight scar at the base of his right thumb.

"Yeah, me too, but I can't put my finger on why. Incidentally let's do a side-by-side with the composite on the man they saw standing still outside, when the old goatsucker with the gun ran them out past him. The one he shoved into the backseat later."

Salvador's eyebrows went up as the pictures showed together. "Are they *sure* that's not the same person? It's an easy mistake to make, in the dark, with the right clothes."

His partner nodded; it was, surprisingly so under some circumstances.

"Looks a lot like Dark Mystery Woman, eh? But it was a guy, very certainly. Wearing a dark zippered jacket open with a tee underneath. Mrs. Lopez said he looked real fit. Not bulked up but someone who worked out a lot. She got a better look at him than at the woman, they went right by. Nothing from the databases on either of them, by the way, but look at this."

His fingers moved on the screen, and the two images slid until they were superimposed. Then he tapped a function box.

"Okay, the little machine thinks they're relatives," Salvador said. "*I* could have figured that out."

"But could you have said it was a ninety-three-percent chance?"

"Sure. I just say: 'It's a ninety-three-percent chance.' Or in old-fashioned human language, *con certesa*. Okay, back up to what Mystery Woman was doing earlier. She and Tarnowski get in Tarnowski's car and drive off around five thirty, a few minutes earlier?"

"Mystery Woman was driving. Tarnowski looked shaky." Cesar consulted his notes. "Yeah, Mrs. Lopez said Tarnowski looked like she was going to fall over, maybe sick, the other one helped her into the car."

"That's *two* people who have to be helped into cars. This smells."

"And then two and a half hours later someone runs in waving a sawed-off shotgun, while Mystery Woman's brother or cousin or whatever was standing outside ignoring everything and talking to himself in a strange language—"

"Strange language?"

"They just heard a few words. Not English, not Spanish, and not anything they recognized. He talks in the strange language, falls, goatsucker with the gun gives him a hand, they drive off, and then the place just happens to burn down a few minutes later."

Salvador sighed and turned up the collar of his coat; it was dark, and cold.

"I need a drink. But get an APB out on Ellen Tarnowski and flag her name with municipal services and the hospitals statewide. Also the old gringo with the sawed-off shotgun, use the face-recognition protocol for surveillance cameras. We can get him on a reckless-endangerment charge, trespassing, uttering threats, suspicion of arson, bad breath, whatever."

"*Sí*, and littering. The Mystery Woman and the Mystery Man too?"

"Yeah, why not? Let them all do a perp walk and we can apologize later."

He sat down on the tailgate and began doggedly prodding at the screen. The first thing tomorrow he'd start tracing Tarnowski's life. So far nobody had died, and he'd like to keep it that way. The employer was a good first place.

In the meantime, he could try to get some sleep. He snorted quietly to himself. After dredging up this many memories, much chance there was of *that*.

Dream.

Eric Salvador always knew it was a dream; he just couldn't affect it or get out of it or do anything except watch and smell and taste and feel an overwhelming sick dread as it unfolded. There hadn't really been a burned-out MRAP at the end of the village street by the mosque. That had been somewhere else, that little shithole outside Kandahar he'd seen on his first tour, and it had been there only one day. It was a composite of all the bads, building up to the Big Bad itself.

A couple of other things are right for the day, he thought.

The way Olsen flicked the little Raven surveillance drone into the air, and the buzz of its engine as it climbed to circle above them, and the dopey little smiley-face button with fangs he'd glued to the nose of the corps' thirty-five–thousand-dollar toy airplane. He'd tried to put little fake Hell-fire missiles under the wings, too, and Gunny had torn him a new asshole about it. The way the translator was sweating and his eyes were flicking here and there, and you wondered if it was just the heat or generalized fear or if he knew something he wasn't saying.

Christ, I've had this fucking nightmare so many times I'm starting to sound like a movie critic.

Smith always went into the door of the compound the same way, the way he really had. Regulation, the two of them plastered on either side, Jackson taking out the lock on the gate with a door-knocker round, *whump-boom,* the warped old planks smacking inward as the slug blew the rusty lock into the courtyard, Smith following, his M-4 tucked into his shoulder and Jackson on his heels.

The explosion was always silent. Silent, slow-mo, the flames leaking around the fragments of wood and the two men flying and just enough time to realize, *Oh, shit, this is a bad one,* before a giant's hand picked him up and threw him backwards until there was the impact and the pain.

Only this time was different. This time *something* walked out of the fire to where he lay with the broken ends of his ribs grating under the body armor that had saved his life.

The shape twisted and its wrongness made him want to scream out the bloody foam in his lungs, but the eyes were flecked yellow. And the voice *slithered* into his ears:

"Who's been a naughty boy, then?"

He began to sink into the dry dusty earth, and it flowed into mouth and nose and eyes, the dust of ages and of empires.

"Naughty!"

"Christ!"

He lay panting in the darkness, smelling his own sweat and waiting to be sure he was awake—sometimes he dreamed he was, and then the whole thing started cycling through his head again. It was blurring away already, details fracturing like sunlight through a drop of water. His hand groped for the cigarettes on the bedside, and then remembered he'd stopped.

"Go back to sleep," he told himself. "Dreaming's no worse than remembering, anyway."

Christ.

"I wonder where Tarnowski is?"

He didn't really want to know; kidnap victims usually didn't end up anywhere good.

CHAPTER TWO

When Ellen came out in a too-large white cotton robe with a towel wrapped around her hair he had the breakfast table set, in the big airy room that led out onto the balcony. The *pensione* was perched high on the slope above Amalfi's little cove, and the Tyrrhenian Sea sparkled an impossible blue to the west; white buildings tumbled down the hillside to meet it, down to the Duomo and the half-Romanesque-Byzantine, half-Saracen cathedral.

She felt much better now; the hot water had driven the last of the grue out of her mind and the stiffness out of her muscles, and she found herself eager for the day, sniffing the scent of the coffee. When she tossed the towel aside the mild warm breeze tumbled through her curly blond hair.

"Good morning, Mrs. Brézé," Adrian said.

"*Salut*, Monsieur Brézé," she replied.

"And *buongiorno*," they added in unison; this *was* Amalfi, after all.

"You look enchanting. And dressed like that, you also look about twelve."

"Not really," she said.

Ellen struck a pose with one hand behind her head and a leg showing through the slit. Adrian's gaze lingered on it. She was twenty-four; she was also five-foot-six and thirty-six/twenty-seven/thirty-six, taut from tennis and cross-country running, with a face close enough to a certain fifties actress that it had been embarrassing in NYU's art history classes when they came to study Warhol's famous portrait.

"No, on second thought, of a perfectly legal age," he said, after clearing his throat.

She sat, and began to eat. The breakfast was more or less Italian, except for the chilled mango, ripe figs, crisp crumbly *frese*, slightly sweet and flavored with anise, *torta di nocciole e limoni di Amalfi*, rich with hazelnuts and tart with lemon, rolls, jam.

"Well, that's certainly blatant," Adrian said after a moment, a slight prickle of danger in his smooth voice.

"What is?" Ellen replied.

"This."

He showed her his tablet across the remains of their breakfast. She took the reader and held the thin sheet between her hands. *This* was an announcement in the *Corriere della Sera* that the . . .

"*Ikhwan al-Fajr al-Aswad* is to meet in Tbilisi, Georgia," she murmured, yawning. "Next year, about this time."

It was late morning, which was a compromise between their preferred hours; Adrian might be a Good Guy, but his genes gave him a thoroughly Shadowspawn preference for waking up around noon and

17

not becoming really active until sunset. By no coincidence whatsoever, that was a preference shared by many eccentric artists and mad dictators. She'd always been an early-to-bed, morning-type person. Marriage required a lot of meeting in the middle; going to bed late sometimes left her tired despite eight hours' sleep, even when it hadn't been interrupted the way it had last night.

Nobody at the inn objected to their schedule, even though it must have played havoc with their housekeeping. They had long experience with eccentric foreigners, and Adrian had used this place before. Mostly for prolonged recoveries and convalescence, after missions for the Brotherhood during his years fighting the Council.

"It's pronounced *Ikkhh*—"

He repeated the name as a rapid series of gargling gutturals and rough breathing.

Mountains ran north and south from here, blue and dreaming in the Mediterranean summer warmth that brought odors of rock and citrus and stone pine through the open French doors that gave onto the balcony terrace. She shivered a little; places like this made the contrast between how the world *seemed* and how she now knew it really worked all the more dreadful. With an effort she cast the thought away.

Besides her native coal-country Pennsylvania English, Ellen could speak fair French and some Italian; those were the legacy of an undergraduate degree in art history from NYU. And a little Spanish, from years spent in Santa Fe. Adrian was fluent in over a dozen languages that she knew of.

"Show-off," she said sweetly, and kicked him in the ankle under the table. "And *don't* repeat it in Tibetan."

"Merde alors!" he yelped, startled. Then he smiled: "I thought that it was you who enjoyed pain, *chérie.*"

She smiled back. "What can I say . . . I swing both ways when it comes to lovely hurting. That's why it's called *sado*masochism, dear."

Then more seriously: "Anyway, what does it mean? *Ikhwan al-Fajr al-Aswad?*" she added, trying to get the throaty sounds right.

"It's Arabic," he said. "For Order of the Black Dawn."

"You're right, that's blatant. That's an elevated finger to the whole planet. The secret conspiracy of evil that runs the world is actually announcing its meetings to the news services?"

"They *do* want everyone to know . . . at least, every one of the people who are supposed to attend. Many of whom are both eccentric and hermetic recluses, or quite mad."

"Why not send an e-mail around?"

Adrian chuckled. "My sweet, people don't change much after their twenties. And many of the ones attending this affair were born before the First World War, and intend to live . . . well, exist . . . forever."

"Of course *they* don't change. They're *dead.*"

"Only technically."

Ellen laughed ruefully herself. "I remember Adrienne saying something about the Old Ones disliking technology, or at least any technology that didn't involve shoveling coal into a boiler."

"Exactly. Also this announcement, it is a boast. They draw closer to the day they need not be secret. When they can rule as demon-gods once more."

"Why in Arabic? I thought French was the Council's official language."

"A slight unblatancy or minor disguise," he said. "That's the Arabic version of the original . . . *Ordre de l'Aube Noire*. It's the term the al-Lanarki clan uses, too. Probably one of them thought it was amusing; they have an odd sense of humor."

"Odder than yours?" Ellen said sardonically. "In which I include your disreputable relatives, my love."

"My ancestors thought they were magicians and *loup-garou*, before they ferreted out the truth. The al-Lanarkis thought they were *ghilan*, until the Order of the Black Dawn contacted them and showed them how to reconcentrate the genes. It shows in their . . . subculture, you might say. As the Tōkairin thought they were Ninja sorcerors."

"Ghilan?"

"The translation would be . . . ghouls, roughly."

"Ech," she said. "Graveyards and corpses and that?"

"Not quite. The *ghūl* of the East is not exactly the ghoul of the West. It is a thing that can assume the guise of an animal, lures unwary travelers into the desert wastes to slay and devour them. *Ghūl* rob graves, drink blood, and take on the form of the one they had fed upon to deceive the living."

"Sounds familiar."

"The Shadowspawn are the source of all legends. Tbilisi is near their bailiwick, they operate out of Beirut for the most part, and they often get handed jobs like this."

He had a slight accent in English; Ellen thought it was charming and distinguished. It went well with his looks, raven black hair, olive skin, a slim build muscled like a cat, and no more than an inch or so taller than her five-six. Of course, he had a slight accent in every one of his many languages, as far as she could tell, including French, which was more or less his first. First if you counted a sort of quasi-Provençal patois from the Auvergne as part of that language; it was what his *technically* dead but still very vocal great-grandparents had spoken to him in his childhood along with the standard tongue.

"My Mhabrogast is utterly faultless, darling," he murmured, picking the thought out of her mind.

"Yes, but that's the *lingua demonica*," she teased. "What they speak in Hell."

"Bah, mere superstition. It may be the operating code of the universe, I admit that."

Then he took the reader back and flicked the pages down with one finger.

"Mmmmm . . . name of a black dog! They're even specifying that it's to elect new members to the *Shura al-Khayal*!"

"Council of Shadows, right?"

"Yes."

Ellen sighed. "And then they decide on which version of their end-of-the-world-as-we-know-it plan to implement."

"Which we must stop. I like the world as I know it."

"So do I, especially now that I'm with you. I knew the honeymoon couldn't last forever. Damn."

Adrian reached across the table and took her hand.

"Only in the narrowest sense," he said, kissing the fingers one by one. "Metaphorically we *can* keep this up forever."

The kisses sent little tingling feelings up into her hand and arm.

Which is a good sign after a week of really energetic *honeymooning, when I didn't have the collywobbles. And the way Adrian takes care of me then . . . that's even better, in a way.*

"And there is nothing we can do immediately. Especially if we do not wish to attract attention. We will move slowly, cautiously, until it is time to strike."

Then he leaned back in his chair, completely at ease. Sunlight dappled across his bare torso and loose chino drawstring pants; he tapped a slim brown Turkish cigarette out of a pack on the table and crossed one ankle across his knee. The bare foot was slender, like his hands, and high-arched.

"Gag. Retch. Cough," she said. "Ak. Ak. Pthft."

He raised one eyebrow but didn't put the cigarette back. Instead he held it up before his face, concentrating, frowning a little with a fixed expression in his eyes, which were brown, almost black, save for tiny gold flecks. After a moment smoke began to curl up from the end of the tube, an acrid pungency with an aromatic undertone. She had to admit it wasn't entirely unpleasant; it was tobacco but very *good* tobacco, and it had been treated with rum.

"Show-off," she said again. "You only do that so you can look like a François Truffaut character."

He smiled at her through the smoke, drew, and let it trickle out of his nostrils.

"But, darling, I grew up on Truffaut movies," he said. "*L'Histoire d'Adèle H.* was the first one I ever went to on my own."

Ellen blinked; occasionally she forgot that Adrian was over fifty. He *looked* twenty-something, like her. His breed aged more slowly, even in their original bodies.

"It's still a disgusting vice," she said lightly. "And not even one of the fun disgusting vices. Plus it's dangerous."

"It's perfectly safe for me," he pointed out, gesturing elegantly . . . very much like a Truffaut character, in fact, probably deliberately. "I can't get cancer. Or heart disease. Or lose the sensitivity of my taste buds, either."

"I can get cancer."

"Yes, but I could cure you."

She put her tongue between her lips and went *pffffthtttt!*

Adrian let his head fall back and stared at the white plaster that overlay the arched stone of the ceiling as he smoked; this place had started out as a nobleman's house six centuries ago, built into the steep almost-cliff above the little city. He was obviously in deep-thought mode, and he hated to be interrupted then. Which was fair enough. She loathed interruptions when she was working too.

Ellen poured more coffee, picked up her cup and saucer and walked out on the terrace, under an arch of arbor thick with hanging bougainvillea, purple and crimson and white. Gulls flew by below the stone balustrade, and above the strip of lemon trees on the terrace below. The polished *mosaico hidráulico* tiles felt comfortable on her bare feet, as if the green and blue floral pattern were a smooth stroking. She lost herself in the moment and the view.

This is a very long way from Swoyersville, Luzerne County, Pennsylvania, she thought happily. *Or even from Allentown.*

"Eek!"

His fingers caressed the nape of her neck, touching the fine hairs there—the rest of his hand was curled up on her head. Then he stripped the robe down, pinning her arms behind her back. She shivered, and then gasped as he gripped the knot of hair and bent her head back. His other

23

hand stroked her. Anyone looking up from the roadway below—anyone with a good set of binoculars, at least—was going to be getting an eyeful of natural blonde having a very good time.

Which added to the excitement. And technically, she had a government license—though not one for *in public*.

"*Con il suo permesso?*" his voice murmured in her ear.

"*Oh*, yeah."

A slight sting at the base of her throat, and hot fire ran through her body like a wave.

"That could get addictive," she said some time later.

"It *is* addictive," he pointed out, head resting on her stomach.

Ellen lay propped against the carved olive-wood headboard of the canopied bed and sipped at the red wine; it was an excellent way to keep your blood cell count up when your husband had . . . special needs. It was also around two in the afternoon, which meant she wasn't starting too early.

"Oh, I don't mean just your feeding on me and the drug in the bite," she said. "Though that *is* very satisfying. I mean the whole setup. Strolls along the seaside, the fantastic sex, we wander off to the Trattoria da Ciccio for lunch, the fantastic sex, sailboating down the coast, the fantastic sex, we go ramble around some quattrocento palace full of murals I've only ever seen in prints and on the Web, the fantastic sex, you buy those prawn things and Mrs. Boriello cooks them up for us with her handmade pasta and we have dinner on the terrace and watch the moon rise over the sea, you drink some of my blood, then the fantastic—"

"Stop, stop, you are turning me into a satyr again!"

He began trailing kisses up her torso.

"You need help for that? Not that I've noticed!"

"I needed your help to stop feeling conflicted."

"Well, c'mon, then, tiger. The safe word for the day is *whoa*."

Adrian laughed. "I find I like the safe-word concept very much."

"So do I, but why 'very much'?"

"It assures me I'm not being a monster."

"Not the bad kind, at least. Well, c'mon!"

"Not now, my sweet. It is time to begin preparing you. This holiday can last longer if we make it a working vacation . . . or a working honeymoon."

She sighed. "I'm supposed to take a level in badassery, right? Starting now?"

"Just a few precautions. An unprepared . . . normal . . ."

Human, she thought, and he nodded.

". . . is too vulnerable to a Shadowspawn. Even one who isn't an adept."

"*Tell* me. I was your sister's prisoner for six months, remember. Of course, she *is* an adept."

He snarled. She jerked back in involuntary alarm for an instant; it was *literally* a snarl, a predator's warning sign, showing teeth that weren't quite human. Not her variety of human, at least: Shadowspawn were hominids, but they had evolved to prey on Homo sapiens sapiens. They were as territorial as you'd expect a specialist predator to be, too. He loved her and hated his sister, but at an instinctual level he was also furious at another hunter poaching his turf.

"Sorry," he murmured, forcing his face back to calm.

"'Sall right. I killed her, after all. *Pop* goes the hypodermic in her foot, *in* goes the poison. God, that was satisfying! Thank you, thank you, *thank* you for giving me the opportunity. And the hypodermic."

He laughed ruefully. "It is an accomplishment for which I will always envy you. And as you remembered it, your thoughts grew remarkably predatory too."

Well, humans are *predators. The Shadowspawn are very* predatoresque *predators. Like supertigers evolved to hunt lions. Predators on top of predators, on true humans and on Neanderthals and Homo erectus and maybe on those funny little things on Flores,* she thought.

"All of them." He nodded. "For a very, very long time. A hundred thousand years or more. But Adrienne . . . knowing she is no longer in the world has lifted a great burden from me, my love."

He rolled onto his back, one arm behind his head, looking at the ceiling. Ellen propped herself up on her elbows.

"C'mon, there's something there, lover," she said. "*I* can't read minds, so I have to ask you."

He was silent for a long minute. Then: "You are not the only one to have bad dreams about Adrienne," he said. "Or to have good reason for them."

Her brows went up. "She tried to kill you a lot, didn't she?"

"That was not the problem. It was war, and we were on opposite sides. We . . . were antagonists as well as enemies. Counterparts, almost, in command of our respective operations, outwitting each other. That meant negotiations, from time to time. She kept trying to *turn* me, as well as kill me. Appealing to our memories of our childhoods . . . oh, not blatantly. Very subtly."

"Hey, you didn't tell me about this!"

He shrugged and reached for a cigarette with his free hand. "I do not like to think of it. Then in Calcutta . . . Operation Black Hole. I was cut off for some time. So was she—a rogue Shadowspawn was involved, one outlawed by the Council as well as hunted by the Brotherhood. I made a very bad mistake; I trusted her."

"You *did*?"

"Only tactically, but it was enough. She launched a mental attack on me. I *think* I was her prisoner for some time, but escaped; Harvey found me wandering. Naked, scarred, bleeding and half-mad."

"Oh," Ellen said, and laid her head on his shoulder. "That sounds like your sister, all right. Adrian . . . I haven't asked before, but you remember when you contacted me mentally, just after Adrienne took me to Rancho Sangre?"

He nodded without looking at her.

"And I told you that she had two kids? Why did that affect you so strongly?"

He let smoke trickle from his nostrils. "Because," he said very softly, "they may be mine as well. I am not certain. My memories of those days are scrambled. Fragments, some that must be nightmares, others that were true—I had the scars for some time—and some that might be either."

She nodded. "I thought so. They . . . really looked like you, especially the boy. He even *moved* like you."

"That does not make it certain. Shadowspawn are inbred, the Brézés in particular."

"I couldn't prove it, but I'm morally certain," Ellen said carefully.

A sigh. "And me also," he said. "What were they like?"

"Creepy," she said bluntly. "But, ummm, sort of creepy in an *innocent* way. Charming, even . . . in a creepy way."

"That is the hell of it, this war. So many innocents. So many, and it is so seldom that we can do anything to protect or help. Even Adrienne, once . . . It haunts me, that if *she* had been the one Harvey rescued, I might be on the other side even now."

"Well, for a girl she's really hot stuff, lover, but I *still* wouldn't have married her. Not even in California and not even if she'd been the Good Guy who rescued me. A brief passionate fling in Saint Barts, maybe, with a bittersweet teary farewell; marriage, no. God, whole *decades* of 'Who took my Tampax?' No way."

"I am glad to hear it."

He laughed as she poked him in the ribs, then crushed out the cigarette.

"And . . . there is a shadow in my mind when I think of those children. Perhaps it is merely my emotions speaking. Perhaps the Power; it can be hard to tell the difference. Shadows within shadows . . ."

"Sometimes I think your mind is mostly made up of shadows. And *don't* make the obvious pun."

She tickled him ruthlessly in the most sensitive spot she'd found, just below one armpit. They wrestled for a moment, and then he said briskly:

"Enough. Now, the protections against the Power will come later. Let us begin with the physical side."

He lay back on the bed and crossed his arms on his chest, each hand to the opposite shoulder—the shaman's posture. She lay back herself, closed her eyes, let her mind float downward into her tired body—

—and was elsewhere.

This was the image he used as the entry to what he called his memory palace, a duplicate of the main living space of his mountaintop retreat near Santa Fe, New Mexico. One side held a huge fieldstone fireplace and a polished-concrete sitting shelf before it; a low fire crackled on the andirons, fragrant piñon pine. The other wall was a stark expanse of glass, rising eighteen feet high.

The smooth stone-tiled floor ran right out past it to the narrow terrace beyond; after that the ground fell away two thousand feet in crag and ravine and piñon and dwarf desert juniper, down to the lights of a little town lost amid the empty moonlit expanse. She enjoyed the view for a moment. Then:

"Hey. I just realized—you have a thing for scenic dropoffs outside the room, don't you? Here in Amalfi, and in your house in Santa Fe. You like to be in a high place, looking down."

He paused, blinked, and nodded slowly in agreement.

"You are right, dear one. I had not realized." A grin. "At least I do not come out on a high *balcony* and make demagogic speeches to adoring crowds."

She tossed here head. "I like it here, though. It felt so *good* while Adrienne had me, when you came and . . . brought me here. An escape."

He sighed agreement. "But frustrating, that I could do no more."

"You *did* more, eventually. That was more important than hurrying and failing!"

"Yes. She never . . ."

"Took me into her memory palace? No. Told me about it, and said we'd go there when she wanted to get more . . . extreme."

Ellen shivered a little, and Adrian put an arm around her shoulder. Seriously:

"We must begin your training now. I have no objection to rescuing and defending you, my darling, but you should be able to defend yourself. I may not be enough, someday!"

Ellen nodded emphatically. "Yeah, I like *playing* at being helpless sometimes. The real thing's not nearly so much fun."

"And we will have work to do that will involve risk. I hate the thought, for you, but—"

"Hey, buster, your sister and her friends are trying to destroy the *world*, remember? You think I'm going to stay in a bunker or . . . or some *resort* sipping margaritas and let you do all the work? You're older than you look, but you're not *that* much of an antique sexist, I hope!"

He laughed, and touched the tips of his fingers to her cheek.

"No. Knowing you as I do now, I would expect you to want to fight by my side. This will involve a great deal of effort, though. You must learn how to fight—fight in a number of ways—how to hide, how to pursue, everything from defensive driving to forged documents. And I must show you a number of things about the Power."

"I don't have enough of the Shadowspawn genes to use it, you said."

Adrian nodded. "But I can help plant . . . artifacts . . . in your mind that will render you less vulnerable to it. Wreakings, localized permanent modifications of reality. I *am* an adept, and both more powerful and better trained than nearly anyone of my generation."

"*That's* comforting," she said. "Is there an advantage to doing it here in, ummm, your head, though?"

He nodded. "How long have we been here?"

"Oh . . . three, five minutes?"

"Four and a bit, to us. Back in the real world . . . less than five seconds. I can stretch the perceived duration. By the time we leave for Paris in a few months, you will have had *years*."

She thought for a moment. Something nagged at her.

"Hey, maybe that's where the Elf Hill legends came from? But look, this is as real to you as it is to me, right?"

Ellen took a breath, tapped one foot on the tile of the floor. Heat from the fire on her legs, thin mountain air in her lungs, scent of burning conifer wood in her nostrils. You *couldn't* tell this from reality . . . until something impossible happened. And she'd learned over the past year that her previous idea of what constituted the possible out in the real world was far, far too limited.

"Yes."

"And you can shape things here just by thinking about them?"

He made a gesture and they were *elsewhere*. This was a huge room, like a converted warehouse. Metal beams overhead, light from high dusty windows around the top of the metal box, a floor of coarse concrete, with reed mats rolled against the walls and big swinging doors opening on a vista of palms leading down to a river. There were wall mirrors in some places, gymnastic equipment elsewhere, ropes dangling from the rafters, odd-looking staffs and swords and various esoteric Eastern-looking things racked neatly around the tall rusty steel pillars.

The air had a warm, moist feel, scented with spices, frangipani blossom and wet earth, and a hint of diesel fumes. Then she looked down at herself; she was wearing an outfit something like a *gi* but not quite, loose trousers and a jacket whose sleeves didn't quite come to the wrists. The coarse tough cotton slid over her skin. . . .

Real. All five senses.

"So," she said. "How come Shadowspawn bother with, like, ruling the world and stuff? Can't you have everything you want *here*? Better than you possibly could in the real world? Sort of like TV, only full-sensory and you're directing the program."

He nodded. "But those vulnerable to that temptation didn't breed very successfully," he said. "We are a very old species, considerably older than modern humans, shaped by both evolution and the Power. To one of us, this is . . . fundamentally unsatisfying, after a while. Or perhaps satisfying only in limited doses? I think the ability to build this interior reality is a side effect of other aspects of the Power, perhaps the tele-pathic organ."

"Okay. Second question, it's just my *mind* here. I know from tennis—"

At which she was a more than decent player at a level that would have let her go pro if she'd wanted to devote her life to it.

"—and running that the body has to learn too. If I learn something here, will my body know it?"

"Your nerves and reflexes and memory will. Somatic memory trans-fers very well. Your body is already in excellent shape from the tennis and the cross-country running. . . ."

He looked her up and down with frank appreciation and snapped his teeth at her. Ellen shuddered with a complex of emotions, plea-sure and fear. He wasn't the first Shadowspawn who'd used that gesture around her. It was playfully flirtatious in a way that might be sexual or not . . . unless it wasn't friendly, in which case it was a sign you were being given the sort of look a chocolate-coconut macaroon got before the first nibble.

Bad Shadowspawn liked to play with their food; strong emotions and sensations made the blood taste much better. Like a wink, context was all.

"So this will cut down on how much you have to train. . . . You will need to build more upper-body strength, work on your flexibility, yes, and some real-world repetition to key the lessons into muscle memory, but not much beyond that."

His face went somber: not exactly cold, but a little remote.

"Understand, Ellen, that while we are training I am not your lover or your husband, or your friend. I am the *teacher*, and what you are learning may be the difference between life and death—or between life and eternal damnation. You accept this?"

"Yes." She stopped herself from adding, *darling*.

"And it will be very hard work."

"I'm not afraid of that."

"There will be pain, *serious* pain."

"Okay, understood. Look, Adrian, I know you're a lot older than I am and have all sorts of knowledge and power and . . . and shit. If I weren't okay with that, I'd have said, 'Thanks for the rescue, fuck off,' not 'Yes, I'll marry you.' So here, you're Yoda and I'm the padawan. Right. I've assimilated that. Let the hard stuff commence."

"Understood."

He reached out, plucked a knife from the wall, turned and threw in a blur of speed. The hard impact knocked Ellen back. She could see the black hilt standing in her right shoulder, and her hands tried to grasp it. Then the shock passed and there was pain, enormous, all-pain, everywhere, the floor rushed up and her head went *thock* against it and she screamed—

—and she was back on her feet. Her hand went to her smooth, un-marked shoulder.

"You son of a *bitch*!" she shouted. "That *hurt*!"

"It does," he said somberly, and laid a hand on her shoulder. "But here I can . . . reset, undo. My darling, training is wonderful, but the only way to learn to fight well is to *fight*. And learn, *if* you survive. But here you can fight, lose, die, and *still learn from the mistake that killed or crippled you*."

"Oh," she said. "Okay, remembering previous words here. Unless I get too blasé about it because I know it's not real."

"You will not. The fear and pain operate below the conscious level."

"Okay, if you say so . . . Where is this, if it's based on anywhere real?"

"The training salon . . . dojo, though the Thais don't use that word . . . of a man named Saragam, in a little town north of Bangkok."

Adrian made a gesture, and the place was gone. Others flickered by. A crowded street in a European city with a blare of noise and a waft of pastry baking, a tiny atoll with a single palm tree and cerulean waves breaking white on a sugar-grain beach, a pine forest stark and silent with winter, snow freezing cold on her feet and heavy on the boughs. Then the converted warehouse again.

He sighed. "Harvey Ledbetter took me here, not long after my . . . foster parents died, as part of *my* training for the Brotherhood. The real here, that is. I miss him."

Ellen felt her mouth quirk. "I realize Harvey's your wise grizzled mentor and second dad and comrade in arms and all those manly bonding things, and I like him myself. He helped save my life. But he's *not* welcome on our honeymoon, darling."

Adrian grinned at her. "Actually, I had a very bad crush on him for the *longest* time. He was a strikingly handsome man then, you know, and very charismatic. There were attempts at seduction. All failures, alas."

She laughed, a startled gurgle. "What did he think of *that*?"

"Quiet horror and loud irritation, my sweet, and the odd swat upside the head. Now let us begin. First, how to stand—"

What felt like twelve long hours later Ellen opened her eyes, and spent a moment being astonished that she *wasn't* exhausted. For a moment the tiredness was there, like the ghost of sensation, then it faded completely and she stretched, refreshed from sleep. Adrian was sitting up and looking at her, twining a lock of her curly blond hair around one finger and smiling. She made her face grow thoughtful, almost awestruck, and spoke solemnly:

"I know . . . kung fu."

He frowned for a moment. "Saragam's style is not really—"

Then he winced. His film experience wasn't *entirely* with Euro classics.

"For that, I should make you fold Paris in half. Or spank you," he said.

"Not until after dinner. I'm hungry, too."

CHAPTER THREE

"I look like death," Adrienne Brézé said softly, shifting in the clinic bed and wincing a little. "I *feel* like death incarnate, and not in a *good* way."

"At least you're not speaking in SMALL CAPITALS," Tōkairin Michiko said from her chair beside the bed.

There was a pickup overhead, and Adrienne had routed it to the big screen at the foot; the view out through the French doors into the courtyard with its fountains and bougainvillea was pretty, but it got boring after a while. She *did* look like death in the screen's pitiless image, and not one of the more glamorous versions. Skeletally thin, and having good bones didn't make that any more attractive. Not to mention the discolored, peeling skin and the glistening ointments and the fact that every hair on her head and body had dropped out.

Like a famine victim, only not so funny, she thought.

She ached. Her digestive system felt as if it were packed with mud from the back of her throat to her lower intestine. She *itched*. Not just the amputated foot where the regeneration was starting far too slowly, but all over. Having several dozen milligrams of silver solution and radioactive waste pumped into you would be bad enough for a human, but the Shadowspawn metabolism was more vulnerable to both. If she'd gotten the full dose . . .

"You do look pretty awful," Michiko said. "It's a good thing I cut your foot off in one swell foop."

Then she giggled. "I only beat Dale to it by a second or two because I had a wakizashi on me. Dale was going to use his bowie, and Dmitri just went around roaring and waving a chair in the air."

"He was a silverback gorilla at the time. It's easy to get lost in the beast when it's that close to your own form."

"*Especially* with Dmitri and gorillas. But one advantage of all that old Japan stuff grandfather liked is that I had the short sword on me."

"That was quick work," Adrienne acknowledged. "I'd have died if you had not cut the foot off before much of that Hell-brew got into my circulatory system—and I might have been too distracted to go postcorporeal in time, too. Even the best plans and probability fluxes are . . .irritatingly uncontrollable at times."

"Well, your darling brother was involved, which screws the Power. Why don't you just spend more time inside while you're healing?"

"Because it's *boring* playing games in my head after a while, Michi," Adrienne replied. "So I ration myself, that way it's a relief when I do it. Besides, I have to keep track of what's going on and make decisions."

"You could night-walk and then sleep away the days," she pointed out. "Your night-walking manifestation is so good even I can't tell you're out-of-body unless I really concentrate."

"Night-walking . . . my body's still too weak to have the personality gone for long, it needs me in here concentrating on healing. Unless I want to go postcorporeal for good, and I don't, not yet. It would be inconvenient. I'm going to stay corporeal until I get *old*."

Michiko wasn't being very considerate—but then, they were both Shadowspawn, and empathy simply wasn't their breed's strong point; Michiko was nearly as purebred as the Brézés.

There's always Monica or Jose if I feel like sympathy.

The other Shadowspawn was also looking disgustingly sleek and contented, dressed in a pale silk summer dress and strapped sandals; she'd turned her hair blond again—a minor Wreaking—and it fell in silky waves past her high-cheeked Asian face.

"Now, to business," Adrienne said. "My father and mother say things are going smoothly."

Michiko nodded. "The Tōkairin clan's accepted me . . . and Ichirō . . . without much trouble. Only had to kill a few, and no Final Deaths," she said. "I can't be *too* friendly to the Brézé interests yet, of course. I'm supposed to be here talking to your parents, warning them not to try anything while we settle down under the new management. Nobody suspects you're not gone, as far as we can tell."

"Good cover. And after all, *you* didn't kill my parents, your grandfather did, so it would be easier for you to negotiate with them now that he's dead all the way."

Under Michiko's grandfather the Tōkairin had ousted the Californian Brézés as the primary Shadowspawn group on the West Coast in a neat little coup over a generation ago. Most of the Tōkairin liked it just fine that way. Fortunately Michiko accepted that Adrienne had her mind on larger things, and besides that, they were on the same side of the great Shadowspawn generational divide. As her now thoroughly deceased grandfather had learned, far too late and very briefly.

Michiko went on: "We're gearing up for the Council meeting, and we won a lot of support for the way we acted when the Brotherhood terrorists killed Grandfather."

A mental communication passed between them: not words, more like a snigger.

"That's good. . . . I'm a little tired now, Michi."

"Get better soon. I'm not up to heading the Progressives on my own! Besides, we could go clubbing."

"Better I remain dead-dead for a while, to the rest of the world."

The sickroom was part of the *casa grande* of Rancho Sangre Sagrado, the mansion in the little California town that had been the first Brézé property on the West Coast, back in the eighteen sixties, when they brought the message of the Order of the Black Dawn to this part of the New World.

"Oh," Michiko said. "And the police in Santa Fe are sniffing around about that lucy of yours . . . the blond one whose blood smelled so edible . . . those marvelous tits and the way her brain fired when you hurt her . . ."

"Ellen. Who did *this* to me, don't forget. Take care of it for me, would you?"

"*De nada.* I'll set our renfields in the government on it. Do them good. I can look in if it's more than they can handle quietly, we do want to keep people—"

By which she meant *their* kind of people, of course.

39

"—from thinking too much about Adrian. Since I'm the head of the ruling clan in the area, nobody can object."

Adrienne shut her eyes and sighed as her friend-ally-rival left. One of the advantages of being sick was that nobody expected her to take care of business. Whatever was happening in Santa Fe, for example, where Ellen and Adrian and Adrienne between them had been fairly . . .

Blatant, she thought.

It was still important not to be too conspicuous. Not for much longer, though. Not after the Empire of Shadow returned in force.

Then it'll be just one long party. Except for the ones on the buffet.

The various monitors and the tubes and catheters gave a tang of ozone to the medicine scents, overriding the greenery from outside. A doctor came in, middle-aged and ginger-haired, with a stethoscope looped around her neck and the head tucked into a pocket of her green scrubs.

"It's time for your feeding, *Doña,*" she said briskly, a slight Scots burr still roughening her voice.

The hunger was there, but curiously muffled. *I never thought I'd get* bored *with blood,* she thought. *I want to* hunt *now and then. Or maybe it's just that I crave some solid food as well for variety.*

A postcorporeal could survive on human blood alone, but even they didn't *want* to, usually, except for a few superstitious antique types. Corporeals needed ordinary nourishment at least every now and then.

"I wish I could eat something more tangible as well, Dr. Duggan," she said, a little fretfully. "I'm starting to have dreams about steak, or some crab claws, or sweet-and-sour pork. Or even *vegetables.*"

"Intravenous will have to do. You're not ready, though you should be able to take broth soon," the renfield doctor said. "I'm still amazed you survived, even with the whole-body transfusions we did. Entire organs kept . . . nearly . . . shutting down. But once the corner was turned the recovery has been very rapid, and it seems to be accelerating. Astonishingly rapid, in fact, as if your body is chelating the poisons somehow."

"The Power was helping, but on an unconscious level," Adrienne said. "I can direct it now, and that'll speed things up, and the more I get rid of the toxins the more my command of the Power will return. It's a positive feedback cycle."

Duggan nodded, obviously taking mental notes. She had been the primary physician at Rancho Sangre for two decades now, and she'd always been intrigued by the Shadowspawn.

"I *am* feeling a little blood-hungry," Adrienne went on. "Now that you mention it."

Plus, of course, you needed blood to do more than the most basic Wreaking with the Power. Otherwise you risked draining your own reserves dangerously.

I wonder why that is, she thought.

One of her lucies, Peter, had been—still was—a physicist. He had some interesting ideas about how the Power functioned. What had he said . . .

The Shadowspawn mind is like a transistor. It modulates the forces it draws from the quantum foam, it doesn't create it. But the modulation itself draws from the energy matrix of the personality.

He wasn't a biologist, of course, so he hadn't been any help with the physical mechanisms, or why human blood was essential. And she was using the Power to heal. She should take as much blood as her stomach could handle.

"Who's on the schedule?" she asked. "I've sort of lost track."

"We were using pickups at first. You weren't really conscious and there was some incidental damage while you fed."

"Are any of my lucies ready? I'm in the mood for comfort food."

"Yes." Duggan consulted a clipboard. "You fed on Peter the day before yesterday, the spare before that, Jose the day before *that* . . . so Cheba and Monica are both past due, actually. That's stressful."

"Cheba, then," Adrienne said. "Don't let me overfeed if I go into fugue; my control is still shaky."

And she's the one I'd miss least if I do go all mindless-voracity.

Cheba was Mexican and from Coetzala in Veracruz, mestizo with a touch of African somewhere, dark and slim and very pretty, a girl Adrienne had bought from a coyote people-smuggler with a job lot of refreshments for the party where the previous head of the Tōkairin had died four months ago. She came through the door with Duggan holding one arm, but there wasn't much struggle; after repeated feedings the addiction had her strongly, and she was quivering a little with the need. And averting her eyes in horror from what lay on the bed, but Adrienne couldn't really blame her for that.

I'm not exactly aesthetic at the moment. Very ungrateful of Ellen to treat me this way, after all I did for her! I will have to punish her quite severely when I get her back, which will be a lot of fun. Still, it's a stroke of luck in the long run. Everyone thinking I'm dead makes it all so much easier.

"Sit here, lassie," Duggan said; there was a padded rest beside the bed. "Then lean forward and present your throat for the *Doña*."

She did. The scent was enough to make Adrienne feel a little more alive: fear in complex layers, shuddering disgust, and something musky that was probably self-loathing. The emotions she could feel directly were a lovely roil too, though Adrienne knew her telepathic sensitivity was still deplorably weak, and she could barely pick up the conscious part of the thought stream at all.

The cinnamon-colored throat came closer and closer . . . a tear dropped into her mouth, and then the contact of skin against her lips brought the taste of sweat, a sting in the cracks. Her mouth moved in the precise grace of the feeding bite, and the microserrations on the inside of her incisors sliced the taut surface.

The girl's whimper turned into a hoarse moan mixed with sobs. Adrienne growled deep in her throat as the blood flooded into her mouth, salty and meaty and sweet and as intoxicatingly complex as a glass of Bollinger VVF 1999, the taste of *life*. The burst of ecstasy flared in the victim's mind and resonated in hers, mingled with terror and despair, swirling down to a warm contentment as the blood flowed, a delicious yielding. Her mouth worked against the skin. . . .

"That's enough, *Doña*."

Adrienne growled again in protest as the doctor's hand pressed her head back to the pillow. Cheba slumped down on the padded stool and leaned against the edge of the bed, breathing deeply, smiling with a soft, dreamy look on her face. The small cut on her neck clotted with unnatural speed; Duggan ignored it for a moment as she wiped Adrienne's chin and lips with a cloth; the antiseptic stung a little in the cracks.

"*Merde*, am I dribbling?"

"Just a little." The Scotswoman looked down at Cheba. "She'll be fine. You took about a pint, I think—aye, as much as you can handle now."

"Good, I do *not* want the nausea back. Though I'd like a kill as well, when I'm fit enough. There's nothing quite like it for setting you up."

She yawned; she *was* feeling better, but from experience she knew the torpor and discomfort would return soon. Duggan was feeling pure scientific curiosity under her impassive exterior; it was a curious emotion, tasting like mineral water or mountain ice, eerily detached. Peter had a similar mind-set when he was working on a problem.

"Will you want Cheba for the kill? If I could dissect afterwards, there might be something interesting in the neurological changes. . . ."

"Oh, no, that would be wasteful, for several reasons. Cheba is progressing nicely. But I'll see if there's anything left for you to poke and prod at of whomever I kill."

"Thank you, *Doña.*" A sigh. "Less likely to be anything noticeable . . . Shall I call the orderlies to remove her?"

"No, not yet. In about an hour, and she'll probably need a sedative then. I'm going into trance now and taking her with me."

She sank back and crossed her arms on her chest, moving slowly and cautiously. The first sensation of withdrawal was like falling into dark softness, like sleep.

Then she was standing in the entrance to her memory palace, and for a long moment she just focused on feeling *good*. The fact of her illness faded to the faintest of memories at the back of her brain with a practiced effort of will. The somatic memories tried to manifest here, but she could overcome them.

The mental construct was a pool edged in white Carrara marble, with man-tall alabaster jars standing at intervals; at one horseshoe-shaped end a colonnade of Corinthian pillars supported a roof of bronze fretwork woven with flowering wisteria to make a walkway, with a plinth in the center pouring more water through the mouth of a copper lion. Tall umbrella pines stood around it, and then oaks amid asphodel-starred meadows, fading away to rocky hills purple under a clear blue sky; the warm air was scented with sap and hot rock and arbutus, birds warbled and insects clicked and buzzed.

Cheba staggered and stared around. Her eyes cleared quickly; now that her mind was running on Adrienne's wetware it wasn't saturated with MDMA analogues and serotonin boosters. When she was fully alert she looked surprised for a moment, then sullen. In here Adrienne's senses felt as if they were functioning normally, and the waves of murderous hate tingled along her nerves.

"I'm much prettier here," the Shadowspawn said, looking down at herself. "This is how I'm *supposed* to look. Really, being sick is such a bore, *tout court.*"

I wish she'd killed you! Cheba thought. *Or that man did, that* brujo.

"I don't doubt you do," Adrienne said happily. "Though really, with dozens of Shadowspawn running around uncontrolled and upset you'd probably have died."

It would be worth it!

Adrienne laughed, and the girl went on: *Where . . . where* is *this?*

"My—" Adrienne thought for a moment; Cheba was intelligent but not very well educated. "Inside my mind. In my head. Or you could think of it as Hell. It's where your kind got the idea for Hell, most likely."

It doesn't look so bad, Cheba thought, and looked around again.

While she did the first tentacle slid out of the water, black and glistening and as thick as her leg below the narrow questing tip. With a movement as quick as a lunging cobra it threw a loop around her ankle and jerked.

Cheba screamed as she fell to the marble, but she wound her arms around the nearest vase and held on with frenzied strength, kicking at the tentacle. More exploded out of the water in a tower of spray and lashing flesh and spoiled-seafood stink, dozens, falling on her like whips and tearing at her clothing, squeezing, thrusting—

"Aiiie. A *Thesaurus* is come. Maim, strangle, violate," Adrienne said as she walked over and smiled down at her. "George gets so lonely here," she explained. "He's quite dead outside, you see, so he's here until my own Final Death. Which will be a *very* long time, I think. That's why your kind thought Hell could go on forever."

Then, louder: "George, what did I tell you? Not unless I say you can!"

The mauling continued, and beneath it the choked, muffled shrieks. Adrienne sighed and looked at the water, frowning. It turned from crystal blue to a rosy pink, and steam began to rise from it. After a moment it boiled, and the tentacles withdrew with a sudden rush, as quickly as the first attack. The water smoked and roiled, and from beneath it came a bubbling shriek of agony as the creature cooked and cooked but could not die.

Cheba was pushing herself backwards, naked, her body streaked with blood and welts, her mouth working, and white showing all around the dark irises of her eyes. Then she stopped and froze. A moment later she felt behind her.

"It's quite fetching," Adrienne said, as Cheba's fingers made contact with the fluffy white doe's tail at the base of her spine. "And symbolically appropriate for your role in this little drama we're about to have."

Cheba bolted upright, pawing frantically at the sides of her head. The ears she felt there were tall and pointed and furred, and twitched.

"*¡Dios mío, Jesucristo!*"

"I'm the only deity here," Adrienne said, feeling the other's control crack. "Ooooh, yes, that's right. Panic, despair, horror, very stimulating, you saucy, sexy minx. Now you run away, sweetie. And when I catch you, I do some really *awful*, wonderful things to and with you."

Cheba turned and bolted through the trees and into the scrub. As she did a line of wasps rose from the underbrush and followed her, malignant shapes as long as a human hand, whining as they flew.

Adrienne watched her go, then clapped her hands together thoughtfully under her chin.

"Darkness," she said.

The sunlight faded, and sunset cast long shadows through air the color of burnt umber. She'd always liked that time of day; it was so full of little magics and possibilities.

"Not quite perfect," she mused. "Something . . . it needs just a little something. . . ."

A delighted laugh. "I know! She's phobic about spiders. Spiders it shall be! About the size of Chihuahuas, I think. Anything bigger would be kitsch."

A sobbing scream of loathing came echoing towards the pool. Adrienne laughed again, and *willed*. The change was easier and smoother than when she was night-walking in the real world, and here the sun was her imagination and not a deadly enemy to the aetheric form.

The great timber wolf raised its head and sniffed the air, snarled happily, and loped through the trees with its tail wagging.

One of the joys of a policeman's life, Eric Salvador thought the day after the Tarnowski case opened, wishing he'd taken more Tylenol with his breakfast. *You meet all kinds of people. Most of them hate you. Así es la vida. At least she's not likely to try to blow me up with a fertilizer bomb.*

Giselle Demarcio was in her fifties, with a taut, dry, ageless appearance and a slight East Coast accent, dressed in a mildly funky Santa Fe look, silver jewelry and a blouse and flounced skirt.

Sort of a fashionista version of what my great-grandmother wore around the house, Salvador thought cynically.

His family, the Spanish part, at least, had been in Santa Fe since the seventeenth century.

Everything old gets new if you wait long enough. Rich Anglos get off the bus and live in pimped-up adobes and you end up in a double-wide on Airport Road.

There was a dash of Irish in his background too, on his mother's side, and the *indio* part of the Salvador line had probably thought, *There goes the neighborhood,* when the *conquistadores* showed up asking about those gold mines the pueblo down the river had sworn existed around here.

She had a white mark on her finger where a wedding ring would go, and she fit in perfectly with the airy white-on-white decor of Hans & Demarcio Galleries. He was *not,* he noticed, being invited back to her office; this was a semipublic reception room. The art on the walls was something he could understand, at least—actual pictures of actual things. Not the cowboy-pueblo-Western art a lot of the places on Canyon Road had either, mostly older-looking stuff. There was a very faint odor of wood smoke from a piñon fire crackling in a kiva fireplace. The whole thing screamed *money.* It had been a very long time since Canyon Road attracted artists because the rents were low.

Santa Fe, the town where ten thousand people can buy the state and fifty thousand can't afford lunch, he thought.

"Jeanette, take care of the Cliffords, would you?" Demarcio said to a sleek-looking assistant. Then: "Coffee, Detective?"

Wait a minute, Salvador thought. *She's not really hostile. She's scared for some reason. Not of me, but scared silly and hiding it well.*

"Thank you," he said, and took the cup. "That's nice."

It was excellent coffee, especially compared to what he drank at home or at the station, with a rich, dark, nutty taste. He enjoyed it, and waited. Most people couldn't stand silence. It wore on their nerves and eventually they blurted out something to fill it. Salvador had learned patience and silence in a very hard school.

"I'm worried about Ellen," the older woman said suddenly.

The detective made a sympathetic noise. "Ms. Tarnowski worked for you?" he said.

"Works. She's my assistant, even if she didn't show up this morning, that's understandable with the fire and all. Not a secretary, she's an art history graduate from NYU, and I was bringing her in on our acquisitions side. I'm . . . She's a sweet kid, but she's gotten mixed up in something, hasn't she?"

"You tell me, Ms. Demarcio," Salvador said.

"I never liked that boyfriend of hers. She met him playing tennis at the country club about a year ago and they, well, it was a whirlwind thing. He gave me this creepy feeling. And then his sister showed up—"

Salvador blinked. *The sister . . . the woman who was with Tarnowski?*

"Boyfriend?" he asked.

"Adrian Brézé."

"Ah," Salvador said.

As he spoke he tapped the name into his notepad's virtual keyboard and hit the rather specialized search function. He'd long ago mastered the trick of reading a screen and paying attention to someone at the same time.

"Now, that's interesting. Do you have a picture of him?"

It was interesting because Salvador *didn't* have a picture; or much of anything else. Usually these days you drowned in data on anyone. There was nothing here but bare bones, a Social Security number, a passport number and an address way, *way* out west of town. Just out of Santa Fe County, in fact. A quick Google Earth flick showed a big house on a low mountain or big hill, right in the foothills of the Sangres, nothing else for miles and miles and miles and miles. The state real property register was a mess, but a check on that showed what seemed to be a single parcel of several thousand acres at least, a chunk of an eighteenth-century grant.

Not even a passport picture to go with the number, and he owns ten square miles of scenery. Someone likes his privacy, he thought, looking at the address. Then: *Hey, if you had enough pull, could you blank yourself out? Nah, nobody can evade the Web.*

Demarcio hesitated, then pulled a framed picture out of a drawer. The glass was cracked, as if someone had thrown it at a wall.

"She told me she was going to break up with him. Couldn't take the emotional distance and lies anymore. Then she didn't show up to work yesterday."

"So she's missing the day before the fire," Salvador said, looking at the picture. "She didn't call in? Just nothing?"

"Nothing this morning. That's not like her. She's the most reliable person who's ever worked for me."

Only she's gone and the place she lived in is a scorch mark, which conveniently shit-cans all the evidence.

The photo beneath the cracked glass showed a youngish man, though on second thought perhaps Salvador's own age. Or maybe somewhere between twenty-five and thirty-five. Dark hair worn a little longer than was fashionable these days, a vaguely Mediterranean-looking face that could have come from anywhere. Handsome, perhaps a little too much so, though not quite enough to be called pretty.

Androgynous, that's the word. But there's something dangerous-looking about him too. Like a cat, like a snake. Or a weasel, or a razor blade in an apple.

"He's . . ." Demarcio frowned. "You know, I met him a dozen times and I listened to *her* talk about him a *lot* and I really can't tell you much. He's wealthy . . . very wealthy, I think. Some sort of old money, but that's an impression, not knowledge. He wouldn't tell Ellen anything about that either, just some vague bullshit about 'investments.' American born but he has a slight accent, French, I think, which would fit with the name. I know he speaks French and Italian and Spanish . . . and yes, German too, all of them very well. I couldn't tell you where his money comes from, or where he went to university or, well, anything."

Salvador looked at the photo. Unobtrusively he brought up the composite picture on the notepad. The resemblance to the reconstruction of the man the Lopez family had seen standing motionless outside their house just before the fire was unmistakable. He scanned the picture into the notepad, and the program came up with a solid positive when it did its comparison.

"Would you say this is Adrian Brézé?" he said, and showed her the screen.

"Absolutely," she said.

"And this is his sister?" he said, changing to the composite of the woman the Lopezes had seen with Ellen Tarnowski earlier.

"Well . . ." The picture wasn't quite as definite; they'd glimpsed the face only in passing and through a window. "Yes, I'd say so. It's a striking resemblance, isn't it? Like twins, only they'd have to be fraternal."

"Have you seen *this* man?"

The composite this time was the older man with the gun who'd frightened the Lopezes out of their home . . . and probably saved their lives, considering how fast the building had gone up.

"No, I can't say I have. That is, he's similar to any number of people I've seen, but he doesn't bring anyone immediately to mind."

Salvador grunted; it was a rather generic Anglo countenance, in fact. Offhand he'd have said Texan or Southern of some sort, there was something about the cheekbones that brought Scots-Irish hillbilly to mind, and the long face on a long skull, but even that was just an educated guess. The corps was lousy with that type.

"Do you think Mr. Brézé is capable of, mmm, violent actions?"

She paused for a long moment, looking down at her fingers. When she met his eyes again his alarm bells rang once more.

"I think he's capable of anything. Anything at all."

"Had a temper?"

She shook her head. "No. He was always a perfect gentleman. But I could *feel* it. Sort of a, um, potential."

Which would be a big *help in court.*

"Now, you saw Ms. Tarnowski later that evening?"

Now Demarcio flushed. "Yes, with Ms. Brézé . . . Adrienne Brézé. At La Casa Sena, they were having dinner at a table near mine."

That was an expensive restaurant on Palace, just off the plaza, in an old renovated adobe that had started out as a *hacendado*'s town house. Not the most expensive in town by a long shot, but up there.

"You didn't speak with them?"

"No. They, um, didn't seem to want company." Her eyes shifted upward and she blushed slightly. "They seemed sort of preoccupied."

Ah, Salvador thought. *That sort of preoccupied. Is this an arson case or a bad movie? Sister catches her on the rebound from her brother, so brother burns the house down? Where do this sort of people come from? Do they step out of TV screens or do the screenwriters know them and use them for material?*

"You knew Adrienne Brézé socially?"

"No. I'd never seen her before. Didn't even know Adrian had a sister."

"Then how did you know the woman's name?" he said.

An exasperated glance. "I asked the maître d'hôtel at La Casa Sena, of course! I'm a regular there. So is Adrian."

He hid a smile. *I think Ms. Demarcio is a nice lady. She's concerned about Tarnowski. But I also think she's a gossip of the first water.*

"Thank you, Ms. Demarcio—"

"Well, aren't you going to *tell* me anything?"

He sighed. Usually you *didn't*, but he needed to develop this source.

"We're investigating the circumstances of the fire at Ms. Tarnowski's apartment, and trying to find where she is."

Her eyes narrowed slightly; that meant, *We think it was torched*, without actually saying it.

"I talked to the Lopez family, and there was a man with a *gun*."

He sighed. Santa Fe was a small town. "True. We've got Santa Fe and Albuquerque and the state police all looking."

She hesitated, twisting her fingers together. "I . . . I got a call from Ellen today."

Salvador came alert without tensing.

"You did?" he said, the sort of polite verbal placeholder you used to keep people talking.

"She . . . she called me on a videoconference link. She said she was staying at Adrienne Brézé's place in California. That she was . . . working for Ms. Brézé now, cataloging her family's art collection."

Aha! Salvador thought. *And again, aha!*

"We'll need the address," he said.

"I . . . I'm afraid I don't *have* an address. Just a phone number. But Ms. Brézé said not to use it very often."

This is one scared lady, Salvador thought. *And I really don't think she's naturally a scaredy-cat.*

He thumbed the number into his phone as she gave it, then spoke: "Here's my card."

He slid it across the low table. "Please let me know immediately if Ms. Tarnowski contacts you again, or you get any other information."

"Detective," she said as he rose to go.

He turned, raising a brow, and she went on: "Remember I said Adrian was capable of anything at all?"

He nodded.

"Well, his sister struck me the same way. But worse." A swallow. "Much, much worse."

Outside Cesar met him, and they walked down towards the end of Canyon, then turned right across the bridge over the small and entirely dry Santa Fe River with its strip of grass and cottonwoods. That led to Palace just north of the cathedral, the reddish sandstone bulk of it towering over the adobe and stucco of the neighboring buildings. Salvador jammed his fists into the pockets of his sheepskin jacket and scowled, pausing only to give the finger to a Mercedes that ran the yellow light and nearly hit them. Right afterwards a rusting clunker with the driver's door held on with coat-hanger wire did the same thing.

Then he keyed the number into the police net, the service that gave you locations. . . .

Not listed, it said.

"This is screwy," he complained, after he'd filled his partner in.

He looked at it again; California area code, south-central coast. But . . .

Not listed.

"You try, Cesar."

Not listed.

The next time Eric tried, a string of garbage scrolled across his phone.

"Now that," he said, "isn't just fucked-up. That is enemy action."

Cesar raised his hands palms up and made a weighing motion; he wasn't as paranoid as his senior partner. *Maybe*, it said.

"But at least we've got names to go with our composites. Adrian and Adrienne Brézé," Eric conceded.

"That is fucked-up, too, *amigo*," Cesar said cheerfully. "Because the databases are *still* not giving us anything even though we've got the names. They don't have e-mail addresses; they don't have bank accounts. . . . You did send them out?"

"Yeah, local, state, Fart, Barf and Itch, and Homeland Insecurity, which means the spooks. It can take a while, even now that they've got the whole system cross-referenced."

"It shouldn't take a while to get *something*. Everyone leaves footprints. The question is, my friend, should we be thinking of this as an arson case, or some sort of kidnapping?"

"A little early for that. According to Demarcio, she's wherever-it-is of her own free will. 'Sorting paintings,' if you know what I mean."

"Yeah, only we can't *reach* wherever she is, and anyone will say anything if they're persuaded right. But!"

Cesar grinned and showed his notepad, a picture of an elderly but well-maintained Prius. "Abandoned car on Palace, ticketed and towed about an hour ago. Registered to—"

"Ellen Tarnowski."

"So maybe, it's not so early to think about maybe some slight element of kidnapping."

Salvador's notepad beeped. "Well, fuck me. Take a look."

The picture was from the security cams at Albuquerque International Sunport, the airport in the larger city an hour's drive south; the face-recognition software had tagged it.

"That's Brézé and our mystery man with the gun, all right. Still in the black leather outfit. Nine thirty to San Francisco last night, just opened up and the request got it. Wait a minute—"

He tapped at the screen. "*Fuck* me."

"What's wrong?"

"They didn't have tickets. Look."

"Could be tickets under someone else's name."

"No, there were two vacant first-class seats, according to the ticketing record. But look, when they cleared for takeoff they recorded *all the first-class* seats as full. But there aren't any *names* attached to these two. Which isn't supposed to be possible. Breaks three laws and twenty regulations."

Cesar made a hissing sound of frustration. "*Mierda*, for a second I thought we'd get a name on Mr. Shotgun. What about the other end?"

"Flight got into San Francisco International . . . nothing on the surveillance cam there, and it *should* have gotten them."

The younger man grinned. "Maybe they got out on the way, *¿sí?*"

"Yeah, at forty thousand feet. So . . . possible kidnapping, by one or two different parties. Or possibly the Brézé twins are acting in concert. One or the other of them's responsible for the burn, I'd bet my cojones on it."

"Okay, we got her last-known location in Santa Fe. Here. Let's go see how Demarcio's story holds up."

The building that housed La Casa Sena and several upscale shops was mainly nineteenth-century, adobe-built with baked-brick trim, rising around a courtyard patio that featured a pool and a huge cottonwood. Originally it had comprised thirty-three rooms of living space–workroom-storeroom–quasi fortress that presented a blank defensive wall four feet thick to the outside intended to repel Apaches, bandits, rebels and tax collectors, whether Mexican or gringo. Now there were a wine boutique, several stores selling upscale jewelry and foofaraw, and the restaurant occupying two sides of the rectangle.

Iron tables stood out under the cottonwoods, vacant this time of year; the flower beds were sere and brown as well. A glassed-in box near the entrance covered the original well that had supplied water to the complex. He glanced at the menu posted beside the door; they weren't open for lunch yet.

"Ever eaten here?" he asked.

"Twenty-five for a *ham sandwich*?" Cesar said, peering at the prices. "You *loco*?"

"I had dinner here once. An anniversary, the last one before Julia divorced me and went off to Bali to Find Herself."

Cesar snorted. "You can't find yourself in New Mexico, you aren't going to find anything different in Cincinnati *or* damn Bali."

"Yeah. But the food was actually pretty damn good."

"Jesus, if lunch is like this, what's dinner for two cost?"

"About the price of a trip to Paris." Salvador grinned and read the small print: "And the ham sandwich has green chile aioli, ciabatta, aged Wisconsin Gouda—"

"It's still twenty-five dollars for a fucking ham sandwich. Okay, a ham and cheese. I don't care if the butter was made from the Virgin's milk."

"Can I help you?" a young woman in a bow-tie outfit said, opening the door. "Lunch doesn't start seating until—"

They flashed their badges. "The manager, please."

That brought the manager out quickly. "I'm Mr. Tortensen—"

After the introductions the manager showed them through to his office, though Salvador felt as if half the contents of his wallet had vanished just stepping over the threshold of the front door into the pale Taos-style interior. Even the office was stylish. The man was worried, brown-haired, in his thirties, lean to the point of emaciation, and licking his lips.

What sort of restaurant manager is skinny? Salvador thought. *Well, probably this far up the scale the customers don't like to think eating can make you fat.*

"What can I do for you, Officers?" he said.

Salvador leaned back in the chair. He knew he could be intimidating to some. People who'd led sheltered lives particularly. He didn't have to *do* anything, even if they were people who'd consciously think of him as something they'd scrape off their shoe on a hot day.

"You had two guests at dinner yesterday," he said. "From a little after five thirty to seven thirty. Ellen Tarnowski and Adrienne Brézé. I'd like some details."

The man started very slightly; then his mouth firmed. "I'm afraid our clients' confidentiality is—"

Cesar cut in smoothly: "Ms. Tarnowski's house burned down last night, and there's suspicion of arson. Her car was found and towed from a parking spot not too far from here. We have independent confirmation that she was here last night, and she's a missing person with this as her last-known location."

Salvador nodded. "So we'd *really appreciate* your cooperation in this arson and possibly kidnapping investigation."

The manager started; short of shouting *terrorism* it was about the best possible way of getting his attention.

"Let me make a few calls," he said, pulling out his phone.

Cesar worked on his notepad. Salvador crossed his arms on his chest and enjoyed watching the manager sweat as he tried to get back to *his* routine. People came in to talk to Mr. Tortensen about purchasing and things that probably made perfect sense. At last a harassed-looking man in his early twenties came in; he was slimly handsome, but looked as if he really wasn't used to waking up this early. Which, with a night-shift job like waiting tables, he might not be.

"Ah, this is Joseph Morales, Officer," Tortensen said. "He had A-seventeen . . . their table . . . last night."

Maricón, Salvador thought; clinically, he wasn't bothered by them.

There had been one he knew who was an artist with a Javelin

59

launcher. *He could put a rocket right through a firing slit, which has a good dirty joke in it somewhere.*

"Pleased to meet you," Morales said to the policemen with transparent dishonesty, but he was at least trying to hide it. "How can I help you?"

The restaurant manager started to speak, and Salvador held up a hand. "We're interested in a party of two at one of your tables last night."

He held up his notepad with Tarnowski's face.

The waiter laughed—it was almost a giggle. "Oh, *them*. Yes, I remember them well. They ordered—well, Ms. Brézé ordered—"

He rattled off a list of things, most of which Salvador had never heard of. He held up a hand.

"What did that come to?"

"With the wines? About . . . twenty-five hundred."

The manager was working his desktop, and nodded confirmation. Cesar gave a smothered sound that had probably started as an agonized grunt, passed through indignation, and was finally suppressed with a tightening of the mouth.

"Tip?"

"Very generous. Seven hundred."

Outside, Cesar shook his head. "Seven hundred for the *tip*? And you *went* there?"

"I was starting to get worried about Julia, wanted to show her I thought about something besides my job. Didn't work. Three weeks later she told me I was just as far away living here as I had been when they deployed me to Kandahar."

"Ai!"

"Yeah, sweet, eh? And I didn't leave a seven-hundred-dollar tip, either."

"What's the next stop?"

"I'll try to see if anyone around saw the van that Adrian Brézé and Mystery Man in Leather were using after they left the burn site."

Salvador laughed. "And *I'll* get back and catch up on my paperwork, and keep trying to locate that phone number. Don't you wish this were a TV show?"

"So we could just work one case at a time? *Sí*, the thought has crossed my mind. Along with a lot else. Like, who was the old guy in black leather? How does he fit in?"

CHAPTER FOUR

Harvey Ledbetter leaned against his pickup and pushed the sunglasses up on his forehead before he crossed his arms on his chest. He was a lean, grizzled man a little below six feet, his close-cropped brown hair shot with iron gray above a long, bony face, extremely fit for his early sixties. His eyes were startlingly blue against the weathered tan of his face.

Hot metal pinged in the engine, and the summer sun was pleasantly warm, without the humid rankness he'd grown up with. The breeze from the west held a little coolness; the Big Sur coastline wasn't far away. This dirt road ended in a field of long golden yellow summer grass that smelled like old hay, above a ravine that cut down through a redwood grove to the sea. Wind soughed through the grass, and birds chased insects in swift, swooping curves.

He drew on his cigarette and savored the harsh bite. The Wreakings that shielded his mind were a teasing feeling at the corner of perception's eye, like a slight continuous buzzing. Nicotine helped long-learned mental disciplines to keep him reasonably calm, despite the knowledge of what was coming towards him. A click sounded through the bud in his right ear: *alert.*

It was *some* comfort to know that hidden snipers were covering the meeting site with rifles firing silver-jacketed .338 Lapua magnum rounds. Some comfort, but not too much. Tōkairin Michiko was a pureblood. She could sculpt the probabilistic foam underlying reality at a level that made his own meager talent look like a toy water pistol compared to an Apache gunship. Despite defenses as elaborate as he could make them, at close range she could probably simply make his ticker give out, or block a vein in his brain for a few crucial seconds. She could *certainly* do it if given time to use glyphs and Mhabrogast to focus the effect, or if she used something preactivated.

A quiet burble of engine, a singing and crunching sound of gravel under wheels. The car snaked up the switchbacks of the road towards him, trailing dust. His brows rose a little when it was close enough for him to see the make: a Nissan GT-X, low-slung sleek elegance, with a double-turbocharged engine that put out more power than most armored personnel carriers weighing twenty times as much. You *could* use that on dirt country roads, but . . .

*Tacky. Very fucking rich-bitch, Michiko-*sama.

It was chrome yellow, with a license plate bearing the *mon* symbol of the Tōkairin clan and the black sun pierced by a jagged trident that was the sigil of the Council of Shadows.

On the one hand, it won't mean anything to anyone who doesn't know already. On the other hand, it's worrisome that they're so confident now. The last generation was a lot more careful about hiding. Michiko's bunch just doesn't give a shit. I wonder if they'll register it as the official Trademark of Evil one of these days.

The sports car pulled to a stop ten yards away, the quiet sound of its engine dying instantly. Harvey noted without surprise that the position would block one of his snipers and give the other the worst possible shot; Michiko probably wasn't even consciously aware that she'd done that. He threw his cigarette to the ground, twisted it under his heel and moved to the tailgate of his pickup, which would put her back under both scopes.

She got out of the car with a lithe catlike motion and walked towards him, smiling. She wore low-slung black Key Closet skinny jeans, which he admitted she could bring off, and a sleeveless silk shirt. It all showed the sort of figure high-bred Shadowspawn females tended to have, slim but high-tensile.

All right if you like weasels with small tits, he thought whimsically, fighting down a hundred thousand years of instinctive terror. *In her case, blond Japanese weasels.*

He bowed his head slightly as she approached. She took off her sunglasses, tucked one arm of them in the neck of her shirt and returned the gesture, a little more deeply.

"Hoping the water will fall out of my head?" she said, in pluperfect Californian English.

"Well, you may notice I'm not offerin' cucumbers," he said dryly, the Texan Hill Country rasp strong in his voice.

It was only in his imagination that she smelled of rotting blood. There wasn't any *physical* way of telling her apart from any rich Yonsei girl, unless you counted the tiny golden flecks in the irises. The Tōkairin had thought they were ninja sorcerers until the missionaries of the Order of the Black

Dawn arrived in the early Meiji era and told them where their powers really came from, and how to make the next generation stronger.

"You're being very unfriendly. I can sense hostility even with those tiresome shields," she said, pouting slightly. "Is this any way to treat a friend?"

"No," he said.

After a moment she shrugged. "Oh, well, if you want to be all tiresome and businesslike. I've got the preliminary schedule for the Council meeting in Tbilisi. Who's coming in, when, and where they're staying, plus the security protocols."

He raised his brows. "They've settled on those already? Bad tradecraft."

She shrugged. "It's a *protocol*. The older generation . . ."

He nodded. Shadowspawn tended to be fanatically conservative, more so as they got older. Many of the current Council lords had been youngsters when their parents carefully directed Archduke Ferdinand down the wrong road in Sarajevo.

"We've made a formal request for a security review, warning that terrorists might strike, but they turned it down. Of course."

"We?" Harvey asked.

"Ah, the . . . Progressive Party, we're calling ourselves. Or the whippersnappers, to the other side."

Harvey laughed; it was quite genuine, and he wished it back.

One slim yellow brow went up. "I notice that you're not exactly the official Brotherhood yourself, Mr. Ledbetter," she said. "They're not nearly imaginative enough to try using us against one another the way you have. Perhaps you're not as different from us as you'd like to think."

He hid his wince, but it was her turn to laugh; the silver tinkle was like splints shoved under the fingernails of his mind.

Don't talk to them beyond the bare necessity, he repeated to himself. *Don't show any reactions. Don't emote, don't engage. They're naturally good at getting inside your head even if you're warded, and they play games and manipulate the way they breathe. Don't give her leverage to fuck with your mind. Just the minimum.*

He held out his hand. She extended hers, with a memory stick in it; his came back before skin could touch skin.

"Now I'm hurt. Don't you *trust* me?" she said archly.

" 'Bout as much as I trust a cobra," he said.

"Hsssssss!"

The sound was startlingly realistic. He waited, immobile, until she tossed the little data-storage unit. He caught it out of the air, then waited while she walked back to her car with a taunting swing of the hips. The superchargers whined, and the long yellow-and-black shape seemed to stretch, vanishing in a spray of dust and gravel as she tapped the accelerator. Harvey dropped the stick into a plastic baggie, tucked it into his pocket and sighed, then produced a handkerchief to wipe his face.

"Tough?" a voice asked in his ear.

"Strenuous," he replied. "Just a mite strenuous, I'd say."

And I don't know whether I'm glad Adrienne is dead or not. She was just as much a monster, maybe more, and a lot smarter. On the other hand she was more rational, so maybe a bit easier to anticipate. Michiko might have killed me just because it felt good.

Harvey's covering squad waited a half hour before they came in, which was good fieldcraft. Both had scope-sighted rifles with them, angular military models with chassis of carbon fiber and aircraft-grade aluminum; the Mhabrogast protective glyphs and silver threads were decidedly nonstandard.

They broke them down, fitted them into the shaped and padded recesses of the carrying cases and slipped them into the compartment behind the rear seat of the pickup. Otherwise they were in the sort of thing hikers might wear, tough cotton drill in neutral colors and laced boots. Traipsing around Big Sur in a sniper ghillie suit would be a bit conspicuous.

"I could have gotten her easy," Jack Farmer groused.

He was a thirty-something hard case with cropped blond hair and a snub nose, and Harvey didn't like him.

He's trustworthy, and he's good at what he does. I just don't like him, because he's a son of a bitch. I suppose his mother *loved him. Before he learned to talk, at least.*

His partner was a woman named Anjali Guha, South Asian dark, athletic, and, in Harvey's opinion considerably smarter. Or at least less driven and obsessed, which was more important than sheer IQ. Your mind could do only what your emotions let it. Character was more important than the size of your vocabulary every time.

"The plan is to use her to get a chance at a lot more of them," Harvey said patiently. "We *did* use her . . . and through her, Adrienne Brézé . . . to get Hajime."

"She and her husband stepped into her grandfather's shoes," Farmer said. "Does that mean we used her, or she used us?"

Guha gave him a barbed glance. "That's a distinction without a difference, Jack," she said sharply. "We got Adrienne Brézé too, who is, was, a bigger fish."

"Ellen Tarnowski got *her*," Harvey pointed out, which made them both pout a little at being outclassed by an amateur.

"And anyway," Guha went on, "if you'd really *intended* to kill her, something would probably have happened to stop it. You'd have had a stroke, or a wasp would have stung you just as you were squeezing the trigger, or some tourists would have tripped over you, or you'd have been assaulted by a wild sheep that suddenly decided it was an arse-bandit queer for humans. You know how that works, yes, indeed, you do."

"Yeah," he said, half snarling with frustration. "But I just want to *exterminate* them."

Harvey sighed. "You're around thirty on the scale, aren't you?"

The Alberman Scale ran from fully human at zero to absolute pure-bred Shadowspawn at a hundred; there were around a hundred and thirty-seven genes involved, mostly recessives. Professor Alberman had developed the scale and the automatic DNA sequencing test for the Council of Shadows, but both sides used it.

The Brotherhood operative was tanned, but he could still flush; thirty was more than twice the average in the general population. It took twenty-five or higher to use the Power consciously, not just have premonitions or the occasional tweaking of probabilities. Harvey was a twenty-seven.

"Yeah, I am. Your point?"

The point is that I keep having to remind you of things, Harvey thought. *That's the problem with talking politics—which this is, down and dirty. People have to be continually mentally reinforced if you want them to absorb knowledge that contradicts what they want to hear; otherwise it just sort of slip-slides away, gets blurred down to the noise level of their viewpoint. It's a pain in the ass.*

It wasn't an accident that Harvey was known as the Brotherhood's loose cannon.

"The point is that you'd have to exterminate the human race to get rid of the Shadowspawn genes," Harvey went on patiently. "Startin' with the ones like . . . oh, the three of us. Humans're too mixed; hell, being a stable Shadowspawn-human mix probably *defines* us as a species and has for twenty thousand years. If the bad guys hadn't spread their genes around during the Empire of Shadow, humans . . . mostly humans . . . probably wouldn't have been able to overthrow them in the first place. Why do you think we're the only surviving type of hominid? I suspect it's because they preferred fucking us to Neanderthals or the rest."

I need to keep Farmer on-side. On the other hand, he's not stupid, exactly. He just filters out things that don't fit the story as he'd prefer it. Shit, that just makes him human. For that matter, Shadowspawn do that too.

"In fact," he went on, "if we weren't mixed, we'd probably be sitting around in caves splitting mammoth bones for the marrow and eating the lice out of one another's hair. Notice when civilization started?"

"When we overthrew them!"

"Yeah, which was just about the same time they finished diluting themselves until it was pretty hard to know who *was* them and who *was* us. A lot of the first pharaohs and kings and high priests and whatnot had a lot of Shadowspawn blood, judging from the way they acted. And if the Council Shadowspawn weren't mixed, they'd be less of a problem—they wouldn't be able to cooperate or care about long-term group interests even as much as they do."

"We can kill all the purebred ones," Farmer said stubbornly; he had the ghost of a Midwestern accent under the California. "There aren't more than a few thousand of them. The ones in the Council clans, in their breeding program."

Guha snorted as she snapped the last of the latches on the battered rifle case.

"Jack, back in Victorian times *you* would have been a purebred. Most of the original Order of the Black Dawn weren't any stronger than you when they discovered Mendel and Darwin and started to use the Power to reconcentrate the heritage. They let in anyone who could lift and turn a feather then. And even if we *did* get rid of the ones who think of themselves as Shadowspawn, the whole thing might happen again. The genes themselves are lucky. They *want* to recombine and they'd still be there."

"Sort of like the One Ring," Guha put in.

"Yeah, all we have to do is reeducate them," Farmer jeered. "They'll become members of PETA—People for the Eating of Anthropoids."

Harvey checked the hidden compartment to make sure nothing was visible to the naked eye; it was a pity this wasn't Texas, where a gun rack was routine. Hiding was one thing the Brotherhood was *very* good at, though Farmer could probably simply tell a cop that these weren't the droids he was looking for and get away with it.

There was a cooler in the back of the pickup. He pulled out beers, a hefeweizen he'd picked up in Los Gatos, plus shaved-ham sandwiches on sourdough rolls, and handed them around.

"That's pretty much what I did with Adrian, Jack," he said, biting into one and savoring the sharp-smoky-meaty flavors.

If hunger was the best sauce, danger survived came a close second; it made you horny too. Luckily that wasn't as big a nuisance when you were over sixty, though it didn't go away either.

"I got him around puberty and raised him," he pointed out mildly. "And he turned out all right."

A lot more like a human being in the positive sense of the term than you,

Jack, he thought to himself. *I suspect if you were just a little higher on the Alberman, if you could feed and get any benefit from the blood and nightwalk, you'd be off to the other side like a shot.*

Guha nodded. "And *Adrian* has killed more Shadowspawn than you've had beers, Jack, yes, indeed. He scares the hell out of me, but not like he's going to boil my eyeballs just for the fun of seeing me run around bumping into things."

"Yup," Harvey drawled. "The problem with the Shadowspawn isn't really their instincts. Hell, *I* feel like killing people pretty often—who doesn't occasionally want to kick some asshole into oblivion? The problem is that the Order of the Black Dawn started as a bunch of black-path occultists. Just because they stopped worshiping Satan and started worshiping themselves after they found out *why* they could do what they did didn't make them any less assholes, and they raised their kids that way."

Farmer took a swig of the beer and shrugged. "So long as I get to kill the bastards, I'm satisfied. And you two give me more opportunities than I'd get if I stayed on the reservation. The Brotherhood's gotten too much like a fucking rabbit in the headlights, you ask me. The Council's planning to wreck the world and all they're doing is trying to build a bolt-hole so they can survive the apocalypse."

Guha nodded. "That's why I'm with you, Harvey. But I notice you don't tell *Adrian* about your little talks with Michiko-*san*," she pointed out.

"I did my job too good. The boy's idealistic."

They all chuckled. "So," Farmer said, "what's your solution for the ones we *can't* reeducate?"

"Oh, we kill 'em all," Harvey said cheerfully. "And Tbilisi is goin' to be one *fine* opportunity for that. A lot more than Michiko and her hubby think. I got a project going along those lines. You guys in?"

"In," Farmer said.

Guha shuddered. "In. But it also means we'll have to walk into the biggest nest of them that's gathered for generations. With enough Power in the air to make all the molecules dance in their favor."

"Considering the alternative, I don't think there *is* much of an alternative. At least Adrienne isn't going to be around. She was too smart for comfort and she had a lot more self-control than most of her friends."

Guha sighed. "I said I am in, too. Deep in doo-doo."

CHAPTER FIVE

Adrian and Ellen crossed the Loire heading north towards Paris in the early evening; the rain had stopped and the lingering twilight of September had a liquid washed-out quality to it.

"I'm glad we didn't take the A6," Adrian said. "It is a nightmare this time of year."

The sun was setting westward, across a low, rolling landscape of vineyards showing red and yellow, reaped fields and autumn-tinged woods, villages and the occasional château. They both ignored the petrol stations and other modern excrescences.

On their right the sunlight caught a line of hills in the distance, turning them blue flushed with a slight tinge of pink towards their tops. Adrian handled the Ferrari F50 with his usual verve; it would do zero to a hundred in eight seconds, and he liked to do exactly that. It no longer drove Ellen to the verge of lost bladder control, and she'd finally started believing that the police wouldn't pull them over either.

Well, he's got reflexes like a leopard, when he isn't literally *being a leopard,* she thought, as he touched the accelerator and the g-force shoved her back into the upholstery in a scent of fine leather. *Plus he can warp probability. It's still a little scary.*

She chuckled as they zipped around a large truck and back into the left-hand lane, and he looked over at her.

"I was just remembering that while I was at Rancho Sangrón—"

He chuckled in turn; she'd coined the pun on the place's name, turning it from Ranch of the Holy Blood to Ranch of the Asshole.

"—Adrienne took me on that motorcycle cruise up the coast to San Francisco. Scared the shit out of me, and that was only *just* a metaphor. You Brézés have a thing for speed and risk, don't you?"

He stiffened, then shook his head. "You're right. For too many years I defined myself in opposition to her; yet we are . . . were . . . similar in many respects."

"Your evil twin."

"Exactly! I can afford to acknowledge things like that now."

"Now that she's dead."

"Since you killed her." Adrian laughed.

Ouch.

Ellen winced inwardly. Half the time she remembered plunging the hypo into Adrienne's foot with savage glee. The other half it made her queasy. Not so much the fact that she'd done it, as the way it had felt for her.

Which was very damned good. And yes, she deserved it—God, did she deserve it!—but should I have enjoyed it so much? Should I enjoy remembering *it so much? Yeah, I was so scared all the time and it was* such *a fucking relief to get away from the mad, sadistic bitch, but I did* kill *her, after all. I always used to put spiders and centipedes out in the garden instead of squishing them. I totally lost it when my cat brought me a dead bird.*

And now I'm killing people. *And enjoying it. Okay, Adrienne only just qualifies as "person," but still.*

He put his hand on her shoulder and squeezed for a moment. It would have been even more comforting if they weren't doing nearly two hundred kilometers per hour with only one of the driver's hands on the wheel.

"I am sorry, my sweet. I forget sometimes that you were not brought up to this war. Most of those close to me have been born into it, but you were not."

"Yeah, I'm not a conflict junkie. Even to get out of the coal country I never seriously considered enlisting. And now I'm a supercommando fem-ninja in training."

He laughed aloud at that. "You have natural talent," he said. "But I would not go quite that far."

"And I feel a little, mmm, guilty about all the people we left in that horrible place."

Adrian shrugged expressively. "My sweet, you *are* in the war now. And you are on the side of the guerrillas. We cannot afford sentiment. If I had tried to smuggle out . . . oh, say, little Cheba . . ."

She shot him a dark glance, half-serious. He'd been impersonating one of Adrienne's guests, and he'd had to take the girl as *refreshment*.

I believe he didn't have sex with her. He's actually a bit of a Boy Scout about that—which, considering what it would be like to be a teenage boy able to play orgasmatron games with girls' brains, says something very good

75

about him. But I find I'm jealous of his putting the bite on her, too. Mine! Mine! All mine! And when I'm short, you stick to the blood-bank product no matter how bad it tastes!

". . . it would have aroused suspicions."

"Well, she's dead now too," Ellen said. "Poor girl . . ."

There was a *quality* to his silence this time.

"She's not?"

Adrian shook his head, his eyes commendably on the roadway.

"No?"

"No," he said aloud, reluctantly. "We have a base-link."

She nodded; being on the receiving end of a feeding attack wasn't just a matter of the Shadowspawn drinking your blood or the euphoric drug. There was a mental joining, a feedback loop; she'd heard Adrienne use the phrase *quantum entanglement*. The feedback could get seriously disturbing, and not only for the human victim. Ellen suspected that was why Shadowspawn had evolved clinical sadism as their normal personality type; otherwise feeling their prey's emotions would put them off their food.

"Not like we have?"

"No, not nearly so close. That was a high-link, with very detailed transference that let us communicate directly. That takes long interaction. I get . . . generalized feelings from her. She is being used for feeding and—"

He shrugged his shoulders.

Yeah, a feeding attack means you usually also get the full explosion-in-the-kink-factory sex-object treatment, like someone playing with their food, World Wrestling Federation style. Fun when it's a game with Adrian, pretty horrible when it's real. Well, there was a lot of pleasure involved, technically, but in a sort of squiky, self-loathing, terrorized, half-crazy way. Definitely not fun.

"Poor girl doubled, then," Ellen said.

Adrian frowned. "There was a toughness to her," he said. "Resilience."

"She'll need it," Ellen said, feeling a rush of sympathy. "At least I can *wake up* from my nightmares now."

CHAPTER SIX

"I wish we could have rescued them all," Ellen said. "You sent those two Brotherhood types away before the end . . . couldn't you have sent Cheba with them, at least?"

"Possibly. But *possibly* that would have aroused suspicions, and I could not take that risk. Not with your life at stake. Shadowspawn are paranoid, not least about one another; even when she believed I was another, Adrienne would have watched me carefully for the slightest sign of intrigue. You would not believe what a black brew of murder and madness, incest and sadism and depravity their lives are."

"Oh, I got some faint tinge of an idea," she said dryly, and she could sense he flushed a little. "What with the torture and the rape and mortal terror and mass murder for fun and so forth."

"In any case, you must learn that the mission comes first. This is hard, yes. It is also essential."

"Yeah, I can see that. With my head. My gut's only half convinced."

Adrian looked eastward again. "And not far away is where it all started," he said.

"The Brézé château?"

"Yes. My great-great-grandfather's lair. Grand adept and commander of the Order of the Black Dawn. Diabolist, murderer, genius."

"Hey, fella, don't brood while you're driving at this speed! I think what's really bothering you is thinking about what you might have been like if Harvey hadn't rescued you. Or kidnapped you. Taken you away from your family before you really knew what they were, at least."

"True, that thought haunts me sometimes. And he was supposed to *kill* me, by the way. That was the first time Harvey dangerously exceeded his mission brief. Not the last, of course."

"Kill you?" She sat as upright as the reclined seat and the safety harness would let her. "Wait a minute, you never told me *that*."

Adrian shrugged. "Harvey was playing a hunch . . . and to be sure, by then he knew me, and as he said, killing a young boy he actually knew was . . . difficult. Despite what his orders were."

"Well, good for him, and to hell with the Brotherhood!"

"They thought . . . still largely think . . . that purebreds like me are damned." In profile she could see his mouth take on an ironic twist. "And there's considerable evidence in favor of that hypothesis."

"And you to disprove it. That's . . . that's *racist!*"

"There, my little cabbage, is the one sin of which neither Shadow-spawn nor the Brotherhood can be accused, at least the younger generations. Not as far as fripperies like skin color are concerned."

"You *look* like the original variety, don't you?"

"Probably, though the first Empire of Shadow is so far in the past that nobody can be sure. Only broken fragments of legends were handed down among the secret clans. When the back-breeding nears nine-tenths purity, this set of looks and build tends to crop up. But they're not closely linked to the Power, or the personality traits. It's one of the most common human phenotypes anyway; I could pass for a Provençal or a Spaniard, a Sicilian or Greek or Turk or Arab or Kurd. It's the . . . inner drives that count."

"Adrian, I can see half my job's going to be convincing you that you're *not* a monster."

"Oh, but I am," he said softly, barely audible over the low, humming growl of the engine. "But I'm a humanist monster, of sorts."

Ellen frowned several hours later. "Isn't it sort of . . . well, blatant of *us* to stay in Paris?"

"No more than anywhere else, if we're not under deep cover," Adrian said. "Why should the local Shadowspawn, who are incidentally ruled by the European branch of the Brézés, care about us?"

"We killed Tōkairin Hajime," she pointed out. "And Adrienne."

He shrugged, eyes on the narrow street. "Hajime killed my parents . . . admittedly, not the Final Death. And Adrienne had tried to kill me more than once. As long as I'm not officially back with the Brotherhood, nobody will much care. It is, you might say, just normal family life. The local Brézés probably considered me only marginally more . . . unorthodox . . . than Adrienne."

Ellen nodded. "I'm beginning to see how the Brotherhood has managed to survive all these years. The Council runs the world, but they don't do it very well."

"They approach it more like managing a series of game parks," he agreed. "Or game ranches. With the neighboring ranchers fighting one another most of the time, when they're not indulging in lethal sibling rivalries."

"Back in California, Peter, the other lucy I told you about, the scientist? He said that humans were apes who'd become more like wolves. And Shadowspawn were like apes who'd decided to imitate cats instead."

"That is quite perceptive; he seems to be a very intelligent man."

"He produced that research I got to you," Ellen said proudly; she'd liked Peter.

"We'll see what Professor Duquesne thinks; it's a good sign that he's agreed to meet us." He sighed. "And that catlike nature is part of my problem."

Ellen made an inquiring sound and he went on: "I have to fight a war and I don't know how."

"Seems to me you've been doing a good job."

"No. Oh, I know how to *fight*, certainly. I was very good working for the Brotherhood—but they pointed me at the targets, and I went after them. I was a, hmmm, black-ops wet-work specialist, not a strategist or even a field commander. A leader of small teams at most. The Brotherhood *should* be doing strategy, but despite what you and I found out for them they are not. They are in a defensive crouch; too many generations of defeat have demoralized them."

Ellen had been impressed beyond words with the way Adrian had rescued her from his sister.

But come to think about it, that was *all fairly small-scale.*

"It's not your genes," she said slowly. "Really. Adrienne, well, except for the XY thing she *was* you, genetically speaking, given how inbred the

Shadowspawn lines are. And I got the distinct impression that she *did* operate on a big scale, with big plans. That horrible synthetic smallpox thing she was working on with Michiko and those other *friends* of hers! But you stuck a stiletto into the plans."

"Harvey and I did," Adrian said. "Harvey is an excellent general, or at least he's been a colonel in this war of shadows. There's only one problem there."

"What's that?"

"Harvey is a bit drastic at times."

Ellen blinked; she liked the big grizzled Texan, and thought he was extremely shrewd behind the Hill Country–boy persona. But to have someone who could be as pellucidly ruthless as Adrian say he was too *drastic* made her think.

"I think," she said very carefully, "that you've been too much in Harvey's shadow, Adrian."

"Merde," he muttered. "I'll concentrate on tactical problems for now. And first let's get onto this ridiculous island."

"I like the idea of staying on an island in the Seine," she said.

"So do I. Unless we have to get off it quickly."

The Île Saint-Louis was mostly inhabited by very reclusive rich people who liked having a front window facing the Seine. The buildings were all seventeenth-century and immaculately kept, stone and brick and mansard slate roofs glistening in the last of the sunlight, with poplars lining the waterfront paths. She half expected to see Porthos and Aramis stroll out from an alleyway with ruff and rapier, with a link-boy trotting in front of them.

Adrian laughed when she mentioned it. "The period is right," he said. "And this was a dueling ground before it was completely built up, too. But it undoubtedly smells much better now."

He dropped into French, and quoted: "'If you walk along the streets of the Île Saint-Louis, do not ask why you feel gripped by a sort of nervous sadness. For its cause you have only to look at the solitude of the place, at the gloomy aspect of its houses and its large empty mansions. . . .'"

"Ah . . . Adrian, you didn't lock the car," she said, as they left it by the curb. "And I don't think that's a parking spot."

His teeth glinted white in the semidarkness. "It's *my* car, darling."

"Oh. And I don't think these mansions look *empty* anyway. Painfully well kept and fully booked, from the looks of things."

"The Île has effectively become a cruise ship permanently anchored in the Seine, for some time. The Rothschilds have a pied-à-terre here. Besides which, Balzac just liked portentous gloom. I enjoyed his work much more as a young man; adolescent weltschmerz, I presume. Baudelaire lived here for a time as well, rooming with Gautier and smoking hashish."

"I remember about Baudelaire," Ellen said. *"Et je vois tour à tour réfléchis sur ton teint / la folie et l'horreur, froides et taciturnes,"* she quoted with relish. "Either that, or you've got gas."

"'And I see in turn reflected on your face / Horror and madness, cold and silent.'" He laughed. "Am I that bad?"

"No, just grumpy sometimes."

His hand squeezed hers. "You are stronger than I, my Ellen."

"Oh, I dunno. You rescued me just in time, I think."

The streets were moderately full, too; a footbridge led to the Île de la Cité northwards, and the towers of Notre Dame beyond. Besides the tourists there were . . .

"Is that a Captain Ahab look-alike with an accordion and a harpoon?" she asked. "Beside the fire-eater."

"Indeed. And mimes, those street lice of Paris."

She privately agreed with that, though she supposed her brief visits made them seem more tolerable; he'd lived here off and on, and gone to university. One of them was complete with black beret, white pancake makeup and the horizontal-striped jumper, doing the supremely annoying I-see-a-glass-wall-in-front-of-you act to a harried-looking woman with a couple of baguettes sticking out of a string net shopping bag. She heard Adrian muttering under his breath.

Then the fire-eater turned, apparently fascinated by something on the river below and letting the burning stick droop. The mime was devoted to his art; it took him several seconds to notice that his fellow street performer had set the seat of his baggy trousers on fire. The mime dashed in circles, beating at the flames with both gloved hands.

Half a dozen people stopped to watch. Ellen bit down on her hand as they started to applaud, wondering how many of them thought it was part of the act.

The mime's efforts grew more frantic; then he dove over the rail into the Seine headfirst, with a high-pitched scream. A moment later he came up, standing chest-deep with water running down his greasepainted face. Both hands were underwater, presumably clutching at his seared buttocks.

"Adrian!"

He grinned sheepishly. "It is the first time, my sweet. I have fought the temptation for more than thirty years."

They came to another of the mansions, this one split up for furnished apartments. A motherly-looking Frenchwoman in her well-kept seventies greeted Adrian with a *bonsoir* and a kiss on both cheeks in the entranceway, and then gave Ellen the same and a long, considering look as she handed over the keys.

"Everything is in readiness, Adrian," she said in French. "But it will be a long time before I forgive you for starting your honeymoon in *Italy*, of all places, rather than here. And giving me only a few days' notice!"

"Ellen, an old friend from my time here as a student, Madame Noémi Lasalle. Madame Lasalle, my wife, Ellen, née Tarnowski."

"It is a pleasure," the older woman said in English; then she dropped back into French. "Even if you married an American, Adrian, at least your Hélène is beautiful, beautiful! May your lives have much happiness."

The old lady drooped one eyelid at Ellen, who chuckled in reply. Adrian missed the byplay, for once.

"Madame Lasalle, *I* am an American by birth, as were my parents and grandparents," he said, exasperation in his tone. "It is appropriate that I marry an American as well, *hein*?"

"Bah. Jesus Christ was born in a stable; does than make him a horse?"

"Ah . . . She also speaks French, Madame Lasalle."

"Of course," Lasalle said with a sniff. "You are a man of impeccable taste. Could you *marry* a woman who did not speak the language of civilization?"

Ellen laughed aloud and spoke . . . in French. Her accent wasn't too strong, and her grammar was good if slightly formal and slow. She'd been speaking it with Adrian for some time now, to gain fluency.

"You have reason, madame. I was a student of the arts by profession, and French is inescapable if one is serious."

"Indeed. I would also expect Adrian to marry a woman of solid good sense. I have stocked the *appartement* Henri IV so that you need not leave it if you wish."

"There is *glace* Berthillon?" Adrian asked.

"Of course there is Berthillon! Did I not know you as a youngster?"

He smiled; Ellen blinked a little at the fond expression.

Well, I do have fifty years of stuff to catch up with.

"What flavors?"

"*Agenaise, Banane, Café au whisky, Café Dauphinoix, Cannelle Cappuccino, Caramel, Caramel au beurre salé, Caramel au gingembre, Chocolat au nougat, Chocolat blanc, Chocolat du mendiant, Chocolat blanc du endiant, Chocolat noir, Créole, Feuille de Menthe, Gianduja à l'orange, Gianduja aux noisettes, Grand-Marnier, Lait d'amande, Moka, Marron Glacé, Noisette, Noix, Noix de coco, Nougat au Miel, Pain d'épices, Pistache, Plombières, Praline au citron et coriandre, Pralieé aux pignons, Réglisse, Thé Earl Grey, Tiramisu, Turron de jijona, Vanille . . .*"

"You did *not* stock the entire selection! There would not be room!"

"No, but enough that you will *think* that I have: the new smaller containers. Go, go, you two are newly married! You do not wish to stand talking to an old woman."

The elevator was another antique, though not quite seventeenth-century; there was a sliding accordion-joint door, with wrought-iron curlicue gates at each floor. It clunked and creaked upwards, and Ellen leaned into Adrian's shoulder.

"I wish this *were* just an extension of our honeymoon." She sighed.

"Me also."

"What's Berthillon?"

"The best *glace* . . . ice cream . . . in Paris. Which is to say, in the entire world. Made here on this island, by hand."

He laid a palm on the apartment's door for an instant, closing his eyes and concentrating; she felt a nearly irresistible impulse to smooth the lock of black hair that fell over his forehead. Then she noticed that her right hand was resting under the tail of the windcheater jacket she was wearing, on the hilt of a knife whose blade was inlaid with silver and etched Mhabrogast glyphs.

Wow. All that inside-the-head training really has *started to bite!*

His eyes opened and caught hers. "Welcome to my world, my dear one. I am sorry."

"Well, I'm *not*," she said, grabbing his ears and giving him a brief fierce kiss. "Let's unpack and have some dinner. We have to go meet this atom wrangler, but we've got an hour or two yet."

He laughed and lifted her across the threshold.

"Very well. I will fix us something to eat, and you unpack?"

"Done," Ellen said. "You'll have to give me cooking lessons sometime."

"I find it soothing to cook, but of a certainty, my sweet."

The apartment wasn't grand, despite the mildly pretentious name, though it shone with expert care and smelled slightly of sachets and wax. A hallway, a living room with windows on the plane trees of the courtyard and the Seine, a modest but superbly equipped kitchen, a study and a bedroom. The floors were polished hardwood, with a few Oriental rugs, and the furniture mostly plain in a subtle way that said expensive and old. One of the paintings on the wall opposite the fireplace was very good, but by a nineteenth-century Academic she couldn't quite identify. French, certainly, and pre-1900.

Wait a minute, she thought. *Wait a minute . . . Yup. It's by William-Adolphe Bouguereau, all right.*

It was a pleasure just to be an art history student again for an instant, and the Academics had become hot enough again to be a big part of her second-year course on French painting, to the scandal of old-fashioned Impressionist/Postimpressionist/avant-garde–succession worshipers still in thrall to the Whig narrative.

This one had a lot less of the slick surface that he used for his mythological pictures; it showed two barefoot girls, one eleven or so and one a few years younger, sitting in a wood. They wore rather plain realistic Victorian-era peasant costumes colored brown and off-white, what working countryfolk actually used every day rather than the Offenbach-operetta exaggeration of festival-day gaudiness the genre usually showed. Their faces were done with a delicate realism that actually gave you a feeling for their personalities.

Though of course they don't have the dirty, calloused feet or grime under the fingernails and their hair is far too neat and clean. Still for Bouguereau it's practically The Stone Breakers. *Not one of his better-known ones. It'll come to me, it'll come to me . . . Ah, it's* The Nut Gatherers!

There was probably a story about how it ended up here, and she wasn't sure she wanted to hear it. The casual way Shadowspawn just appropriated what they liked from galleries and museums still made her angry—which was odd, considering the *other* things they routinely did, but it hit her at a level below conscious ethical priorities. This was a really fine piece of work; whether you considered it a great painting depended on what you thought of the Academics, but there was absolutely no doubt that Bouguereau had total mastery of his technique.

The paint does exactly *what he wanted it to do,* she thought, with a smile. *The question is whether he* should *have wanted it to do that.*

There were times she could just stand and look at something like this for hours. Instead she threw the traveling cases on the bed and continued her tour of the apartment. The only real luxury was a large bathroom, featuring a bathtub carved from a block of some silver-gray stone and shaped like a futuristic gravy boat.

Just big enough for two, she thought happily.

Adrian was already busy in the kitchen; she wandered in, took a carrot and nibbled on it while she perched on a stool and watched him work.

"I get a man who's soulfully beautiful, with a body like a Greek god, knows *just* how to tie a girl up, he's rich *and he cooks*. There's no justice in the world and for once I'm the beneficiary."

"Of a surety there isn't, or you would have better," he said, pouring her a glass from the bottle of red wine he'd opened. "But this is scarcely cooking; mere unpacking and setting out. Noémi has been very thorough. Hand me those tomatoes, would you?"

She did, then hooked her feet up on a rung, sipping and watching the smooth fluidity of his motions, chuckling occasionally when he added a flourish like flipping a knife up to the ceiling and catching it as it fell; it was a pleasure with a slight frisson, when she recalled the things she'd seen him do with the same assurance. For a moment the wine distracted her.

"What *is* this?"

"Domaine de la Butte Bourgueil Mi-Pente 2003," he said. "That was a wonderful year, but perhaps . . . No, it's still at its peak. That hint of chocolate is nice, eh?"

They sat and ate: salad, olives, charcuterie of dry sausage and cured ham and rabbit terrine with herbs, a round loaf of *pain Poilâne* that crackled when you cut it, butter, a hard dry white cheese that bit gently at the mouth. She looked down again when he served the ice cream and she took her first taste. Dense, rich, tasting of actual cream and fruit . . .

"My *God*," she said.

"I told you so."

She tried to kick him beneath the table, and found her foot trapped under his. "You mustn't become predictable, my sweet."

Noémi Lasalle gave them another set of kisses when they left. It was full dark now, or at least as dark as it got in a major city, with the tall buildings of La Défense showing to one side in the middle distance and the lower-rise center of Paris to the other. The granite paving blocks glistened in the light of the cast-iron street lamps, and the heavy, silty smell of the Seine was all around them. It was cool enough to make her jacket comfortable; that also made her less self-conscious about going armed. Beneath it she wore a silk shirt, and tights and a pleated skirt and soft black pumps.

And a knife and an automatic pistol. Welcome to married life, she thought mordantly.

Ellen tucked her arm through Adrian's; the wine bar they were looking for was at 1 Quai de Bourbon, which put it at the corner with the bridge leading off the island. She looked to her right; the site of the Bastille was that way.

"Don't tell me the Shadowspawn were to blame for *that*," she said lightly; there were advantages to a husband who could sense your feelings.

"No. Too early. Though the Marquis de Sade . . ."

"At last, something good they did!"

He shook his head and staggered slightly, unlike his usual cat gracefulness. She put out a hand.

"Adrian?"

"I . . . am a little confused."

"Why?"

"This meeting is a nexus of . . . possible events. Events which depend on our decisions and actions; they will close some possible paths, open others, make some more or less likely. But there are other decision points crowding in: more and more and more, in the immediate future. I have never felt anything quite like it. And they are *blurred*. So many minds, so many of them with the Power and striving to warp the path of the future."

He shook himself slightly, as if to brace himself. *Au Franc Pinot* had a narrow blue-fronted entrance, and the steps led down to an atmospheric vaulted-stone cellar. It was pleasant, in a funky, run-down manner, though there was a very slight but definite odor of damp stone, and the tables were islands of candlelight.

Adrian sighed a little as they sat. "I used to come here while I was at La Sorbonne," he said. "It was a jazz club then, and a very good one. Though the food was execrable, but of course nobody goes to the Île Saint-Louis to *eat*."

"It's a bad-food zone?"

"No, not quite that. You can get a decent meal here. Not one of the famous *gastronomique* areas, though, nothing to attract someone looking for a special treat."

He flicked a finger in the air for two glasses of white wine and settled in to wait with a hunter's patience. Ellen took out her notepad instead, and found herself looking at a headline for want of anything better to do.

"It's amazing how she's aged," Ellen said, looking at the president's picture. "They all do."

Adrian leaned over to take a glance and nodded. "And I know why. A day or two after their inauguration, they get a visit in the White House from the Council's representatives."

"You're kidding," Ellen said.

I knew they were pulling the strings from behind the scenes, but they put the gimp on the president *in the* Oval Office? *I thought that meant something more subtle.*

"Yes. In fact, they require him, or her these days, to make a human sacrifice just to drive the lesson home, and for amusement. From the time of . . . Mmmm, I think Woodrow Wilson was the first."

"Wilson?"

"Note that he was elected on a promise to keep America out of World War One. Then he declared war on Germany. *He* turned into an old man overnight. Then he had a stroke. I suspect he tried to assert himself, and that is why he took so long dying."

Ellen turned her head and looked at him. *Sometimes he does these convoluted practical jokes. . . .*

His face was dead serious. She winced.

"This stuff just keeps getting worse."

I mean, what I went through with Adrienne was worse for me, *but that gives me an idea of the* scale *we're talking about.*

"And you wondered why I was always so gloomy," he said.

"Darling, before . . ."

Before you told me anything, and then I left you because you wouldn't open up, and then Adrienne kidnapped me on the rebound, as it were.

". . . I thought you were fascinatingly, broodingly, insanely, irritatingly romantic."

"And now?"

"Now I just think you're depressive and it's going to be my mission in life to keep you from turning in diminishing circles until you vanish up your own fundament."

He smiled at her, and she simply sat for a moment appreciating. A man cleared his throat.

"Monsieur Brézé?"

The man was middle-aged and thin, with an unfashionable grizzled ponytail and an aquiline face; in Santa Fe she'd have typed him as one of the inevitable aging hippies, though he was dressed rather better in a Euro-casual way. His brown eyes were uncomfortably acute, as well as holding the usual male appreciation. Her experience with Peter Boase at Rancho Sangre had taught her that physicists were no more likely than artists to live up to their stereotypes—less so, since artists were more prone to doing it deliberately.

"Professor Duquesne?"

The man nodded, and they exchanged names and handshakes all around in the European manner. Duquesne remained silent for a moment afterwards, studying them both. At last he spoke:

"So, monsieur. You have persuaded me to talk with you." A slight smile. "A quarter of a million euros will buy even a crank an evening of my time."

Adrian shrugged expressively—money was more or less meaningless to him, since he could have as much as he wanted. He also suppressed a movement that was almost certainly a reach for his cigarettes. Duquesne's eyebrows rose fractionally; Paris had held out on no-smoking rules longer than most other first-world places, but the changeover wasn't exactly recent. A man of Adrian's apparent age should have been used to it.

"I think I can convince you that I am, at the least, not a crank, Professor," Adrian said. "Have you examined the files I sent you?"

"Interesting. Rather as if someone who actually knew quantum mechanics had written the draft of a science-fiction novel in a documentary style, disguised as research notes whose bizarre quality increases as one goes on."

"Peter certainly knew . . . knows . . . his physics," Ellen said.

The Frenchman looked at her in surprise. "Peter?"

"Peter Boase, ScD from MIT." She didn't say *doctor*; in France that applied only to physicians, dentists, apothecaries and vets. "Later he worked at the Los Alamos laboratories. I was the one who, ah, acquired his notes. Long story."

"I know of him, a very sound young man, if adventurous . . . but he is dead, surely? Several years ago."

"Not as of this spring, although it was put about that he died. I came to know him rather well."

Adrian interrupted. "We could save a good deal of time by a little practical demonstration." He looked at her. "Two days, is it not, my sweet?"

"Red cell count doing fine, so Power away, darling, and the drinks are on me tonight."

"Then this is justified. Professor, that is a perfectly ordinary water glass, is it not?"

The older man nodded briefly; it was, of a long-stemmed type.

"Then please observe closely," Adrian said, and murmured under his breath: "*I-Moh'g, tzee, sha.*"

Oh, how I hate the sound of Mhabrogast, Ellen thought. She could see

Duquesne wince too, though he didn't know why. *You wouldn't think a symbol set could sound evil, but it does.*

Then Adrian frowned in concentration. Duquesne waited skeptically, glancing between him and the glass. Then he blinked.

Slowly, and without any fuss, the water was beginning to run *up* the inside of the glass, a thin film inching evenly up the surface. The physicist's eyes went wider and wider as it reached the rim and flowed over it and rilled down the stem, leaving a spreading stain around the base. The last of the water in the bottom froze with a crackle.

Duquesne reached out and touched it. "Cold . . ."

"Some of the energy came from subtracting the heat from the rest, I suspect," Adrian said.

"You *suspect?*"

The physicist sounded scandalized. Adrian shrugged again.

"The process is unconscious. But tell me, Professor Duquesne, how long would you have to wait before the molecules in a glass of water spontaneously behaved in that manner?"

Duquesne sat silent for thirty seconds, his eyes locked on the spreading blotch on the tablecloth.

"Not until proton decay and the end of matter," he whispered at last. "I am assuming this is not some sort of hoax. Though I very much wish that it were."

"No. You will require further proofs, of course; extraordinary claims—"

"—require extraordinary proofs, yes," the professor said. "For the sake of argument I am willing to grant for the moment that this is genuine."

His face lit with enthusiasm. "This phenomenon must be studied! Evidently Penrose was right after all! A quantum consciousness—"

Adrian shook his head. "I am very sorry, Professor, but study is not possible. Not in the sense you are using the term."

Before Duquesne could boil over Ellen put a hand on his. "Professor Duquesne, you're not a biologist. But consider, how would such an ability arise?"

"If there was something for evolution to work with, a means whereby the mind could affect quantum states, the obvious selective advantages— Oh," he said.

"Exactly." Ellen took a deep breath and closed her eyes. "I had it explained to me as . . . 'A long time ago, when humans first spread out from Africa—which was far longer ago than the archaeologists think—a small band of hunters was trapped in the mountains of High Asia, a few families, perhaps twenty or thirty in all. Each year the glaciers rose around their plateau, and the food was less, and the cold was more. It was most likely that they would merely eat one another and die. But one was born who was lucky. . . .'"

"Why would the whole human race not have such abilities by now?" Duquesne asked.

"To a certain extent they do," Adrian said. "As you said, consciousness is a quantum process. My . . . subspecies . . . has taken this to another level. Unfortunately, it arose very long ago as a bundle of abilities associated with, how would one say, a particular ecological adaptation."

Duquesne had an abstracted look for a moment. "Predation on human beings?" he said. "But why . . . Ah, the same phenomenon would make a human consciousness easier to affect, eh? And once committed to that, path dependency would maintain it even if it was no longer essential when the ability had grown. A legacy system, as it were."

Well, he's a cool one! Ellen thought. Then: *Well, judging by Peter— which is to judge by a sample of one—the stereotype is true to the extent that physicists really can get lost in an idea. But then, so do artists. Or even art historians like me. Or anyone in a field that requires really deep thought and intense commitment.*

"I am deeply sorry, but by involving you in this matter, I have endangered you, Professor Duquesne," Adrian said gently. "You now know of our existence, and of the Power. . . ."

"The Power?"

"The term for the ability in general."

The man made a dismissive gesture. "Let me develop my line of thought. So, if this phenomenon is instinctive, it is not well understood even by those who possess it?"

"No. There are many techniques for amplifying the effect, but no real scientific understanding." He smiled bleakly. "My breed is many things— paranoid, sociopathic, sadistic—but we have produced no scientists that I know of, though some have been scholars. It is only a few generations since the whole business was thought of in superstitious terms, as magic."

"If I could do such things"—Duquesne nodded towards the glass—"I might not have developed a scientific sensibility either."

He thought for a moment. "The information you sent me . . . in retrospect, and taking them seriously, the sections on the—"

Duquesne was still speaking French, but Ellen lost him after half a dozen words. She could see Adrian do the same a few seconds later.

"Professor, you are speaking to scientific illiterates," Adrian said. "Can you put this in layman's terms?"

The academic made a quick impatient gesture. "No. Not without complete misunderstanding."

"There is nothing you can say?"

Another string of technicalities, ending with *phase shifts*.

"And that is why silver resists the Power?" Adrian asked.

"From what Boase said, the transuranics should as well. Fascinating!"

"No less fascinating is that the memory stick itself had . . . I find myself in the same position as you, Professor . . . it is hard to express . . . a feeling of no feeling. Usually anything linked to a significant nexus of probabilities in the future has a *feeling* of importance. Or of nonimportance if it does not. This information simply did not show either."

"Fascinating," Duquesne murmured again. Then he laughed. "Perhaps it is as it was with the Large Hadron Collider. The future is interfering with the present to prevent certain information from being accessible."

He stopped laughing when they both stared at him expressionlessly.

"That was a *joke*, monsieur," he said.

"I'm afraid it isn't." After a moment Adrian went on: "You are willing to continue this research?"

"Ah . . . well, that is a difficult matter. I have commitments to other projects. I certainly cannot do research in isolation, without informing colleagues. . . . It would all be completely irregular. Things are not done in such a fashion. But if a project can be arranged—we must think and plan in some detail."

"Of course," Adrian said soothingly.

After a little more conversation Duquesne left, still shaking his head.

"The poor man," Ellen said wistfully. "This is his last normal moment, isn't it?"

"Yes, alas," Adrian said. "Wait . . . wait . . . *now* we follow him."

"How many?"

"It's not quite certain yet," Adrian said as they went out the door and turned right into the bustling night; Duquesne was walking towards the nearest metro station. "The world-lines are coalescing . . . yes. Two normals, renfield muscle, and a Shadowspawn. He will intervene only if the normals fail."

"You'll take care of him?"

"Exactly. I'm afraid you must keep the normals occupied."

Gulp.

"I wish Harvey were here to help."

So do I!

CHAPTER SEVEN

"**Y**ou!"

The man who called himself José Figuerez froze in the corridor with a spray of files against his chest. Harvey Ledbetter raised his hands in a soothing gesture.

"Hey, Dhul Fiqar—"

"You know my name?"

"Obviously."

"How did you get in here?"

The man's eyes darted to the stairwell. Obviously he was wondering how Harvey had gotten up here unnoticed; there was an inconspicuously armed guard on the front door and at the vehicle entrance, and the rear was locked, with steel reinforcement on the inside. Nothing out of the ordinary here in Veracruz, though the concealed stash of automatic weapons would raise eyebrows if anyone knew about them.

"I walked," Harvey said. "Let's talk, shall we?"

The man waved him through the door of the office. There were only two chairs in the little third-floor room, the office model on casters that Dhul Fiqar went to behind his desk, and a plain molded-plywood-and-wire type near the louvered window that cast bars of savage light and ink-black shade on the plain polished concrete floor. The air that came in past it was hot and rank-heavy with rancid smells, traffic stink and petrochemical plant effluent and the smell of a warm sea not far away and far too full of rotting garbage and raw sewage and the odd dead pig, dog or inconvenient human.

Veracruz was *big*. Not quite the thirty million–plus monster that Mexico City was, but bigger than New York or Tokyo, with a lot less in the way of frivolous infrastructural luxuries like sanitation than a first-world city.

The Arab seated himself behind the desk, keeping his hands on the edge. His left thumb was pushing an alarm trigger that would alert some of his followers, or at least would have if Harvey hadn't bent the path of some electrons, just *so*. The other was twitching with readiness. Which meant . . .

Yeah, gun in the upper right drawer. And that's making him feel safer, Harvey thought. *He probably thinks he's got me trapped. Silly bastard.*

"How did you find us?" the man behind the desk said tightly.

"Well, Dhul, ol' buddy, consider that we got seventeen kilos of weapons-grade plutonium out of Seversk—"

"*Seventeen* kilos?"

"Y'all weren't the only destination. Sorry, fourteen kilos for you."

I used the rest to kill Brâncuşi. Well, kill his postcorporeal energy matrix. Sorta debatable whether that was the same him *who was a bouncing baby boy 'round about 1911.*

He went on aloud: "We brought it all the way to Port-au-Prince with every security service in the world lookin' for it, and handed it over to you intact. . . . Are you really surprised we can find out what we need to?"

Dhul Fiqar—the name meant Sword of the Prophet, and Ledbetter assumed it was a nom de guerre—was quite believable as a Mexican here in Veracruz even apart from his accentless command of the local Spanish dialect; he was olive-skinned and had a few gray hairs in his bushy black mustache.

In fact he was from Lebanon, originally, and Harvey suspected he'd been placed here as a sleeper agent by an organization that no longer existed to any great extent. He was extremely fit, even a little gaunt, with the face of someone whose compulsions were eating him slowly from the inside. Right now he was obviously thinking hard.

"Perhaps it is not so surprising," he said after a moment. "You knew to whom you were selling the material?"

"Is that a surprise either?"

Contempt glinted in the dark eyes; he might as well have sneered *mercenary* aloud. Then a hint of caution. *But a capable one.*

"You were well paid," Dhul said. "Ten million euros is a great deal, even in these times."

"Yep. And you *did* get the material, and it's the real goods. That's a first."

Light kindled in the man's face, an exultation that nothing could suppress for long.

"Always, always before something has blocked us. The most accursed strokes of bad luck! But by the Lovingkind, the Compassionate, this time victory will be ours!"

102

"You reckon?" Harvey asked, leaning against the wall with his arms crossed.

"*¿Perdóne usted?*"

"You think so?"

"It is fated!" An effort at control, and Dhul went on. "But sit, sit, my friend," he said; the affability sat very poorly on him, if you could sense emotions directly.

"Thanks, but I won't be here long," Harvey replied.

He's certainly been a busy little bee, and he's built up quite a little operation on his own. They're like cancer cells—usually there're a few left to grow back.

"How'd you manage to machine the plutonium?" Harvey said.

This was an older section, near run-down docks but not very close to the modern container facilities. Most of the buildings, were from the same period, built during the booming days of the Porfiriato from blocks of *piedra muca,* coral stone. Some were pocked with bullet holes under the cracked stucco, from the revolution and the brief American occupation that had followed, or the drug wars of recent years. Nowadays they held a tangle of struggling small businesses or cheap rooming houses with the odd spot of renovation. The metal desk and antique ASUS-S6 computer would fit right in.

"When you love death more than life, these things are not difficult," Dhul Fiqar said.

Ah. A suicide machinist. Wonders never cease.

Plutonium was toxic chemically, violently dangerous as a radioactive substance, and a stone bitch to handle—for one thing, if you exposed it to moist air it was liable to more than double in volume as it turned into a flaky paste of hydrides that would then spontaneously burst into flame at room temperature. The job wouldn't be impossible, with computer-controlled machine tools as common as they were these days. You could set up an improvised clean room for it, though you'd be well advised to use a cellar and pump it full of concrete afterwards.

It would all be much easier if you didn't mind the operator dying a couple of weeks later. And this bunch had the advantage of being completely obscure—that was why he'd picked them, rather than hire some unemployed Russians or whatever. They had the best possible reasons not to talk, too.

"Besides, it was already formed," Dhul Fiqar acknowledged. "You saved us much time with that, since we had only to alter the angles on the wedges. I would like to know how you gained access to those components!"

Well, you make a deal under the table with these werewolf-vampire-sorceror-psychopath types, then—Harvey thought ironically.

Dhul went on: "You will receive the last payment as agreed."

"Well, that's what I'm here about. We'd like to discus the possibility of delivering it for you. With an additional fee, of course. After all, we got the material to you in the first place, right?"

A wave of savage suspicion and utter refusal roiled through the man's mind. Harvey sighed, though he wasn't surprised. When Dhul spoke, his voice was smooth.

"I will consider your offer to transport it to the target for us."

Dhul Fiqar was lying; the Texan had enough of the Power to tell that easily, from someone without protections or shields. Harvey smiled wryly; he'd expected the man to try to kill him to provide a cutout for anyone on the trail of that missing metal. But it would have been so convenient if he *had* agreed, of course. Always better to have someone hand the goods over to you rather than take them by brute force.

"You really should have taken me up on that," he said regretfully. "Or at least been willin' to consider it. But I suppose if you was reasonable, you wouldn't be in this exact line of work."

He ignored the trickles of sweat running down his face and flanks. He'd spent a lot of his life in hot, humid, smelly places, starting with Texas. The Brotherhood had been obligingly incurious as to how *much* plutonium he'd smuggled out of Seversk; the organization had always been decentralized. Part of the hell-metal had gone into the coffin bed of a postcorporeal Shadowspawn lord, which had been Harvey's official mission. The rest had come here, and there was more than enough for a critical mass.

"Didn't I get you the finest ex-Russian bomb components? And after all, we got the stuff to you without a problem. That shows we can handle transit security."

"I said I would consider it!" Dhul Fiqar snapped.

It surely does alter your interactions with people when you can sense whether they're fibbing, Harvey thought. *Could* that *be the reason I keep getting divorced?*

"Where are y'all keeping the bomb?" he asked with a guileless smile.

"Far from here."

Another lie, and the Arab's mind had jumped sideways at the word *bomb*, a feeling of anxiety reassurance.

"And it is not yet assembled."

Bingo, lie number three. I thought he'd work it this way and it turned out I was right. The bomb's ready and it's in this building. He wouldn't want it out of reach.

"Okay, time to cut the comedy," Harvey said.

His hand went under his embroidered, khaki-colored linen guayabera; he was wearing it three-quarters unbuttoned over a black T-shirt printed across the chest with very small white letters:

Yes, I am *carrying a concealed handgun. (Pursuant to CH 411.172, Texas Government Code.)*

The hand came out with a Colt Commander .45, a customized model with a Caspian Arms titanium frame and an integral laser sight that came on when you took up the trigger slack. The little dot came to rest on Dhul Fiqar's chest, and the man froze with *his* hand halfway to an open drawer. There was nothing quite so intimidating as knowing exactly where the bullet would hit: in this case in the cluster of big blood vessels just above the heart.

Harvey knew he wasn't nearly as fast as he'd been thirty years ago, but he was still pretty good, he had the priceless advantage of moving first, and the Arab wasn't a pistol expert anyway. If he had been he'd have carried at all times rather than leaving his gun uselessly in a desk, and Harvey would have made a different plan to begin with. A firearm where you couldn't reach it was about as useful as one on the cold side of the moon; you might not need it often, but when you did you needed it *very badly.*

"Now kick back from the desk, friend," he said. "That's right, lean back in the chair. Relax, and we'll have us a talk."

There might be some position that made it more difficult to move quickly than sitting back in a swivel chair with your feet off the ground, but he couldn't think of one offhand. Dhul Fiqar was sweating, but his eyes were steady and burning with hate. The fear in them was well under control, and Harvey could see him note how the gunman's back was to the open door. A shout would bring armed help.

"You know, it's a relief sometimes to deal with folks who *can't* hex firearms," he said.

The important thing now was to keep hitting his opponent faster than he could respond until his mental balance went completely to hell. He grinned.

"Sure, yell for help if'n you want to; that alarm you pressed had a little malfunction. The more, the merrier."

"You are mad," the plutonium buyer whispered, though he obeyed and kept his hands visible. "You will die for this! Die *slowly*."

Then, louder: "Rashid! Jasim! Come quickly! Alert the others; the Jews and Crusaders are here!"

There was a brief burst of fire from below.

MP-5, Harvey thought. *'Bout half a clip.*

It was racking-loud inside, but through the thick coral-block walls a casual ear would miss it, or mistake it for a piece of machinery stripping a gear.

Harvey shook his head with a *tsk* sound. If you could Wreak, even the little he and the other two could manage, you shouldn't need to shoot.

"Guha, bring Jasim in, would you?" he said, speaking normally. "It ain't polite to keep friends apart."

To the man in the chair: "I took the liberty of havin' some company of my own along on our little visit. Sorta forgot to mention it, on the off chance you'd be unreasonable."

The pickup mike was in a little skin-colored patch on his throat. The bud in his ear was similarly tiny and inconspicuous. The Brotherhood might make its operatives fly coach, but they didn't stint on gear.

A woman's voice with a singsong accent spoke: "Jasim's in bad shape, oh, yes, indeed. Will this much of him do?"

He could hear her voice twice, through the radio and from the door

107

behind him as she walked through and tossed something through the air. It landed on the desk with a wet, meaty thump.

"It's very *big*," she went on.

Which was what *Jasim* meant: big, or huge or strong. The man had probably taken the name because he was a six-four slab of muscled beef. Dhul Fiqar scrabbled backwards a little in his seat; the head of his follower was wrapped in a piece of burlap sacking, but that fell away to show the blank-eyed contorted face. A spray of blood whipped across his cheeks and mouth, and he scrabbled a hand at it in involuntary reflex. The metallic-coppery scent was suddenly heavy in the damp hot air, and flies buzzed downward.

That's more Farmer's style, really, Harvey thought. *But I suspect Guha is a bit prejudiced about these folks. You can take the girl out of Hindustan, but you can't take the Hindu out of the girl. Come to think about it, her family were Kashmiri Pandits back a ways, if I recall correctly.*

Theoretically once you knew about the Shadowspawn-Brotherhood war and the reality behind the false front of history, human tribes and nations and religions shouldn't matter anymore. The ancient enemy was more important, and besides that, you learned how they used human rivalries to keep the prey species down. In practice it didn't always work that way, not for humans, sometimes not even for Shadowspawn.

And I can't fault a severed head for technique. It's classic. Now we have to keep our friend Dhul Fiqar psychologically off balance well and truly.

"There was a machete," she said half apologetically. "I think he was using it to open coconuts and then tried to open me."

The front of her cotton blouse was soaked and dripping with sticky red. It clung to her body so closely that the blouse was transparent, and he could see her navel and the outline of her sports bra.

"It seemed bloody appropriate to use it on him," she finished.

She chuckled, and Dhul Fiqar flinched a little. It probably didn't help that she was a woman.

"Rashid! *Rashid!*" he shouted.

Farmer came in with Rashid stumbling before him; Rashid was thin and dark and probably quite quick. He was bleeding freely too, from a pressure cut above the eyes that more than half blinded him with the stinging, sticky fluid. The sort of injury you got when you turned around at a sound behind you and got pistol-whipped in the same motion; his hands were secured with a one-way loop, a variety that could be yanked tight with a tag but couldn't be removed without cutting it.

"The others?" Harvey said.

"Dead," Farmer said. "A little Wreaking and they didn't suspect a thing until too late."

"Evidence?"

"Nothing that'll show from the street until they start to smell. The truck they've got will do fine to get us to Lopez's boat with the package. It looks like a piece of crap but the engine's in good shape, the cargo compartment is well shielded, and they've got a knock-down lifting tackle inside."

"Looks like they were planning on using it for exactly what we'll do. Secure friend Dhul Fiqar here. We wouldn't want him to get reckless in his disappointment, and we do need a mite of information from him."

Guha had her knife in one hand, ten inches of slightly curved steel with a dimpled bone hilt. The man's eyes tracked it as she approached, being careful to keep well out of Harvey's line of fire and looking like an image of Kali with the front of her body splashed red. She produced a larger loop of the type around Rashid's wrists and dropped it neatly over his shoulders, working it down to his elbows. When she jerked it tight it sent the swivel chair spinning; she stopped that with a flicking kick to the man's ankle. Then she stepped close and put the point of the knife against the bristle of five-o'clock shadow under his chin, undid his belt with her other hand, made that into a loop and used it to strap his knees together. Duct tape finished the job.

"Now," Harvey said, kicking the other chair over, straddling it and leaning on the back. "At this point, you've probably realized we are not the CIA or the Mossad."

Dhul Fiqar jerked slightly; the American had switched into perfect, colloquial Arabic, the dialect an educated man from Damascus would have spoken.

"You speak Arabic . . . but . . ."

Harvey shook his head.

"That trick of saying things like 'you bastard son of a sow and an ape' and calling my mother and sister nasty names to test whether I could understand you is played out, my friend. Where did you get it, an old Kamal el Sheikh film? I really had trouble not laughing out loud in Haiti."

He dropped into verse, rolling the throaty sounds:

> The happiness of children
> When embraced by parents is like
> The happiness of a thirsty man
> When drinking water
> And the happiness
> Of suckering an asshole like you.

He switched back to English: "That last bit don't scan 'cause it ain't in the poem, but you get the idea."

Dhul Fiqar gathered himself a little. "You are not the Jews or the Americans?"

"Course not. The Army of Northern Virginia would have been more formal. You know what I mean—guys in black body armor rappellin' down on your roof in the night, drones, android surveillance chipmunks in the plumbing. The Mossad would just've killed you, if they didn't retroactively kill your granddaddy before you were born. And neither would *ever* have let you near real plutonium. You know that."

That struck Dhul Fiqar hard enough to draw a grunt. "What do you want with me, then?"

"We don't care a bucket of warm piss about *you*. We just want a functionin' *bomb* in the twenty-five-kiloton range. That's what all this was about; we sold you that plutonium so's you'd build it for us. Give me the control codes and your specs now, and I'll even let you and your fella Rashid here live. We'll just take the gear and head on out. Last offer. If Jasim there could talk, he'd advise you to say yes."

"Who *are* you?" Dhul Fiqar whispered.

"I don't have time or inclination to tell," Harvey said.

While he spoke he reached under his guayabara with his left hand; the X harness held two clips of ammunition under his right armpit, and a cylinder-shaped pouch the size of a very large cigar. He took the suppressor out of it and screwed it into the threaded recess around the muzzle of the Colt while he went on:

"Let's just say we're the anti-djinn squad. Now, the information, please, or things will get unpleasant."

"Never! I am not afraid of death! I will pass the gates of Paradise while—"

Harvey sighed. "Y'know, Dhul Fiqar, ol' buddy, this ain't to the death. I believe you when you say you're not afraid to die. This is to the *pain.*"

"You cannot make me talk."

"Oh, bullshit. There's times when torture don't work so good. Then again, as I suspect you know from experience, there's times when it does; like, when all you need is specific information, quick. Particularly since I can tell when you're lyin', so you can't fool me none. And seein' as you were planning on blowing up London or New York or Tel Aviv or something of that order, I really don't have much sympathy to spare for the way you're about to suffer."

"What are *you* planning on using it for?" Dhul said a little wildly. "A fireworks display?"

"Oh, we'll use it for the greater good of humanity," Harvey answered.

Bit hard on the bystanders in Tbilisi, but omelettes and eggs and all, seein' as the Shadowspawn are planning to kill off at least half the human race in the immediate future.

Harvey nodded, and Farmer stepped away from Rashid. The Texan extended his arm, sighting in the old-fashioned single-armed grip. Then he fired one shot, letting the recoil ride up.

Phut!

Suppressors didn't silence a gun. They did knock the sound down a fair way from the hearing-damage level of a shot in a confined space to something like a door slamming or a heavy book being whacked down on a tabletop. The big .45 hollow-point slug ripped the thin Arab's kneecap away and he toppled like a cut tree, clutching at it. After a moment he began to shriek, high-pitched and astonishingly loud. Farmer stepped forward and put his foot on the man's throat, pressing just enough to cut the sound down to bearable levels.

Sweat was pouring off Dhul Fiqar's face, but he remained silent except for the heavy sound of breath whistling in and out through flared nostrils.

"Oh, hell," Harvey said wearily; the adrenaline of danger was fading. "Jack, take over. Break him, and do it fast."

"Sure thing!"

Farmer drew back his foot and kicked Rashid in the temple, hard. The body jerked a few times and went still; Harvey could feel the life fading out of the brain stem, entropy randomizing the signals for a moment until they faded away. Then Farmer stepped over to the desk and swung his light nylon backpack onto its surface and began to unpack it.

Dhul Fiqar's eyes were fixed on the hypodermics and ampules, the surgical instruments and the tools. Farmer whistled between his teeth as he worked, and then drew on a pair of thin-film gloves, stripped off a piece from the roll of duct tape and slapped it across the prisoner's mouth. Guha sighed and went to stand by the window, looking outwards.

"They've got a bathroom here," she said. "All right if I go and shower?"

"Good idea. Make it quick," Harvey said. "I want you driving, and it'd be a nuisance coverin' up the way you look."

"And the smell."

Harvey kept his eyes on the man in the chair as she left—if he could order it, looking away would be cowardice—but he let a Mhabrogast phrase fall through his mind. A slight burring sensation flickered behind his forehead for an instant, and his consciousness of the other's emotions faded.

He hadn't done it to isolate himself from Dhul Fiqar's pain; it was

Jack Farmer's pleasure in what he was about to do that he really didn't want inside his head.

Give Jack his due, he don't torture people for fun. He doesn't even let himself do it in the line of duty unless a superior orders him to. But it does sorta make you queasy to share the jolt it gives him when he's got an excuse to cut loose. Halfway between digusting and . . . tempting, which is worse.

Farmer cut the arm of Dhul Fiqar's shirt away and injected him twice in one of the swollen veins near his elbow, where he'd been straining against his bonds. The dark eyes went wide, and then the pupils expanded until the iris was a thread-thin rim around them.

"Anytime you feel like talkin', Dhul Fiqar, just nod vigorous-like," Harvey said heavily.

Farmer smiled as he raised the battery-powered electric drill and held it before the captive's face, letting the motor whir with a touch on the trigger.

The vehicle was a Chinese-made Foton Aumark with a lot of miles and hard use on it, the 2010 model, a cab-over-engine type with a van body and a five-ton capacity. Someone had worked over the Cummins diesel until it burbled happily, though, despite the heavy load. Dhul Fiqar's suicide machinists had made something that would work, and at least it wasn't leaking radiation, but it wasn't exactly a suitcase bomb either.

"So, we've got the bomb," Guha said, driving carefully down the narrow street.

She could pass for a mostly *indio* Mexican if you didn't look too closely. Farmer was in the back with the long crate. This wasn't a tourist area, and blond German-American Midwesterners were conspicuous by their absence around here. Harvey was slumped in the passenger seat himself with a billed cap drawn down over his face, for the same reason in its Scots-Irish Texan Hill Country incarnation.

"The question is, my big boss, how do we get it to the target? Cannot you *feel* the threads of destiny on it? And this we will plant among thousands of Shadowspawn adepts? Perhaps we should carry it in on our shoulders, wearing red noses and big floppy shoes?"

"The adepts'll cancel one another out, a bit."

Guha snorted. She was right; the overlapping abilities with the Power would help, but not that much when the wielders were all threatened with the same onrushing death casting its shadow backwards through time.

Harvey went on: "Adrian's workin' on that."

Though he don't quite know what he's working on hiding. Come to think of it, the world bein' what it is, there's a lot of people who don't know the truth of what they're dealing with. And God help the ones who stumble across the truth, or part of it.

"Okay," Cesar said. "Guess what? Something funny on the Brézé case."

"Tell me something funny. I could use it."

Salvador sipped at a cup of sour coffee and looked out the window at a struggling piñon pine with sap dripping from its limbs; they were having another beetle infestation, they happened every decade or two. Firewood would be cheap soon; he could take his pickup out on weekends and get a load for the labor of cutting it up and hauling it away.

The prospect of an afternoon spent with a chain saw was a lot more fun than the case he was working on now.

Man beats up woman, woman calls cops, woman presses charges, woman changes mind, couple sue cops to show how they're together again. Tell me again why I'm not selling insurance.

"The funny thing is the analysis on the DNA from the puke I found in the Dumpster behind Whole Foods," Cesar said.

"Ain't a policeman's life fun? Digging in Dumpsters for puke?"

"*Sí, jefe.* Nice clean white-collar job, just what my mother had in mind for her prospective kid when she waded across the river to get me born on US soil. Anyway, there's blood in the puke."

"I remember you telling me that. The attendant says it was *Adrian Brézé's* puke, right?"

"Right, he saw him puking out the rear of that van, thought he was drunk. I'm pretty sure that Brézé paid him something to forget about it—he sweated pretty hard before he talked, and I had to do the kidnapping-and-arson dance. He saw the blood in it, too."

"So he's got an ulcer. Even rich people get them. How does this help us?"

Cesar scratched his mustache, and Salvador consciously stopped himself from doing likewise.

"I'm not sure it does," he said. "But it's *funny.* Because the DNA from the puke is not the same as the DNA from the blood. In fact, the DNA from the blood is on the Red Cross list. One of their donors, a Shirley Whitworth, donated it at that place just off Rodeo and Camino Carlos Rey. It seems to have gone missing from their system. They clammed up about it pretty tight. We'll have to work on that."

Salvador grunted. "Let's get this straight. The *puke* is Brézé's—"

"Presumably. Male chromosomes in the body fluids. But there's no Brézé in the DNA database."

"That's not so surprising; they only started it a couple of years ago, and it just means he's not a donor and hasn't been arrested or gone to a hospital or whatever. But the *blood* is definitely some Red Cross donor's?"

"*Sí.* So, funny, eh?"

"Funny as in fucking weird, not funny as in ha-ha. Because it had to be in his *stomach*, right?"

They both laughed. "Good thing we know he comes out in daylight, eh?" Cesar said.

"Yeah, and he doesn't sparkle. I'd feel fucking silly chasing a perp who looked like a walking disco ball. . . . But he did drink it . . . maybe some sort of kink cult thing?"

"So I'm not surprised he puked," Cesar said, still chuckling. "It'd be like drinking salt water, you know? Blood *is* salt water, seawater. My mother used salt water and mustard to make me heave if I'd eaten myself into a stomachache."

Salvador could feel his brain starting to move, things connecting under the fatigue of a half dozen cases that were never going to go anywhere. Then his phone rang. When he tapped it off, he was frowning.

"What's the news, *jefe*?"

"The boss wants to see us now."

The chief's office wasn't much bigger than his; Santa Fe was a small town, still well under a hundred thousand people. The office *was* on a corner, second story, and had bigger windows. The chief also had three stars on the collar of his uniform; he still didn't make nearly as much as, say, Giselle Demarcio. On the other hand, his money didn't come from San Francisco and LA and New York, either.

Cesar's breath hissed a little, and Salvador felt his eyes narrow. There were two suits waiting for them as well as the chief. *Literally* suits, natty, one woman and one man, one black and one some variety of Anglo. Both definitely from out of state; he'd have put the black woman down as FBI if he had to guess, and the younger man as some sort of spook, but not a desk man. Ex-military of some type, but not in the least retired.

She's Fart, Barf and Itch. Him . . . the Waffen-CIA, but ex-Ranger, maybe?

"Sit down," the chief said.

He was as local as Salvador and more so than Cesar, and might have been Salvador's older cousin—in fact, they were distantly related. Right now he was giving a good impression of someone who'd never met either of the detectives, his face like something carved out of wood on Canyon Row.

The male suit spoke. "You're working on a case involving the Brézé family."

"Yes," Salvador said. "Chief, who are these people?"

"You don't need to know," the woman said neutrally; somehow she gave the *impression* of wearing sunglasses without actually doing it. More softly: "You don't *want* to know."

"They're Homeland Security," the chief said.

"Homeland Security is interested in weird love triangles?" Salvador said skeptically. "Besides, *Homeland Security* is like *person*, it's sort of generic. You people FBI, Company, NSA, what?"

"You don't need to know. You *do* need to know we're handling this," the man said.

Wait a minute, Salvador thought. *He's scared. Controlling it well, he's a complete hard case if I ever saw one, and hell, I've been one. But he's scared.*

Which made him start thinking a little uncomfortably that maybe *he* should be scared. The man was someone he might have been himself, if things had gone a little differently with that IED.

"Handling it how?" Salvador said, meeting his pale stare.

"We've got some of our best people on it."

"Who, exactly."

"Our *best* people."

"Oh, Christ—" he began.

"Eric, *drop* it. Right now," the chief said.

He's scared too.

"Hey, Chief, no problem," Cesar cut in. "It's not like we haven't got enough work. Right, drop it, national security business, need to know, eh?"

The two suits looked at each other and then Salvador. He nodded.

"Okay," he said. "I wasn't born yesterday. Curiosity killed the cat, that right? And unless I want to go, 'Meow-oh-shit,' as my last words . . ."

"You have no idea," the woman said, almost whispering and looking past him. "None at all."

Then she turned her eyes on him. "Let's be clear. There was no fire. There is no such thing as a Brézé family. You never heard of them. You particularly haven't made any records or files of anything concerning them. That will be checked."

"Sure." He grinned. "But check what? About who?"

Salvador waited until they were back in the office before he began to swear: English, Spanish and some Pashto, which was about the best re-viling language he'd ever come across, though some people he'd known said Arabic was even better.

"Let's get some lunch," Cesar said, winking.

Yeah, Salvador thought. *Got to remember* anything *can be a bug these days.*

"Sure, I could use a burrito."

They shed their phones; when they were outside Cesar went on: "How soon you want to start poking around, *jefe?*"

Salvador let out his breath and rolled his head, kneading at the back of his head with one spadelike hand. The muscles there felt like a mass of woven iron rods under his hand, and he pressed on the silver chain that held the crucifix around his neck.

"It's fucking Euro-trash terrorists now, eh?" he said.

"Yeah. Euro-trash *vampire* terrorists. Maybe Osama bit them?" Cesar said, still smiling.

"Or vice versa."

"What sort of shit is coming down?" Cesar said, more seriously.

"Our chances of getting that from those people . . ."

". . . are nada."

"Somewhere between nada and fucking zip."

Cesar looked up into the cloudless blue sky. "Maybe these Brézés are just so rich they can shit-can anything they don't like, pull strings, some politician leans on the FBI and the Company? Call me cynical. . . ."

"Nah," Salvador shook his head. "You can't get that *just* with money. Not with those people, the spooks. They know they're going to be there when any given bought-and-paid-for politician is long gone. You need heavy political leverage. Whoever they were, they *were* feds, and not your average cubicle slave either. They're not going to tell any of us square-state boondockers shit. The chief didn't know any more than we did, he was just taking orders."

"You sure?"

"I've known him a long time. We're related, cousins."

"You old-timers here are *all* related," Cesar said. "It's not fucking fair."

"You people who just got off the bus don't understand the strength of our family feelings. Can I help it if we're descended from *conquistadores*?"

"Fast *conquistadores* and slow *india* girls. Hell, my family goes right back to Cortés too."

"It does?"

"Sure. One of my great-many-times-grandmothers was squatting in the dirt grilling a guinea pig when he rode by on his horse."

Salvador's grin was brief; his eyes made a to-business flick.

"So . . ." Cesar said. He leaned back against a wall. "How long do you want to let it cool before we start poking in violation of our solemn promise?"

"Couple of months," Salvador said. "First thing, get all the data on an SD card and make some copies and let me have one. Scrub your notebook and anything you've got at the office. None of this ever goes on anything connected to anything else."

Cesar grinned. "I like the way you think, *jefe*."

CHAPTER EIGHT

Ellen kept her breathing deep and steady against the fear that made her want to pant as she walked the streets of Paris behind the professor.

The professor who's about to be ambushed by werewhatsits and hired killers. What a way to See Europe and Die Screaming. The other parts of this honeymoon trip were a lot more fun.

She pulled the raw, chilly air deep into her lungs, freighted with traffic and cooking and old stone. A little fog lay on the river, with the running lights of boats shining through it like a blurred Impressionist cityscape, and wisps of it were pooling along the cobblestones. Beads of moisture starred her eyelashes, and a lock of hair came out from under her floppy hat and stuck to her brow.

"He's crossing the river on the Pont Marie and heading for the Saint-Paul metro station," Adrian said. "Not long now."

They followed. Already Ellen had a sense that she was in a bubble of nonspace, and it grew stronger with the thronging life of Le Marais moving around; it was that kind of neighborhood. Ellen kept her head slightly down, avoided eye contact, neither hurried nor dawdled.

She spotted the professor's ponytail as he walked along, deep in thought, his hands in his jacket pockets and his head down. The street life was busy this early in the evening, dense traffic, thronged sidewalks, light from lamps on curled wrought-iron brackets reaching out from the walls. Nothing was high-rise—older stone-and-stucco buildings for the most part, in pale colors. But it felt densely urban in a way that even far more built-up American cities didn't, as if you could feel the layers of time here beside the Seine, all the way back to the Lutetia Parisiorum of the Gauls and Romans. The latest included a restaurant that had a menorah in the window and advertised, BLINIS, SAUMON, ZAKOUSHKIS ET VODKAS, and some remarkably well-stocked gay-themed fetish stores.

She eeled through it all, keeping her target in sight without being obvious about it.

God, it's like I've done this a thousand times before! she thought, unconsciously sliding away from Adrian so that they wouldn't be together to jog the target's memory if he turned around, pausing now and then to pretend to look in a window. *And I have, in Adrian's head.*

Tailing, detecting a tail, losing one, in cities that had included Paris and a dozen others, or the equivalent skills in forest or desert . . . that and a hundred other things, things more arcane and terrible. There in her mind, ready to surface when she needed them.

And I'm not even very frightened. I was frightened at first in there, because it was all so real, but I could keep it under control because I knew consciously that it wasn't. Now when it's really real I'm just . . . just taut and ready. And a bit apprehensive in a sort of reasoned way, as if this were something I was used *to doing. I've even beat* Adrian *at it a couple of times, the non-Power parts, at least.*

"This is *weird*," she murmured almost inaudibly. "Hey, isn't it a cliché that marriage doesn't change you? Well, it has changed me, already!"

Adrian had turned. Now he lounged past her, heading in the other direction, then leaned against a wall like any man out for a stroll and eyeing a pretty girl.

"You are doing splendidly. They will act soon," he said quietly as she passed. "And if we had not married, *I* would still be sitting on a mountaintop brooding."

Then he ducked behind an elderly Jewish couple, came back through a gaggle of Chinese teenagers chatting in French—there were a lot of East Asian immigrants around here—and strolled slightly behind her. His looks made it easier for him to blend in; her blond height and figure always attracted attention.

Duquense was speeding up when he suddenly turned left into a narrow alleyway.

Wreaking, Ellen thought with a shiver. *There was a* possibility *that he'd do that, no matter how remote. So a little push with the Power, and he* does *do it, willy-nilly.*

Ellen walked past it, stopped and stooped as if to fiddle with her shoe an arm's length along the next building. Adrian came up behind her and turned directly into the narrow curving backstreet. She reached under her jacket and laid her hand on the butt of the little Five-seveN automatic, drew it, then turned and followed him in, holding it down near her thigh. The heavy silver amulet around her neck was tingling, seeming to itch at her skin.

A tableau was frozen for an instant as she and Adrian entered the alley. Three men and Duquesne. The academic's hand was raised in futile protest as one of the men drew a long knife from under his jacket and the other held him by an elbow and the back of his neck. Adrian faced the third, farther in, who'd been standing with his hands resting on the knob of his walking stick as he surveyed the murder-in-progress.

Shoot the one with the knife, her training told her. *He's the immediate danger. Don't assume he'll go down with the first round.*

Ellen blinked at the calmly ruthless thought, even as her hands came smoothly up with the gun ready. The two men threatening Duquesne were unremarkable, except that they both looked very dangerous, moving like lethal dancers—one squat and a little darker than Adrian, the other with the drawn blade taller, with oddly silver hair.

Even the single glance aside as she brought the weapon up and aimed showed that the man her husband faced was different—he could have been Adrian himself, aged a decade, and dressed in an opera cape, tails, white tie, gloves, gold-headed ebony cane, shining topper and gleaming shoes with spats, a white flower in his buttonhole . . . the complete outfit of a boulevardier from the earlier part of La Belle Epoque.

All that as her eyes flicked across. The man with the blade who'd been about to stab Duquesne snarled.

"Hold him, Joko," he said; he spoke in French with a British accent. "I'll handle the bitch."

Then he was coming at her, knife held low with the point up, fluid and sure—only three long strides away. She was slightly crouched, leaning into the weapon with her left hand under the butt. . . .

And her finger froze. *This is real! That's a human being! I can't do it!*

The knife caught a glitter of distant streetlight. That made her act, and without thinking. Without thinking with the forward part of her brain, the one that was a good small-town girl with a slather of self-made junior-grade artsy-academic across it. A chunk of her hindbrain had met knives before, in the memory palace.

They *hurt*.

The somatic memory didn't give a damn that the experience had been imaginary; it knew exactly what it was like to die with seven inches of blade through the lungs. Her finger contracted just as the man's shoulders tensed to drive the steel home. That put the muzzle barely a yard from his chest.

Crack!

The little pistol didn't have much recoil, but it was *loud*. The sound slapped back and forth between the limestone facades of the buildings on either side of the narrow little street, like someone snapping an elastic right into her ear. The flash was almost blinding through her slitted eyes, flicking through the dimness like miniature lightning.

The sequence went automatically after that. *Crack! Crack! Crack! Crack! Crack!*

Six shots into the center of mass. The man turned as he fell to come down on his face, and the knife skittered away, ringing on the granite paving. The little sharp-pointed hypervelocity bullets deformed and tumbled through bone and flesh like miniature saws: six neat holes in the shirt, and a shower of bone and flesh fragments punching out his back to leave a crater the size of her paired fists.

Some distant part of Ellen's mind thought: *I just shot someone! A real human being, and he's dead for real!*

The rest of her was moving, a swift half skip sideways to get a clear shot at the squat man who held the professor. *That* part of her had shot hundreds of men—and women. Just projections of Adrian's mind, or sometimes his mental image of himself, but the sight and the feel and the very *smell* were the same, the acrid scent of burned nitro powder, the jerking thump of impact, the tang of blood and the boneless finality of the dead body.

My subconscious thinks I'm a mass murderer and this is all in a day's work. Jesus!

The platinum ferrule on the ebony cane in the dandy's hand poked towards her; she grunted at the impact of an impalpable force. Her mind seemed to blur, as if her brain had been invisibly shaken, and the amulet was uncomfortably hot now. Everything from a slip and a cracked skull to a stroke, epileptic seizure and heart attack trembled on the verge of *realization.* Adrian's hand moved, and the instant passed, but the trigger froze under her finger as something malfunctioned.

The second renfield killer had wasted a instant staring incredulously at his dead comrade, and another drawing a gun and firing at her. It jammed too. Ellen dropped her weapon, leapt backwards and drew the knife from under the tail of her jacket, where the sheath lay point-up along her spine. The steel came out and up, leading; she stood with the right foot a little advanced behind it, crouched, left arm held across her chest with the hand stiffened into a blade.

"You kill Chance, *putain,*" he growled at her.

He chopped Duquesne under the short ribs with the edge of his hand, paralyzing his diaphragm, then shoved him at her. She swayed aside and let the Frenchman fall; time enough to help him later. He thudded into the wall and slid down it, struggling to breathe, his eyes wild.

"If that was his name," she said, much more calmly than she felt; any delay was welcome.

"*Salope*," he snarled, which meant *bitch*, more or less. "I will cut you deep for that."

He drew a knife, a balisong that skittered through a sinister metallic *chink-click-click* as he flicked it open and locked it. The angry rush she half expected stopped before it began. He saw the stance, the way she held the blade and kept most of her weight on her back foot. She could see it flowing into his mind along with the way she'd shot his partner and dodged Duquesne.

All moving instantly into his fighting gestalt as: *Much more dangerous than she looks. Don't take any chances.*

He advanced warily, his own weapon held in a different grip, point down with his thumb on the pommel.

"*Vous êtes une pomme de terre avec le visage d'un cochon d'inde*," she said.

She'd always wanted to call someone that: it meant, *You are a potato with the face of a guinea pig*. It was much more insulting and less funny in French.

He cut and stabbed, a horizontal slash and then a backhand punch of the knife towards her face. She leaned back, just enough to let the steel pass.

Whoa!

It was disconcertingly as if someone else were operating her body, and doing it by fits and starts. *Stopping* doing it when she thought about it.

Then stop thinking or you'll die! she scolded herself desperately.

The thickset man had staggered a little as the counterattack he expected didn't come, then almost ran himself onto her knife as she let the conditioned reflex thrust underarm towards his belly.

Just more practice, she told herself. *You can get hurt, but the pain's all there is to fear. No real people involved.*

As they circled and feinted another part of her was hoping desperately that Adrian would finish whatever he was doing and come to the rescue, fast.

"Nephew," the Shadowspawn said, slinking a pace closer.

"Great-uncle Arnaud," Adrian acknowledged, with a slight inclination of his head. "Looking as vicious and depraved as ever, I see, *mon tonton.*"

"You always were a charmingly polite lad."

The other man looked solid; Adrian could even smell his rosewater cologne. But there was a something, a glitter that the eyes did not quite see. . . .

Of course, he's been postcorporeal for seventy years. But I'd know it anyway. Not really a man there, something that looks *like a man because the hindbrain remembers.*

"And I always did hope I'd meet you like this," Arnaud said amiably. "Killing you will be an intense pleasure in a life grown a trifle dull."

His hands turned the walking stick, and nearly a meter of narrow blade slipped free. The gloves must be insulated very thoroughly; there were silver inlays on the blade as well, and there were preactivated glyphs, warping probability towards bane and ruin and sickness. Adrian could feel them buzzing through the fabric of things, drawing the paths negative. His own blade came into his hand, a Brotherhood-style tanto. He excluded all worry for Ellen from his consciousness; it would do her *no* good at all if he lost this fight, and it would take all he had.

"As I recall," Adrian said, "killing me wasn't quite what you had in mind last time we met."

"Oh, the two are related," Arnaud said. "You were a beautiful boy."

He fell into a fencer's pose—an exceedingly old-fashioned one, knees bent at right angles, like a Victorian duelist—and whipped the cloak around his left arm, keeping the sheath in that hand.

Watch that, the fighting part of his brain reminded him. *Arnaud was always good at* la canne *too.*

"And perhaps I had a killing in mind as a finale at the time, eh?" the older Shadowspawn said.

The point of the sword darted towards his eyes, fluid and swift and sure. If that sliver of graven steel went home in his brain, it would be the Final Death. And Adrian had more than his own life to save.

Ting, as the long knife beat the slender spike aside, a shivering quiver up the nerves of his right hand.

He whirled inside the thrust and struck with the knob that tipped the tanto's hilt. Arnaud parried it with the sheath portion of the sword-cane; for a moment they were locked, faces inches apart. Then Arnaud broke back, whirled in again with a looping elliptical *savate* kick. It was blindingly quick; Adrian took it on his crossed forearms, and it was like being kicked by a horse. He rode it in a double back somersault and came up again, breathing hard.

"Bah, an *apache* weapon, that knife," said Arnaud as he came back on guard. "Could you at least not use a decent stiletto?"

They circled. The steel whipped down towards Adrian's foot; he danced over it, and felt his mind automatically snarling through Mhabrogast phrases as he did. Their psyches grappled, slid, retreated, baffled. Nature reasserted itself as the Power canceled out.

I am more purebred, but he has been beyond the flesh for long and long. They grow stronger as they age.

"Why kill the human?" he asked.

"Why not?" Arnaud shrugged. "It seemed a lucky thing to do, and I was here in Paris and had no pressing engagements."

Which made perfect sense, in Shadowspawn terms. He could even sense lack of will to deceive in the words, though with an adept you never knew.

Another lunge, and then a whistling blow with the sheath. Adrian threw the knife, and as Arnaud blocked it he threw himself forward and down, heels to buttocks and head to knees with his arms wrapped around his shins. Rolling like a ball, the pavement battering at him, and then into the other man's legs. Arnaud managed to catch himself on his hands, but the younger man was already turning, leaping his own height in the air, driving one heel down between the shoulder blades . . .

. . . of an empty dinner jacket.

"Merde!"

He hissed the curse in pain, as his foot slammed into the pavement, only slightly cushioned by the empty clothes, and nearly pitched over backwards. The impact jolted all the way into his pelvis and up his lower back, pain just short of tearing gristle and cartilage. A wrenching effort let him regain his feet and stance. Something like a cross between a seven-foot weasel and a great cat ran up the wall and paused to hiss at him before it disappeared over the roofs.

Ellen, he thought, spinning away.

That gave him just enough time to see the second renfield turn and run four paces away from her, then spring up into the angle two walls made. He scaled it in an acrobatic zigzagging rush, looking as if he were walking up the vertical surface by vaulting from one wall to the next, then twisted backwards over her head in a somersault.

Le parkour, Adrian thought. *Very impressive if—*

Ellen did *not* let herself be hypnotized by the seemingly impossible arc. Instead she turned calmly beneath it, and was waiting as the man fell out of the sky. There was a strangled shriek as her tanto flashed, and then the man staggered away out the mouth of the alley. Screams of alarm came from the crowd outside.

Adrian suppressed his grin; Ellen was looking shaky as she wiped her knife and retrieved the automatic, and wouldn't appreciate it. He could sense the bubbling horror beneath her control, and stepped up to lay a hand gently on her shoulder.

"You did splendidly, my dear," he said softly. "I could not have dealt with all three of them."

She nodded jerkily, taking deep, deliberate breaths, as she'd been taught.

"What *was* that thing? The thing that ran away?"

"A giant fossa, a predator from Madagascar. Arnaud was there for a while, nearly a hundred years ago. . . . No matter. We must see to Duquesne."

The professor was slumped against a wall, his face wet with sweat and glazed with horror as he stared at the bleeding body of the man who'd been about to kill him, and then up where the fossa had gone. He'd been looking directly at Arnaud when he transformed, too. An ordinary human wouldn't see anything but instant change.

"That . . . that *thing* . . ."

Abruptly he turned and vomited, the sharp stink cutting through the smell of blood. Adrian waited, and then offered his flask.

"This will help, monsieur," he said.

The man accepted it with both hands after he'd wiped his mouth on a handkerchief. "My God, what *happened*?" he mumbled.

"Alas, you have become a danger," Adrian said.

Indignation drove out some of the bewilderment. "A danger? To whom? *How?*"

"To . . . the people we were discussing. It is not necessary that they know why or how you will be a danger. The fact itself casts its shadow in their minds."

"Then why didn't they kill me when I was a baby?" Duquesne asked skeptically.

Adrian clapped him on the shoulder; it was a good question, and a good sign that the man was thinking again.

"Because the possibility was faint, one among an almost infinite number. When you took the first steps towards investigating that data . . . *then* the fan of might-be narrowed down enough to be noticed."

"They . . . That man, that *thing*, was going to kill me just on a *suspicion*? They can do such things? The police, the authorities—"

"Monsieur Duquesne, I cannot give you all the details of the last century and a half in this alleyway. Think of this: men who can walk through walls, read thoughts, transform themselves into the likeness of carnivorous beasts, bring ruin and death with a thought or a touch . . . are they likely to be constrained by the authorities?"

"No," he whispered.

"It's a shock," Ellen said sympathetically. "But you've got to get going and accept it, Monsieur Duquesne."

"And they have noticed me," he said.

Fortunately, you are not blaming me for that, Adrian thought. *Yet.*

"And if they take notice they act," he confirmed. "Your life is less to them than a cockroach. Arnaud would have sensed it because he was close to you, like a scent drifting through time. And that closeness, it may have been the Power influencing *his* choices. Though he always did spend much of his time in Paris."

Ellen crouched to put her face on the same level and took the man's hand in hers.

"I know it's awful to find the world isn't what you thought it was, Professor Duquesne. It was for me, too, when the curtain got raised and I saw, saw the *things* underneath. But you've got to *think* now, no matter how hard it is. Or you'll end up like . . ."

She swallowed, then visibly recovered by an effort of will.

". . . like *him*," she concluded, and pointed to the corpse of the man she'd shot.

It lay with limp finality in a spreading pool of blood.

"Not that he didn't deserve . . . Well, more about that later."

She pulled him up. "Come with us if you want to live."

"I . . . My colleagues . . ."

"Your family?" Adrian asked sharply.

"I am a widower, my parents are dead, and so is my only sister. No children . . ."

"Then you are relatively immune to pressure through your loved ones, Professor. Now *come*."

They turned and began to walk rapidly, almost hustling the stunned academic between them, down the opposite way from the way they'd entered the narrow alley. Behind there was a rising chorus of voices; a bleeding man had staggered out into the crowds and collapsed.

That was *not* common in this part of Paris; they were far away from the *banileus*. By the time they were among people again he was walking almost normally, but Adrian could feel the stuttering tension in his mind, a sensation as of thoughts breaking off into fragments, almost like free association.

Adrian looked over his shoulder. *Was that too easy?* he thought.

"Well, now we've got a physicist, lover," Ellen said.

Her color was better now, but her mouth looked drawn. *Pauvre petite,* he thought, not for the first time. *Caught in the contentions of demons. Poor humanity, nursing its own nemisis in its bloodstream, unawares.*

"Yes," he said. "And perhaps he can actually *do* something. The very fact that Arnaud was moved to kill him indicates that he might."

She frowned, a single line occurring between her brows; he'd long since concluded that she was even more intelligent than she was beautiful. The Power didn't make you any smarter, and it often made its possessors intellectually lazy. Why bother to shed skull sweat when you could just *sense* the best course of action, like guessing?

"Funny that nobody else has ever thought to study the Power scientifically."

Adrian grinned. He was beginning to feel exhilarated; Great-uncle Arnaud had tried to nip off a negative pathway . . . and he'd ended up expediting Adrian's purposes instead, swinging the course of events to favor his enemy more than if he had not acted at all. It was often so when adepts clashed; physical defeat was less than half of it.

"Not so odd," he said. "There are so few Shadowspawn, and modern physics has existed for only a few years. Probably your Peter was the only scientist who has ever been so closely exposed to someone with the Power who was willing to tolerate curiosity."

They turned out of the far end of the alley. Behind him he could hear the distinctive *oooo-an, oooo-an* of French police sirens.

"Nothing else has worked," he said. "Perhaps this will."

"I wish we had Peter, though," Ellen said wistfully.

CHAPTER NINE

"*Maman*'s a woof!" Leila shrieked.

The little girl flung herself at the great beast's neck; a hundred and twenty pounds wasn't much for a human, but it was very large indeed for a wolf.

Adrienne ducked into a crouch as the small body landed on her back and clung with hands and feet. Then she jumped and bucked and swung back and forth mock-growling; carefully, just short of throwing her off, leaving her squealing with delicious terror. Leon laughed and darted in, grabbing at her tail.

Ouch, she thought. *Well, they are* my *children!*

That would have been obvious even to someone Power-blind; they had her olive complexion, regular high-cheeked faces, straight noses, Cupid's-bow lips and hair the color of a crow's wing. They resembled their father too, of course.

A *twist* within, and she was an Arabian mare. Leila drummed heels on her ribs, and Leon pulled over a footstool and used it to scramble up behind her. They whooped as she trotted out the open French doors and into the garden courtyard of the nursery section. Then she broke into a slow, even gallop—running was *fun* when you were a horse—on the turf around the pool. The night was even dimmer to horse eyes, but she knew the terrain, and the juicy-sweet scent of the grass and the cool air were exhilarating.

At last she halted by the doors. Transforming back to your own etheric form was always easiest, and the children tumbled onto the soft carpet with more laughter. A surge of effort overrode somatic memory and made the body she wore like her normal one, not the still-healing physical frame.

"More, *Maman*!" Leon said. "Be a tiger!"

"No more, my little weasels," she said firmly. "It's one o'clock. Go get ready for bed, and I'll tell you a story."

Leila pouted a little, then sighed. "You don't go to sleep yet," she pointed out hopefully. "We missed you a lot."

"My body is still a little sick, so I sleep nearly all day, little weasel one. And I need to feed after you go to sleep; turning into animals takes a lot of Power."

"Who will you bite?" Leon asked with interest.

"Peter," she said. "And then perhaps Monica, for dessert."

"Monica's nice," Leila said. "She smells like cake. I don't think Peter likes us, though. I can feel it in his head. He feels real scared, too, even if he doesn't look that way. That makes my head . . . all prickly."

Adrienne smiled, full of pride. Six was young to be that sensitive. She suspected Leon would have a little more raw strength when he was grown, though they'd both be very formidable. But the Power was a saber, not a club. Without subtlety, it could be dangerous to the wielder.

"What're you going to do to them to make them taste good?" Leon asked, slightly ghoulishly.

"Things that will make them have very strong feelings," Adrienne said. "Starting with chasing them. That's how you prepare humans for feeding."

"Like putting ketchup on *frites*?"

"Yes. It spices their blood with things we need and that taste very good, and you can . . . mmmm . . . get inside their minds and sense their feelings. That's a lot of fun too."

"Not for the human," Leon said, with a smirk.

"Sometimes it is, sometimes not," Adrienne said. "But it's what they're for, after all. They're our food."

"If we drank more blood, could we do more things with the Power?" Lelia asked hopefully. "I *like* the way using the Power feels. I can keep the feather up for a whole minute now. Maybe—"

"No," Adrienne said again, firmly. "You have to wait for that. You have to grow up and become strong first."

This time she used a little of the Power herself, cloaking herself for a moment in shadow and awe and a tinge of fear; the two children blinked their yellow-flecked black eyes and looked away. She could feel their minds roiling, slightly startled, instinctive childhood deference and an equally inbred defiance. More pressure, until their eyes dropped.

You had to be *careful* with purebred Shadowspawn children, and there had been none so pure as these for twelve thousand years or more. Not since the Empire of Shadow. More than one Council member had argued that they should be destroyed before they reached adulthood as too dangerous. It probably *was* going to be trying when they hit puberty, but if the world didn't like it, the world could do the other thing.

Inwardly she bared teeth at the universe; let any *try* to harm her get! And at the thought her spine bristled, the little hairs trying to come erect. She blinked at the thought, grasping with the Power for the thread of possibilities, but it spun away into infinity. Children were *made* of potentials, and these more than most.

"You're too young for more than a sip of blood now and then," she said, bending and putting a hand behind each head, locking their gaze with hers. "It'll be years yet before you can really feed, or night-walk. You have all the time in the world to wait. Now off with you!"

The two slight raven-haired forms scampered away to don pajamas and brush their teeth. She picked up a robe and threw it over herself as she walked into the bedroom; it opened on a balcony with a chest-high balustrade of carved marble fretwork, and over that in the distance she could see the moon setting over the Coast Range hills.

The room was big, and there was a spray of toys, shelves of picture books and murals of children's stories from the manor's last rebuilding in the 1920s: Bre'r Rabbit squealing in bulging-eyed despair and agony in the jaws of Bre'r Fox, Cinderella trimming the feet of her stepsisters as they screamed and writhed, Jack stamped beneath the giant's foot, Hansel and Gretel burning in the witch's oven. . . .

All the classics, she thought. *Tradition does have its place.*

The children returned, smelling of soap and toothpaste and virtue. She gave each a hug, and then they climbed into their beds. Leila cuddled her doll, and they both rolled over to face her with the covers drawn up as she sat on the chair between them.

"Story!" Leila said, her voice carrying a hint of her mother's firm tone of command. "You promised."

"Yeah!"

"But certainly," Adrienne said. A moment's thought, then:

"'Once there was a little girl with a red hood. She was a pretty girl, with pale skin and veins that showed, and she smelled like flowers and hamburgers and chocolate-chip cookies, just *scrumptious*. But everyone knew she'd come to a very bad end, and she did!'"

The children grinned, their eyes alight. Their mother went on:

"'Well, one day she was walking to her grandmother's cottage in the woods. Her grandmother was old and useless, but a beautiful strong wolf broke down her door and chased her around and ate her right up, yum! yum! Then—'"

Eyes drooped as an active day took its toll. She put the book down and began to rise. Leila was snoring, but Leon blinked at her.

"Maman?" he said, his voice slurred.

"Yes, my darling?"

"What's Papa like?"

Ah, she thought.

"Well, he looks a lot like you," she said. "And a lot like me. And he's very, very powerful. His name is Adrian."

"Will Papa ever come and live with us?"

"I don't know, sweetie. I hope so, someday."

"I would like that," Leon said. "I dream about him, sometimes."

Leila murmured drowsy assent, and Adrienne felt the Power prickle at her nerves again, a message too faint to read, like a sound not quite heard in a nighted forest.

When she felt the minds of both children spiral down into deep sleep she walked to her own chambers—through the walls for practice's sake, pausing a moment before each to will them open. It was really more a matter of making *yourself* impalpable, but that was the way she'd always visualized it and you didn't alter what worked. A glitter, the solid plaster and stone fading, and the slightest tug as she walked through— the probability matrix that made up an etheric body interpenetrating with the gross material atoms of the structure.

When her corporeal form opened its eyes she stretched.

"Now I'm *hungry*," she said.

"How do I look?" Adrienne Brézé said a few hours later, glancing over her shoulder at her nude image in the mirror. "Sort of a butch thing, perhaps, with the hair still short?"

Hmmm. I'm still too thin; it's the Case of the Amazing Disappearing Tits. And I do not like my hair only an inch long. If I want to look like a man, I'll night-walk and turn into a man.

That was easy enough; all you needed was an individual's DNA to copy him or her in etheric form, and it was slightly easier with a human than a wolf or a tiger. It could also be a lot of fun, though if she had had to choose one or the other she'd have picked female without hesitation.

We're more flexible, literally and metaphorically, she thought. *Fortunately, I can take my pick.*

She had a remarkably wide selection of templates. Biting someone did nicely, and semen was even easier than blood as a source sample. Any body fluid would do in a pinch.

And my new foot is still a little smaller than the other and disgustingly pink and gets sore easily. Still, I look much better than I did a few weeks ago. And my appetites are coming back, I feel almost normal as long as I don't overexert.

Peter Boase mumbled from the bed, three-quarters unconscious. The room smelled of sweat and blood and musky sex, and strong, sweet lady-of-the-night jasmine in great terra-cotta jars outside the glass doors. This was his own house on Lucy Lane, not her chambers in the *casa grande* above; logically enough, it was where her lucys lived. The houses were comfortable, middle-class buildings in the same Spanish Revival style as the whole of the town, about twenty-five hundred square feet, with rooms grouped around an interior courtyard patio; those backed on the outer wall of the estate gardens.

She walked back to the bed and climbed onto it, onto the man there, and straddled him, resting her chin on her palms and looking down at him. He was short, only a few inches taller than she, perhaps five-six, blond and fine-featured and slim. His skin felt warm, almost flushed, compared to the cool linen on her knees and shins.

"Peter," she whispered. And, within: *Peter.*

He was deeply asleep, wandering through evil dreams. She touched the surface of his interior dialogue delicately, her eyelids drooping as she let the rhythms of consciousness synchronize. You couldn't *talk* to someone's mind like this—not if they weren't Shadowspawn of fairly pure blood—but you could suggest things. The thoughts were one. You could persuade. . . .

Adrienne is dead.

A startling leap of joy, life, freedom—the sort of pleasure that came when a long-existing agony was relieved. Then crashing despair.

No. She's alive. Sick, but alive.

Adrienne is dead.

Make it his *own* thought; not a wish, the ring of conviction.

I saw her die. Overtones, joy . . . not too much, not the savage exultation she'd feel herself watching an enemy perish, add a little revulsion.

Now guide, gently, gently. The mind *wanted* to believe, and they were deep-linked, by pleasure, by pain, by the bond of blood.

The heavy bullet ripped Hajime's head open, and the Shadowspawn lord disappeared, *a fucking* sabertooth *leaping at him as he died.*

All that was real, that had happened.

Gone, gone, Hajime just gone, *Monica down and Jose protecting her with his body, get between her and the danger too, another bullet going by with an astonishing* crack *sound, not a bang at all, not like anything he'd ever heard in a movie, and a* peeeenngggg *sound as it hammered off stone. Shadowspawn running riot, the night-walking or postcorporeal guests transforming into a nightmare collection of beasts and birds.*

The thoughts/memories/images/sensations ran faster and faster, with the iron taste of truth.

Ellen's face contorted with rage and smashing the foil-sheathed hypo down on Adrienne's foot, the great silverback gorilla standing roaring with the bench in its hands, Ellen riding *the sabertooth as it leapt for the roof of the pavilion—*

Adrienne jerking, screaming, slumping in death—

No.

Yes. That happened—

An image of Michiko leaping forward with the wakizashi raised—

To fight the sabertooth, holding it out two-handed, looking around in terror. Adrienne just lay there, and she breathed a few more times, then her chest jerked and there was a sound in her throat and it stopped. Her eyes, the pupils didn't dilate anymore. Dead, dead . . .

Yes.

Yes. Saw that. Saw that. Fear since, fear of her parents, they're dead *but somehow they're alive. . . .*

His mind trailed off into a matrix of equations, trying to understand how a neural net could float free of the flesh that had given rise to it, wrap a synthetic body around itself to go forth and feed. Curiosity burned almost as strong as the need to live, somehow tied into reproduction and the life-death cycle down in the base of his hindbrain.

His mind was almost as unusual as Ellen's, in its way.

Withdraw, withdraw, let the pattern repeat, repeat. Memories uncoiled as they were recalled, reknit as they were stored, again and again. Memory wasn't a recording, it was a song, a story the mind told itself, very slightly different every time. Croon it into the shape of desire . . .

Got to get out, got to get out. GottoGETOUT!

Pushing on an open door. She drew herself back and he turned on his side, drawing into a fetal position, his arms wrapped around his chest.

Chuckling, she let thoughts trickle through their linked minds, tumbled images of her mother baring her teeth—it would be easy enough to mistake one for another, and he'd been appropriately frightened when introduced to her postcorporeal but very much alive and hungry parents. Thoughts of pain, fear, the terrible unwanted ecstasy of feeding. Then the car in the garage, the money in the drawer. Decision firming.

Backwards inch by inch, letting his mind flutter down deeper into sleep, breaking physical and mental contact. His eyes were flickering here and there in rapid eye movement, real dreams, but she'd seen how they would be shaped. Humans had such odd dreams, so . . . so *uncontrolled.*

It could be enormous fun to ride their nightmares, in a subtler way than taking their personalities into your own memory palace, but Peter had had enough. This was business.

Soon she was standing at the foot of his bed. "Poor Peter, I'm going to miss you," she murmured. "But perhaps we'll meet again, eh? *Bon chance*, little physicist."

She turned and walked out into the dark courtyard, stretching with her arms over her head, blinking and yawning and favoring her tender new foot a little. The night was fairly young: around three o'clock, which was halfway through her waking cycle in normal times. There was more than enough light to see by, the glow from the town's streetlights and a few on the *casa*'s grounds; even a human could have made his way, and it was enough for a Shadowspawn pureblood to read by, if the print wasn't too small. She took a long breath of the air.

Now I'll pay Monica a visit . . . no, I'll have her up to the casa *and play a little while I'm night-walking. Then a nice light meal, an omelette perhaps, maybe look in on the children, then some sweet, restorative sleep. And first a shower. Ah, the bourgeois pleasures!*

She let herself through the gate and walked upwards on a sweeping stone staircase between rows of cypresses.

More night-walking, now that I can safely leave my body to take care of itself. The scents are lovely this time of year, with a nose that really works.

And there was always the details of her plots. Plots and plans and intrigues, and so many crossed threads that even she had trouble keeping track of them. Nudging them through the web and warp of probabilities, towards . . .

"The part where I get to be God," she mused. "Not just *a* God as I am now, but *the* God, with my face carved upon the moon."

In the meantime, it was extremely convenient that everyone thought she was dead—including Peter, now, ready to walk out like a ticking bomb that her enemies would hug to their hearts.

And Peter gets to be very, very brave and suffer a great deal. What a tragedy!

"Fix us a drink, *chérie*," Adrienne said.

Muffled sounds; she concentrated, and things that *might* have happened did, even if they wouldn't have by themselves before the sun expanded and then collapsed into a red dwarf.

The effort moved her hunger into the sharp, demanding phase; she'd drawn on her inner reserves for that. Adrienne *suspected* that metabolizing some sort of trace element was involved, but nobody had ever done much research on the biochemical pathways.

Buckles unfastened and snaps clicked free. Monica lay for a moment panting around the gag before she pulled it free, wiped her face on a towel and rose from the great bed and walked stiffly towards the sideboard. This was Adrienne's own chambers in the *casa grande*, pale arched Fragonard-esque elegance and *space*, which she'd missed so badly while she was sick and crowded by machines and people.

Monica's step swayed more as she stretched, and she glanced aside at herself in one of the eighteenth-century mirrors in its ormolu frame.

"And to think I once thought 'spank me rosy' was a figure of speech," she said playfully.

Adrienne laughed. "It's your fault for having such a delectably elegant posterior."

Michiko was right, she thought. *She does look remarkably like Ellen apart from the hair color, and they both* do *look like Monroe, and I'd never thought of that before she mentioned it; Michiko can be disturbingly acute sometimes, when she bothers to make the effort.*

"Anything in particular?" Monica said. "Your word is my command."

"Use your imagination, *chérie*. You're good at that."

Monica laughed and struck a thoughtful pose, like Rodin's *Thinker* but standing up and female.

Or Monica looks like Norma Jean before she became Monroe and went blond, whereas Ellen was a natural platinum. But the figure is very similar, allowing for Monica being a few years older than Ellen. Odd. But then, it's logical that Adrian and I should have similar tastes, no? I don't think I have any particular type *when it comes to males, except of course that they be pretty in one way or another. And their minds are* almost *as important.*

Adrienne put her hands behind her head and looked down at her toes; the left set was only a little paler than the right now, and no longer sore. She wiggled them with some satisfaction; it wasn't worth the trouble to override somatic memory when the waking form was so nearly back to normal.

"Cocktail?" Monica asked. "One of those antique styles your parents like?"

"Splendid idea. Retro can be amusing."

She went to work with bottles and shakers, making a little dance of it, which was entertaining.

Next to the bed was a painting; French Symbolist, showing the death angel bending over an old grave digger in a snowy cemetery, a soul-light in one cupped hand and her black wings making a counterpoint to the leafless branches; he'd dug his last grave, and it would be his own.

Schwabe's *La Mort et le Fossoyeur* had always been a favorite of Adrienne's. For the obvious reasons, and for another: the model the artist used for Azrael's face had been her great-aunt Zoé. Who had long since died the Final Death, a matter of a little family disagreement, but Adrienne remembered her fondly from her own childhood.

"Champagne Apricato," Monica said proudly, handing her a cocktail glass and drinking from her own.

Adrienne took hers and sipped the chilly tart-sweet mixture. Champagne, apricot liqueur made on the estate, gin and the juice of fresh-squeezed lemons from just down the hill.

"A bit too sweet for constant consumption, but superb of its kind," she said. "Much like you, Monica."

The human blushed and smiled as she sat down on the edge of the bed.

"In fact, when I was tucking Leila in earlier, she said you smelled like cake."

Monica laughed. "They're wonderful children," she said. "So cute and smart . . . Do I really smell like cake?"

"To a child. To me . . . a little. Definitely *tasty*. Perhaps a little more like kebab with a honey-mustard glaze. Also like sex on two legs, right now."

"You *are* feeling better," Monica said as she sipped at her drink. Softly, glancing over her shoulder: "Will you kill me when my looks go, *Doña*?"

They locked eyes. "Possibly. Or maybe not. But I'm going to swallow your soul in any case, so you'll never *really* die."

Adrienne tickled her delicately with a toe—the pinkish, new one—and the human shivered.

"That'll be . . . interesting, dying and knowing I'm not *really* going to die."

"I can assure you that at the time you'll be *very* focused on the physical side of things."

Another shiver. "But we get to go on with things together."

"True. Of course, who knows what I'll be like in a few thousand years? Or what you will be? But we're both going to find out."

The human's mind roiled, longing, lust, fear, adoration, and far down a faint screaming from the deeply buried core personality. She put her drink down by her feet; Adrienne knelt behind her and grabbed a handful of her hair, bending her head back. A shiver as the last of the cocktail was poured along her neck . . .

Sometime later Monica sighed drowsily and wiped at a drop of blood on her forehead with the back of her hand. The delicious coppery smell of it mingled with the earthier body musk and sweat.

"It's lovely to have you so *active* again, *Doña*," she said. "It's been a little lonely on Lucy Lane."

"It has?"

"With Jabar . . . gone . . . even if he wasn't very friendly."

Well, he shouldn't have tried to run, Adrienne thought, and grinned. *Though it was a nice bonding experience to hunt him down with Ma-man and Papa when they arrived from La Jolla. How he cursed and then squealed, there at the end when we ran him to ground in those woods. Papa was so inventive! I wouldn't have thought a reptile could do that.*

"And Ellen too; it was nice to have another girl as a neighbor."

"Cheba might be described as a girl," Adrienne said.

"Cheba . . . Cheba isn't adjusting very well."

"I thought you had her enrolled at all those ESL and adult-education classes at the high school? She's a veritable Horatio Alger story of immigrant success, in a way."

"Yes, that's working out, but . . . There's Jose, of course, and Peter, they're both dears. I was going to ask Peter if he wanted to go up to San Francisco and take in the opera, if that's all right?"

"Alas, I'm afraid Peter will be going too. You won't be seeing him tomorrow, in fact."

Monica went very still; Adrienne tickled the back of her neck, savoring the chill of despair.

"No, I'm not going to kill him," Adrienne said. "Not anytime in the immediate future, that is. He'll just be going away for a while."

"I didn't think . . ." Monica said, over a rush of relief.

"That I ever let anyone go? I don't."

Like a cat with a mouse, Monica thought.

"Exactly. And you should be prepared for some travel in the immediate future."

"Paris?" Monica said hopefully.

"Among other places. I've got a new plane, you'll enjoy it. An Airbus A380."

"Oh, that sounds like a *dream*."

"One of the better ones," Adrienne replied. "Though nightmares have their charm."

Me llamo Eusebia Graciela Cortines Angeles. Nanotoca Eusebia.

"I name Eusebia."

Cheba sat at *her* kitchen table, in *her* kitchen, in *her* house . . . in a country and state and town very, very far away from where she had been given her names.

"I am practice my English. I . . . I *am practicing* my English . . . *¡Qué lengua más estúpida!*"

Before her, scattered over the table, were books, a computer pad, notebooks and paper, all dappled with sunlight from the garden outside.

The building wasn't totally unlike what she was accustomed to seeing, nor ones that her mother had occasionally scrubbed floors in: rooms grouped around a courtyard, pale stucco walls, red-tile roof. Nothing like anything she'd ever lived in, of course. This *kitchen* was bigger than any house she'd ever lived in before; at least, it smelled more the way she was familiar with now, cinnamon, cardamom, of fresh peppers and the strings of dried ones over the stove, poblanos, pasilla, chipotle, serranos, negros. A pot of corn was boiling with a hint of cal, chicken bubbling in a stew.

Every detail was wrong, though. Better than the *barrio*, she had to admit. No wood smoke, no kerosene. The town wasn't big, but it made her feel alien and exposed.

As for what lived here—

Her hands began to shake, and she stared at them stubbornly until they stopped. She had not slept very well. You didn't, when you were *waiting* for . . . No.

Then she took up the pencil again. Her teacher had told her that handwriting was one of the best ways to make her new words sink into her brain.

"I'm not feeling very smart today."

Early in the morning, well before dawn, Monica and her mother had had a screaming fight out in the street. Cheba hadn't understood much, but she hadn't been able to get back to sleep. It was best not to think about that. She frowned at the last sentence instead. It wasn't right. She tugged on the gleaming black curl she'd wound around her left forefinger.

¡Inglés! she thought in exasperation.

It had auxiliary verbs. *And they don't make sense! Oh! My, it is "my" name,* mío! *And my father's and my mother's.*

The words hit her in the chest, squeezing, as memories opened and bled, and a single coughing sob burst out before she choked her lips shut. Images—

Father, happy drunk and mean drunk.

They'd lived with her mother's parents in a brightly painted little cinder-block hut, on the edge of a small village. The dusty unpaved steet outside ran from the tiny town center to the hot, humid green jungle. Her mother, Alma Marta, had been an only child, and her husband had expected to inherit the lands from his father-in-law. But it hadn't happened. The elders hadn't liked his drunkenness, or the slovenly way he worked the lands for his father-in-law, and a cousin of hers had been granted the lands by the *ejido* when her grandfather had died.

Unitario Cortines Cruz had left the village to find other work. She and her mother had stayed with the cousins.

The only thing Papá *found was his way into the grille of a very large truck. And I cannot even pretend it wasn't his own fault. He was probably looking at it and laughing when it hit him.*

That had been near Papantla, Veracruz. The news arrived at the village a few months later.

Alma Marta Angeles Zapatero had found only cold charity with her cousins. She and her surviving child had walked and hitchhiked to Tlacotalpan.

I do not remember the village all that well. We were hungry there, sometimes, yes. But it was not like the homeless camps and the shantytown. And selling those ugly baskets to the tourists for centavos on the peso didn't pay any better, and we had to buy everything. Everything stank of sewage. Even the sun and the rain were worse, all crowded together, and never any quiet, never a place to be alone even for a moment. Waking up and the bugs crawling on me and eating the calluses off my feet. I had to come to el Norte. *The thieves, they were as bad as the bugs, and as many as the rats and pigeons and seagulls. The rats stole our food and the thieves stole our money.*

"Mama, you saved everything, for years. Sometimes you would tell me you had eaten when you hadn't, so we could put a little more in the box."

She squeezed her eyes shut again. The final day had been hot and muggy even to her, raised in the coastal lowlands; just like all the others before it, but worse. She had danced across the great highway first, carrying most of the baskets, the fresh straw smell strong as she peered around them.

I could see it on the men watching. They were looking at me, at my legs, and then their eyes went up and they saw behind me and they shouted.

Brakes squealing and engine roar and tires skidding across the hot asphalt screaming like a trapped rabbit. Her own voice shouting, *No, no,* as she dropped the baskets and turned. The heavy, meaty thump came through the air like a blow, like a fist in the belly. A crackling with it, like sticks being twisted off a bush. All that before she could even turn and see, see what she knew and would not believe even when she saw it.

There were baskets scattered all over the busy fairway, and she stood, teetering on the edge of the curb, watching the broken rag doll tossed into the air and rolling, bouncing and banging, under two more cars before traffic split about the shattered body. The screams of the sirens had echoed through her head, the flashing lights had played on her eyes as she stood frozen, watching the emergency crew bag the body up and bundle it into the back of the ambulance. The police had held people away, but they hadn't asked questions and the great truck was long gone.

Who cares for the death of one more useless old india? *And now, I have my truck. Her name is Adrienne*, she told herself mordantly.

The doorbell chimes startled her out of the fruitless reverie. Like everything in this *maldito* country; they were wrong! Who would have tooting, galloping horns for a knocker! She stumped through the living room and opened the door, scowling. Jose was there.

They try, she thought. *They try to be so nice. And I try, try to be polite to them.* She silently stood aside to let him in and waved towards the kitchen.

She frowned as he sat down; there was a blanched look to his skin, and the small wrinkles at the corners of his eyes were tight and tense.

"*¿Una chela?*" she asked.

He nodded and wagged a finger at her. She stuck out her tongue, feeling as awkward as usual. He was Hispano like her, she should feel at home with him, but it didn't happen. He didn't feel like a *bad* man; she had experience enough and to spare with those, and you could tell. But he was different.

"*¿Una cerveza?*" she asked instead.

He opened his mouth and then wagged his finger again. She sighed.

"*Bien, bien.* Do . . . you . . . like . . . the . . . beer?"

"Would you like a beer?" he corrected her. "Don't sigh, Cheba. It's really important you work at fitting in. Yes, there are many who can speak Spanish in this town, more than in most places around here—"

"Why?" she asked.

"This was a rancho . . . hacienda . . . long ago, before the Americans came. Under Spain, under Mexico. After that it was out of the way, not close to any of the cities. Anglos settled here only slowly; then the Brézés came, long ago—more than a hundred and fifty years—and since then, not many people leave, not many come in, we are a bit apart from the world. But it is still California, and if you cannot speak English well you are like someone with only one eye or one leg. Also my *tía* Joan has spoken to me about you."

Cheba went to the refrigerator and took out a bottle of the beer with the pretty label for Jose and a Jarritos soda pop for herself.

"Your *tía*? Is she a sister of your father or mother? And why does she care?"

He took a long gulp from the bottle. "My father's older sister. As to why . . . Because . . . it's part of being human?"

Cheba snorted. "Not like your *tía* Theresa?"

She had met the Brézé household manager that terrible day the people-smuggler Paco had delivered them to Rancho Sangre. They called them coyotes, but he'd met *real* shape-shifters. He had deserved to die; the others hadn't.

He laughed. "Theresa? There's a story here that a snake bit her once, a rattlesnake."

"What happened?"

"The snake died."

That made *her* laugh, a brief, unwilling snort. Jose leaned forward, speaking earnestly.

"Listen, Joan lived in Mexico for many years, studied there and all. She owns an import business, goes back a lot. She asked me what you did all day. I didn't understand why; but she says that the women of the villages are never idle. They always have something in their hands, embroidery or crochet lace, or weaving, but never idle."

Cheba closed her eyes, seeing the brightly embroidered blouse her mother had been finishing, soaking up the blood, turning from white to dark red, and shuddered unexpectedly.

"It costs money," she excused herself. "And I am . . . sad all the time. I like to crochet, and sometimes embroider."

"Money . . ." exclaimed Jose. "You know you have as much as you want. And making things that are pretty will make you less sad."

"But, where?"

Jose sighed and waggled his finger at her again. She laughed, a bit sourly.

"You mean, where would you buy the stuff? In town, of course. There are three or four shops that sell craft stuff. Monica would take you, and love doing it."

He looked at her and she dropped her eyes to the papers on the table. Her classes were over the Internet, she didn't need to go out and try to mix. Jose had taken her to the library and introduced her to the librarian. Cheba had not been back.

Jose made an exasperated sound. *"¡Mira, tú!"* he said with some heat in his voice. "We are all trying, but you are not."

Cheba bit her lip and tried to stop the tears. "What should I try? Try to be a *puta* and food?" she asked, feeling the raw anger crowd forward. "I had to leave my village because my papa was a drunk and died . . . walked in front of a truck. My mama died crossing a street . . . another truck, so, I took a truck up to here, trying to get away from the bad luck and a new life. And look what picked me up!"

"Yes. But now you have that new life. A house, a life, things to learn, people to meet . . . What is wrong?"

"It's all wrong!" Cheba shouted. "It's not the right size, or shape; the rugs are dirty! There aren't nice floors to sweep, the kitchen is closed in; the windows too big; the lights too bright; the roads . . .

"I want to feel the dust between my toes, the sun on my back, pick the corn and beans in my grandfather's *milpa*, hear the voices of the village, of the market, of the children. . . ."

More tears threatened and she held them back with her scowl.

"But what did you expect?" he asked her, a puzzled note in his voice. "Of course it would be different!"

She looked around, surprised, and thought back to that day, the day of death when she had carefully stolen ten wallets, carefully, oh, so carefully, and added the money to her little hoard and begun her flight north. What had she expected? Difference, just something different from her real life.

"I guess, different; I wanted something different. No more poverty or living like an animal? To be rich."

"And in comparison, here you are rich!"

"But it is not rich like I know rich! It is wrong. . . . Everything is different, yes; but evil!" Cheba shook her head and watched Jose take a quick gulp of beer.

"Yeah," he said, surprising her. "It is." A grim smile at the look on her face. "Do I look stupid?"

"But if you hadn't fallen in with *La Doña*, you'd have been slaving in the fields, living crowded cheek by jowl in tar paper shacks, hiding from *la migra*, eating worse than you ever have in your life . . . and raped, often, by the men who hire the wetbacks. That man Paco who sold you and your friends to *La Doña* was not interested in taking you *anywhere* good. I don't have to draw you a picture about that, no? So, it kinda balances out."

Cheba clenched her jaw. *He is right, the trip across the border and to here taught me that!* This piece of logic of Jose's she could follow; she couldn't always understand his thoughts.

"*La Doña* is better than working in the fields? A *bruja*, a *chupacabra*, and I am not a goat!"

"You are a goat." Jose's voice was flat. "Or you're a bird and she is a cat. We all are. And it is better than the fields. At least she doesn't roast us over fire; just over the coals of our emotions. Rape is rape, and that hasn't changed."

"There's a lot you don't understand and we've tried to tell you. Not just my *tía* has sent me to talk to you. *La Doña* called me in and told me . . ."

"She confides in you," Cheba observed sourly.

He hesitated and then shrugged.

"I was born here, and my ancestors. One chance, Cheba. You have one chance left. If you don't do what *La Doña* orders you to she will eat you up tomorrow."

He took another swallow of the beer and Cheba glowered at him; this nice young man who looked so much like the young men in Coetzala and Veracruz and was so very different in how he saw the world. She couldn't help herself.

"You are gringo, *gabacho*, you don't understand!"

"I know that! And it bothers me. What don't I understand? You're

159

india; you and your people have lived for twenty, thirty generations as conquered people, on the edge! Where do you get that pride?"

"We still live!" she flashed back at him, and scowled as he dissolved into hearty guffaws. "What is funny?" she demanded.

Jose shook his head. "It's from a TV show, or a movie or something. It's used as a joke and also as defiance."

"Well," she said, glowering at him, "I'm defiant and it doesn't sound funny to me."

Jose shook his head and finished off the beer. "Look, you've survived for generations as a people, now you need to survive as a person. Independent, yes, doing things, being alive, or *La Doña* will eat you up."

"Then I'll be dead; grateful release!"

"Really? Hasn't *La Doña* taken you into her memory?"

Cheba made an involuntary movement and barely managed to catch the Jarritos bottle before it went flying across the kitchen. She started to say something and paused.

"Yes, you've met George, I see. Take what time you have and can use. My aunt says that the Shadowspawn, *los hijos de sombra*, she calls them in Spanish, were the kings and priests of the old ones before the conquest. So it really isn't new, even to you, from that little Huasteca village."

"So, they are *chupacabra* and we their goats! Nyyahahaha . . ."

"Yeah, pretty much. We are their *barbacoa*."

"It's worse than flames what she makes me do!"

Jose looked surprised. "You were a virgin? I'm sorry. It must have been very hard to learn the perversions she likes, not knowing the loving pleasure most of us can share."

Cheba snapped angrily, "No, I wasn't a virgin! Paco took care of that, he and five other men!" She turned away from his shocked eyes, picking up and draining the soda pop. She hesitated and waggled the bottle at him.

"How do they get the drugs into it? And what is it called?" she asked.

"Drugs?" he asked.

"If she doesn't like what I do she takes away the drugs. I never smoked, drank, did *drogas*! And now I am shaky, angry, confused, and she will only give me the drugs if I do what she says. But I don't know which drug or how it gets into me. If I knew, maybe I could run away. I thought it was in the Jarritos and that she took away the ones with drugs if she was angry at me. But now I don't think that's it."

"Ooohh, *niña*," exclaimed Jose. "It's the bite itself. *La Doña* is the drug. It's in the spit."

"*¡Ai!*"

"See, I told you, they're *made* to prey on us, like jaguars on deer. You remember the night you came here, what happened—"

He pointed eastward. She remembered it, the killing hall, and *La Doña*'s guests . . . feasting.

"Well, you're lucky the Brézés don't always kill. *I'm* going to live a long time."

"What do you mean?"

"*La Doña* hasn't bitten me for five days, now. It hurts and I'm restless, and angry . . . and trying hard not to yell at you, you stubborn goat!"

"Oh," she said. "Then . . . why?"

"Because she says my time as a lucy is over. Now I go back to my life, get married, settle down. *Protected*, you understand? All the people born here are, the renfield families who serve the Brézés. And you could be. Or you could end up dead, or worse than dead—like George."

"You look sick," she said suddenly.

"I'm going to get a lot worse before I get better, and it takes a lot of work and other drugs to stop the addiction."

He shrugged. "Pain I can stand. There's pain in life, you know that. You let it be your master or you make yourself its master; there is no other way."

Cheba frowned. The blanched quality she'd noticed earlier was getting worse, and she could see pain lines etching themselves on his face.

"*¿Eso te pasa?*" she asked sharply, feeling sick to her stomach as she understood.

He took the bottle to the sink and turned. "Yes. I was born here. I get to live when she is done with me, just like my uncle. You don't. If she had died, you, Monica and Peter would have been killed by her parents."

"Will . . . will it be very bad? I feel . . . itchy now. And I saw people at home who had no money for their drugs."

"Yes, it is very bad. Some kill themselves because of the pain; I won't, and I have the doctor to help me as well. Give me your cell phone."

Jose snatched it out of the air when she tossed it over to him.

"When I call you it will play 'Tilingo Lingo.' That's loud enough to wake you no matter what."

He tossed it back to her. "So, I am going through withdrawal. It's getting really bad, I've got a few more days before I begin screaming. Do you take this chance? Or die?"

Cheba looked at the gray and sweating man standing by her—her!—kitchen sink. He, and Monica and even Peter had all tried to be nice to her.

No, she thought, *were nice to me, helped me, tried to support me, teach me . . . and I was mean and nasty and sullen back to them. They are not her. I don't dare be that way to her.*

"I don't know what to do," she said.

"If that means, yes, then go see Dr. Duggan tomorrow at eight a.m. Say it with words."

"Yes, yes, I will take care of you. And not because *La Doña* says so; but because you took care of me and I wasn't good back."

Jose's eyes were dark brown pools of pleading fear, and Cheba put out her hand. Hand in hand they walked through the house. She opened the door and they walked out into the late-summer day.

She looked over at Jose's house and the one beyond it. "Monica is still asleep. Her mother was pretty mad, last night," she observed in Spanish to Jose.

"It's hard; most lucies don't have kids. Monica tries to make sure they are always taken care of. I don't know what will happen next. *La Doña* will be traveling and she always takes Monica with her."

He shrugged. "She's sent Peter away somewhere, to do something for her. Poor guy; withdrawal will be hell for him, all alone. You might go with her and Monica—if you can get along with Monica. Try! Monica is a very nice person, and if you can't make her want you there, you might die, after all."

Jose walked to his house and gave her a small wave as he walked in.

She stood, troubled, on the doorstep, turning the cell phone over and over in her hands . . . hands that wanted work; a crochet hook, some thread, a pretty collar and some cuffs, a doily growing steadily, extra money as the tourists admired her mother's embroidered napkins and her lacy trims on them.

¡Chupacabra! she thought. *¡Y yo, chiva! Cheba, la chiva, cabrita chula!*

163

Calling herself a nanny goat, a cute little kid, didn't really make her feel any better. She went back to the kitchen, rinsed the bottles out and took them to the recycling bin on her back porch. The little orange cat that had belonged to the *brujo*'s wife, Elena, peered out at her from under the bush. She called it *imizton, that woman's cat* in Nahuatl, and fed it out of pity. She wondered what Elena had called it; Monica hadn't known.

She returned to the house and closed the door, frowning. The house was clean. The annoying rugs that couldn't be swept were vacuumed with the loud machine several times a week, her kitchen spotless. . . . She grimaced, wishing for her grandmother's open-air kitchen, four poles, a thatched roof, a table and a little charcoal stove. Then she looked around the bright little room and scolded herself. It wasn't what she had wanted, or expected, and it was full of the . . . of Elena's things. But Elena had good taste and they were pretty and comfortable things. She should stop being angry, all it did was give her *bilis*.

One day, she thought, *one day I will find a way to kill* La Doña, *and free myself. Elena nearly killed her, and what she could do, I can do! Until then I will take what I can and use everything I can find. I will be clever before I can be brave; then I will be brave and clever.*

She nodded sharply and looked down at her clean brown foot, neatly shod in a pretty gold leather sandal, a light anklet around her right ankle with a little charm made out of amethysts. Her lilac pants, ordered with Monica's help off the Internet, were something Monica had called "pedal pushers," and fit perfectly. She had on a nice shirt in a soft gold color. Her feet were clean, her toenails and fingernails manicured, her hair soft and wavy, pulled up into a long ponytail; she had many luxuries she had never had in her life.

She shook her head thoughtfully, remembering the little stream where she and her mother had bathed every night in the warm, smelly waters that ran into the Gulf of Mexico, carefully using harsh yellow soap under their clothes; never undressing all the way. It had been hard to keep themselves clean, but they had managed that much.

Now, she thought. *Now, I must make friends with Monica. How can I do that?*

She stood by the living room window and craned a bit, looking towards Monica's quiet house. Generally Monica had the house open to the air and sun, nice smells coming out as she cooked a little snack for her children.

Oh! Cheba remembered. La Doña *called Monica to come to her last night and she called her mother and her mother came but yelled and yelled at her. I hope they didn't wake the children. So Monica must be really feeling bad. . . . A session with* La Doña *right on top of the fight with her mother. I guess her mama doesn't really know what* La Doña *is. Will the children travel with them or stay with their grandmother? What about* La Doña*'s children?*

Cheba thought about Monica for a moment and then nodded to herself. She stuck the cell phone back into her pants pocket and walked out and down the lane.

Ringing the bell of number one wasn't as hard as she thought it would be. She wasn't a petitioner, a stupid from the bottom of the heap anymore. She was somebody who could help, and help in a real way.

The other woman's overly familiar manner and bubbly personality made her feel just like the orange cat backing away from her the first few days she'd been stuck in number five. But she could take it; it was well-meant. She firmly pursed her lips and pushed the button. Monica's ringer was something cheerful that sounded like kids' cartoons.

Monica didn't look much better than Jose when she opened the door: pale, moving a bit carefully, her hair tousled, and her sweatsuit rumpled.

"Oh, hi, Cheba," she said flatly. "What can I do for you?"

Am I too late? Does she already hate me? No, no, this is just her being tired from last night. The kids are going to be home from school in just a little bit.

"I am the sorry," she said. "I . . ." Exasperated with the difficulties of trying to speak proper English, she flipped over to Spanish. "I am sorry, I know you understand my language better than I speak yours. I woke up last night when your mother yelled. I have come to say, I will help you if I am not helping Jose. Can I help now? You need to sleep and I can look after the children. They are nice children and a pleasure to watch."

Monica sagged against the doorframe. "You'd do that? I can pay you! Oh, Cheba!" Tears leaked down her cheeks. "I've been so afraid somebody will tell *La Doña* what Mom said."

Cheba nodded firmly and pushed Monica into the house. "Go, go take a nice bath, listen to soft music, sleep. You do not need to pay me money; that we have.

"I will clean for you today, make dinner, watch children. This I can do and will. Then later you will help me buy things so I can make you some crocheted lace collars or trim an apron for you. And we will become friends; friends help each other. Now I pay you back for those first terrible days when you helped me so much."

Monica gave a sudden sob and clutched Cheba to her in a strong hug. Cheba stiffened, but held still. With a big sniff Monica let go and rubbed her face with a hanky.

"Thanks. Thanks. I know you don't like it here, but, oh, Cheba, I'm so lonely and alone. Ellen was nice. And she's gone and she can never be a friend again. Adrienne will just tear her to pieces when she catches her. . . ."

Cheba turned the babbling woman around and pointed her down the hall. "Bath," she said firmly, and felt the first glow of positive action in a long time.

CHAPTER TEN

Twelve days after he fled Rancho Sangre, Peter Boase stumbled into the bathroom of the motel and fell to his knees before the toilet bowl, retching. The heaves came again and again, even though he had nothing in his stomach but a little water. When that was gone it felt as if his guts were coming up, as if something were going to tear inside and he'd spew blood and bits of organ meat into the bowl.

Only clenched teeth kept him from screaming as the waves of misery swept over him; the nausea, the blinding headache, the fierce itching feeling as if his skin were crawling off his bones, the way the bones *ached* with little jabs of pain in the joints. The flickering of the dim fluorescent light seemed to strobe in rhythm with the gasps that drove themselves through his throat.

I'm not going to die, he made himself think. *I'm not going to die.*

Part of him *wanted* to die. Most of the rest of him wanted the bite, knew that if Adrienne were to appear he'd beg for it, do anything for it. Everything was *wrong*, the whole world was *wrong*. The crooked hang of the shower curtain hinted at obscene possibilities, the grinning fangs beneath the surface of the world. Tendrils crawled at the edges of sight.

She's dead. I'm not going back. Thank God I got too sick and weak to go back before the craving got unbearable.

He managed to choke out a grunt of laughter. He'd placed himself in a situation where he *had* to endure the unendurable. The cheap motel room didn't even have a phone in the room to call back to Rancho Sangre and tell *La Doña's* parents—

You don't have to think of her as the Lady *anymore. That sadistic bitch's freaking undead monster parents.*

—to come and get him and please, please feed on him. And he was too weak to get dressed, much less go ask for a line at the desk. He'd made his own phone inoperable without more concentration than he was capable of right now.

The nausea died down a little, and the universe stopped trying to buckle in on him in waves of squirming horrors. He crawled to the sink, the cracked bad-smelling linoleum of the floor gouging at his naked skin. The stinks of dirt and stale urine and old sweat and bad, distant ghosts of greasy food set his stomach in a knot again; his senses were superacute now, touch and smell especially.

Peter waited out the spasms and reached the sink and hauled himself up. He didn't want to look in the mirror, but he couldn't help it. The blond stubble on his face was a lighter color than his hair, a tinge of orange in it. The face beneath had fallen in on itself, the skin showing the skull beneath, and his hair was lank and greasy and plastered to his forehead with cold muck and sweat. Dried tears marked streaks down to his chin, and his lips were cracked.

Always thin, his body was skeleton-gaunt now; he hadn't been able to keep any food down for nearly a week. Moving very carefully, he turned on the tap, shuddering at the sound the water made as it hit the discolored porcelain of the sink. For a minute or so he leaned with his hands on the side of the sink, panting. Then he put a light plastic cup under the flow and waited until it overflowed. It took both hands to raise the water to his lips, and he sipped cautiously between breaths.

Oh, God, it's going to stay down, he thought. *I'm dehydrated. I need this water.*

Slowly he reached to a capful of pills. They were a prescription sedative he'd taken from Monica's bathroom before he left; it felt obscurely like a betrayal, although she'd have no problem getting more. The dose was two; in his present state he didn't dare take more than one. Another cup of water to wash it down, and an anxious wait until the nausea didn't grow any worse. He shuffled his feet around, feeling dizzy as he turned despite the caution.

One step to the bathroom door. Grip it, lean, pause. A slatted window across the room, a stained carpet, a chair and table, the mess of blankets and sheets on the bed. Step. Step. Step. Then a slow lowering onto the messy surface.

It's not *a mass of flesh-eating beetles. It's not a pit of black slime. It's a* bed*; you're imagining things.*

He startled himself by yawning. Then he turned onto his side, grabbed a pillow, and held it to his stomach as he curled around it. Sleep was an escape, a door he longed to dive through, but only by relaxing could he seek it. The sedative helped, a little. He forced himself to take slow breaths instead of panting. Let the pain flow through. No stopping it along the way, not magnifying it by paying attention. Just let it go as another physical sensation. Another yawn. He shut his eyes and looked at the random patterns on the inside of his eyelids.

Think about the way your retinas discharge randomly in darkness. It's soothing.

A deeper darkness. When he awoke the sun was bright outside the window. He raised his head to look at the clock; it was two, which must mean the afternoon.

I feel better, he thought. *Which is to say, I feel like absolute shit.*

Stiff, sore, weak, headache, dry grainy eyes. His hand rested before his eyes, and it was like a yellowing spider, the knuckles enlarged like the swellings in a root. Moving it hurt, and parts of it felt as if he had deep paper cuts.

"Sit up," he murmured, and then stopped at the shrill squeaking sound of his voice and the way it hurt.

And feels like it's echoing down a tunnel, with something waiting at the other end. Stop that!

Still, he sat up. The room swam for an instant, and then steadied. He braced the mummy hands against his knees; they were knobs in the middle of sticks, and he could count every one of his ribs along the way. *Push, very carefully.* He came erect, tottered, and walked to the door of the bathroom. Fresh misery washed over him for an instant at the effort, then receded. He clung to the doorjamb and laughed weakly, a croaking like something that lived in a summer pond back in his parents' Minnesota home.

Then he arranged himself and walked two steps to the sink. That was triumph, and he felt himself grinning idiotically. His throat was dry and raw; he sipped three cups of water carefully, and felt it sinking into his tissues, bringing them back to a painful life. Outside in the room were the supplies he'd laid in before the withdrawal symptoms got too bad, and he made his way there. A can of chicken broth with a pop-top lid; he was panting and trembling again before he got it open, but he did, and spilled only a little to run down his chin as he drank it. The rich fatty salty goodness of the clear fluid was almost too much, and he fought to keep it down with deep breathing.

Back to the bed. Sleep, a falling into a welcome darkness.

But yellow-flecked eyes waited there.

This time the misery was less when he woke, but for a moment Peter couldn't tell where he was. Twelve, Christmas, lying sick with the flu while the rest of the family was down in the living room. The model of the *Enterprise* hanging over his bed, the Hubble photograph on the cupboard door, the Xbox on the desk, the shelf with his Jack London and schoolbooks. Mom would come soon, and spoon some of her chicken soup into his mouth, and change the cloth on his forehead—

No. I'm not twelve. I'm thirty-two.

Cold clarity, and tears ran down his cheeks again in reaction.

I want my mom, I want my mom! Oh, shut up, Peter!

He coughed, deep, and had to spit as dryish sticky phlegm filled his mouth. Fastidious reflex made him blunder into the bathroom to use the sink for it, then he forced himself to stop and move with the aching care of a very old man. A clinical appraisal told him he was a little more mobile, but just enough to hurt himself if he wasn't cautious. For the first time in a while his bladder was full, and there was a stinging pain at the beginning of the dark yellow flow.

He drank more water, more broth, blundered back to bed and collapsed as if bludgeoned. His dreams were memories: ice spray whipping in a glittering veil off a hillcrest under moonlight as he crested it on his skis, gray slush on a city street, a canoe and big mosquitoes and white birch trees. A chocolate bar forgotten in one hand as he stared at a textbook and suddenly he *understood* what that theorem meant, the multilayered elegance of it clicking home in his mind. Ruth's shy smile . . .

But all with a sense of *wrongness*. It faded as he woke, coughed, and wrinkled his nose at the smell of stale ancient sweat that filled the room. Flies buzzed near the ceiling. He hadn't noticed those before, but now his eyes tracked them for minutes at a time.

For three days he kept up the pattern, sleeping, eating what he could—he graduated to crackers as well as broth—sleeping again. When he was stable enough for a shower the relief was inexpressible, though going back to the smelly sheets was hard for the moments it took to tumble into unconsciousness.

"You say you don' want the maid," the manager of the motel said; he was a short, thickset dark man in a stained T-shirt.

"That was then. This is now. Now I want the room cleaned," Peter said.

The office had a tall, dirty glass wall that turned it into a solar furnace. The air-conditioning unit in a side window rattled and wheezed, laboriously dumping the heat back out into the environment and leaving a slight smell of mildew in the cooler air. Peter reached carefully into his hip pocket and took out his wallet, then fanned another three hundred dollars onto the desk.

"Okay," the man said.

"And that covers the next week."

"Maybe you should pay extra," the manager said.

"Maybe I should pay less. Maid service is part of the standard charge."

There was open contempt in the motel operator's gaze; he might as well have said *junkie* aloud. After a moment he shrugged and swept up the money.

"Okay, one more week."

"Is there anyplace in town to get something to eat?"

"This isn't like the city, mister," the man said. "Hell, it ain't even like it's a town."

Peter managed to smile; his lips weren't so dry and cracked now.

"The place I grew up was about this size. Just a lot colder and greener."

"There's Teresa's. The truckers stop there. Out past the gas station."

"Thanks."

"*De nada.*"

Of course, probably Teresa's your cousin or your aunt.

Heat hit him like a club as he pushed open the nonfunctioning automatic door and walked out of the little patch of shade flanked by the dry twigs of something dead in two concrete planters. It must have been at least a hundred, but it felt good, as if it were sinking into his bones and driving out lines of ice crystal there. He walked cautiously into the white light, a dozen steps at a time and then a moment's rest.

The little sun-faded Arizona hamlet held the one run-down motel, a scattering of old crumbling adobes, and some trailers and doublewides sandblasted by years of the desert winds, along with a few spindly bushes that were trying to be trees, their silvery gray leaves turning in the slight hot breeze. Beyond was nothing but rock and sand, occasional tufts of reluctant hardy vegetation, and things that glinted in the brilliant sunlight and might have been old broken bottles or flecks of mica in the rocks.

It also held a gas station–cum–convenience store, and beside it a blocky white single-story structure labeled, T RESA'S. He *supposed* that had originally been, TERESA'S, and it was definitely a restaurant. A bell tinkled as he pushed through the screen door; from the silence he guessed that it wasn't air conditioned, but it was oddly cool. After a moment he felt his mind function again; the wall had been three feet thick. This was adobe, and excellent thermal insulation.

The big surprise was that it didn't smell. Well, not of anything but food; the interior was plain, and some of the furniture looked like it dated to the eighties or even earlier, but it was dim and cool, and his stomach clenched in anticipation at the prospect of solid food, helped by the smells of spices and frying meat and onions. Everything seemed reasonably clean, though. Presumably truckers stopped here, or maybe smugglers. He sat at one of the plastic-topped tables and panted a little, exhausted by the brief walk. There was sweat under the straps of his light knapsack; the damp patches felt cool with evaporation for a moment as he sat and controlled his breathing.

"I'll have . . ." he croaked.

The waitress could have been Mexican or Indian, in her thirties and built like a rain barrel. She looked at him incuriously.

"A burrito. And a glass of water. A pitcher of water, please. Just a little ice."

She waited expressionlessly until he put a twenty by his plate, even though he was clean and he'd thought he looked much better once he shaved. Evidently *much better* still didn't mean *acceptable.*

The food came fairly quickly, which wasn't surprising, since he and the waitress were the only humans visible. There was a cat in one corner, but it was firmly asleep on a mat, stretched out to "sleep thin." Nothing moved, except the overhead fan in its eternal slow revolution, giving off a slight *squee* and wobble with each turn.

"Careful, careful," he muttered to himself when the plate arrived.

It was a long time since he'd had much solid food. Peter swallowed painfully, aware that he'd been nearly drooling; it was as if he were an old rusty outboard engine that had finally caught and was stuttering and letting out clouds of blue smoke but turned the propeller nonetheless. The thought made him smile a little. Despite years in the Southwest, his mind still used Land O' Lakes visual metaphors!

One bite, and he almost moaned with pleasure. Chewing, chewing, making himself go slowly and not bolt it and overburden his shrunken stomach. The burrito was Mexican-style, not surprising this close to the border, smaller and thinner than the American variety, and holding only *barbacoa*-style pork and onion and refried beans. A pause while he monitored his stomach; it was going to stay down. He finished and licked his fingers, and then just sat sipping at his water for twenty minutes, feeling relatively *good* for the first time since the symptoms started to hit.

"Okay, work," he muttered to himself. "You're supposed to be a logical thinker. At least about physics. At least, you *used* to be."

His hands still wobbled a bit as he slid his workpad computer out of the knapsack on the chair beside him. A gentle tap to the screen projected the virtual keyboard onto the table. He slid the foot down to put the image at the right angle and adjusted the distance. The battery had a three-quarter charge.

"I should have remembered to leave it plugged in. Hell, am I fit to do *anything* right now? Doc Duggan said the withdrawal was rough but there usually wasn't any permanent damage. *Usually* is sort of an unpleasant word. And I sort of liked Duggan, we had things in common, but she's a renfield. She works for *them*. How trustworthy was what she said?"

Although she hadn't been born into the Shadowspawn-worshiping cult, like most of the inhabitants of the town of Rancho Sangre Sagrado. Some of those people were all right, if you stayed away from their . . . well, not quite a religion, but nearly.

The Shadowspawn are creepy enough if you know *that what they do isn't really supernatural. I mean, they* do *drink blood and they* can *assume other shapes and move things with their minds and affect how chances turn out. . . .*

Jose Villegas, one of his fellow lucies, had been a decent guy, what they'd called a regular Joe in his grandfather's day, though he'd been born and raised there. Others, like the household manager Theresa, were rabid weasels, as bad as Shadowspawn in their way—maybe worse, given that they didn't have all the king-predator genes pushing them. A *lot* of them were really screwed up in one way or another, functioning neurotics with weird forms of denial. He suspected that suicide was a major health problem there.

"Okay, Peter, think logically."

He stared at the screen as the system logged onto the Web—the area had phone reception, and that was all it needed.

"I can't be Peter Boase again."

The thought of resuming his researcher's life at Los Alamos was wonderful beyond belief, but every bit as impossible as being twelve again. Peter Boase had kept prying into anomalous phenomenon despite *strong hints* that he shouldn't. Peter Boase had been marked for death by the Council of Shadows, and Adrienne had come in to kill him because she was the one who happened to be closest.

Stroke, heart attack, traffic accident, slipping on the soap in the shower; they didn't have to make it *look* like an accident, they could produce a *real* accident.

If I was a tub of unwashed lard like, say, Bob Heigel or a pencil-necked geek with adult acne like Johnny Wong, I'd have died right there no matter how interesting my mind felt to her. But Adrienne was a collector and she took a fancy to me. Making me one of her lucies was as good as killing me. Probably just a slow form of killing me. Monica had been there on Lucy Lane for eight years, but that was the longest. We never talked about the others.

The changes that intrigued him had been in certain constants; now he knew it was the effect of so many Shadowspawn mucking with the quantum foam, making probabilities blur into one another. Homo sapiens nocturnus was the source of all legends in more ways than one.

The tales of leopard-men and werewolves and blood-drinking ogres and evil sorcerers came from them, from the Empire of Shadows in the dim pre-Neolithic past, or from chance recombinations of the genes in the ages since producing someone with half-understood powers and inhuman hungers. But the weird, arbitrary, anything-can-happen world of the legends was a folk memory of the way the world was when there were many powerful Shadowspawn in it, enhancing chaos just by *existing*.

A world where trees could speak and gingerbread houses with ovens for stray children waited in the woods and water flowed uphill . . . which was happening again.

Concentrate, dammit! he thought savagely. *Okay, my old life's gone. And if the Brézés back at Sangre ever get their hands . . . or talons or claws or tentacles . . . on me, I'm* worse *than dead. I know Ellen's boyfriend, Adrian, is supposed to be a good guy, more or less, but I don't think I'll be able to contact him, he'll be hiding too hard and he's Adrienne's equal with the Power, which means he's consistently* lucky. *If he doesn't want to be found, a normal human would never, ever stumble on him; it's the damned* luck. *Now, what else did I hear. . . .*

Ah. At the party . . . someone had mentioned a Harvey Ledbetter. And this Brotherhood thing, some sort of resistance group.

"Oh, risky. But I can't just wander around until *they* find me or I run out of money."

Still, you could find almost anything on the Web, with a little patience.

He took a deep breath and poised his fingers over the keyboard.

He was screaming. The voice in his ear whispered:

"You love it, don't you, Peter. Tell me how much you love the lovely pain when I—"

Still screaming, he sat bolt upright. The clean sheets were sopping again, and tears streaked down his cheeks. After a moment he bolted for the bathroom again and vomited into the toilet. Then he spit, rinsed out his mouth and sat on the lid.

"Great," he said to himself. "I'm over the addiction to the drug in the bite. Now all I've got to worry about is the post-traumatic stress syndrome turning me into a wreck. And I thought I'd be home free, yeah, right, that's the way the world works, Peter."

He looked at his watch; it was four thirty in the morning. Not all that long to dawn, and he'd gone to bed early. It wasn't that surprising; he had enough memories to give him nightmares and shakes and attacks of depression for a *long* time. He looked over at the pill bottles, then shook his head violently.

No. That's all *I need,* another *monkey on my back, one I put there myself.*

"All right to use them for physical pain," he muttered. "The rest I'm just going to have to tough out. I can't get a therapist, and if I did they'd just put me in an asylum . . . and something would come walking through the walls to get me there. Something with lots of teeth. There really *are* shoggoths in the places between."

Instead of trying to sleep he showered, then lay and watched the light grow gradually on the roof, trying to think.

"I need facilities. I'm about ready to go experimental, in a small way. I need an experimentalist to work with, too. Lots of computer time. And ideally I'd need one of *them* to work with, as well. . . . Wish for the fucking moon while you're at it, Peter. Wish you smoked, it would be something to do."

At least he felt *physically* better than he had, although there seemed to be a weight on his mind, turning his thoughts sluggish. After a while he abandoned the attempt at serious thought and let strings of disconnected images float through his consciousness. Most of them turned out to be the bad parts of his life. Oddly, that was comforting. *Nothing* had really been as bad as what happened after Adrienne turned up. With that perspective, messy ends to soured relationships and not getting the grant you lusted for paled into the minor toe stubbings they were.

When the sun was fully up he rose and dressed in shorts and a T-shirt and running shoes. The computer was plugged in this time, and he'd set it to activate at exactly seven o'clock—checking every five minutes would make the time crawl even more unendurably.

His breath checked in his throat. There *was* a message: *Wait there and don't make any waves. From the Giant Rabbit.*

"Okay, calm down," he told himself. "Don't exhaust yourself emotionally. You can't afford it, not now."

Of course, it might be from the wrong people. But he remembered Adrienne raving about how most of the older Shadowspawn hated using information technology. Most of them *were* older, as you'd expect in a species that aged at about half the human speed and then could survive indefinitely after the death of the physical body. The median age must be well over sixty.

He frowned thoughtfully. *You know, that could be a real disadvantage,* he thought with some hope. *Younger people tend to be more imaginative and innovative.*

That was certainly true in physics; most did their best work before they got beyond middle age.

"So they'd be a bunch of Strudlebugs, eventually."

He wondered what it had been like in the old Stone Age, the hundred thousand years when Homo sapiens nocturnus had dominated the planet as the predator of the apex predator. After a while, almost all of them would be postcorporeal, ageless parasites hiding in caves by day and emerging by night to hunt and feed. The organic phase would be sort of a pupa breeding stage in their life cycle.

"Not as much of a disadvantage then," he said to the air. "Nothing changed much back there from millennium to millennium. Or it might be the other way 'round—nothing changed because they were in charge. Maybe that's why it took so long for a human civilization to emerge."

Eventually it was late enough to head out to T RESA's for breakfast. A little gaggle of children stopped to stare at him. He heard giggles, and when he turned away a pebble bounced off the back of his head. It was enough to sting, especially in his weakened state.

"Hey!" he said—tried to shout, and heard his voice crack. "What was that about!"

The children ran off, laughing, all except for one girl about seven. She stood looking at him solemnly from under the brim of a floppy hat, her hair in two glinting blue-black braids over her shoulders, dressed in a loose pinafore-style dress the worse for wear.

"What was that about?" he said again.

Her face was narrow, weasel-like, and her eyes were large and dark.

"Yor a stranger," she said, in a strong accent like a West Texan rasp. "You otter move 'long."

"Hey, I'm staying here."

"Strangers don't stay here," she said, and walked away.

He shrugged off an unease and headed for the restaurant. Fortunately he had his personal library with him on his machine, and he could use a lot of time to get his strength back.

Peter looked around. The momentary enchantment of the desert dawn was fading, heading towards another baking white day.

There probably wouldn't be much else to do here . . . and even his sleep was likely to be unpleasant.

Bad dreams are bad enough, he thought. *It's when the nightmares spill over into the waking time that things get really unpleasant.*

CHAPTER ELEVEN

"**A**re you sure we should accept the invitation?" Ellen said.

Adrian shook his head. "No," he replied frankly. "But when my great-grandfather issues it, I am sure that the consequences of refusal would be worse. If he simply intended to kill us, we'd probably be dead already."

He left unspoken the knowledge that there *were* worse things than death, and that his technically dead ancestor might simply be toying with them.

"Ah . . . honey . . ."

He turned and looked at her, concern in his dark gold-flecked eyes.

She took a deep breath. He wasn't in the least a bully, not even unintentionally, but his strength of personality could make you feel uncertain about arguing with him just by existing.

"Honey, I don't think you realize just how much I *don't* want to meet any other Shadowspawn but you. You're the only one I've met who doesn't make me want to kill them, or run screaming, or . . . And I'm afraid of flashbacks. This great-grandfather of yours, he's the Big Bad, right?"

He nodded. "Grand master of the Order of the Black Dawn and the Council of Shadows," he said. "He has been for over a century."

She closed her eyes. "Okay, this is the guy behind World War One and Two, the Holocaust, the killing fields, the Congolese wars, the Seoul thing, the . . . the just about *everything*. And we're supposed to go have *dinner* with him?" Almost pleadingly: "Look, couldn't I stay here and watch over Professor Duquesne or something? Rather than having dinner with werewolf Hitler and his vampire bride?"

He took her hands. "My dove, for one thing I want you to be safe. Or as safe as possible."

"*Safe?*" she said.

"This place . . . the Pavillon Ledoyen . . . opened in 1791," he replied. "Great-grandfather has been coming here all his . . . well, life. And postlife. He brought me there on a visit when I was ten, during our annual summer trip to Europe."

Which was forty years ago, Ellen thought. *That keeps tripping me up.*

Adrian went on: "It's one of the favored spots for Shadowspawn in Paris because of the continuity; there's a truce for the restaurant and grounds. That's one of the main reasons I agreed to this, instead of running immediately. I do not want you anywhere else without me.

"More, I feel stronger with you beside me, also," he said. "We are comrades-in-arms now, as well as lovers. And . . . you are my link to normalcy, to sanity, to all that is good. Merely being *around* my great-grandparents is to fall into an alien dimension, ethically."

She hugged him. "Okay, when you put it like that. Sorry for the collywobbles."

"It is nothing."

"Odd to get a dinner invitation from the emperor of the Earth," she mused.

"First among rivals, rather," Adrian said. "And by aspiration, more of a living god. Or unliving god."

"You're frightened, aren't you?" Ellen asked.

He glanced at her quickly. "Anyone who is not afraid of Étienne-Maurice Brézé is an idiot," he said quietly. "And Seraphine is only marginally less dangerous, if at all."

Then he smiled a crooked smile. "Yet at least you look lovely."

Even with the tension, that could make her feel a flush of pleasure, and she turned slowly; she was wearing a turquoise sheath, shoulderless, tight above and with a slightly flared skirt three fashionable inches below the knee that showed off her hourglass figure. Her antique shawl shimmered with silver paillettes, and the choker silver necklace held aquamarines laid out in Mhabrogast glyphs, bringing out the deep blue of her eyes.

It was all rather fetching, and the choice of precious metal was *not* an accident, either. It wasn't precisely that silver was toxic to Shadowspawn; they certainly didn't sizzle at its touch. But the Power couldn't affect it, or could only by massive and painful effort, and silver weapons affected them as ordinary ones did her type of human. That went doubly for night-walkers and postcorporeals, who could make themselves impalpable to ordinary matter with a little warning.

Her fair brows drew together a little, and she paused to adjust Adrian's bow tie—he was in formal evening dress, and looking very fetching in an archaic, rakish James Bond sort of way, especially with the deep red cummerbund.

"Honey, there's something that sort of puzzles me. You can walk through walls, right?"

"Yes, when out of the body, with a little effort."

"Then how come you don't drop right into the ground when you do?"

To her surprise he looked a little alarmed; rather the way a claustrophobic would if confronted with the thought of being buried alive in a small coffin.

"You can, if you're careless, though there's an . . . instinctual reluctance to let the soles of your feet go impalpable while they're in contact with the earth. And you can go palpable very quickly if you fall over. It's usually a fatal mistake if you don't."

"Why?"

"Because when you're *in* solid matter you have to *stay* impalpable. You're sliding through matter and can't affect it, there's nothing to *push* with. Total darkness, no air . . . the night-walking body needs to breathe eventually too, remember, even if not as often as the corporeal one."

He took a long breath. "It's an instinctual fear, with us. Those who didn't have it didn't live long enough to breed."

She thought about it for a moment, then shuddered herself. "What happens?"

"Nobody knows. Presumably you slide down until you lose consciousness and your energy matrix disperses in death; it has mass, and gravity affects it. Or until you reach the center of the earth, though the heat would randomize you first."

"Ow. Well, at least there're *some* disadvantages to the package!"

She took a deep breath and looked around the apartment. They'd been there only a few days, but already it seemed like a home, a welcome refuge against a world larger and colder, stranger and crueler than it was easy to comprehend.

"Will the professor be okay?"

"Probably. I've warded this place as much as I can. He's certainly safer than he would be anywhere else. Safer than he would be if we brought him to my great-grandfather's attention! You, they know about. Him, they do not, as yet."

They rode the elevator down in silence, holding hands. The hired limo's driver held an umbrella over them as they walked out to the curb; a light pattering of cold rain fell on it, and a few drops that evaded it raised gooseflesh on the bare skin of her shoulders. The silk shawl was draped elegantly but uselessly over her elbows; she pulled it up with a gentle chime from the paillettes.

Mentally, she ran through the etiquette of meeting the grand master of the Order of the Black Dawn and the Council of Shadows.

Honey, here's my great-granddad, the emperor of evil, she thought. *Oh, well, you know what they say—you fall in love with your fiancé but you're stuck with his family!*

She shivered slightly, and had no impulse at all to repeat the thought aloud. As attempted jokes went, that cut far too close to the bone.

Pavillon Ledoyen was just off the Champs-Élysées, fronted by a strip of lawn and gardens, surrounded by huge old chestnuts, and then by flowers in pots. It was not far from the Petit Palais; her training immediately classified it as late-eighteenth-century neoclassical in origin with a lot of Victorian work. The side facing the street had a high pediment supported by caryatids in the form of white-robed women, a sculpted architrave above and LEDOYEN in white on blue. The arched glass awning over the main entrance looked a little more like art nouveau work, the ribs cast as elongated silver maidens. Their limousine swung into the circular driveway, past a fountain with a central statue.

"It's been here awhile, eh?" she said to Adrian, clutching at her purse. "Seventeen ninety-one?"

"With a major renovation in eighteen forty-two," he said.

The blade within the purse was a slight comfort. Her fringed shawl was welcome in the cool autumnal evening air, though the rain had stopped. Streetlights glistened on the pavements, and there was a musty smell of damp fallen leaves from the gardens.

She took a deep breath and let it out slowly, forcing calm as the doorman bowed them through, and an attendant in a dress almost as elegant as hers escorted them up a grand curved staircase. The main dining room walls were about half floor-to-ceiling windows draped in carnelian curtains with beige blinds; there were oxblood marble pillars against the walls between, and some fairly good period paintings, including what she thought from a brief glance was an actual Watteau.

Napoléon III, basically, but a restrained example of Second Empire style.

There was a very low murmur of conversation from the widely spaced tables; arrangements of striking hibiscus flowers rested between the place settings, and the cloths were white damask over burgundy. She caught more than a few discreetly admiring glances. And a few yellow-flecked eyes lingered on her as well, with a different hunger added.

Oh, great. The chic Shadowspawn hangout. What wine goes with human blood? Or does the blood count as wine and go with food?

Two figures sat at a table set for four, watching her and Adrian approach: a man and a woman with their faces underlit by the candlelight. That wasn't all that made them appear rather sinister, but it didn't hurt the effect, either. Nor did the fact that their eyes weren't *flecked* with gold. They were the burning hot-sulfur yellow she'd noticed with Adrian's parents at Rancho Sangre, like windows into a pit full of lava; evidently that was a mark of the postcorporeal, unless they deliberately controlled it.

Wait a minute, she's—

"Great-grandfather," Adrian said.

Étienne-Maurice Brézé, also born heir to the Duc de Beauloup, looked . . .

A lot like Adrian, Ellen thought, dazed. *That family has to be* seriously *inbred.*

He rose for a moment, and inclined his head slightly, with a lordly insouciance.

Oooof! Talk about presence. *It's like getting punched in the gut, psychically speaking. You can't look away, and it's not just those fires-of-Hell eyes.*

The little hairs tried to stand up on her arms and down her back. She took a deep breath and let it out slowly through barely parted lips, struggling for control.

A little older, I'd say he was thirty if I didn't know better, a bit . . . coarser, perhaps. More rugged. An inch or two taller, enough to be just average instead of a bit short like Adrian. Though I suppose when he turned twenty in 1898 he was tall by the standards of the day.

He was certainly *dressed* differently from his descendant, in a full ankle-length wide-sleeved robe of some rich black velvet, a color that swallowed light, embroidered with black YLI silk thread in sinuous vine patterns around the hems, neck, cuffs and down the front panel. It caught subdued flickers as he moved, looking at Adrian with his head tilted slightly to one side. His long raven hair was pulled back at either side and pinned by a gold-and-ruby clasp at the rear of his skull, with the rest flowing loose beneath it down his back.

The robe was slit halfway down, and fastened with black-and-gray catches of Brazilian onyx. Beneath the black velvet was a high-collared shirt of white silk showing at cuffs and neck. The only other touch of color was a golden ring, set with the jagged trident and black sun.

As the mouse put it: Say what you like about cats, but they've got style.

"Great-grandmother."

This time Ellen blinked a little in surprise, the interrupted thought registering.

Seraphine Brézé was *black*. Specifically she was that dark chocolate color combined with a tall, slim build and sculpted aquiline thin-nosed face that was common in the Horn of Africa, Somalia and Ethiopia and Eritrea. Against it the yellow eyes were like windows into a world of chaotic fire.

She was dressed in a halter-top gown of an old-gold color that showed off the long slim neck and body, slit from ankle to thigh to give a glimpse of a leg like a gazelle's. A broad belt of platinum and blazing blue tanzanite cinched her narrow waist, and more of the blue jewels shone in her mane of sculpted, curled hair.

I could have sworn Adrian said she was French, or at least as much as Shadowspawn can be any human nationality. And . . . Wait a minute . . . they've both got swords with them, hanging on the back of their chairs, and nobody's noticing!

Adrian bowed with a hand on his heart; Ellen sank into a carefully practiced curtsy, spreading her own long dress of robin's-egg blue a little as she did. It couldn't hurt . . . and this *was* approximately the ruler of the Earth and his consort, or something much closer to that than she'd thought there could be.

A little informal family tête-à-tête with the masters of the universe. Or the chief ranchers of humans.

The Shadowspawn touched fingertips, evidently their equivalent of shaking hands; she'd seen it before, and then exchanged the air kiss on the cheek.

And I don't feel in the least slighted by not being included. I'd rather tongue-kiss a tarantula.

Adrian made the introductions, calmly naming her as "Ellen Brézé," and "my wife." Both the Shadowspawn looked at her. . . .

Uh-oh. There's that chocolate-coconut-macaroon look again. Why do these people . . . things . . . whatever . . . find me so attractive, or appetizing, or both? They all want to eat *me, metaphorically and then literally. I don't mind it with Adrian, except when I get the flashbacks about his lovely sister and her winning ways, but* he *doesn't want to* kill *me as as part of the peak experience.*

But they nodded acknowledgment and murmured polite words. Adrian held her chair, and put her purse on the handbag stool; it was all very Old World. Étienne sighed.

"You always were the most willful boy," he said, in a smooth, rich voice that vibrated with undertones of power. "Willfully eccentric, as well."

"It is a Brézé characteristic, Great-grandfather," Adrian said lightly. "After all, belonging to the Order of the Black Dawn was an eccentricity in its day, is it not so?"

"And your parents?"

"Well, the last time I saw them. Though that was rather under false pretenses, as I was infiltrating their house with a view to a kill."

Both the older Brézés laughed indulgently; rather as if listening to a child describing a prank.

Which, to them, is pretty much the truth.

"Ah, yes, your father has written an amusing letter about how you deceived him and killed Hajime," Étienne said.

The sommelier came and popped the cork from a bottle of champagne, holding it expertly tilted to keep the noise and foam to a minimum. Then he filled their flutes; it was a Réserve Blanc de Blancs d'Aÿ Brut Millésimé 2000 Grand Cru, tickling her palate with citrus and honey.

Étienne sipped, nodded approval, and continued: "It was about time that someone put the little yellow monkey in his place. We did not reveal the secrets of Power to the swine so that they could raise their hands against their betters."

Ellen choked, then coughed to cover it as the pair looked at her.

Okay, gotta remember this guy was born when Ulysses S. Grant was president and the Eiffel Tower was daring modern architecture. He was my age when Wilbur and Orville were making plans for a flying machine. Plus he's just plain evil, of course.

Gold and beige tableware was set out, and the *amuse-bouche* bites arrived: langoustine arranged in a little pyramid, an almost liquid mozzarella cheese, miniature samosas, beetroot as well as cheese and olive chips, with a choice of four types of bread: cereal, baguette, shrimp and bacon bits.

"Still, it's good to see family now and then," Étienne said. "Particularly your children, one imagines."

Adrian's hands didn't even pause as he broke a piece of bread, but his nostrils flared slightly.

"I did not have that pleasure. I was under an assumed identity, after all."

Seraphine made a *tsk* sound. "Ah, well, your parents . . . our grand-children, after all . . . will take excellent care of them. Perhaps better than Adrienne would have, not being either as busy or as ambitious. They much valued their time with you two when you were young, despite having to maintain the pretense that they were your aunt and uncle."

"No more fosterage?" Adrian said.

Ouch, Ellen thought. *Adrian really loved his foster parents, even though they were renfields. He still blames himself for their deaths. I don't think he killed them, and Harvey doesn't think so either and he was there, but Adrian still feels responsible.*

"No," Étienne said. "That has fallen out of fashion in the past generation. The gap between the powers of child and parent is no longer what it was in *our* generation, so there is less need for precautions."

Seraphine nodded. "We killed our own parents, of course, as soon as we were adults, the tiresome creatures, but that would be much more difficult now."

Ellen knew a moment's vicious satisfaction. The parents of the . . . things . . . she was talking to had been human beings. Very *bad* human beings, with a lot of Shadowspawn in them, but still not really the ancient predators reborn. They'd used what Power they had to make those genes meet and match . . . and they'd paid an exquisitely appropriate price for it at the hands of those offspring. The hands, not to mention the teeth.

What did they expect? she thought.

"I am sure they will ensure . . . forgive me, my descendant . . . that your little ones have a more *conventional* attitude to things than you did," Étienne said.

Like, conventional for a sadistic monster. Of course, he is a sadistic monster. Normalcy's all in the point of view, I suppose.

Whatever their moral state or age or background, the Brézés certainly ate in the grand old French manner, in fact almost in the *antique* French manner—religiously, and with only light conversation so as not to distract. That left her thankful for the chance to observe without offering more than the occasional commonplace.

She'd had a little trouble following the talk at first. Adrian's French was slightly but noticeably old-fashioned. His great-grandparents' version was *extremely* so, and not only in the way they used contractions. There was a hint of a rolled harshness to the vowels, occasionally words like *moé* instead of *moi*, as if they were a considerable way back towards the Middle Ages. Or at least towards the world between the Revolution and the fall of the Second Empire, before the accent of the Parisian bourgeoisie completely triumphed as the standard form.

"How did madame come to meet the *duc*?" Ellen said at last.

Seraphine raised one elegant eyebrow. "We are cousins, of course. . . ."

Wait a minute, there were black *Brézés in Belle Epoque Paris?*

At Ellen's look of incomprehension: "Ah, you mean my outfit! Beautiful, is it not?"

We are definitely *talking at cross purposes here.*

"It's a beautiful dress," she said.

"Oh, no, I mean Ayan," she said, and touched one finger to the opposite arm. "Gorgeous, *n'est-ce pas?*"

For a moment the gesture itself distracted Ellen's attention from its meaning; the way Seraphine held her wrist and moved the finger was . . .

Exaggeratedly feminine. Effeminate, in fact; sort of like a drag queen or a really old silent film of Sarah Bernhardt . . . Why would she . . . Oh, that's it. It's Edwardian body language, or even Victorian. It's what drag queens imitate *these days, passed on down by generations of convention while the way* actual women *hold themselves and gesture changed. That's the sort of posture that she picked up from her mother as a little girl, before she grew up and tortured her mom to death. She's the real article in more ways than one.*

Seraphine went on: "We acquired her near Djibouti shortly before the Great War, when I was still corporeal. Actually bought her as a slave from some nomads, a strange experience but intriguing. Beautiful, and of a fierceness . . . She lasted an entire year and died exquisitely, such defiance mingled with the pain and despair."

Ellen paused with her fork halfway to her mouth, looked down at the little samosa on it, and doggedly chewed and swallowed.

She's wearing *one of her victims like a* dress, she thought. *Oh, new vistas of ick-ness open at every turn!*

Then: *Adrienne could have been wearing* me *for the next thousand years when she felt in the mood, calling up my body's DNA from the memory bank; she certainly drank enough of my blood . . . and whatnot. God, but I'm glad she's dead. Actually all-the-way dead.*

Seraphine turned to Adrian for a moment. "Your Ellen has the most intriguing mind, but what have you been *doing* with it? The surface is like the armor of an ironclad, there are so many wards and blocks and traps!"

"Elementary precautions, my dear Seraphine," Adrian said.

Suddenly Ellen felt a warmth inside. *He's just tolerating them,* she thought. *Even* they *can't tell, but I can. And he's flaunting me partly just to piss them off, which I find I don't mind at all.*

Étienne went on: "But killing your sister, and the Final Death at that . . . perhaps a little excessive, *mon fils?*"

"It's not as if she hadn't tried to kill me often enough," Adrian pointed out. "Serious attempts. And not only in the line of duty, as it were."

"Ah, well, sibling rivalry," Seraphine said tolerantly. "Who can avoid it? I still remember how annoying little Anaïs was when we were children, taking up our parents' time and being tiresome. And how often I tried to drown her or push her out of windows or set her on fire, even when *Maman* scolded me for it. What I am really annoyed about, *mon chouchou,* is that you have neglected us so long. Admittedly you were involved with those horrible Brotherhood vermin, but still, after the closeness of your childhood visits, it is a wounding."

The next course arrived: *terre et rivière,* a sea urchin–and–avocado dish, and *truffe blanche d'Alba, gnocchis légères, eau de Parmesan,* with beetroot and eel.

"These Brittany sea urchins are unrivaled," Seraphine said. "The current chef here is Breton."

"Oh, they're better than the Santa Barabra variety, a little," Adrian said. "But in my opinion those of Hokkaido are fully as good, if not better. The gnocchi are delicious, but extremely un-gnocchi-like."

Odd, Ellen thought. *I can actually* enjoy *dinner under these circumstances. Am I getting callous? Or just . . . case-hardened? Or am I braver than I thought I was? Or has Adrian turned me into a compulsive foodie? Or all of the above?*

The contrast between the buttery richness of the avocado and the sea-kissed taste of the urchins was certainly arresting. They finished the champagne, and she cleared her mouth with some of the bread.

"Ah, turbot with black-truffle emulsion," Étienne pronounced. "Now with this, Meursault. Les Tessons Domaine Michel Bouzereau 2007, I think. It will serve admirably for the *Noix de Saint Jacques en coquille senteurs des bois* and even for the *Jambon blanc truffe spaghetti au parmesan* as well. One must not be a purist, like some visiting . . . foreigner."

He was about to say visiting American, *I think,* Ellen mused. *Well, miracles never cease. Tact.*

The sea scallops in their shells were barely steamed, soft-textured and fragrant, with wild wood vegetables, salsify, tomato, turnip and black truffle.

"I do prefer the ham," Seraphine said, looking down in pleasure at the smoked meat in its rectangular nest of al dente spaghetti, with cèpe mushrooms and black truffles standing like the masts of a ship. "One grows nostalgic for a sauce that is a true *sauce* rather than an ethereal wisp, and the truffles are of the earth. I grant you that this is no longer the age of Escoffier, and one must move with fashion, but yet . . ."

The white Burgundy blossomed in Ellen's mouth like the scent of apple orchards in the springtime.

"I notice Arnaud was not included in this little family gathering," Adrian said. "It would, perhaps, be a little awkward just at the moment."

Ellen closed her eyes for a moment, remembering the way the dead man had fallen, and the other coming for her with the knife. And the mindless killing malice behind the fossa's snarl. When she opened her eyes Seraphine's yellow gaze was on her, avid, and her tongue came out to moisten her lips in what was *probably* an unconscious gesture; she returned the look with a bland smile and mentally elevated a finger.

"Arnaud, Arnaud," Étienne said with a regretful sigh. "I fear he is more and more a creature of impulse; and impulse always did govern him more than is good. He is unlikely to see the twenty-second century at this rate."

A smile that was at once cultured and feral. "Surely, my dear boy, you do not imagine that if *I* sought your death I would proceed in so amateurish a manner?"

"Granted, Great-grandfather."

The table was cleared and the desserts came: a concoction of meringue, white chocolate and almonds, pastries filled with chocolate and an iced pistachio side, and a fantasy of cooked and raw grapefruit and lime sweet as palate cleanser. Then coffee, *noir* for the three Shadowspawn, and *noisette* for her in deference to American sensibilities, and cognac.

She hadn't liked brandy before she met Adrian—in fact, with her family history, she'd been at least mildly prejudiced against anything distilled.

Of course, before I met Adrian I didn't get Frapin Cuvee 1888 Rabelais, either.

A taste of dried fruits slid across her tongue, nuts, candied oranges, and a wash of cacao and flowers and soft spices; it made you think of hot tropical sunrises seen past the curve of a sail,with the sea breaking white beneath your bowsprit.

Étienne sighed. "Eighteen eighty-eight was a marvelous year . . . but perhaps I recall it so because I was young, eh? And this . . . like all the greatest pleasures, it is fleeting, impermanent. Little of this remains; perhaps only a few bottles, and once they are gone it will exist only in memory. As one accumulates experience, more and more resides there."

"I can see that you have reason for cultivating such an outlook," Adrian said carefully.

"Perhaps we come to the meat of the matter with the *digestif,* eh?"

Ellen took a deep breath. Adrian went on, calm, his tone conversational.

"I have no interest in who is selected to fill the vacant seats on the Council," he said. "Save as it affects the plans for Operation Trimback."

"You are acquainted with that?"

"Yes. Ellen received the details from Adrienne, and I have had Seeings."

"Ah." Seraphine lifted her brows. "Strong ones? Apparently you remember my teaching."

"Very high orders of probability, and tied to my sister. Our worldlines were deeply entangled at the time."

"And which do you favor?" Étienne said. "The plague, as your sister did, or this rather drastic use of nuclear weapons to shred the humans' electronic devices?"

"The EMP attack," Ellen supplied.

The Shadowspawn master waved a hand. "I have no interest in the terminology."

"You should be interested in the effects," Adrian said. "Have you Seen?"

"Nothing immediate. That is a matter of subtlety rather than raw Power; dear Seraphine has always been more sensitive, doubtless you derive it from her. I have had glimpses of the far futures that might be. Quite pastoral and attractive, most of them. A few rather grisly—"

Christ, what would he *consider grisly?*

"—but those of much lower probability."

"Great-grandfather and lord, I do not think you appreciate just how *much* would be destroyed if the structure of the technological world were removed at once. Runaway nuclear reactors—scores in France alone!—ruptured oil refineries . . ."

The older Shadowspawn began to laugh. Adrian merely raised a brow, but Ellen felt a surge of fury. It died as she realized that this wasn't, or wasn't merely, the usual schadenfreude and sadism. There was a genuine irony here.

"I laugh, my dear boy, because I did *not* grasp the implications. I was quite taken with a return to the medieval period, with us as the *noblesse*. After all, the Power can do a great many of the same things as the humans' technology. Until your sister carefully explained the problems to me."

He shook his head. "The al-Lanarkis are the primary advocates of the, ah, EMP. Trimback One. She demonstrated convincingly that they argued so because *their* primary territories would be least affected, and so all the other Shadowspawn would be weakened. They would probably have done it themselves, if I had not strongly hinted we would exterminate their clan down to the babes in arms if they did."

"And the humor?"

"Well, Adrian, you *did* kill her. And here you are, repeating her so-convincing arguments to me!"

Seraphine sighed. "I will rather miss Adrienne. She reminded me of myself at that age, so passionate and enthusiastic about her causes, yet so carefree and merry and natural."

Yeah, she longed to unleash a tailored supersmallpox on the world so she could take it over and be worshiped as a goddess, and she had a deep, care-

free, merry enjoyment of . . . actually doing *things to people that would be squicky even if you just played them. Doing them to* me, *in particular. And I'm not puritanical about that sort of thing* at all.

Étienne continued: "But something must be done. The humans are breeding like cockroaches and threaten to destroy the Earth. And while I could . . . how did Adrienne put it . . . turn myself into a guinea pig, walk into a steel box, and have Arianespace launch me to the moon, there would be no food and little amusement there."

Ellen surprised herself by chuckling. That *was* the sort of thing Adrienne would have said. It was easier to appreciate her sense of humor when you weren't having your head held underwater as foreplay or being chained up and flogged.

Though she was actually pretty good at the chaining and flogging. It was just the knowledge that she might decide to go on until I was dead or crippled. God, I'm glad she's dead. How many times have I thought or said that? Not enough, dammit! I expect to spend the next sixty years being glad she's dead.

Adrian continued earnestly: "Yet you are the grand master. The human governments are under your control. Surely you could take other measures, slower and surer? Our great advantage is that we are not pressed for time."

Seraphine laughed again. "This is a game of intellectual musical chairs! Now you are taking *my* part, when we discussed this with Adrienne. I thought that the plague scenario was also somewhat risky. Things rarely go as smoothly as one plans, and we would be relying on human scientists doing work we did not understand ourselves."

Her husband looked at her with a crooked smile. "True. Since we are all Brézés, I suppose it to be expected that we find ourselves echoing one another's thoughts. Though in Adrian's case, I suspect his deplorable sentimentality about the cattle is involved."

Adrian shrugged. "True."

Why did he admit that . . . ? Oh, they're telepaths. I suppose true/false is easy to detect, even with screens.

"But that does not affect my argument. Why take the hideous risks, when slower and surer methods are available?"

Étienne shrugged again; it was worthy of Charles Dullin, and Ellen dropped her eyes to her brandy. The gesture was entirely natural, and it reminded her of how *old* this . . . manlike creature was.

And Adrian will not die when his body does either, and he could Carry my soul forever. . . . Stop that! You don't have to think about that for de-cades yet! The world may end in the interim. In fact, it probably will *end in the interim.*

"It has been tried. The Chinese one-child policy, for example, which our good *taotie* allies implemented. But while we can make any particular government perform any particular action, we cannot force most of them to adopt *many* consistent policies over many *years*, which they are violently unwilling to do. Our puppets would be overthrown, and if we forced their successors to do the same then *they* would be overthrown . . . and meantime, our existence would become painfully obvious."

Seraphine sighed. "It is a paradox; we have all power, but only so long as we do not use it very often. It would be much more convenient if we were worshiped openly. Of course, that would also have certain dangers."

"Our existence will become very obvious indeed, if *either* of the Trimback options is used," Adrian said.

His ancestor nodded. "Yes, but by then the humans would be much weaker. We would be in a position to use the crisis to take control more directly."

Ellen swallowed. Adrian had shared his Seeings with her. They weren't exactly prophecies, the future was a spray of alternate possibilities and not one fixed path, but they did represent the trend of events, the balance of possibilities. Most of them showed a wrecked world; many a world under the open rule of the Council of Shadows. Those were like Hell come to earth, in ways more horrible because they were quiet.

"And besides," the Shadowspawn archimage went on, "Adrienne also convinced me that if the humans are allowed to play with their scientific tools and toys much longer, they will stumble across us anyway. Neglecting to keep an eye on that monkey curiosity of theirs let them develop nuclear weapons, to which we are so vulnerable."

"Which was the result of the Council's starting the world wars," Adrian said. "Shadowspawn perceptions of the future do not altogether free us from the law of unintended consequences."

"Granted. Though the wars were amusing as well. . . . But that is all the more reason to end the project of science. It will let them acquire far too much understanding of the Power. That we cannot allow, and killing too many individual scientists again risks revealing presence by absence."

"Then you will back the EMP attack?"

"No, no. You—and your sister—are quite right there. Far too dangerous. Let it be the plague; we and our servants—" He smiled grimly. "Our *renfields*, as the younger generation put it . . . Did I ever mention that I met the man Stoker? He was invaluable to us. . . . In any case, we will be prepared, and when the humans despair we will step forward and stop the pox . . . when their numbers have been culled sufficiently. One-sixth or one-fifth the current total, that would be more than sufficient. As many as there were when I was your age."

Seraphine smiled; the long, lean, aquiline face of the Somali girl she wore made it extraordinarily wolflike, and her yellow eyes glowed.

"And then the world will be as we wish it, wild and free. Enough humans for servants and food and amusement, enough to make the things we need. Few enough that once more the world will be sweet and uncrowded, the air and water clean, with many plains and woods and mountains empty save for great numbers of beasts. *We* will have the jets and yachts and things for our palaces and estates, and the humans will have just as much as we choose to give them, and they will worship us. As we wish it, forever."

Ellen sipped more of the brandy. *The horrible thing is, that isn't even the worst possible alternative.*

"Ah . . . would you need science for that?" she asked. "Ignorant serfs wouldn't be much use in keeping the central heating going."

"No, no," Seraphine said. "Not science. Only engineering, really. Science we could gradually abolish. A tiresome thing, in any case."

Adrian sighed. "I suppose I must support your position, then, Great-grandfather," he said. "Option two it is."

He and his progenitor locked eyes for a moment, and then he finished his brandy.

"It will be useful to have your support in Tbilisi, my descendant. You inspire a good deal of fear, which is of course in the end the basis of all respect."

Adrian's bow was graceful. "Thank you for the excellent dinner."

"You would not care to join us for other fare?" His molten-gold eyes paused on Ellen. "Your . . . wife could participate, in a number of different ways."

"A thousand thanks, but not tonight," Adrian said.

Ellen buried her face in her hands and huddled against Adrian in the back of the limousine.

"Oh, *Christ*," she said.

"You were splendid, my sweet. You were brave as a lioness."

His arm went around her shoulders, and she could feel the chuckle rumble through his throat. "And it is because of *you* that we know about the plague that Adrienne and her conspirators developed. And even now the Brotherhood is preparing."

She took a shuddering breath and let it out slowly. "Yes. Will they have enough vaccine?"

"Enough, and knowledge of how to make more. The Council may plan to step in as saviors; instead they will be exposed, and their numbers are so few that even the Power would not be enough, not against a humanity knowing what they are and united against them. Nothing is certain, but it may be the turning point in this long war!"

"Well, *that's* good to hear. At least this wasn't a complete wash."

"No. And—" He frowned.

"Aha! That's your *portentous* frown."

"I had a flicker. When Étienne mentioned the children. Something . . . yes, portentous. A shadow from the future. Something involving them; some decision I will make concerning them. That is . . . is becoming . . . a crucial point on which much will turn."

"What sort of decision?"

He smiled. "That is impossible to know at this point."

She punched his shoulder; it was like striking a layer of resilient hard rubber through the fine cloth.

"In other words, you know it'll be important, but not *how*. And you don't know whether deciding one way or another will make things good or bad!"

"It is often that way when many adepts surrounded a nexus. The most fortunate choice will gradually become clear."

Ellen made an exasperated sound, and then a little squeak as his hand gripped the nape of her neck.

"Perhaps you worry too much, and about the wrong things, my sweet."

Ellen fluttered her long fair lashes. "Why, *whatever* could you mean, good sir?"

CHAPTER TWELVE

*D*ream.

The sense of sick dread got worse as the flames erupted through the door and Eric Salvador was flung back to lie helpless in the dust of Afghanistan that had eaten so many soldiers' bones in so many wars. This time he could see the figure who walked through the fire.

It was a woman, young, naked, her face doll-like and pretty, with slanted eyes, hair piled up on her head in an elaborate coiffure that looked Asian. If he'd seen a picture like that he'd have gotten horny. Instead he felt as if giant fingernails were screeching down slate everywhere in the universe, as if he should run and run and run, and there was a *stink* that wasn't physical at all, and he retched hopelessly.

"Who's been a naughty boy?" she crooned. "Naughty, naughty. I'm naughty too, sometimes."

Then she knelt by Johnson's body, only it wasn't Johnson anymore, it was Cesar, and he was naked too. They rolled in the dust, coupling like dogs, but Cesar was screaming. When she raised her head, blood masked her mouth and dripped from her chin and poured from Cesar's throat. Yellow flecks sparkled in her dark brown eyes.

"I just *love* brave men," she said. "They're *delicious*."

"Christ!"

This time there were cigarettes under his searching hand. Eric fumbled the lighter twice. The dark coal glowed like an eye as he sucked in the smoke. He fumbled for the light switch and sat with his feet on the floor, then pulled the smoke into his lungs again, coughed, inhaled again. After a while his hands stopped shaking, and he looked at the time. It was just three o'clock, which meant he'd been asleep a bit less than two hours. The air in his bedroom smelled close, despite the warm breeze that rattled the venetian blinds against the frame of the window. Sweat cooled on his back and flanks.

He looked at the phone. "I'm not going to call. Cesar puts up with a lot, but *he's* not sleeping alone this last month. I can't tell him I had a bad—"

The phone rang. He picked it up.

"*¿Jefe?*"

"There's anyone else at this address?"

"Get over here. I've got something you need to see. About the Brézé case."

Eric Salvador knew something was wrong. He could *feel* it, a prickling along the back of his neck. Cesar's house was completely dark except for the light from the street lamp, which was very damned odd even at three thirty, since Cesar had just called him. His partner's new Chinese import was parked in the driveway; the ground between the road and the house was gravel, with a few weeds poking through. The neighborhood was utterly quiet, and the stars were bright. A cat walked by, looked at him with eyes that turned into green mirrors for an instant, and then passed. Nothing else moved.

Shit, he mouthed soundlessly, and pulled his Glock 22, his thumb moving the safety to *off.*

Then he touched the door. It swung in. He crossed the hallway, instinctively keeping the muzzle up and tucking his shoulder into the angle between the bedroom door and the wall. Then the smell hit him. He looked down. It looked black in the low light, but the tackiness under his foot was unmistakable.

"Are you certain, Herr Brézé?"

"Yes, I am, Herr Müller," Adrian said. "And no offense, but how often have we had this little conversation over the years?"

The *conversation* was in English, the easiest common language. Professor Duquesne had boiled with indignation for an instant when it turned out that Müller's French was only passable, worse than Ellen's. The middle-aged German banker spoke English with near-complete fluency, if also with an accent that reminded her irresistibly of Christoph Waltz in *Inglourious Basterds,* which one of her roommates studying classic film at NYU had played obsessively despite complaints. He even looked a little bit like the actor, though heavier-set, and with thinning blond hair combed over the top of his head.

It was a good movie for its day, even in 2D. But not thirty-six times!

Müller sighed. "I hope our wealth-management section has not disappointed you, Mr. Brézé."

The Commerzbank Tower gave an excellent view of downtown Frankfurt, being nearly a thousand feet tall, complete with open gardens every twenty stories or so and a central atrium. Müller's office had a prestigious amount of exterior window, and let you see that unlike most European cities the center was dominated by skyscrapers, if not to a Manhattan-esque degree.

"I've never been to Frankfurt before," she said, partly to defuse the heavy tension. "It's very high-rise. Not at all like most central cities over here."

"Ah . . . there was extensive rebuilding after the Second World War," Müller's secretary said with a discreet cough.

She was named Saraçoğlu and she was youngish, about Ellen's age, with even more of an hourglass figure. The cool gray business suit tried to play that down; she had black hair cropped very short, gave off an air of efficiency and was almost as dark as Adrian. There was a slight guttural accent to her English, German and French.

Ah, Ellen thought. *Speaking of wars. Even in the twenty-first, that was a bit tactless of me.*

Urban renewal courtesy of the 8th Air Force and the RAF, and the rebuilding in the three generations since had reached for the currently gray and drizzly sky around the gray and flowing River Main.

Less for the historical preservationists to preserve. Though in a lot of Europe stuff that looks like it was medieval or Renaissance or baroque is post-1945 restoration of buildings that were blasted down to the basement. Prague's the only one that wasn't *heavily damaged, if I remember correctly.*

There was silence for a moment and then Adrian addressed the banker:

"Quite the contrary, it's been very satisfactory. I have my own reasons for new arrangements that are not, strictly speaking, of a business nature. Let's leave it at that."

The decor in the big room was old-fashioned icy-modernist with very subdued PoMo flourishes, probably because times hadn't been flush enough to redo since the last renovation in the early years of the century. Müller's desk was a glittering expanse of dark stone, for example, and so was the oval conference table. On a plinth there was a small sculpture that looked like a length of bronze intestine, and a faint smell of the flowers in Bohemian crystal vases.

"In good conscience I cannot advise moving substantial assets into gold at this point, much less distributing them as you propose," Müller said. "And why pay a premium for coin and small bars? And silver . . . not a good investment at present."

Adrian smiled. "I appreciate your concern, Herr Müller. I don't expect to make much return on the transfers."

"You realize that Swiss bank security is, ah—"

"Not what it was, yes. That is why I'm diversifying the locations, and not just to the Caymans, you will note."

Another sigh. "As you wish, *mein Herr.*"

His secretary opened an accordion file of black leather and began producing documents, along with a print-and-retina scanner that she plugged into a secure link on the table.

"First," Müller said, "the signing authority for the initial fifty-million-euro tranche under the Aegis Project fund, to be held in short-term commercial paper until drawn. You and Frau Brézé will both have full discretionary authority, and Herr Doktor Duquesne unless and until you remove him. All payments authorized by Monsieur Duquesne will be listed as withdrawn from the project's funds, whose ownership will of course be strictly confidential."

They signed and entered their biometric data and DNA samples; Duquesne was looking a bit stunned at the amount he was being given to play with, just for starters. Plus an official salary of a hundred thousand euros a year personally, which was extravagant for a European academic.

"And here is Frau Brézé's power of attorney and authorization to access the other funds, and her personal account as per your instructions."

She darted a quick glance at Adrian, and found him smiling with that odd quirk-mouthed expression, half-teasing.

"I thought you might want to pick up a few pictures while we were in Europe, my sweet," he said. "You deserve it more than I, in any case. You will derive more pleasure from it; and that will give *me* great pleasure."

Ellen read the papers before she put her name to them. Essentially Adrian had irrevocably signed over an undivided half interest in everything he owned worldwide. And there was a personal account she could use for day-to-day needs with a total draw of . . .

She choked slightly at the amount. Day-to-day needs like buying Nob Hill, or possibly Oahu, given the way the real estate market had tanked again lately.

Money doesn't really mean anything to him, she reminded herself. *He can pick stock market winners by intuition. But it does to me! I grew up* poor. *Trailer-trash poor, except that we had Granddad's house, which was what a retired miner could buy in Swoyersville in the nineteen sixties. My father was a no-good drunk and a sponger and I clawed my way into uni-*

versity working three jobs and getting scholarships in my spare time. Now I can collect Old Masters if I want to.

Of course, there were drawbacks.

Monsters who can walk through walls are going to keep trying to kill me, I have to shoot people in alleys or stab them with knives. . . . On the other hand, I get Adrian, who's worth it all and more. And someday it may be fun to be very, very rich, if civilization hasn't been destroyed in the meantime. If I can ever manage to feel unguilty about it. Maybe I'll endow a foundation. . . .

She laughed and signed her name with a flourish. The prospect of enough leisure and safety to wallow in upper-class guilt and go around contributing to good causes was fairly remote right now.

"Thank you, Frau Saraçoğlu," Müller said.

Not Fräulein, Ellen thought. *That's dropped out of use for anyone except little girls.*

"These to the secure vault now, *bitte*," he continued, indicating the documents.

Adrian's phone rang, a soft sequence of notes from a famous piece by Delibes, one that was a bit of a joke if you knew how it had been used in the movies. He tapped it, and she could faintly hear:

"Pooka here."

The way his face went blank made her sit up and take notice. Duquesne didn't catch it, and Müller was unreadable because he always looked like a truck had just run over his puppy, but Saraçoğlu noticed something.

"Pardon," Adrian said, and walked over to a corner of the room.

The conversation was minimal; from the way his eyes flicked to the screen, text was coming through as well, or possibly a visual. When he tapped it closed and returned to the table he was frowning.

"Herr Müller, we'll need to charter a jet. Something with transatlantic capacity, and immediately. Whatever's available."

Müller looked even more lugubrious, but his secretary/assistant merely nodded and began tapping at her keyboard even before he prompted her.

"Any specifications, Herr Brézé?" she asked.

"That it fly all the way," Adrian said dryly. "The flight plan is Hamburg to Tucson, Arizona. Earliest possible departure."

In the elevator on their way to the ground Ellen looked at him.

"Harvey," he said to her; which told Duquesne nothing.

Then to the professor: "It seems you'll be having a colleague sooner than we thought, monsieur."

Peter! Ellen thought with a stab of delight.

He'd been the only friend she'd had at Rancho Sangre Sagrado . . . unless you counted people who were obscenely evil, batshit crazy with variations on Stockholm syndrome, or both. Certainly the only one she'd been able to talk freely with, Jose, had been all right, but he was born a renfield.

The Frenchman was looking at his own notepad; Adrian had transferred a list of suppliers and locations.

"Sweden?" he said. "An abandoned *military base?* And *underground?*"

"*Discrétion, monsieur. Toujours discrétion.* Remember what happened in Paris."

He shivered a little. "And these people, these suppliers . . . are they reliable?"

"Entirely, as long as they're paid. Will there be a problem with logistics?"

"I am familiar with that aspect, and there are some individuals I could hire to handle administrative matters, perhaps?"

"I leave that entirely in your hands. I wish results, and quickly; I don't care how. More than our lives depend upon that, but certainly our lives, at least."

Duquesne's expression was dubious, some fear, with a hint of exaltation. From her acquaintance with Peter Boase she understood that. Anyone who'd spent his adult life fighting for every penny of grant money would be attracted by the prospect. It was a peculiarly rarefied and intellectual form of greed in the service of pure curiosity.

"But it is—" he began.

"Most irregular, I know. You are not . . . how do the Germans put it . . . you are not operating in a *salonfähig* fashion anymore."

When they were alone for an instant waiting for the cab, she leaned close to Adrian.

"He's alive?" she asked. "Peter's alive?"

"Yes. Evidently my parents . . . acquired him rather than killing him. Possibly because of the research he was doing for Adrienne. And he has escaped."

"He escaped? He's safe, then?"

"Escaped, but not at all safe; he contacted Harvey, and that makes it entirely likely the enemy will be on his trail as well. That's why we have to get there as soon as possible, while Monsieur Duquesne gets his project started here."

Peter Boase gripped the silver table knife convulsively. The night was much cooler than the day even here in southern Arizona. Outside the night was silent, save for the hoot of a great horned owl once as it glided past. He tensed at the sound, relaxed as he realized what it was, then tensed again.

It's not paranoia. They really can *turn into birds. That would be a good way to scout around.*

His eyes flicked to the ancient LCD beside the bed. One o'clock in the morning. Hours before the sun would come up and . . .

Make things just a little less dangerous. There's absolutely nothing to prevent one of them from walking in at noon and just fucking shooting me. *Or one of their hired guns. That would make me just as dead. Adrienne had that platoon of mercenaries working for her. Plus the police in Rancho Sangre. Plus probably they could have the* government *send people to kill me. No, make that certainly, from what they said around me, and they had no reason to lie. It actually explains a lot of things, once you know they're pulling the strings.*

Maybe it *was* paranoia. How could you think about this stuff and not go crazy? There was even a slight impulse just to slash his own wrists with the sharpened table knife and get it over with. It wasn't the animal escape from pain that had tempted him while he was undergoing withdrawal. Now the impulse came from the knowledge that he probably *was* going to die anyway, and very painfully, and the sheer tension of waiting every second.

He hadn't bothered to close the window. The fresh air was worth it, when the people . . . things . . . he feared could walk through walls. He'd gotten thoroughly sick of the smells in this room, too.

But the wall-walking thing meant they could be right behind him. Right *now.*

He turned quickly. Was that a noise?

"Nothing. Sheesh!"

Peter straightened up with a shaky laugh and turned back towards the door.

The front six feet of the giant python were already reared up man-tall. He had just enough time to see the head flash as it struck like a trip-hammer into his shoulder, and the knife went skittering across the floor. Then the coils were whipping around him, like trying to fight a berserk steel cable, around his ribs and his left arm, squeezing, squeezing. . . .

"Isn't it wonderful that Peter escaped?" Ellen smiled.

She lay back in the deeply padded recliner and fought not to sleep as the engines rose to a muted scream outside and acceleration pushed at her.

The aircraft was an Airbus A321 Elite, a two-engine wide-body that had served as the toy of an oil prince, before being sold on the rental market when he tired of it and bought something more recent; he'd probably moved up to an A380, because judging by this, the concept of restraint wasn't one of the files on his hard drive.

"Perhaps it's your Power operating without your knowing it?" she asked.

Effectively the plane was a luxury penthouse with wings, complete with gym, study, entertainment center and two huge bedrooms, with an air of jasmine and ozone. Half the cargo compartment below was extra fuel tanks, which gave it more range than a B-52. She felt a little guilty using it for the pair of them—the normal complement of passengers would be over two hundred—but it was the first thing that had been available, if money were no object.

"Yes," Adrian said. "That could well be so. The Power"—he smiled grimly—"operates in mysterious ways."

This thing reminded her a little uncomfortably of Adrienne's private jet, though it was bigger, and the decor—Birdseye marble tile in the bathroom, Persian carpets in the lounge area—was considerably less restrained. Gaudy, in fact, though extremely expensive and very well maintained.

"Particularly where many purebreds, many adepts, are involved," he went on. "Strokes of *luck* may happen, yes, but they may be . . . ultimately . . . lucky for someone else than the first recipient. Coil upon countercoil."

Wow, Ellen thought. *It takes a bit of getting used to, strokes of luck that really happen.*

He frowned a little. "Even so, it seems rather odd, since normally my parents would have killed any of Adrienne's lucies who survived her. Granted, I am more purebred than they, but they are *there* and the Power attenuates according to the inverse-square law, generally."

Ellen winced at the thought of the orgy of slaughter that had probably followed her escape. *Poor Monica.* The den mother of Lucy Lane, with her brownies and her sympathy . . . and Jose . . .

Jose might get off. He's a native, born into the service of the Brézés. God, I hope Monica's kids are okay. They don't feed *on kids but that doesn't mean they wouldn't hurt* them. *Adrienne's parents . . . Adrian's too . . . they were always charming, and I got the distinct impression they'd watch people thrown to crocodiles and make witty repartee about it.*

There was no way to tell for sure, of course. It had taken all Adrian's command of the Power and the Brotherhood's resources just to *find* the main estate of the California branch of the Brézés. None of them was going into that maze of traps arcane and physical again if they could help it; plus Adrian's parents were there now, which put two adepts in charge instead of just one. They were postcorporeal, but that wasn't much of a handicap.

Still, I wish I knew what had happened.

Adrian quirked a smile at her. "You are a refreshing change from the people I have associated with most of my life, my sweet."

"Honey?" she said.

"You *are* sweet," he said. "Empathetic. You care for people. Even people you met in a very horrible place."

"So are *you* a sweetie. You've just . . . not had much opportunity to show that side of yourself."

"The running and hiding and fear and killing and death do tend to limit opportunities for emotional expressiveness. . . ."

"I could *hit* you sometimes, Adrian!"

"You see what I mean."

She laughed. "Besides, the people you knew can't have *all* been bad. Those Brotherhood types are on the side of the Good, Pure and True. Right?"

"So were the men who saturated Dresden and Tokyo with incendiary bombs until streams of melted human fat ran in the gutters," he said. "One becomes hardened, if you live at all."

Then he surprised her a little by reciting:

> In bombers named for girls, we burned
> The cities we had learned about in school—
> Till our lives wore out; our bodies lay among
> The people we had killed and never seen.
> When we lasted long enough they gave us medals;
> When we died they said, "Our casualties were low."
> They said, "Here are the maps"; we burned the cities.

He shook his head and snorted a little. "Living with you challenges me," he said. More softly: "And shames me. I have not *dared* to feel deeply, for fear of loss. That is unpardonable cowardice."

The rental came with pilots, maintenance and cabin staff; she suspected Adrian would have done without the latter if he could, and it had meant keeping certain parts of their luggage locked and in the bedroom. Even with a private charter like this, people would talk if you carried an assortment of lethal hardware on board openly. Which reminded her . . . "What about going through customs?"

This time his smile was a little ironic. "My darling, I can use *both* the Brotherhood's and the Council's . . . safe words. Codes that will tell the officials to turn a blind eye and wave us through. They undoubtedly think—"

"—that we're spooks," she finished, and thumped herself on the forehead with the heel of her hand. "I feel like *I'm* walking through walls all the time. The bottom dropped out of the world, but as a compensation I get to go through all these cool secret doors. I suppose I'll get used to living down the rabbit hole. Only it's not Wonderland, it's WonderHell."

"I hope you don't have to live so," he said. "Not for long, at least."

She noticed that he didn't say she *wouldn't* spend the rest of her life doing just that. One of the things she liked about Adrian was that he didn't overpromise.

The staff brought them dinner and retired quickly at his glare; Adrian was usually gracious in a sort of de haut en bas way, but this time he was deliberately cold, to keep them out of contact as much as possible. It was unlikely that more could endanger them, but there was no reason to take extra chances with bystanders.

Ellen looked down at the meal; steamed asparagus with herb sauce, *Kasseler Rippchen*—smoked, brine-cured pork chops in an egg-and-crumb crust—finger-length golden-brown potato *Schupfnudeln*. . . .

She began to laugh. At Adrian's raised eyebrow she ate a bite of the pork, savoring the smoky, salty richness, and then spoke:

"I was remembering my first cattle-car-with-wings across the ocean. NYU was by-God going to expose us art history types to the original font of *kultcha*, even if we had to suffer for it. My seatmates on either side weighed three hundred pounds each, and . . . Well, I wasn't picky about food then, but . . ."

Adrian winced. "I could not endure it. No, literally. My, ah, reflexes would be too likely to get the better of me. We do not adapt well to crowding, my breed."

Thoughtfully: "One can go into trance, of course. But that leaves you so helpless."

They finished with *kranz* ring cake, sweet buttercream frosting studded with toasted hazelnuts, and a filling of cherry preserve. After a moment they were feeding each other forkfuls across the table.

"This is *weird*," she said, using a napkin. "We get honeymoon crossed with deadly peril."

"Spice added to spice," he said.

The dark yellow-flecked eyes burned at her, and she felt a shiver prickle over her skin. She reached into a bag and smiled.

"Recognize this?"

He blinked in puzzlement. "No . . . some medical device?"

"It's made for people suffering from anemia," she said, and stuck her finger in it. "Frau Saraçoğlu had it expressed to the plane for me. God knows what *she* thought I needed it for."

"Did she ask?"

"Yes. I said you were a vampire, but considerate."

Adrian gave a shout of laughter. That gave *her* a spike of pleasure; he wasn't exactly gloomy, but it wasn't exactly a common thing to see him lose himself in a moment's humor, either. A little light shone green and the digital display lit up.

"Ah, red cell count normal, pressure normal, flow normal, viscosity normal . . . Think of it as compensation. With you having the Power, I don't have to worry about birth control. I *do* have to keep track of blood loss."

He raised a brow. "It would be advisable for me to be . . . fully charged. Though we have blood-bank supplies on board."

Ellen grinned at his involuntary grimace; she knew how loathsome cold, dead blood tasted to a Shadowspawn. Adrian was the only one she'd met who would use it at all.

"C'mon. That double king-size bed is calling our name. We're going into danger. So first, let's *party*."

CHAPTER THIRTEEN

The reticulated python of Asia was the world's largest snake. For a flashing instant some part of Peter Boase's mind contemplated the irony that his last thought would be a totally irrelevant piece of data like that, culled from a random Wikipedia search years ago.

Then he was rolling on the floor with four turns of the thigh-thick, thirty-foot body around him. It threw a loop of its tail around a leg of the bed for leverage and the needle teeth bit into his captive shoulder. Air wheezed out of his lungs as the terrible pressure squeezed inward.

His scrabbling right hand came down on the knife, gashing his fingers. He gripped it and flailed at the snake's diamond-patterned body, cutting himself again, and then slashed at its head. But the tip penetrated the taut skin, and the long head came up with a hiss. It whipped aside and the nose struck the base of his thumb like a jackhammer;

the hand spasmed open and the weapon went flying a second time. That gave him a single instant to gasp in a breath before the pressure resumed.

Cold reptile blood spattered his face. He wheezed again, and waited for the cracking of ribs and death.

Crackcrackcrackcrack.

Peter thought the stutter of harsh elastic snaps was the end, his own bones giving way like green sticks; then the intolerable constriction eased. He lay struggling to draw in air with his diaphram half-paralyzed. The python blurred as it thrust itself at the wall. . . .

He blinked. It had gone *through* the wall, as if it were diving into a horizontal pool of water. Then it was gone. Hands gripped him under the arms and threw him into a chair; two dark-clad figures sandwiched him, backs towards him and pistols leveled outward in professional two-handed grips. Their sweat stank of fear.

"You get him, Jack?" the third man asked, his voice the rasping drawl of rural Texas.

Like them he was in nondescript dark outdoor clothing; his long, bony face was battered and weathered, and gray streaked his cropped brown hair. He threw several packs on the bed as he spoke.

"Clipped him," one of the men said in reply. "Tail, I think. He didn't have time to Wreak on the guns. And using a snake's brain probably slows your wits."

"He *will* Wreak first if he comes back," a woman's voice said.

"He'll be hurting," the one called Jack replied.

The older man nodded. "Even so. Blades. Guha, you do the walls. Careful about the floor join, there's no crawl space but . . ."

"I know, big boss," the woman said.

Her voice was singsong, the accent of someone who grew up speaking Hindi along with English, possibly added for emphasis.

They holstered the guns beneath their jackets and took out long curved knives; they looked like they were wearing some sort of body armor under their clothes as well. The woman went to the packs, shrugged one onto her back, and unclipped something that looked like a spray-paint attachment. That turned out to be exactly what it was. She started on the door and worked her way steadily and swiftly around the walls; there was a sharp creosotelike odor in the air, and everything turned a dull silver-gray beneath the nozzle.

Silver, he thought, and croaked it aloud.

"Yup," the older man said. "Harvey Ledbetter, Mr. Boase. My friends here are Jack Farmer and Anjali Guha."

The Indian woman . . . or more probably Indian-American, from the way she moved . . . finished her task. The whole inside of the little room was covered in the silver paint now, and the sharp chemical stink filled the air; the three strangers seemed to relax fractionally.

"We're safe?" he said hoarsely.

Guha handed him a glass of water; he drank it while she checked him over with impersonal skill. He winced and bit back a moan a couple of times. He'd been hurt worse whitewater rafting once, and another time while he was rock climbing, but not lately. Plus he was in generally lousy shape, weak and vulnerable.

"No broken bones, no serious sprains or tears," she said. "I will fix this bite."

He stifled another yelp when she ripped back the T-shirt over the red stain and applied antiseptic and a bandage from a kit in one of the knapsacks.

"This . . . this isn't enough to readdict me, is it?"

Harvey looked at him with what he thought was considering respect.

"You went cold turkey? No wonder you look like shit. You don't have to worry about that. Reestablishing the dependency would take a lot more." A grin. "And since Shadowspawn ain't infectious, like in the stories, you don't need to worry 'bout the next full moon either."

Peter let out a long breath. Right now, he was more afraid of the addiction than death; that would be preferable to going through withdrawal again.

"So we're safe?" he asked again.

"Safe? Yeah, you might say so. Unless our snaky friend has an RPG—"

At his puzzled look, the man clarified: "Rocket-propelled grenade launcher. Or somethin' of that order. Not likely. They mostly don't think that way."

"Adrienne liked technology."

"She was unusual, and thank God she's dead. So we're safe until he figures out what he feels like doin' next. But that's one heap powerful adept out there. A lot of them don't study on *how* to use the Power, they just wing it by instinct, but this one does have the full postgraduate course. I could sense it. He's likely to have all the luck—literally."

"You're the, um, Brotherhood?" he asked, as Farmer and Guha started spray-painting again.

This time it was in black paints, spiky symbols around the edges of the room that seemed to twist and hurt his eyes, until he had to blink and look away. They murmured as they did, in whining, throat-catching syllables.

A thought occurred to him: *Wait a minute, that's Mhabrogast! These guys are using the Power too!*

Harvey seemed to sense it. "Yeah, we're the Brotherhood, more or less. *La Résistance.*"

"Ah," Peter said. "A ragtag band of heroes who'll overthrow the evil empire?"

"Nah, mainly we're a nuisance not worth the effort of squashing 'cause we're really good at hiding. A lot of us have enough of the genes to use the Power—not enough to night-walk or feed on blood, though. Think of us as ferrets up against a timber wolf."

That's comforting. Peter thought. *Not.*

"What about Adrian?"

"He's somethin' of an exception. And I hope he's here real soon now. 'Cause otherwise we are well and truly fucked."

"Good to see you out and about," Dmitri said, leaning on a boulder after he assumed human form once more. "And as lovely as ever."

"Flattery, my snake in the grass," Adrienne chuckled.

She leapt atop it, her own head-height, and squatted in an easy crouch next to her kit to talk to him.

"Besides, this is my etheric body."

She was justly proud that even another adept couldn't tell it from the corporeal form without probing.

"I'm still not completely back to meat-normal."

The night was on the comfortable side of chilly; the dry desert air lost heat rapidly. The stars overhead glowed in colors someone more human—less her type of hominid—could not have seen. Steel blue, red, pale green, the almost harsh-bright of the three-quarter moon; Shadowspawn had always been more nocturnal than their prey, and even in the flesh saw better in darkness. The etheric form's eyes were more sensitive still.

"The plan proceeds," she said.

"Except for the unplanned elements, such as my being shot in the arse and having my throat cut. That is a role reversal I do not relish."

"A mere detail," she said, and they both laughed.

"Though I did get a taste of your lucy. In any case, we'd better scout the place again," he said, shifting to Russian.

"*Da,*" she said, in the same language. "Good idea, Dmitri Pavlovitch. We must make their hairbreadth escape completely convincing."

Learning new tongues was easy for their breed; the same enlarged speech centers that let the telepathic facility read the code of another brain helped the learning process.

"But cautiously," she said; Dmitri tended to be reckless.

And then she *willed*, reaching within for the familiar template.

"*Amss-aui-ock!*" she snapped, a purling, spitting sound.

Mhabrogast, the *lingua demonica*, the language that mapped and compelled the hidden structures of the world. Potential-being-becoming, an arrogant command directed at the stuff of reality itself. You convinced your mind that you were something, and the mind made it real. . . .

Or close enough to real for government work, she thought whimsically. *Close enough for biting, rending, tearing. Close enough for blood.*

Pain thrilled along her nerves, a shivering almost-pleasure, a dissolution like sleep or orgasm or death as her very self ceased to exist for nanoseconds. Sight dimmed as her quasi body folded and stretched.

Sound exploded outward, and smells—it was much easier to tell Dmitri was night-walking when his very scent had a sharp metallic overtone, like a small thunderstorm.

A real wolf would have snarled and cowered; she let her long red tongue loll over her fangs and jerked her nose upward. The scurrying rustle of a field mouse nibbling the papery cover of a seed yards away was distinct; so was the growl of a heavy truck's diesel near the distant mountains on the western horizon. The clean scents of the desert's sparse life flowed into her nose, a tapestry even more powerful than hearing, and one that made sight almost irrelevant. The human reeks from the little hamlet a few miles upwind were harsh by contrast. But though the body was a timber wolf, the mind wrapped around the brain stem was Shadowspawn; the thin black lips skinned back from long teeth as she smelled human blood. Warm, spicy, enticing . . .

Business, she thought. *Mere prowling terrorism must await happier times.*

Da, Dmitri replied; at close range telepathy was easy and swift. *Let us continue our little charade. Ah, if only Michiko-sama were here!*

She's attending to something else, Adrienne said. *Besides, I don't think she reciprocates your affection, Dmitri.*

I'd be waiting for her *to get silver in her buttocks,* the male Shadowspawn gibed.

He'd been rubbing at his arse—she had to admit it was a fairly nice one, taut and muscular, though right now marked with red where the silver bullets had grazed the snake's tail. He was taller than most, nearly six feet, and his hair was long and white-blond. It tossed like hers in the grit-filled wind that coursed by. Then he threw his arms upward. Form sparkled for an instant too brief for even her senses to fathom, turned into something like a mist with eyes, and then the eight-foot wings of *Aquila chrysaetos simurgh* whipped at the air.

She reached down to her baggage and took out a small shape in her teeth. They closed on it, and the wolf's powerful neck muscles tossed it a dozen feet upward.

Talons closed on the metal oblong, and the extinct golden eagle of Pleistocene Crete soared upwards.

The wolf leapt down and loped to the west.

The Humvee was old but well maintained. Adrian drove it into the shadow of a tall boulder and parked. The engine ticked slightly as cooling metal contracted; even in the tail end of summer the Arizona desert could be chilly at night. Ellen swung out of her seat and looked around at the moon-silvered landscape and breathed the cool sage-scented air with its hints of caliche and dust.

Adrian's mouth tightened as he glanced around likewise. She had her night-sight goggles pushed up on her forehead, but he could pierce the darkness on his own. The lights of a very small town or medium-size hamlet glittered in the middle distance. Somehow they emphasized the loneliness of the spot the way the passing of a train did, a peculiarly American desolation—it made you think of dust blowing over the cracked concrete of a gas station and people looking out a window over their fifth cup of midnight coffee.

I really am an artsy, Ellen thought. *Here I am about to fight for my life and I'm making comparisons to Hopper paintings.*

"This is an abortion of a mission," Adrian said. "There is at least one night-walker out there, perhaps more. I can scent them."

Oh, thanks, honey, Ellen thought—and then hoped that Adrian wasn't listening.

He was usually scrupulous about her mental privacy, at least as far as words went: sensing her emotions was something he just couldn't help.

It's a compliment in a way, she thought. *He's* really *treating me as a comrade-in-arms. I guess this is that soldier's bitching you hear about. Goes with the gallows humor, I expect. And I may not have thought seriously about enlisting in high school—the university money wasn't quite tempting enough—but I've been well and truly drafted.*

It all made taking a permanent holiday in that flying penthouse look pretty attractive. Her instincts were telling her things about why the night was dangerous, and she knew the source of those genetic promptings better now.

Things were out there, things far more dangerous than any tiger or lion. They'd hunted her human ancestors like rabbits while the glaciers came and went and came again. She'd had personal experience with them, and only the training inside Adrian's mind was letting her control her fear. It was there, lurking in her mind as the predators did in the night.

"Let us get ready, then," he said.

She helped him get their gear out. Part of it included a high-impact oblong of composites. She knelt and unlatched it. A sniper rifle lay within, and she let her hands occupy themselves snapping it together. It was beautifully crafted and scrolled with silver inlays that would look like ornament to a casual gaze. But it was also a single-shot weapon that broke open like a shotgun, a thing of stone-ax simplicity; the fewer moving parts, the less for the probability-twisting Power to grasp.

While she completed the mechanical task she was conscious of

Adrian moving in the background: the scrape of colored chalks against the rock behind them, the purling whine of Mhabrogast. She turned, the rifle cradled in her arms like a cold lover of walnut and blued steel. The final glyph was sketched on the sandstone surface. It glittered faintly in the moonlight.

"I meant to ask about that. If the Power can't affect silver, how come you can use it for a glyph?"

"That is a glyph of negation, of constraint," he said. "You want it to be unchangeable. This sort of thing involves feedback loops; you can alter the probability cascades keyed to the glyphs on the fly if you're good enough."

She made a questioning sound—she couldn't really understand the Power intuitively or use it herself, but she could learn the theory—and he shrugged.

"Nobody has ever been able to prove whether Mhabrogast objectively helps one to use the Power or whether it's just a focusing device. Latin certainly isn't more than that, and it's useful as a lead-in."

"You mean the *lingua demonica* may be psychosomatic? Or some sort of symbolic placebo?"

"Or the operating code of the universe." He snorted laughter. "We can't even prove that modern Mhabrogast is actually what the Empire of Shadow spoke. The Order of the Black Dawn's adepts used the Power to reconstruct it from a few fragments, back in the nineteenth century. But we know it works."

"Or maybe it works because you know it does. . . . My head hurts when I think about that. . . . What does *that* one do? The silver one."

Adrian smiled grimly. "If someone comes walking through the stone and into contact with it in their aetheric form . . . let us say the consequences will be unfortunate. For them. Think of it as running into a cross between invisible barbed wire and the web of a very large spider."

"Except there's no spider."

He smiled, a remarkably unpleasant expression if you were on the receiving end of the dislike.

"Oh, so there *is* one. That *so* relieves my mind, honey. Having to think about someone fading through solid walls right behind me and then biting me on the ass is sort of paranoia-inducing. Now I feel safe because there's a giant murderous spider lurking in the rock."

"More the *potential* for something that would be *perceived* as a giant, murderous spider. In a way the victim creates it themselves."

"That so reassures me. Not." She took a deep breath and gave him a light kiss on the lips. "Go get 'em, tiger."

"And I have you to make sure I have a body to come back to."

He lay down on the unrolled foam mat inside the semicircle of glyphs, crossing his arms on his chest.

"Amss-aui-ock!"

Adrian was there, lying on the mat in his fatigues, with a webbed belt bearing tools and devices and pouches. And he was *there*, naked under the moon. Another not-quite shift and he was gone. What stood there instead still took her breath away a little: Smilodon populator.

Sabertooth tiger. A cat but not really a tiger, built as much like a bear as a feline, a tawny bulk with huge shoulders coming up to her chin and a broad back sloping down to the hindquarters. The face was a cat from a nightmare, with fangs like curved ivory daggers more than a foot long, serrated like steak knives on their edges. The lambent yellow Shadowspawn eyes didn't help either. Something deep down screamed, *Run*, at the sight.

The great feline weighed as much as a horse—she'd ridden on its back, not least when they escaped from the bloody shambles at Rancho Sangre, after Hajime's death. Now it brushed against her, rocking her back a little, then nuzzled affectionately at her body with its stumpy tail twitching, and nuzzled again in a way that would have been fresh from someone . . . something . . . she wasn't married to.

She leaned the rifle against the rock and used both hands to scratch at its ruff and behind the palm-size ears; there was a rumbling deep in the chest, and it licked her with a great rough washcloth of a tongue. Then it turned and leapt into the darkness, eerily silent for all its mass. Ellen crouched back against the stone, cradling the rifle in her arms.

"There're definitely some kinky elements in this relationship," she murmured to herself. "And I don't mean just the good ol' vanilla B and D. But kinky in a *good* way."

Then she fell silent. That was another part of the training, and one she'd enjoyed after a while; she'd never realized how much she missed by being noisy all the time, not least the noise she made herself inside her head. In a way the listening was like sinking into a painting, opening yourself completely while excluding everything else. Thought went away, until she was floating somehow, but intensely aware of *everything*. Letting it pass through without dwelling on it, her attention suspended until something tripped it.

After a while—later she thought it might have been an hour—something did.

Pain ran along Adrian's nerves like a wave of white fire as he shifted. He fought briefly for control as he took the Smilodon's form, man-thought crowded into the dim, focused brain of the great carnivore. It was easier this time; he'd been using the sabertooth's form for more than two years now, since investigators unknowingly in his employ had succeeded in reconstructing the beast's genome. You could lose yourself in the beast, if it was unfamiliar and you weren't careful—that was one of the many ways the Power could kill you.

It also accounted for a lot of the bad reputation of werewolves.

Hearing flooded in, keen enough that Ellen's quick heartbeat was like a snare drum thudding in the night. Vision painted the desert silverbright, sight as good as a man's at high noon and much sharper than a wolf's; his scent wasn't as keen as the canid model, but it was a thousand times better than that of a man. Enough that her femaleness was like a club across the senses; he walked over, his platter-size paws soundless on the gritty soil, and nuzzled at her. Confused images of mingled human and beast-form mating and feeding cascaded through his mind.

A practiced effort of will thrust down the consciousness of how appealingly, mouthwateringly *meaty* she smelled, something that harmonized all too well with more complex Shadowspawn hungers. Her fingers dug into the ruff around his throat, and he rumbled in contentment, then turned and sprang into the night.

The sabertooth was a young male in its prime years, an ambush hunter made for burst speed. He raced in a series of twenty-foot bounds southwards to leave as little trace on the ground as possible. Then he slowed to a springy trot. The lights of the little hamlet glared with a blue-white radiance that human eyes would have seen as isolated pools of dimness.

Closer, and the rank scents of burnt petroleum and chemicals made his nose wrinkle, whiskers bristling as his thin black lips curled back to show the rest of his fangs. Then the smells of humanity, stale and dirty, the present-but-uninteresting tang of children, others healthy and fresh and insidiously appetizing and tempting, now and then the revolting odor of sickness.

Shadowspawn senses picked up other things: the way sleeping minds whimpered and retreated into nightmare as his form padded down through the thick, cool dust beside the road, the growls or frightened silence of dogs. He could tell instantly where the humans he sought were holed up. The blaring, shrilling *wrongness* of the silver-particle lining they'd applied to the inside of the motel room. He winced and turned the eyes of his mind aside as if he'd stared into the sun. A struggle for a moment; was he supposed to attack those men, or . . .

Defend them. I must defend them.

It seemed odd, alien, unnatural. *Taste fear, scent terror, the hot intoxicating spurt of blood—*

No.

The humanoid energy-matrix mind at the base of the feline's brain mastered it; mastered its own drives as well. He vaulted over a goat-stick fence and into a backyard bare except for a rusty slide and the tattered remains of a children's wading pool, then eeled between the aluminum siding of the house and a pitted Chosan sedan.

A dog whimpered inside the house. Beyond was dense shadow, and he went belly-down on the stained concrete as he approached the motel, as intent as a tabby with a mouse. The slit pupils of his eyes widened nearly round as he scanned back and forth. The Power stretched out too, despite the pain of the silver barrier, seeking—

A tingle. A strumming along the nerves. The feeling of matter turned and constrained, a knot of warped probabilities. Will imposed on chaos and dragging a piece of the universe down the slope of entropy as it did. *Up there.*

The great cat had a different perception of distance than did a man; it was more concerned with what was within one or two leaps, very much with scents, less so with larger patterns. He forced its attention outwards.

Flying.

The huge golden eagle came with a *whoosh* of displaced air to land on the flat roof. Then a naked man was there instead, his long white-blond hair blowing around his muscled shoulders. He kicked something upward as if with a soccer ball and caught it, something that the eagle had carried in its talons. Then he began to walk forward sure-footed towards the other side of the roof, the inner court where the units of the motel faced.

There he paused, looked over the edge, and made a gesture. Hands together, then apart, then dropping something . . .

Grenade, the thinking part of the sabertooth's hybrid mind said. The rest replied: *Kill.*

Huge muscles moved on the creature's bones, and claws flared out as it worked its paws into the dirt. Then he was flying, a bronze streak through the darkness, his mouth gaping open to keep the lower jaw out of the way of the stabbing downward slash. The man toppled forward over the edge of the roof, changing as he did.

The door blew in. Peter tumbled backwards towards the bed; things hit him, astonishingly painful, and he yelped. There was a flash with it, and a crashing *bang!* and a sharp, acrid smell.

"Grenade!" someone yelled.

Lying blinking at the ceiling, all he could think for an instant was: *That's a grenade? That little flash?*

He'd expected globes of slow-motion flame and people flying through the air with their arms and legs windmilling. But the blow had been *hard*; he tasted blood in his mouth again. And loud, his ears were numbed.

What next?

A gorilla smashed through the shattered door, great black fists punching inward and then ripping the broken veneer and particleboard out of the way. Its shoulders sent chunks of the frame pinwheeling as well as it charged into the room, nearly five hundred pounds of black-shaggy silver-backed rank-smelling beast, roaring behind fangs that looked like daggers of white bone and beating its fists on a leathery chest like a great drum. Hair bristled in a roach on the pointed head, and the creature's thigh-thick arms stretched out to grip and crush as it bounded forward on its thick bowed legs in a shambling run.

Gorillas aren't aggressive towards human beings! Peter thought, or gibbered. *I remember that distinctly from that Dian Fossey article I read.*

Guha ducked a fist that would have torn off her head and slashed with the long knife, then went flying head over heels at an openhanded cuff that hit not quite squarely.

But Shadowspawn weregorillas are *pretty damned aggressive, you betcha.*

Peter shook his head, winced at the pain that caused, and looked around for the silver table knife. He spotted it, and began a dogged crawl-roll towards it, ignoring the pain of the fresh bruises on his still-fragile body. The rest he saw in flashes, and heard bits and pieces as his blast-stunned ears began to function again.

Farmer drove at the beast's back with his blade. It whirled and caught him up, holding the man's yelling form over its head, ready to throw him down with enough force to turn his body into a bag of shattered bone and ruptured organs. Something flew glittering through the air and slashed into the gorilla's arms, lapping around them with a harsh rattling clank and a rip of leathery skin. Blood sprayed . . . and dissolved in midair with an iridescent sparkle as the pseudomatter lost coherence.

That was the older man, Harvey. The weapon was a kau sin ke, a Chinese fighting iron; he recognized it from one of his guilty pleasures, the Shanghai action flicks of the late teens. Like a steel whip made from short rods joined by ring links of chain, but this had a silvery gleam, and each of the rods was a cylinder of razor-sharp blades.

The Shadowspawn beast screamed again, a stunningly loud roar even to Peter's abused ears. Farmer tumbled away as it tried to clutch at the weapon, but more blood spurted from its huge hands as they met the sharp silver-inlaid edges of the jointed bars. Harvey turned the fighting iron into a whirling blur between himself and the giant ape, a gleaming circle of menace to protect himself and the injured humans. It filled most of the little motel room; Peter could see the sweat of effort and fear gleaming on the older man's long, craggy face, and the way the muscles bunched and gathered on the gorilla's massive bones. It knuckle-walked a pace back and forth, then stood and hammered its chest again, shrieking.

Farmer crawled away and picked up his blade, long as a short sword, forcing himself back onto his feet; Peter found himself clutching the little sharpened table knife. He looked at the pathetic spike in his scrawny fist and suppressed a hysterical giggle. The gorilla would charge in an instant, even though its hands streamed lines of blood . . . blood that somehow disappeared as it dripped towards the floor. It would charge, and those hands would close on a human body, and that would be the end of it.

He would die free, at least. Oddly, that actually *was* comforting. He propped himself up on one hand and held the little knife out in a wavering attempt at guard.

An appalling shriek filled the room, halfway between a scream and a coughing roar. A tawny thunderbolt came through the ruined door.

It struck the gorilla with a massive thud, and the combined forms went over and over in a ton-weight ball of black and brown and claws and saberlike canines and hammering fists the size of small casks. More blood and black bristly hide and skin covered in short sand-covered fur flew and misted away. For a moment Peter could see the gorilla's hands locked around the cat's throat, holding the dreadful stab of the long canines away, and the sabertooth's hind paws raking at its swag belly.

Harvey threw himself aside with a yell, dropping the kau sin ke. Something hit him in midleap, and he tumbled away to crash into the cheap bureau in a shatter of age-dried pressboard. A twisting in the melee, and suddenly it was two giant cats, rearing on their hind legs and slamming back and forth at each other with their taloned paws, sabertooth against Siberian tiger.

Another twisting, and it was two naked men facing each other, one dark, one fair, both lithe and muscular. Their snarls were as bestial as the animals' had been. Those turned into words as they circled, purling, spitting, their fingers tracing shapes in the air that hurt the eyes to watch. Peter yelled and rolled away off the edge of the bed as the wall behind him suddenly turned freezing cold, the sort of cold that would tear off your skin if you touched it. An instant later the frame of the broken door burst into flames. With a screech the Mhabrogast glyphs around the edges of the room began to *glow.*

Cherenkov radiation! Peter thought. *And they're* changing, *too.*

He felt an impulse to beat his head open against the floor. Images spun through his mind, intolerable glimpses down dark whirlpools that spun through the depth of things. For an instant the flames seemed to melt the blond man's form, making it run. Then he turned and leapt, arms before his face as he dove through the blaze. Through the fire Peter could see him take a dozen strides and then throw himself into the air. A fractional second, and an eagle thrashed itself skyward.

The remaining man swayed and went to one knee. His skin was sheened with sweat, and there was a raw, feral look in his eyes as he panted. That faded, and humanness came back to them.

"Harvey?" he croaked. "I'm not sure I can stay palpable, Harvey. He was too strong."

Then Farmer's voice, sharp with pain and throttled panic: "Guha's hurt! Bad!"

CHAPTER FOURTEEN

Ellen felt herself freeze; she was already motionless, but this was an *inability* to move. Then she took a deep, quiet breath and made herself relax. Less than a second later there was an *impact* behind her. Right behind her, where Adrian had put the final glyph.

Not physical. Nothing had struck her, but something had *wanted* to and started to make the world obey its will. And then been caught in a very bad place.

Scratch one night-walker.

Ellen started to giggle, then jammed it down with an effort of will of her own. Something was walking towards her. Trotting easily . . .

Eeep! she thought as she adjusted the rifle, taking a turn of the sling around her upper arm to steady her aim. *There's another one!*

Then: *It's a wolf. Big fucking wolf with big fucking teeth. I don't* like *dogs, and wolves are even worse. Wolves with a Shadowspawn inside are even worse than that.*

She'd been savaged by a dog as a child. . . .

A blur too swift to be really seen, and the beast became a man . . . more or less. Arrogantly fit, brown skinned, with a broad, hook-nosed, high-cheeked face and black hair falling to his wide shoulders. The eyes shone lambent yellow. They turned down at the ring of glyphs Adrian had drawn around her, and his lips moved in what was probably either a curse or Mhabrogast, if there was a difference.

Dale Shadowsblade, she thought. *One of Adrienne's bully boys.*

She'd met him while she was Adrienne's prisoner, and even by Shadowspawn standards he was nasty; also extremely powerful. His usual day job . . . sort of . . . was to carry out executions for the Council.

"I'm unarmed—" he began, smiling.

"Unarmed? *Good!*"

Crack. The rifle hammered back at her shoulder.

Just as it did, her hand slipped on the rock she was using as a rest; dust fountained up from the desert as the heavy silver bullet kicked into the dirt near Dale Shadowsblade's feet.

The Apache—Apache to the limited extent he was anything human at all—grinned at her, teeth very white in the darkness.

"Not in a chatty mood, eh? I like women with spunk. They fuck good, die well and taste even better."

Doggedly she broke the action open and thumbed in another shell. It was a little depressing that the Shadowspawn just stood and grinned at her at point-blank range. Then his eyes went to the rock face at her back and down to Adrian's motionless form as it lay breathing once every twenty seconds.

"*Szau-ti* glyph! That Adrian has a nasty mind," he said. "Put you in front of it like a tethered goat and see what he can catch while he's off being busy, and you're one tasty piece of meat. Dmitri the apeshit got whupped by Adrian and now he looks like he's got his ass caught in a crack back in there. He's going to be pissed, let me tell you."

Okay, so that's who got trapped behind me. Now if I can kill Dale here, it'll be a prefecta.

She aimed, took a breath, let half of it out, *squeezed* the trigger—

And as she did the man faded away. *Crack*, and the bullet split the night. Then he was there again.

"Pity the glyph worked, bitch. If it hadn't you'd be spending some quality time with my wolf right now, and then Dmitri's would be getting sloppy seconds. Before we drank you dry. Hey, they're man's best friend, right, so why not a gal's?"

Reload. Do not *think about that. Ignore him. They try to play with your mind. Just fucking shoot him. Look on the bright side: before you met Adrian, you* never *got to shoot or knife abusive sexist assholes.*

"But I guess I'll have to rescue him instead, no matter how much fun it would be to leave him there. Think about what you're missing!"

Suddenly he was rushing towards her. *Crack*, but the man was a wolf again. The bullet went over its head, and then it rose in a soaring leap over the semicircle of glyphs. Her head swiveled to follow it, and it vanished into the moonlit rock.

"Oh, man, I do *not* like this," she said, reaching for another shell. An effort made her fingers stop shaking.

"Adrian, what's going on?"

Adrian's body breathed once more, very slowly.

*   *   *

245

"Guha's hurt!"

Harvey went over to her. Peter let the knife drop and hobbled around the bed, vague recollections of Boy Scout first-aid courses in his mind. He stopped, shocked. The Texan's fingers were unlatching and easing away her body armor.

"Aw, shit," he said tiredly.

The dark woman was shaking slightly—shivering, Peter thought, but with an odd mechanical look to it. More like machinery than a human being. There were bubbles on her lips, swelling and popping, but they weren't spit. Even in the dim light of the single remaining bulb he could see that they were red—a very dark red, almost black. Her eyes were open too, and one had the pupil contracted to a pinhead. There was a smell about her, blood and something else.

"Aw, *shit*," Harvey said again. "He didn't just hit her. There's a bane with it, feel?"

Peter felt nothing. . . . *No, I feel terrified.* Farmer ran his hands through the air over the injured woman, and his face scrunched up. It looked as if it were going to crack as it showed an emotion that it wasn't used to: sorrow.

"Right down into the cells," he said. "She's trapped in there. Everything's black-pathed. She's hurting really bad, and it won't stop until she dies, and her duration sense is stretched out so that seconds are days. The physical stuff would be all right but even her blood isn't clotting. All the healing functions are blocked. Harvey, do something!"

"Fucking *what*, Jack? I couldn't touch that any more than I could rip steel cuffs off barehanded!"

There was a stumbling sound behind Peter. The little hairs on his neck tried to stand up. That was just very tired footsteps, but . . .

Fascinating, he thought. *My* body *knows when to be afraid.*

But they were a night-walking *Shadowspawn's* footsteps. Something very far down wanted to whimper and puke and piss itself and scream and plead.

The Empire of Shadow must have been really awful, *for a very long time.*

"Let me see," Adrian Brézé said hoarsely.

The others moved back; Farmer hesitated, and Harvey Ledbetter laid a hand on his shoulder. Adrian crouched, then went to one knee.

"I've known her only a little," he said. "But she was very brave, to go after that thing."

"Yeah," Farmer said tightly; he'd picked up his knife and was looking at it and the injured woman, his face twitching with what he would probably have to do. "She is. Was."

Adrian sighed. His face went completely blank for an instant, and then he held his hands out in the same gesture that Farmer had used.

"Wait a minute, Adrian! You could just fucking *dissipate* if you overstrain, you're night-walking and you're not strong enough after that fight—" Harvey began.

"I will have to be strong enough, won't I?" he said remotely. Then: *"Auii za!"*

Both hands clenched closed. Guha's back arched, and then she was awake and screaming. And Adrian *faded.*

"I wish I hadn't seen that," Peter said, muttering to himself. Then he collapsed backwards on the bed. "I'm a physicist, I was trained to believe in an orderly universe where things make *sense.* I shouldn't see that sort of thing. I shouldn't be squeezed to paste by wereanacondas, I shouldn't—"

"Yeah, you're a physicist."

The light cut out. Harvey was standing over him, and staring, and Peter found that he was a little afraid of *this* man, as well.

"And you'd better be worth all this," he said flatly to the physicist. "You really had better be worth it. Especially if Adrian ain't waking up in his body right about now."

Ellen shivered again. The night felt *empty*. There was the palest pale to the east, over the leagues of silvery desert. She'd never thought how good *emptiness* could feel.

There was a trickle of alarm along her nerves. Then Adrian's body reared up and fell back. A keening sound came from between his clenched teeth. She leaned the rifle against the boulder—guns could go off if you dropped them; that caution was automatic now—and threw herself down beside him.

His sweat smelled rank, despite the chill of the desert night. The yellow-flecked eyes were open and rolled up in his head, and teeth showed white and bare; they chattered, and he shook as if in the grip of a chill. Strings of disconnected words sounded, in half a dozen languages, then French, then English:

"I . . . she was hurt, I had to . . . Too much, too much! The fighting and the healing, too much!"

He had to help someone. He's overdrawn on the Power, Ellen knew. *Which is entirely like him. He talks cynic and acts like Galahad.*

And she knew what she must do; the thought made her mouth go dry with him in this condition, but her voice was steady. His eyes were fixed on her and the pupils had grown to swallow the iris, a thin band of gold around pits of black; his teeth showed, and a line of spittle hung from one lip.

"Come on, darling. I've got what you need."

"No . . . control . . . get away . . ."

"*Do* it," she said, and bent forward, bending her chin back. "Come on, you goddamned Boy Scout!"

He snarled and lunged. Ellen gave a scream that was half moan as cable-strong arms closed around her and teeth scored her throat.

Dawn broke; the air was still comfortably cool, but it had a hint of the day's white furnace, and a scent of dry dust. Harvey Ledbetter walked into the motel's office and held up one hand. The manager was obviously frightened—despite the overcranked air-conditioning there was a sheen of sweat on him—and obviously desperate to know what had happened to his unit in the night.

"There's been a bit of damage," Harvey said aloud.

Meanin' your little fleabag is trashed, he thought.

And saw the same knowledge on the man's face; he'd been out to take a look. A grenade did do regrettable things to cheap construction, not to mention tons of homicidal gorilla and sabertooth rolling around making bad and throwing off Wreakings while they did. Fortunately there hadn't been any flames they couldn't put out, and the bloodstains were nothing out of the ordinary.

Harvey smiled and flicked his right hand. A fan of hundred-dollar notes appeared there; even these days, a C-note wasn't toilet paper. He put them down on the desk, and then rested his index finger on them, friendly blue eyes peering over the tops of his mirrored shades.

"I think that will keep things nice and tidy," he said, and let something else show; he could feel the man's mind jump. "And quiet."

The way the Texan was leaning gave just a hint of the shape of his shoulder holster and the Colt within. The manager paled a little at that and the eyes, then crumpled—not physically, but you could sense the inward collapse. Also his calculations: three people in civilian versions of field gear, their truck, the disturbances, the Humvee that had arrived a few minutes ago. All that said either *police* or *cartels*, possibly both in this part of the country. Or perhaps *spook*, but he'd be less likely to think that.

"*Sí*. Just some friends getting a little rough, eh?" the manager said, and made the money disappear. "A little party. Insurance, I have it."

"Friends? Well, one of 'em was a real gorilla, and I didn't like him at all," Harvey said, and smiled at the other man's uneasy laugh. "And the other was a real cool cat. Just so we understand each other."

Harvey nodded, smiled again—there was no point in pushing the man when he'd gotten what he wanted. Frightening people had its uses, but it was all too easy to make them terrified, and terror was the original two-edged knife. Desperate human beings switched off their minds and got really unpredictable. Besides that, there was no point in taking out his frustrations on bystanders.

He walked back into the bright sunlight, and onto the scuffed cracked asphalt and concrete and bare dirt of the motel's courtyard. Despite the stiffness and the bruises, and the general message his body was sending him about slowing down in his early sixties, he grinned. There was even a *tumbleweed*, and a couple of skittering lizards.

He'd been born in the Hill Country, not far southeast of Austin, which was pretty enough in a spare, rocky way; there were even olive groves and vineyards there these days. And would-be *Tuscanista* rural gentrifiers making organic goat cheese, most of which, in his opinion, was about as much fun to eat as the other caprine by-products.

But there was a certain ugly charm to desolation like this, a sort that could appeal to any country-bred Texan. A Larry McMurtry *fitness*, as if Captain McCrae were about to ride in with a scruffy patrol of Rangers, a Winchester in a scabbard at his knee.

A little unconscious nostalgia there too, he thought. *Back then, all humans had to worry about was other humans, like the Comanche or Mexican bandits. The Order of the Black Dawn was just getting started.*

As he came out Farmer was helping Guha into the van. It was a big, nondescript vehicle, with oversize tires and certain facilities that didn't show; the back could be rigged for casualties, for instance. She'd be some time healing, but it was a big improvement over dying after a subjective month or so of agony and fear. Farmer was moving carefully too, and he was thirty years younger than Harvey; that gave the older man a good deal of satisfaction.

Peter Boase was being cautious, but holding up remarkably well for a civilian who'd just gone through a withdrawal process that made kicking heroin loose nothing by comparison.

And there were Adrian and Ellen, both looking . . . *ridden hard and put away wet,* he thought ironically. *Pale and interesting.* The girl . . . woman . . . moved stiffly and looked washed out, but she and Adrian were still exchanging smiles and glances and touches, almost unconsciously.

Well, that's the real thing, he thought. *And Adrian's actually found a girlie who* doesn't *mind being on the receiving end of a Homo sapiens nocturnus feeding frenzy. Good for him, since he can apparently control even that. And I can't even find a woman who'll put up with all-too-human me.*

There was a hint of irony in his smile. Harvey Ledbetter considered himself an excellent judge of character, including the female variety. As long as he wasn't personally interested in the woman in question. When he was . . .

Three marriages, three divorces, he thought. *Fuckin' perfect record. Of course, not being able to tell the truth about what you do really doesn't help.*

He could talk to Brotherhood women, of course. Weird term, when you thought about it; they'd never gotten around to modernizing the name for these gender-inclusive times. They were another story.

The problem with that was that nearly everyone in the Brotherhood was insane in one way or another.

"He who fights with monsters might take care lest he thereby become a monster. And if you gaze for long into an abyss, the abyss gazes also into you." *Note that the feller who said that ended up wearing a straitjacket and baying out the window of the asylum at the Bavarian Alps. Now, I'm completely sane, I surely am. I'm planning on blowing up a city with a nuclear weapon for* perfectly rational *and highly moral reasons.*

He laughed as he walked over to the vehicles, and Adrian smiled at him. It had always been a charming expression, and it looked better now with some years on him and a bit less of that androgynous beauty Shadowspawn teenagers tended to show. Adrian *looked* like he was in his late twenties—maybe a bit older this morning, after a hard night—but his body language was somehow a little different.

"What's the joke, Harvey?"

"I was just thinking that things were going too smoothly," he said. "And then I backed off a bit and looked at that statement, plus the way we all give a pretty good impression of having been through the cat once, and it struck me as funny."

Adrian laughed himself. Peter Boase started to sputter, then looked around at all of them and chuckled a little himself, wincing when it made a scab on his lip crack. Harvey found himself thinking better of the man for it.

"All right, Dr. Boase," he said. "You're going to Sweden for your new job. Consider yourself a lucky man."

The blond physicist did think about it for a moment. Then he joined in, for the same reason, and they all chuckled; even Guha smiled weakly.

"I am," Boase said. "It's . . . I hate to say it, but from what little I remember it was even worse at Rancho Sangre after Adrienne died. . . ."

"After I killed her," Ellen said with satisfaction.

Quite a girl, Harvey thought admiringly.

Then she went on: "Farmer here will take you to the next stage, Peter."

They hugged, and Ellen kissed him gently on the brow. "You get to work, you hear me?"

"I will. Professor Duquesne is a first-class mind. Though I'll need some test subjects . . . and there will be a *lot* of equipment. . . ."

"We will see that you have all you need," Adrian said. "And you have plenty of motivation, no?"

"*Fuck*, yes," Boase said, his face grim for a moment. Then, a little shyly, he extended a hand. "And thank you too."

"You are welcome, for what it's worth."

"But shouldn't Duquesne have a spunky young daughter, o square-jawed scientist?" Ellen teased. "A redheaded tomboy who can hand you a soldering iron while you cook up the world saver in the hidden underground lab?"

Everyone laughed, except Farmer, who jerked his head brusquely at the vehicle. When the van pulled away, Harvey looked inquiringly at the pair.

"So, you needed to talk to me?"

Adrian nodded. "It was Ellen's idea."

And for a masochist bottom, she surely does rule that boy with a rod of iron, Harvey thought.

"You noticed how disorganized that attack was?" Adrian said.

Harvey nodded. "Shadowspawn usually are. They don't *need* to be better. Probably just came here on *impulse*."

"Or they could have detected Peter's e-mail. He was using one of the pseudonyms he operated under while he was at Rancho Sangre and doing work for Adrienne."

Harvey snorted. "You see either of those two as hackers? Exceptin' in the literal sense of the word."

Adrian shrugged. "Not directly, no . . ."

Ellen cut in: "Theresa, Adrienne's household manager, was *very* good with systems. She could be working for Adrienne's parents now? She was born a renfield there before Jules was, ah . . . killed. Before his body was killed, that is."

"That is possible," Adrian said. "They would be unlikely to kill her, then. She might have given them a heads-up. They *would* have been better organized, if my sister were still running that little faction of theirs. Dmitri and Dale Shadowsblade were both here. I bested Dmitri in the contest of Power, but if they had attacked together . . ."

"We'd be toast," Harvey acknowledged. "Without you, we'd have been toast anyway—or gorilla fodder."

"So Rancho Sangre must be disorganized too," Ellen said firmly. She crossed her arms, took a deep breath, and went on: "And Adrian's children are there."

Harvey grunted and leaned back against the Humvee. "So, you know?"

She shot a glance at Adrian. "He—"

"My darling, I wasn't *sure*. I was Adrienne's . . . captive for a while in Calcutta. Seven years ago. My mind was not my own for much of that time. And—" He sighed. "I feared you were right. Perhaps I did not inquire more because I did not want to know."

"They're not in any danger," Harvey pointed out, feeling a trickle of alarm. "Adrian's parents will take care of them."

"Adrian's parents will turn them into *killers*," Ellen said.

"Well, Adrian . . ."

". . . was rescued, Mr. Ledbetter. By force. Usually I'm not one for removing children by force, but in this case . . . their mother is dead, Adrian *is* their father, and leaving them there is the equivalent of having them raised by Nazis. Not just the risk to them, but the people they'll hurt."

She called me by my last name. Uh-oh.

"And so will Leon and Leila be rescued. Think of what an asset they could be to our side, too."

Ellen's face was beautiful, but right now you could see the bone structure under it, and that was beyond all prettiness. Her blue eyes glinted.

"Look—" he began.

Behind her, Adrian smiled. It was almost a smirk, and he mouthed silently: *Good luck.*

CHAPTER FIFTEEN

"Ol' buddy, this is crazy."

Ellen crossed her arms and glared at Harvey. "No, it isn't," she snapped.

"Harvey—" Adrian began.

All three of them fell silent as the waitress brought their food. Harvey beamed at her.

"Now *that's* a taco," he said, taking a happy bite. "My compliments to the chef, darlin'."

Unexpectedly, the heavyset woman smiled at him as she plopped down a basket of sopapillas and covered it with a cloth to keep them warm.

"We don't have no chef," she said. "All we got here at Teresa's is a cook."

Ellen's nose twitched, and saliva spurted into her mouth; her stomach twisted with a need so intense it was almost nausea. She'd been too keyed up to realize just *how* hungry she was. Still was, despite the energy drinks and nut bars she'd devoured as they drove into town.

What with waiting to be attacked by monsters, shooting monsters . . . well, shooting at monsters . . . donating blood and coupling like mad stoats, she thought. *God, what a movie this would make! Rated R, of course.*

With an effort, she restrained herself from gobbling, the spiced *barbacoa* beef and onions tingling on her tongue. The puffed bread with honey tasted even better.

"Mighty strange how sometimes the best tacos are in these little places you'd swear probably cooked up roof rabbit. I recall this time near Abilene—" Harvey began reminiscently.

"Shut up with the funny, rustic good-ol'-boy thing, Harvey," she said. "I'm a small-town girl myself and it doesn't fool me. And I'm not going to forget those kids because I'm stuffing my face."

She took a bite of her taco and glared. Harvey shrugged; he was about the most imperturbable man she'd ever met. At least he couldn't sense her emotions anymore, not with his limited talent and the protections Adrian had installed.

At last she pushed the plate away and drank the last of her Diet Coke. Adrian looked at it and raised a brow, chuckling.

"What?"

"It just seems a little . . ."

He indicated the plates, now mostly clear of their tacos, burritos, refried beans and much else.

"I just prefer the taste of aspartame. And *you're* not going to distract me either, Adrian. Tell me honestly—will there ever be a better time?"

He sighed and rested his face in his hands for a moment, elbows on the table.

"I am so tired," he said softly. "No. There will not. But answer me honestly, *chérie*. Why do you care? Why are you ready to take risks for children who are not yours? Did you fall in love with them on brief acquaintance?"

"No. I only saw them a couple of times, and . . ." She hesitated. "Frankly, I thought they were . . ."

"Creepy, you said. Then why?"

"Because they're yours, and I love *you*. Tell me you haven't been thinking about this since I first told you about them. You froze then and it's been eating at you ever since. So I think this is something you need to do."

"Yes, I have been thinking about them." Adrian sighed. "It . . . has been obsessing me. I thought I hid it better."

"Honey, we're sorta linked. It isn't all one-way, you know."

Softly he went on: "I try to suppress it because it isn't really concern for *them* in any immediate sense. I think of them, but what the, the eye of my mind sees is myself, as a little boy. Myself and Adrienne, when we were like kittens playing together in the sun. Before we ate of the tree of knowledge and had to choose between good and evil."

Harvey touched Adrian on the shoulder. Ellen fought down a slight pang; they'd been together for a *long* time before she met Adrian at all. It was illogical, but . . .

What was that old saying? The heart has its reasons that the mind knows not?

"Son, you should let that go," Harvey said, his voice quiet but compelling. "You can't help those two kids you remember, even if one of them was you. They're both dead. They became you, you and your sister. You both made your choices."

Adrian looked up at the Texan. "Harvey, I made the choices I did because of *you*. You took me out. Adrienne stayed behind and became . . . what she is. It was a close thing for me even so, sometimes, Harvey. Being good is *hard* for us. It's so easy for you humans—I've known a lot of bitterness, a lot of envy over that."

Ellen laid her hand on her husband's shoulder, beside that of his friend.

"You did manage it, darling."

"But . . . I had the opportunity. Adrienne never did; and the little girl I loved is dead, murdered by the thing she became. How can I leave the flesh of my flesh there, to lose them the same way?"

Ellen nodded. "You can't. And no child should be treated the way they will be."

Adrian sighed and looked down at his elegant, slender hands. "My parents will . . . love them, in their way."

"That makes things worse, not better. You can turn against an outright abuser. Someone who really loves you can lead you into the pit."

"And the children are Shadowspawn, Ellen. Purebreds, even more than I. Perhaps the purest-bred in twenty thousand years. Very powerful, hideously dangerous."

Ellen snorted. "Now, that's, well, racist. *You* aren't a bad man, Adrian. And *you're* extremely powerful and dangerous. There's no reason they have to be bad, no matter what they can do. You're vacillating. It isn't like you." More quietly. "They look so much like you. The boy was like seeing you at that age."

259

"Oh, *Jesus,*" Harvey said wearily. "Do you two do this we-are-the-dyadic-unit thing *all the time?*"

Ellen flushed; she'd become very used to being alone with Adrian. Adrian's face firmed and lost the slightly wistful expression it had worn for an instant.

"And there is a nexus here, Harvey."

The Texan's face altered, going very still. A probability nexus was nothing to take lightly. The fact that they could seldom be pinned down in detail simply made that more essential. Nobody who had enough of the Power to Wreak at all doubted the existence of the precognitive ability, and Adrian had an awesome degree of it.

"What sort?" he said cautiously.

"I am not altogether sure, but a powerful one. Extremely powerful, and growing very rapidly; I can feel it looming out of the spray of futures, cutting across one path after another. And I am increasingly convinced that *not* doing this is black-pathed. When I try to invoke common sense and convince myself not to do it, cold winds blow. Both for me personally and for the world. It has been troubling me for some time; I think that was why I avoided thinking of the children as much as I could. Since Ellen mentioned them it has been forcing its way into my conscious mind."

One of the grizzled eyebrows went up. "You sure your feelings aren't pushin' you there?"

Adrian spread his hands. "No, I'm not sure of that at all," he said frankly. "But one can *never* be sure. Even with an overt Seeing, rather than just an intimation like this. It is enough to convince me, my old. And my subconscious has a lively sense of self-preservation. If the Power is prompting me to do this thing, despite the obvious risks, then there is some hideous danger involved in *not* doing it. We cannot know what the danger is, but it is there. And if we ignore the warning, we will find out the danger far too late."

"*Or* someone stronger than you is tweakin' it."

Harvey held up a hand as Ellen began to speak; she felt a little relief. Even now, parts of her brain screamed, *This is crazy!* at logic like that.

And that's after *I've seen people turn into . . . well, not bats, but things with wings, and walk through walls.*

"All right," Harvey said slowly. "I've got a powerful respect for your precog, Adrian. Plus we *do* have some downtime in a few months, and it *is* the best opportunity . . . which don't make it good. It's an unjustified risk before the Tbilisi thing. Though I can probably even sell it to Sheila Polson."

Adrian raised a brow and said to Ellen: "Did I mention her? The Brotherhood's executive for western North America?"

"Yes. *Bigoted bitch* was the term you used."

Adrian grinned. "I didn't think she altogether liked me," he said. "And I thought that she disliked me for my genes, which I can't help, rather than my actions, which I usually can. Doubly ironic because she has considerably more of the Shadowspawn inheritance than Harvey here. Projected self-loathing is one of the occupational hazards of the Brotherhood. Also a reason I, ah, resigned."

Harvey snorted. "She didn't like you, until you pulled off the Rancho Sangre thing. Hajime *and* the late unlamented Adrienne, that's quite a bit of counting coup. You got real chops with her now, son."

"*We* pulled that off."

"Yeah, it ain't hurt *my* chops with the organization either. There's not a person in the Brotherhood didn't cheer, which makes up for bein' a loose cannon, sorta. A little."

Ellen murmured. "Harvey Ledbetter, organization man?"

"Not so much. More like the Brotherhood's indispensible skunk," Harvey said. "But I think I can sell it to her. Say rescuin' a pureblood and raisin' him right worked with *you*, and there's no reason we couldn't do it again; and we should strike fast, because the younger we get 'em, the more likely it is to work out right. It'd make a powerful difference if we had more major mojo like yours on our side. I can bring her 'round . . . *if* I work at it for a while."

"Ah," Adrian said. "That is good!"

"And I'll go on the op, too, of course."

"No," Adrian said, shaking his head. "You were definitely made as the shooter during the fracas. Not the first time you'd killed them . . . remember how Hajime tried to make me give you up, by name? It takes a great hatred for them to *notice* a specific human that way."

Harvey grinned with happy ferocity. "I don't mind havin' that sort of rep. Still, I know the ground. . . ."

"And it knows you, by now: Wreakings aimed at you specifically. I am fairly sure that the Tōkairin would do so, and my parents. Farmer and Guha would do; they were covered by my penumbra and got out before anyone paid attention to them. Or any reliable Brotherhood muscle. And technical and logistic support, of course."

"That I think I can do, ol' buddy. Properly motivated, that is."

Ellen felt her skin prickle at something in Harvey's smile. "You want something for it," she said.

I didn't watch all that bargaining at the gallery for nothing.

Harvey leaned back and put a toothpick between his lips. "Tryin' to quit," he said in explanation. "And yeah, I do want something."

"What?" Adrian said.

"A promise. I'm goin' along with this against my better judgment. I want a blank check for some operation sometime *you* think stinks. Solemn oath, Adrian, ol' buddy. I call in the favor and you go along with it, no questions, beginning to end."

Adrian hesitated, his eyes narrowing. Ellen remembered something he'd said once: that Harvey could be *drastic* sometimes.

You know, these guys really are *terrorists in a way. I mean, they don't go out of their way to kill bystanders, but they don't seem to give much of a damn about it either, except for Adrian . . . and Adrian can play really rough too, I think. And they'll step on renfields like bugs. Which is fine in one way, but on the other hand that includes guys like Jose and his family, whom I mostly liked. Fighting the Bad Guys is more complicated than I thought, even when they* are *really-for-true evil.*

"You really mean it," Adrian said.

"*Oh,* yeah," Harvey said, relaxed, one arm hooked around the rear of the chair. "That's my price. Take it or leave it."

Adrian glanced at Ellen. "I can deny you nothing," he said, and the words were for her. "My oath, old friend. And I am glad of it, too. Once more Ellen is *making* me do something I very much wanted to do . . . but I doubted my own wanting."

"Okay, first installment on the payback," Harvey said promptly. He pulled out his phone and selected a number. "I can recognize when my talent's prompting me, even if it isn't in your league. Just tell her Operation Defarge is a go. Nothin' else."

Adrian shot him a look, shrugged, and took the phone.

"You have reached Polson Consulting. All of our operatives are serving other customers at the moment; please leave a name and number and we'll get back to you."

"Mowgli here. Lefarge is a go," Adrian said, and snapped off the phone.

"Mowgli?" Ellen said; it had been a *long* time since she read Kipling.

"My code name," Adrian said. "One of them."

"Oh . . . the human boy raised by wolves . . . Bit of an ironic inversion . . ."

He sighed. "We should go back to Santa Fe for a stop. I need to pick up a few things there. Then we'll head to California. It's some time before the Council meets, and . . . I was hoping our physicists would come up with something that might help us there."

"So was I," Harvey said. "When you're ready, I'll come a-runnin' to earn the rest of my favor. Meantime, business calls and it's a far, far better thing."

Ellen turned and looked at Adrian as the Texan nodded and left.

"What was that?"

Adrian frowned slightly. "Harvey isn't any great adept, but he has mental shields like machined tungsten carbide," he said. "There was just a *flicker.* . . ."

Ellen snorted. "You get too dependent on reading people's minds, darling. *My* take is that he was improvising, but he has something in mind you're *not* going to like. At all. Whatever this Defarge thing is, it's going to be a bone in your throat."

Adrian shrugged; then went abstracted for a moment. "The world-lines are tangled, too many Wreaking along them . . . but you are right. Let's get on the road, then. Perhaps we can rest a little in Santa Fe."

"Maybe I can see Giselle? She'll have worried herself sick, and I didn't dare write."

"Perhaps."

Ellen smiled. Then something teased at her memory. It wasn't all that long since her graduation, and she'd had to take English literature courses as well.

Defarge, she thought. *That Dickens book. She's the one who sat knitting by the guillotine during the Terror, while the heads of the aristos fell into the basket.*

Adrian shrugged again. "One of the reasons I liked living in Santa Fe for so long was how *quiet* it is. Little happens there."

"Well, that's unique," the Santa Fe chief of police said.

The forensics team moved around the room. Most of them had more than one hat; Santa Fe's police force didn't run to elaborate hierarchies.

Eric Salvador felt a surge of anger, and throttled it back automatically. It wouldn't help . . . and he'd said the same sort of thing. You did, it helped you deal with what you were seeing. Usually.

Cecile was on the bed. Usually dead bodies didn't have much expression, but usually they weren't arched in a galvanic spasm. They'd have to break her bones to get her into a bag. The look on her face was not quite like anything he'd ever seen, and his experience was broader than he liked. Now he'd have to have this in his head for the rest of his life. He licked his lips, tasting the salt of sweat.

Cesar was naked, lying on his face between the bed and the window. His pistol was in his right hand; the spent brass of fourteen shells littered the floor around him. Most of them were in the coagulating blood, turned dark red now with brown spots. In his left was clutched a knife, not a fighting knife, but some sort of tableware. A wedge of glass as broad as a man's hand at its base was in his throat, the point coming out the back of his neck.

"This is a murder-suicide," the chief said quietly.

Salvador stirred. The older man didn't look at him as he continued.

"That's exactly what it is, Eric."

He doesn't call me by my first name very often.

"Probably that's what the evidence will show. Sir," Salvador added.

I've seen friends die before. I didn't sit down and cry. I did my job. I can do it now.

He hadn't been this angry then, either. He'd killed every mouj he could while he was doing tours on the rock pile, and it had been a lot of tours and a good round number of kills, but he hadn't usually hated them. Sort of a sour disgust, most of the time; he hadn't thought of them as *personal* enough to hate, really.

This is extremely personal. Now I hate.

"Chief."

That was one of the evidence squad. He walked around the pool of blood to them. "We got something on the windowsill, going out. Sort of strange. When did you say you got here, Salvador?"

"Three thirty. Half an hour after . . . Cesar called me."

The night outside was still dark, but there was a staleness, a stillness to it, that promised dawn.

Baffled, Salvador shook his head. The man held up his notebook. The smudge he'd recorded on the ledge turned into a print as he ran the enhancement. A paw print.

"You notice a dog? Or something else like that?"

"No," he said dully. "Just a cat."

"Well, that's not it." The print was too large for a house cat. "Probably just something drawn by the smell. Big coyote maybe, the things are all over town."

"Time of death?"

"Recent but hard to pin down, on a warm night like this. Everything's fully compatible with sometime between the time you got the phone call and the time you called it in."

The chief put a hand on his shoulder and urged him outside. He fumbled in the pockets of his jacket and pulled out a cigarette and lit it.

"You know you can't be on this investigation, Eric," the older man said. "Go home. Get some sleep. Crawl into a bottle of tequila like a worm to get some sleep if you have to. Take a couple of days off and as many bottles as it takes."

"That doesn't last," he said.

"It works for a while, and the pain afterwards distracts you too," the chief said.

Salvador nodded, flicked the cigarette into the weedy gravel of the front yard and walked steadily over to his car. He pulled out very, very carefully, and drove equally carefully to Saint Francis, down to the intersection with Rodeo and the entrance to the I-25. Only then did he pull over into a boarded-up complex of low buildings probably originally meant for medical offices or real estate agents, built by some crazed optimist back in the late aughts or early teens.

"Okay, Cesar, talk to me," he said aloud, and slid the data card he'd palmed into the slot on his notebook; nobody would notice, not when he'd left his shoes standing in the pool of blood. "This had better not be your taxes. Tell me how to get the *cabrón*."

The screen came on, only one file, and that was video. Salvador tapped his finger on it.

Vision. Three ten in the carat at the lower right corner. Cesar was sweating as he spoke, wearing a bathrobe but with his Glock sitting in front of him within range of the pickup camera; the background was his home office–cum–TV room, lit only by one small lamp.

"I'm recording this before you get here, *jefe*, 'cause I've got a really bad feeling about this. I was on the Net tonight and I got a query from the Quantico analysis lab we sent the puke and blood to back when before we were told to back off, you know? They said there were some 'interesting anomalies' and did I want any more information on the Brézé guy, they attached the file. It *looked* like a legit file, it was big enough."

Cesar's image licked its lips; he could see that, but Salvador's mind superimposed how he'd looked with half his face lying in a pool of his own blood.

"Okay, it was a trap and I was stupid. I should have asked them, 'Who dat, never heard of no Brézé, me,' or just hit the spam blocker. But we weren't getting anywhere, creeping into Adrian Brézé's house like we planned would be desperation stuff, so I downloaded. Here's what I got, repeated a whole lot of times."

Letters appeared, a paragraph of boldface:

—youaresofuckedyouaresofuckedyouaresofuckedyouareso—

"I—"

"Cesar!" A scream in a woman's voice from another room, high and desperate. Then: "Don't—don't—*please, don't*—"

Then just screaming. Cesar snatched up the pistol and ran. Salvador heard himself screaming too, as the shots began. Then more sounds, for a long time. Then another face in the screen.

It was the woman he'd seen in the dream; he could tell, even though her face was one liquid sheet of dull red. Only the golden flecks in her eyes showed bright, and then her teeth were very white when she licked them clean.

"You are *so* fucked," she crooned, and the screen went black.

Eric Salvador choked as the tears ran down his face. His hand twitched towards his pistol and he forced it to lie still.

There were far too many people who had to die before he did. People he had to talk to. Adrian Brézé, for starters.

Adrienne Brézé lay back in the big hot tub, watching the high cold stars slip by in the skylights overhead and enjoying the gentle eddies of the hot lavender-scented water. Her toes floated slightly above the surface with wisps of mist half veiling them, but the regenerated foot was now just as large as the other and only slightly pink; for that matter, her hair was shoulder-length again. No trace of the famine-gauntness remained on the rest of her.

"I'm back to my full, magnificent form," she said.

There were three other people in the room with her, besides Monica. Theresa Villegas was a thin, dark woman in her forties and the household manager, which to a Shadowspawn meant considerably more than overseeing the maids, or even scaring up the human refreshments for parties. The household was the instinctive unit of organization for her breed, the way clans were for Homo sapiens. Harold Bates was recorded somewhere as head of security for Brézé Enterprises; that meant he ran her human mercenaries, mostly Gurkhas. David Cheung was young, extraordinarily fit, with the sort of build you saw on gymnasts or martial artists, and sleekly handsome. She used him as a guard and enforcer, among other things; it was a rather unusual arrangement.

But the whole point of being a Progressive is not to be overly bound by tradition, hein?

By her elbow there was a dish of smoked salmon and little spiced shrimp on toothpicks and a glass of slightly chilled New Zealand gewürztraminer—quite extraordinarily good; she made a note to acquire the vineyard as she nibbled and sipped.

"The arrangements?" she said.

"Your great-grandfather agreed to the meeting," Theresa said efficiently, her eyes flicking down to her tablet for an instant. "His personal reply . . . I quote: '*Quelle surprise,* we Brézés are infernally hard to kill.'"

"I think he used *infernal* with malice aforethought," she said, chuckling. "Alas, he retains a sentimental attachment to the satanist part of the family heritage. Emotionally if not literally. Captain Bates?"

The mercenary nodded. "The security plan is ready for implementation, Ms. Brézé," he said in upper-class British tones.

"Good, it would be tiresome if there were interference. I need to consult closely with Great-grandfather and Great-grandmother, without distractions."

"I understand your brother consulted with them first," the Englishman said. "Is that likely to create difficulties?"

"No, no. I wanted him to make his appearance first. It will confirm certain assumptions he has made about my plans. Because, at the time he saw them, Étienne and Seraphine *shared* those assumptions, you see? I did not want to illuminate them for fear he would sense something. He is astonishingly sensitive at times, my dear sibling."

She looked at David. "And we'll need you active when we arrive, so go wait for me. You can sleep afterwards."

The young man grinned, bowed, and left through the door that led into her private chambers. She caught a flicker of verbalization from Bates; they'd been in close enough proximity for long enough that her mind had begun to decode the symbol structure of his.

"I don't think you think much of David, Captain Bates." She laughed.

His mind jerked in alarm; then he tried to focus on a mathematical formula. As a shield, it was pathetic.

"He's very useful as an instructor in hand-to-hand combat," he said neutrally. "Surprisingly so, for someone so . . . academic."

"I've given him the opportunity to fight *for real* quite a few times," she said. "That means he's not just a dojo ballerina anymore. And, Captain Bates?"

"Ma'am?"

"You're really not in a position to indulge a feeling of moral superiority, you know."

"I, ah, have no such opinion of Mr. Cheung, ma'am."

"Oh, yes, you do. Really, you should have realized by now that you can't lie to me. *Gigolo* was among your unkind thoughts. You're a very able man, Captain Bates; you're also quite satisfyingly venal and sadistically murderous, which is why despite the drawbacks you find my employ so satisfying."

She held up a hand. "Not a criticism! Just an observation! And you work for a monster; you can't trust me, but you can't keep secrets from me, either."

"Your service has been . . . educational, ma'am."

"What was that? 'Peeled back the lid'? Yes, I suppose so. And you're helping upend that can and spread a nice thick layer of what's inside all over the world. Do keep that in mind, my little toenail of Satan."

"Yes, ma'am. I'd better get to work on the details if we're traveling overland from Paris."

"By train," Adrienne amplified. "Call it the Orient Express. Then by ship from Istanbul."

Theresa smiled thinly and followed him, her tablet tucked under her arm. The Villegases had been renfields for a long time; one knew where one stood with them.

"But how much more authentic it would be if I were sailing across the Atlantic," she said sourly. "Mthunzi would just love that. Or if I had a log and a couple of humans to paddle it for me. Or I could try being a werealbatross and fry like an egg when the sunlight caught me. And then we could travel by *coach* to Tbilisi, through oceans of mud and streets running with shit."

"*Doña?*" Monica asked. "Mthunzi?"

"Oh, did I ever tell you about him? He's head of the Council eugenics program. He has been for most of the last century."

Monica shivered a little; she preferred not to think about other Shadowspawn. As far as possible she preferred not to remember that they existed.

"He's . . . not a friend of yours?"

"He's a reactionary fossil," Adrienne said. "Compared to him, my great-grandfather is a Progressive."

"What sort of name is that, Mthunzi?"

"Zulu. He wears this *absurd* costume at gatherings, with cow horns and beads and bells, a veritable witch doctor's outfit. Well, Great-grandfather dresses up in that Robe of the Dark Magus, like some Parisian version of Aleister Crowley . . . or Saruman . . . actually it was the other way 'round; Crowley was imitating him, with much poorer taste . . . but at least it looks striking and not just silly, and he doesn't wear a pointed hat."

"He'll be coming to Tbilisi too?"

"Yes. He wants us back in the *caves*. Caves are *boring*. I think he's just as aware of how Trimback One would probably be much worse than the projections as I am. He simply *wants* that."

The phone function sounded a quiet chime. "Here," Adrienne said; not many people had her private number, and she'd gone to a great deal of trouble to encrypt the link.

Or rather, others went to a great deal of trouble. They work, I enjoy the results; it's the natural order.

"Hi!" Michiko's voice.

"Ça va, Michi?"

"Nothing much, you know?" she said, with an utterly Californian rising inflection. "Oh, that Santa Fe thing, a couple of the locals are poking around where they shouldn't. I had the renfields warn them off, but it looks like they're being naughty and trying to keep it secret. . . ."

"Have them killed, then."

"I may go handle that myself. Nice to get in a little plain terrorizing and torture and butchery of unsuspecting ordinary humans now and then. The simple pleasures are the ones that last in the end, like steamed rice. I'm actually going to miss it once we're out in the open, the way their minds dissolve in fear when they realize what we *are*."

"That is delicious," Adrienne conceded. "Still, one can't have everything, and there's something to be said for lifelong dread and cringing fear. Wait, *Adrian* hasn't been around there, has he? That would be . . .

dangerous. The last I saw of him was too close for comfort. We don't want *him* suspecting anything too soon."

"Don't you think I could handle him?" Michiko bridled.

Not in a thousand years, Adrienne thought. Aloud she went on:

"Darling, *I* could barely handle him. He gave Dmitri all the trouble he could take just a few weeks ago. The poor boy is still sulking about Dale rescuing him."

"There is that. Well, he wouldn't be around here, would he? He killed my grandfather; Ichirō and I would be on the lookout for him, even if you were really dead. This is probably just one of those irritating things the humans do now and then."

"True. But he might drop by for his things, or the Power might prompt him; he *is* one of our generation, remember. Do keep alert."

"You know, this is as much my home as anywhere," Adrian said quietly.

They were sitting on a bench in Santa Fe's little central park on the plaza, eating ice-cream cones. The Palace of the Governors stretched in front of them, past the plain plinth of the Civil War memorial and the bandstand. He bit off a chunk of the cone; it was solid and smoothly rich, if not Berthillon, and there were piñon nuts in it as well.

The patch of cottonwoods and grass was drowsily peaceful on a Sunday morning, just cool enough for their Windbreakers to be comfortable on a bench in the shade. The thin mountain air seemed to impart an extra clarity to sight, as if everything were in a hyperrealist painting, sharp-edged and definite but with an unearthly glow to the colors.

"More than Paris?" Ellen said in a teasing tone.

"Much more," Adrian answered soberly.

I am a serious man, by inclination, he thought. *Gloomy and brooding, in fact. Ellen . . . lightens me. Not that she is light minded, but she has more of a sense of proportion. Considering all that has happened to her . . . well, I knew she was a remarkable person.*

"I was a young man in Paris, a student."

"What, Harvey didn't have you blowing things up and . . . Wreaking?"

"Yes. Though explosives are only occasionally useful against Shadowspawn—more often against their hirelings . . . but he thought I should have that experience, to make me . . . how did he put it . . . less of a *fuckin' wing nut* than most members of the Brotherhood. Many are born into the war, you understand, and it does strange things to the mind to be raised so. Others are recruited after an encounter with the Shadowspawn, and that is usually still worse."

"Did you like Paris, being a university student, being normal? Well, relatively normal."

"I loved it. I will always remember the city fondly . . . but there, even though I was estranged from the family, I could never forget that I was a Brézé. The very stones of the place spoke of them."

"And you didn't feel at home when you were a kid?"

"With my foster parents in my childhood I was living a lie—that I did not know it at the time makes no difference in retrospect."

"What about Harvey? He raised you."

"Nomadically, though I loved his place in Texas, the little ranch in the Hill Country. We moved frequently even then. When I became an active fighter for the Brotherhood, we moved every week, or nearly—and that was when I was sixteen. When we were not holed up in safe houses or redoubts. In a place in the Yukon for a whole winter, once, for training, and for the Brotherhood's adepts to study me. Besides . . . though I tried to think of Harvey as a father, he was more like an elder brother to me. We are only a decade apart in age, after all. He was in his early twenties when he . . . rescued me. I was twelve."

Ellen blinked. She knew that, but it was hard to keep in mind when it looked as if Harvey were a full generation older. He could sense a slight discomfort; she'd been startled and put out when she first learned that there were twenty-five years between them, rather than the three or four his appearance suggested.

Which was one excuse I gave myself for driving her away, he thought. *Stop wallowing in guilt, Adrian! It is a self-indulgence and makes for nothing but paralysis!*

By the elbow she gave him in the ribs—quite hard—she was thinking the same thing. Base-link or no, she'd grown disconcertingly able to follow his train of thought. It was a little like telepathy, only shields and blocks were of no use whatsoever.

And I have been an excessively private man, as well, Adrian thought. *It is hard, learning to share. But worth the effort and discomfort, a thousand times over.*

"This was the first place I could be *myself,*" he finished.

She licked her ice-cream cone and snorted slightly.

"Alone, lonely, brooding on a mountaintop. The happiest time of your life!"

"No, the months since our marriage have been the happiest time of my life," Adrian said, and glowed at the smile that rewarded him. "But the years here, they were . . . calm, for the most part. The days, at least. At night I could run beneath the stars, and come to terms with my demons and my past."

"Sounds like you needed it, honey," she said.

I needed to make myself worthy of you, he thought but did not say; even a newly wedded couple had to have *some* sense of restraint.

"I love this place too. It was where *I* was first on my own, making my own living as an adult. NYU didn't really count, there I was working *three* jobs and studying too."

She smiled, her full, curved Cupid's-bow lips were particularly charming with a little smudge of chocolate ice cream at one corner. She licked it up, which was both charming and disturbing.

"I remember the first time I came here, it was for the job interview, and I had lunch over there at the Plaza Café," Ellen said. "It was January."

She nodded towards the restaurant that occupied the center of the block of two-story Territorial-style adobes facing the open space. It had been there for over a century, since just after the First World War, when this square had had the only paved streets in the city . . . town, it had been back then. Oddly enough the food was, and always had been, rather Greek in emphasis.

"I had a gyro, and then a big piece of that heavenly coconut cream pie, and sat and sipped my coffee and watched the snow fall. Big thick fluffy flakes, you could just see the cathedral up there, and then you couldn't as it got dark, and it kept snowing; I didn't know it was unusual, but it wasn't *like* snow in Pennsylvania somehow, the light seemed to make it glow from within, and I remember thinking that I understood a lot of Southwestern paintings that had looked like exaggeration or kitsch. After dark I walked out and it was like being in a snow globe, perfectly silent, all the sound hushed. . . ."

"We will have a day like that together, sometime," he said.

She slid a hand into his. "You know, we should have done all this backstory stuff the *first* time we got involved."

"Ah . . . that wasn't possible. . . ."

"It was like trying to talk to a *lobster*!" she said. "You were the sexiest guy I'd ever met, and the most mysterious, and I *knew* there was something inside, but I could *get* there. Click go the claws, talk to my shell, scuttle away!"

The tone was mock angry, but he could sense a flicker of real grief behind it, and he squeezed her hand in apology; it was all he could do.

"No *wonder* I threw a bottle of brandy at your head and stomped out. Women like to *communicate*, you know. It's a foible we have."

"Men prefer to grunt, belch and scratch themselves," he said, his tone solemn. "It's a foible—"

She freed her hand for a moment and thumped him on the back of the head.

"So, let's go talk to Giselle," she said.

"It may be useful."

"It's *certainly* necessary. She's my Harvey, Adrian. She gave me my first real job and she mentored and mother-henned me and listened to me cry. She did a lot more for me than any therapist ever hatched."

"Born."

"Therapists are hatched, like other reptiles. Anyway, I owe Gis a lot."

And she advised you I was too creepy for words and that you should leave me, Adrian thought. *I should not resent that; it was quite true and simply showed she was perceptive and had Ellen's best interests at heart. Nevertheless I* do *resent it. I must simply do my best to control that.*

They held hands as they walked over to La Fonda, the Harvey hotel on the road that ran up to the cathedral; it was built in the classic faux-adobe-Hopi-Hispanic style of the reconstructionist nineteen twenties, which made it of respectable antiquity itself now. Then right across the bed of the Santa Fe River. Adrian smiled to himself as he felt the little flares of envy from others who saw him with Ellen. It was perhaps not the noblest of pleasures, but still definitely a pleasure.

She chuckled as they crossed the bridge and she looked down at the dry creek bed. Adrian raised a brow, and she spoke:

"I was remembering a comic I heard once, a local, doing an act with a fake Blues song:

> And I was so goldurn sad that night
> If there'd been any water in the Santa Fe River
> I'da jumped right in and drowned.

Adrian chuckled too. "I wish I could have gone with you," he said.

She squeezed his hand. "I noticed that when we were dating . . . the first time, before it all came out . . . you always took me *lonely* places. That time we went to your beach place down on the gulf near Corpus Christi, all the other stuff."

"Habit. You have made me less solitary. Not that I will ever be gregarious."

"I'd die of shock to see you become a people person, honey. You're not cut out to be a glad-hander."

They turned left, uphill this time, along the winding course of Canyon Road. Originally it had been a stretch of little farms, ranchos where Spanish-Mexican settlers and their retainers had used water from the river and the Acequia Madre, the Mother Ditch, to grow patches of grain and fruit and raise pigs and chickens, goats and sheep and burros.

Many of the trees were still there, and the rambling adobe-and-stone houses they'd built to house their extended families, long since converted to other uses as the city grew around them.

Some a little farther back from the road along narrow alley were high-priced residences; over a hundred art galleries and studios stretched along this mile of winding street. The new construction blended in, being low-slung and stuccoed in brown with vigas, wooden beams with their ends exposed, supporting flat roofs. Many of the gardens were lovely, though those were mostly in the courtyards at the back, glimpsed through gateways. The art, though . . .

Adrian grinned at one modernist interpretation of a Hopi or Navajo medicine man, a stick-thin figure with a bulbous mask and antlers reaching for the sky.

"Bullwinkle the shaman!" he laughed.

Ellen joined him for a moment; then he could feel a wave of confusion and fear.

"My darling?" he said gently.

"Adrienne made the same joke. When she had me tied up in my own apartment up there, that day after I ran into her on the road. She'd be *doing* things to me with a sock stuffed in my mouth or duct tape across it so nobody could hear the screams, and then it was this chatty, witty conversation and then back to the screams. . . . *God*, but I'm glad she's dead."

"I too," Adrian said, forcing down his rage.

You cannot take revenge on the dead, he thought. *It is one of the few real disadvantages to killing your enemies. But some of them are too dangerous to let live an instant more than it takes to kill them.*

Ellen took deep breaths and her mind calmed.

"Okay, she's your evil twin, it's only natural you'd see the same joke sometimes."

Hans & Demarcio Galleries wasn't open, but as Ellen had predicted, Giselle was there, working in her office at the back. A little pounding brought her to the front door. She opened the door with her mouth sagging, then turned gray and began to topple backwards towards a plinth that held a vase. It rocked as Ellen threw her arms around the older woman; Adrian felt the Power flow automatically as he lunged forward leopard-smooth to grab the dark feather-patterned piece of pottery out of the air. Not even Shadowspawn reflexes could have caught it before it shattered on the tile floor without his pushing the probability curve.

"Here," he said. "I would not want to destroy an original Maria Martinez."

Ellen gave him a quelling glance and took Giselle's arm. The older woman was still pasty with the shock, and making little gasping sounds. Her former assistant steered her into the office at the rear of the gallery's long rectangle, pushed her into the office chair and hunted up a glass and a bottle of sherry from a cabinet.

Quite passable sherry, too, Adrian thought; it was a Barbadillo San Rafael with tart, leathery scents and the taste of crushed toffee. *A little sweet, a woman's sherry, but very good short of the V.S.O.P. level.*

The gallery owner gulped the first glass as if it were water or a shot of bad bourbon; even then Adrian couldn't help wincing slightly. He occupied the moment and gave the two friends a little privacy by examining the shelves. The room had the orderly chaos of someone who knew where everything was, but probably couldn't have told someone *else* how to find anything to save her life. There were a couple of very good local pieces in spots where the skylight gave adequate light, though; one seemed like pure Abstract Expressionist when he first saw it, but the closer he came the more it looked like a local sunset seen from a tall dropoff.

Giselle Demarcio cleared her throat. Adrian turned around; she was dabbing at her eyes with a Kleenex, and then gave a honking blow.

"I thought you were *dead*," she said to Ellen; her voice held a slight trace of East Coast big city. "*Or* off somewhere with his *creepy* sister."

Adrian sat; the chair was comfortable despite the local rustic make. Ellen sat beside him and took his hand again. She held the paired grip up, so that Giselle could see the wedding ring, and Adrian showed his own.

"You're *married*?"

"Quite happily, Ms. Demarcio," Adrian said.

"And to each other, at that, Gis," Ellen added dryly.

Demarcio was getting her composure back; Adrian could feel the roil in her mind subsiding, the random flicker steadying into the wave-like patterns of coherent thought. He couldn't tell *what* she was thinking, apart from the emotional overtones—that would require days of close association—but he could tell that she *was* thinking, which was impressive.

"After you went off with his . . . with Adrian's sister . . ."

"I didn't," Ellen said, with almost clinical detachment. "She kidnapped me. And burned down my house, nearly killing the Lopez family in the process. Would have killed them, except for Adrian and a friend of his. And she . . . did some very unpleasant things to me. Quiet a lot of unpleasant things for several months. Mmmm, drugs and brainwashing, you might say, besides the chew-toy stuff. Adrian rescued me."

"Oh," Demarcio said again. "Oh, the *bitch*!" Her thoughts spiked, settled into a mixture of sympathy and rage. . . . "Oh, you poor thing!"

Ellen shook her head and smiled. "I'm a survivor, Gis," she said. "You know that."

Demarcio nodded. "I suppose this means you *don't* want me to keep the job open?"

The two women shared a laugh; then the gallery owner turned to Adrian again. He could feel—and could have seen, even if he were mind-blind—her suspicions click into place once more.

"What do the police have to say about this?" she asked shrewdly, her eyes darting between them.

"Nothing," Adrian said. "My sister is dead. And . . . Ms. Demarcio, some people cannot be controlled by the police, by the authorities. By any conventional means. They are too rich, too . . . powerful for that."

Demarcio nodded, and he could feel her agreement; it was something like the scent of mint. Ellen had told him a good deal about her, among other things that she was a rather paranoid variety of left-winger. That didn't interest him in itself—human politics were a smoke screen, self-deluding nonsense at best, and had been throughout the century since the Council of Shadows reached its full monstrous power. But that mind-set *would* predispose her to believe an edited version of the truth.

Since the world really is *ruled by an all-powerful evil conspiracy. Just one of werewolves and vampires and sorcerers, rather than capitalists and generals.*

"But you can deal with them?" she asked him sharply.

He nodded. "I must, I find," he said. "After what happened to Ellen. And my sister was not acting alone. She was part of a, umm, cabal.

283

Of . . . younger members of some very old, very powerful families. Families that already wield great hidden power, you understand; shadowy influence within governments and corporations and intelligence agencies. Influence sufficient to silence or kill those they consider threats."

"Like, for example, *your* family, the Brézés?"

"Yes. I have been something of a family black sheep, you might say."

I actually managed to say all that without outright lying, he thought, slightly amused. *It's even accurate to call Adrienne's followers a cabal. Shadowspawn politics work that way, like a Bronze Age monarchy's court intrigues. Or the other way 'round, since those kings probably had a great deal of our blood. As one might expect from their taste for human sacrifices.*

Demarcio sat watching him for half a minute. "You're not telling me everything, are you, Mr. Brézé?"

"Adrian, I think," he said, smiling and indicating Ellen.

The charm of the smile bounced off her like buckshot off a battleship.

"You're not, are you, Adrian?"

"No. Because you have no need to know more, as yet; and because knowing more would endanger you. Endanger your life."

"Oh."

A flash of apprehension, very little of which showed. "Is this a social call, then?"

He shook his head. "Not entirely, Ms.—"

"Giselle."

A nod. "Not entirely, Giselle. I'd like to know what happened here after we all, how shall I say, *left*. It would be entirely in character for Adrienne to have . . . energetically suppressed any police investigation. Naturally they would have asked you questions; and questions sometimes reveal information as much as answers do."

And naturally you would have found out as much more as you could: out of concern for Ellen, and because according to her you are the biggest gossip in Santa Fe and possessed of an insatiable curiosity.

"There was a detective, two of them, SFPD. They came around, asking questions. And then . . . nothing. When I called, they said the investigation had been moved to the dead-files section. That was . . ." She cleared her throat, then continued: "That was when I thought you must be dead, Ellen."

Her beaming smile died. "Then there was the incident, a couple of months ago."

"Incident?" Adrian said.

His voice was still calm, but there was an edge of danger to it now. He could feel the flux in her mind, the primal fear of death welling up. And a ghost wind touched the back of his neck as well, the Power hinting of risk. An effort of will fought down the instinctive rage that the presence of another Shadowspawn in *his* territory brought. His breed were still more jealous of such things than normal humans, and whatever his conscious convictions, the back of his mind still thought of this place as *his*.

"One of the detectives . . . Cesar Martinez . . . was found dead. With his girlfriend. They're calling it a murder-suicide. The details were, well, pretty gruesome. Then—"

Adrian listened through the description, and called up the newspaper reports on his tablet. His brows went up.

"Thank you very much, Giselle," he said, after they'd made arrangements to meet for dinner. "That was, as they say, interesting. And suspicious."

Demarcio looked as if she'd like to shiver, despite the comfortable temperature. She shook hands with him, and hugged Ellen fiercely.

On the street outside Ellen sighed. "It's going to be rough explaining to her that we're just here for a visit," she said.

"It would be no favor to spend too much time in her presence," he said grimly. "That double murder is a classic. Tōkairin Michiko, at a guess, now that my sister is no longer with us."

Ellen shivered. "Michiko wanted to kill *me*, right there, that evening," she said. "I can remember her waving a crab leg in that restaurant in San Francisco and saying how much fun it would be for the two of them to kill me together, and smiling at me as if I were supposed to chime in with, 'Oh, that sounds hot.' And when Adrienne said she had other plans for me, the mad bitch pouted *at me*, as if she expected me to agree what a poopy stick-in-the-mud killjoy Adrienne was being."

He reached into his jacket and pulled out his cigarette case, ignoring a brace of hostile looks as he lit up. Ellen scowled and pushed her hands deeper into the pockets of her jacket; she'd more or less given up on pressuring him to quit.

"She is not a nice person," Adrian replied. "And her passion for little masterpiece atrocities—"

"Like a pointillist painter. Maybe she likes playing up the dragon-lady thing."

"Precisely. Or her liking for being hands-on. That weakness means that perhaps we can arrange that something not very nice happens to *her*."

"Oh, yeah." Something deadly flickered in Ellen's voice for a moment. Then: "You sure she came and took care of it *herself*?"

"Probably. We will have to check, of course. It might be worthwhile to contact this surviving detective; at need, I could blur his memories afterwards. I do not like doing that, both because of the effort and because it is ethically a little dubious. But one does what one must."

"She's the big Shadowspawn honcho of the west now, she and her hubby, now that her grandfather's dead."

"He is a retiring type. By our standards."

"So how come she doesn't just send a goon to do it?"

Adrian shrugged. "Boredom, perhaps. Shadowspawn don't go in for large organizations, my dear; they don't even make optimum use of the human ones they control. And they act on impulse. A highly *educated* impulse. We must investigate further."

CHAPTER SIXTEEN

"**W**e're well settled in and getting some results," Peter Boase said.

"No complaints about the facilities?" Harvey Ledbetter asked.

"The cook, pardon me, the *chef*, is too good. Fortunately this is a great area for high-impact running and looks like it'll be great for cross-country skiing, too. Otherwise I'd look like a blond garden slug with limbs, but otherwise no complaints, nada. Anything we want appears like magic as fast as FedEx can fly."

Harvey looked around at the pines. Peter had the wiry, tensile build of a cross-country man, and this would be the perfect ground for it. The old base had been tucked away in a remote valley in Dalarna, designed to ride out a Soviet nuclear strike and provide a center for prolonged resistance. It was blasted deep into the granite up where Sweden faded into Norway in a tangle of hills graduating into mountains. The hills were densely green with fir and birch, and he could hear the sound of trick-ling water, smell rock and greenery and sap, watch a squirrel run chat-tering up a tree like a streak of red fire. The sun was bright, though it was well after eight, and it glittered on the long narrow lake below. Snow peaks shone like white salt far to the west, floating like the ramparts of Jotunheim in a saga.

I wish I hadn't thought about that, Harvey thought. *Man-eating Et-tins. Christ. The stories are all about* them, *when you get right down to it.*

"Better be a bit more explicit about that there progress, Professor," Harvey said.

Peter smiled—he looked much better than he had the last time Harvey saw him, which said a good deal for his basic resilience and toughness.

Gotta remember that the opposite of badass is not *weenie,* Harvey re-minded himself. *That's a risky way to think, could lead to underestimating people, which can lead to a bad case of the deads.*

"This isn't like any research project I've ever worked on," Boase said. "No bureaucracy, no nonphysical constraints on equipment, only the security considerations are anything like what I'm used to."

"Glad you're happy," Harvey said. "The Brotherhood hasn't done much scientific research before; we didn't think in those terms."

"I suppose you don't, when you're a *magician*," Boase said.

"It ain't magic. We've known that for generations now."

"But you've been *using* it as if it were magic."

Harvey could feel a combination of fear and resentment and fasci-nation in the other man's mind; he suspected that the existence of the Power just plain *offended* the physicist. That it had been in the hands of black-arts secret societies and their esoteric opposite numbers probably offended him even worse. It was a good thing he'd never seen a meeting of the Brotherhood's leadership, with the white robes and doves and meditation and chanting. The meditation actually served a useful purpose; the rest was pure theater, a relic of their origins as witchfinders. Though you could eat the doves, in a pinch.

Harvey shrugged. "For that matter, this operation is really sorta off the reservation, Adrian bulldozin' his own priorities through. Since he controls the financing, no reason for the leadership not to go along. Now, about the *results*?"

Boase smiled. "I actually got nearly all the theory done while I was at Rancho Sangre," he said.

For a moment his handsome, good-natured face turned savage. "And she'd *really* be going to regret that if she were still alive."

"If she were still alive, you'd still be there. Now, the *results*."

"The essential thing was realizing that the Shadowspawn brain doesn't *create* the oomph that you guys call the Power. It just *modulates* it, like a transistor does electric currents; the basic force comes from the substrate of the universe. Saying that someone is 'strong in the Power' just means they can tap more without frying their neural circuitry, the centers that step it up and direct it. But a brain is a physical object, and what one object does another can do."

"Wait a minute, you've got some sort of computer that can use the *Power*?"

Boase shook his head. "Oh, no. Not for a long time, like two or three paradigm shifts in our ability to process information. Generations, even if the whole world were trying really hard. A computer as we know it, a Turing machine, is far too, ah, too coarse a mechanism. The brain has a subatomic, a quantum element that's essential to consciousness, and it's that part that interacts with the substrate of the universe, the holographic—"

The words stopped making sense; Harvey shook his head impatiently. "Cut to the chase."

"Okay, we'd need a quantum computer as sophisticated as a brain to really handle the Power. With *that* we could fry any protoplasmic adept. We'd be the next thing to God, which worries me a little, but we don't have it and we aren't going to in our lifetimes anyway. But. The way silver screws up the Power, and the transuranics, was a clue. There's one simple thing that we thought we *could* do with the electromagnetic spectrum, provided we—"

Boase lapsed into Old High Technicalese again; Harvey spoke with dangerous patience:

"Don't tell me about the dilithium crystals, boy, just tell me what they can *do*."

Peter smiled beatifically, glanced at his phone's time display, and waved a hand behind him.

"Look," he said. "I was stalling for this."

Harvey turned and did. "Well, fuck me blind," he said mildly, blinking in astonishment.

That was a particularly appropriate oath. The entrance to the complex was disguised as a farmhouse, red painted, with barns and outbuildings of the same, all looking considerably run-down; it had been mothballed most of a generation ago, and the new occupants had left as much of the patina of neglect as they could. The dirt road was more like two ruts through weeds, and only a careful observer would have noticed the wear of a great many trucks last year.

The actual entrance to the tunnels was through the "barn," which had doors big enough for heavy vehicles; the whole thing was splendidly camouflaged, and the power source was an underground water turbine powered by a mountain stream, so there wasn't even much of a heat signature.

None of that meant anything to the Power, of course. Even Harvey's modest talent could sense the minds there, the flow of energies, and feel the bunching of world-lines. It was like a *smell*. The ability had evolved to track down humans doing their very best to hide—in caves, among other things—and to foil competitors equipped with the same brain centers.

Everything had an effect on the world, casting its shadow back from the infinite spray of possible futures into the present. A grain of sand on the other side of the galaxy did, though of course that was far too faint even for the greatest adept to detect. People most of all, because their minds touched the foaming substrate of reality even if they couldn't mold it the way a Power wielder did.

Only now it isn't there and I can't smell a thing, he thought. *It's like the Power doesn't apply there. But not in a way that would be obvious if I didn't already know otherwise. It's just about the most dramatic undramatic thing conceivable, when you think about it.*

"It's like it's vanished," he said, wondering. "Not like a silver barrier. You can *feel* that even if you can't get through it. Silver's like a hole in the universe, or like having a tooth drilled if you try to probe. This isn't an absence, it's as if there's nothing there *to* sense."

Boase was grinning from ear to ear. "How's *that* for accelerated R and D—"

Pop.

Harvey blinked. Everything was *back*, and now he could hardly believe that he hadn't noticed anything before.

"Whoa, that is one odd effect," Harvey said. "Sorta tampering with reality, if you know what I mean. Now you don't see it, now you do, and the whole universe switched over from one to t'other without making no fuss I could detect."

Boase was scowling and punching at his phone. He looked up as he did.

"Says the walking quantum effects manipulator!" he said. "*You* people have been screwing with *my* nice rationalistic if indeterminate worldview for *years* now."

Harvey was grinning too, happy enough that not even being classed with the Shadowspawn annoyed him. He supposed that from the point of view of someone who couldn't Wreak at all, it was fair enough.

"Hey, wait a minute," Boase said thoughtfully, pausing in midprod at the smartscreen. "I think I've just had a thought."

"Happens to most people with functioning brain stems every now and then. What sort of thought?"

"The Fermi Paradox."

"What . . . Oh, why we haven't had little green men droppin' in on us in flying saucers?"

"Yes. We know there are planets around most stars and a lot of them are Earth-like, we know that for sure now. Why hasn't anyone shown up or at least sent a message? But it just occurred to me that it's quite likely any species with a conscious brain would eventually evolve the Power—or some subset of every species would. And that means no science."

"How so?"

"Well, to invent the scientific method, you've got to believe in an orderly, rational, *deterministic* universe. The sort of billiard-ball world Newton and Laplace thought they were discovering."

"Hell, that isn't the whole truth, is it?"

"No, but it's the indispensible first step. But if the Power is around, the universe wouldn't feel that way. It would be *magical.*"

The word sounded slightly obscene in the scientist's mouth. He went on:

"It would be irrational, arbitrary. Mhabrogast glyphs, water running uphill because you *wanted* it to, doing things because they felt lucky, shaping reality by sheer willpower. I don't see how you could even get as far as a Hellenistic view of the world with that stuff around. Not if you're living in a fairy-tale world for real. It would look like Hansel and Gretel all the way down, and that means you'd never discover any way to really analyze the world—or even just the Power. And without that, you'd always be limited to what brains could handle, which means no interstellar flight. And if you had telepathy, would you ever want radio?"

"Phones are a lot less trouble."

"But not at *first*. And you'd never think that way to begin with."

Harvey looked up into the blue arch of the sky. "Oh, great, a universe full of Shadowspawn."

"Except here."

"Except here from the Bronze Age to the Victorians," Harvey said. He slapped Boase on the back hard enough to stagger him a little. "And with your help, Professor, we're going to keep it that way!"

Peter shrugged, embarrassed. "Anyway, the effect only lasted thirty-eight seconds," he said disgustedly. "Come on, Duquesne—"

A conversation happened; Harvey Ledbetter didn't even try to follow it. For one thing it was in New Middle Physics Babble-onian, a language he had never learned, and for another, unless he wanted to Wreak he could hear only half of it.

"What happened?" he said, when the other American pocketed his phone.

"Well—"

Harvey listened to two sentences and then held up a hand. "In Ignoramish!" he protested. "Pretend you're Samantha Carter trying to tell O'Neil something."

"Oh, you watched *SG-1* when you were a kid too?"

"Professor!" Harvey said; and he'd been a young adult, which suddenly made him feel his sixty-odd years more.

Boase stood silent for a minute, obviously lost in thought, then shook himself.

"Ah . . . we blew a fuse."

"That mean what it sounds like?"

"No, it's just a metaphor, and not a very good one either. Equipment failure, let's say. There was a spillover of . . . A fuse blew. But we have proof of concept."

"*Yes!*" Harvey shouted, punching his fist in the air.

When it came down he pointed his finger at the younger man's face.

"Son, if Duquesne *did* have a spunky, red-haired daughter, your handsome assistant ashes would get thoroughly hauled. She'd not only be smooching you, she'd be throwing herself on her back and throwing her heels towards her ears right this—"

"Hey, I'm *not his assistant!*" Boase said. "Hell, I'm his *boss*, if anything. I'm the theorist. He's the experimentalist. And most physicists do their best work in their thirties!"

"Yeah, he's just the man with the soldering iron." Harvey chortled. "You run along now and make one that's reliable for days at a time and doesn't weigh more than half a ton. Something we could put on an eighteen-wheeler truck and not take up more than, oh, half the load would do right nice."

"Wait a minute! Going from proof of concept to—"

"You *git*, you high-forehead wonder, you!"

Harvey stood quiet for a moment and then pulled out his own phone. It had a specialized little program that not only ate all record of the conversation at either end but erased it from the servers in between.

I come from a place northwest of San Antonio, he thought whimsically, as he waited for the acknowledgment icon as the little machines shook hands. *Paranoia County.*

Operation sheet is go, he tapped out.

It is?

Yeah. Fondest expectations and all.

A long pause, and then: *All right. I'll want details on that, but provided you satisfy me, Defarge can proceed. Surprised you got Mowgli to sign off on it.*

I'm persuasive.

He turned off the phone function and did a purge just to be sure, then drew back his arm and threw. The little black oblong soared away, turning in the air and then hitting a lakeside rock with a faint *crack*. The pieces went into the lake like a string of pebbles, and then the crystal blue water closed over them.

"Hallelujah," he whispered.

Deep within his mind an image of a mountain city grew. And a fire brighter than a thousand suns. When he spoke again, for a moment his voice was an exultant shout that echoed off the hills:

"'For I am become death, breaker of worlds.'"

"At last, a place where neither of us sticks out, Jack," Anjali Guha said, looking out the window of her side of the cab. "Here in the entranceway to Europe."

"More like the stinking lower intestine of Europe," he said sourly, slumped behind the wheel of the waiting vehicle; the elevation gave a good view. "Which orifice it uses to eat *and* crap."

"I grant it is not beautiful," she said, and sniffed at air heavy with a mixture of stale brackish water and every variety of hydrocarbon. "Nor is it a rose garden."

Europoort-Scheldt wasn't. The whole area was reclaimed marshland in the Scheldt delta, flat as a tabletop, and covered in gray concrete for the most part to match the gray North Sea just visible beyond the cranes and container blocks, and the gray November sky above. The stacks of shipping containers around them were the most colorful things in sight, their blue and red and yellow in contrast to the many acres of oil refinery, the storage tanks, and the vast coal and iron-ore heaps. Boxy, hulking modern freighters plowed the waters, and heavy trucks and strings of freight cars moved in and out in an intricate computer-controlled dance.

"Still, Veracruz was worse."

"Yeah, it *literally* smelled like shit. This just smells like PetroDystopiaLand."

But they both *did* fit in with the human geography; Farmer had a generic northwest European look, as long as he didn't open his mouth and expose his heavily accented Dutch or French or American-variety English, and the Netherlands' long-standing connections with the east made her South Asian features boringly unremarkable anywhere outside the depths of tulip-growing rural Blondistan.

Besides which, I speak better Dutch than Jack does, she thought a little snidely. *Better English, too, if you want to be picky, and I do.*

They were dressed in stained blue overalls, and they had really *good* forged IDs as well. None of that would help them if some Shadowspawn simply followed a line of *might-be* down to the docks. Her own slight talent was already starting to shrill at her, a feeling like giant snake slithering through her dreams. Or as if her mind had looked too long into the sun, a rolling wave of flame and heat coming at her out of the future. On many of the possible world-lines that bomb was going to send lives by the tens of thousands into the stratosphere in a gout of radioactive flame.

Possibly including all the strongest adult Shadowspawn, she thought with savage satisfaction. *Oh, indeed, yes. Decapitation! So many years of defeat, and at last victory is possible.*

The freighter was the CM *Pavlina,* Panama-registered with a mixed but mainly Filipino crew, currently out of Mexico with a cargo that was officially mainly industrial parts. The Panamax cranes moved like vast robotic elephants as the last of the load came ashore, neatly grouped in rectangles four containers high, half a dozen technicians performing labor that would once have taken hundreds of stevedores days of effort.

The control unit on their dashboard beeped as the code for the container matched that loaded into the truck's computer. In a few years this wouldn't need humans at all . . . or perhaps in a few years this would be broken ruins, with the sea reclaiming it and the metal gantry shapes tilting up out of the mud.

Our job is to see that it does not happen. No wonder my precog is blinded, with Trimback facing us!

Jack engaged the engine and let the big eighteen-wheeler purr forward; it was a nearly new Daimler hybrid, and the all-glass control panel looked like an F-42's. It also prompted the driver in a female German voice that somehow conveyed a grating, hectoring, anal-retentive personality along with a strong Mecklenburger accent.

"Very slow," it said. "Continue strictly on this line—"

A glowing track came up on the screen forward of the wheel, with an outline of the truck approaching a matching form beneath the crane.

"Halt! Reverse ten centimeters!"

"Shut up; it's a fucking truck and I'm only two inches off!"

"Halt! Reverse ten—"

"Shut up, you fucking Nazi bitch!" Jack screamed, hammering a fist on the wheel and punching the controls more or less at random until he found the mute function; then he tapped the *ready* icon on the screen.

"Ve haff wayz of making you stop talkink!" he shouted, then added: "Sorry," in more normal tones.

Oh, my, but Jack is not wired too tightly at all now and then, Guha thought—not for the first time. *At least I only scream when I am dreaming.*

The screen switched to one of the pickups on the cab of the truck, showing the huge four-legged crane as it trundled over on its man-high wheels. The heavy weight spooled down smoothly and landed on the truck bed with a muffled *clunk*. Clamps were inserted and turned. Guha hopped down briefly, did a visual examination to confirm the video and sensors, and then climbed back in.

"You may now proceed to exit gate seventy-six-B," the truck said. "Please follow the indicated route. Do not deviate from the route or Europoort Security will be alerted. A condition of heightened security awareness is in force. Thank you."

"*Fuck* you, bitch!" Jack snarled, as he pulled away.

"It's just a truck, Jack," Guha soothed.

"Then it won't mind me calling it names, will it?" he grumbled.

Guha slipped a hand inside the toolbox and let it rest on the compact little Steyr machine pistol there; it wouldn't be much use if an adept were around, but it would kill stray renfields very effectively. The gray sky began to drizzle, and Jack was driving as much by the telescreens as through the windshield. They slowed again for the exit scan. There were more personnel there than usual.

"Uh-oh," Jack said softly.

The extra personnel were in camo fatigues and body armor; as they came closer she saw that they had C7 assault rifles and wore badges shaped like a burning grenade.

"*Koninklijke Marechaussee,*" she muttered. "So much for machine pistols. And they are not renfields. Not really, they do not know for whom they are working."

"Big fucking difference," Jack muttered.

Koninklijke Marechaussee meant Royal Gendarmerie; specialists in border protection and counterterrorism work, with a well-deserved reputation for professionalism. This wasn't a problem you could solve by slipping a couple of hundred euros from hand to hand.

And they had a van that looked like it was full of some sort of detection equipment to add to the usual scanners; she could sense its buzzing activity. The forty-foot container behind them was lined with lead fabric, among other things, but it *did* have a nuclear weapon in it, and it was a bomb made by amateur fanatics for a one-off use at that.

"You take care of the gendarmes," Jack said quietly. "I'll fox the machinery."

Guha nodded stiffly. "I would guess someone found the little workshop of the jihadi elves in Veracruz," she said. "And the DNA would tell them who made it."

The workshop would have, besides half a dozen very decayed bodies with interesting personal dossiers, an underground facility with unmistakable traces showing that someone had been handling plutonium there. Even if the original theft from Seversk hadn't been detected, which it probably had, the Veracruz thing would have security forces all over the world on the alert; even the Shadowspawn might be concerned, since they were more vulnerable to ionizing radiation than true humans anyway, especially when night-walking or postcorporeal.

Guha smiled grimly. A very long time ago, human rebels had slain Shadowspawn with everything from silver arrowheads to poison, but they had always buried the bodies with carved disks of natural pitchblende—uraninite—in the grave as well.

To make sure they *stayed* dead.

She licked dry lips as the computers in the gendarmes' equipment identified the serial number on the container and shook hands with the truck's own IT system and the Europoort mainframe. One of the military police held up a hand, carefully not standing in the way where a desperate terrorist might have run him down; the road had a pop-up toothed barrier that would rip their wheels to ribbons if they tried that anyway.

Another walked towards her side of the cab, and two more went towards the cargo containers with sensor paddles in their hands.

My, my, would they not get a surprise if they looked in there! she thought, fighting down a hysterical giggle.

"Can I help you, sir?" she said in excellent Dutch as she keyed down the window.

Jack slumped down in his seat; he couldn't go into full trance here, but that was close. And he had the easier task, dealing with the coarse and simple processes inside computer circuits. Though they were both going to be very shaky after this. Using the Power when you didn't have the biochemical equipment to feed on others—or even to use the ghastly stored blood that was a very bad alternative—meant that you were taking it out of yourself.

Guha felt a familiar, complex set of emotions shudder through her hindbrain. A dark longing that could never be satisfied, even if you gave in to it. She had enough of the inheritance to want to feed, but blood would simply be contaminated seawater to her stomach. Best not to think about it. That way lay madness; that way lay Gilles de Rais and Elizabeth Bathory and Jeffrey Dahmer.

I do not know if the ones like Sheila Polson are luckier or even farther down the ramp to Hell, she thought. *She* could *feed. She* does *use Red Cross blood, foul though that tastes, to give her strength. She could give in to the temptation, while I know it would be useless. She probably even feels that she is better because she has a real choice and refuses the power, the ecstasy. . . . I am not a bad person. I am just a good person who wants to do bad things. I know giving in would do nothing except make me hate myself even more.*

But the needs coiled down in the base of her skull knew nothing of reason or consequences. They just *wanted.* And they never went away, though it was worse when she used the Power.

"Goede middag, mevrouw," the yellow-haired gendarme said with a

flat, nasal accent in his standard Dutch, which meant he'd probably grown up speaking Frisian. "Papers, please.

"Thank you," he added as she handed over the manifest and the truck's papers and her and Jack's—false—IDs.

She noticed a *wachtmeester*'s single chevron on his sleeve, which made him a sergeant, more or less. He had a headset monocle deployed over one eye, part of a full mil spec infantry IT outfit; it would be reading her face and running the digitized pattern through the EU database, and matching it to the papers she'd just given him. That didn't worry her; planting data in computers just wasn't very difficult for the Brotherhood's specialists, who combined high-level conventional IT skills with low-level Wreaking. That worked better than the usual Shadowspawn habit of simply making the system forget them. A false positive was much more convincing than mere absence.

She wasn't very worried that they were slightly in violation of EU regulation (EC) No. 561/2006 on driver rest periods either, which just added a touch of authenticity. Nobody could actually abide by all of Brussels' pettifogging micromanagement even if they wanted to; sliding around it was a way of life.

"This all seems to be in order," the man said.

But he's tense. Not very tense, but alert. So if this is but a routine check and everything's in order, why—

"We will be doing a physical inspection of this container, madam," he said. "This is purely routine, due to the heightened state of alert currently in force."

He smiled, politely. So did the woman trooper behind him, with the C7 on the assault sling across her armored torso. Everyone was paranoid about this sort of thing since Marseilles.

The real irony was that if she'd been the jihadi lunatic they were looking for, she'd have a deadman switch rigged to the bomb, and Europoort-Scheldt and much of Rotterdam would cease to exist about now.

Training kept her from snarling. She couldn't just bludgeon his mind the way a purebred might. Instead . . .

Warmth. Such a pretty face. *Yes, you have warm feelings for me. Mother/sister/lover. Look into my eyes. . . .*

Feeling emotions was easy. Manipulating them was much harder; you had to sort of *tie* them to your own, then change what *you* felt. It took effort, and she could feel it drawing on the inner reserve, as if something deep inside her were draining away like blood through a wound. Guha smiled and gazed into his eyes, blue meeting a brown so dark it was almost completely black.

Such a nice young man. He joined the gendarmerie because he wanted to help people, to protect them. We know each other. We trust each other. . . .

The man blinked. "I'm . . . I'm very sorry to bother you," he said, mumbling a little.

The sharp blue eyes had lost their focus. He slurred in his birth speech, enough like both English and Dutch that she could follow along:

"*Mem . . . mem . . .*"

She remembered her own mother: the warmth, the comfort, the security that were like nothing you ever felt again.

"It's just that we're behind schedule," she murmured. "You can see that. And there're all these people behind us, waiting. We don't want to get into trouble. You don't want to cause us trouble. . . ."

She could feel the decision crystallizing in his mind, like a muscle flexing under her fingertips.

"What's the scanner say?" he said over his shoulder.

The woman with the assault rifle glanced at the team with the paddles and whispered, probably into a throat-button pickup.

"Absolutely clean," she said. "But they've got the machinery ready to open the container."

She looked and sounded part Indonesian by background, and was even younger, without any rank badges at all. Her mind felt a little puzzled by her superior's actions.

"Let them by, then."

"Sergeant, we're supposed—"

"We're supposed to stop one-tenth of one percent at random and so far we're over quota. The next but ten will do just as well. Pass this one through."

The truck accelerated soundlessly save for a slight whine of electrics as the barrier went up and the spikes sank into the roadway, then with a low burbling mumble as the turbodiesel cut in. The scraggly clutter of the area around the Europoort faded as they swung onto the A15 *snelweg* that ran all the way to the Ruhr; if you wanted to hide a needle, the best place was in a pile of needles, not a haystack, and this road swarmed with big trucks hauling cargo containers.

"You okay, Anni?"

Guha shook her head, clasping her arms around her middle. "Not so great, Jack. Overstrained. That was a stubborn man."

Cold. Empty, cold, alone. A bit nauseous too.

"Yeah, squareheads are like that. You did a great job. We definitely weren't the droids they were looking for."

She nodded jerkily, feeling his concern and walling it off. They pulled off into a desolate little place with just enough to merit the title of a truck stop, and the European equivalent of a motel; the noise of the thundering traffic was louder when they had parked and opened the door. A youngish man lounging against a cheap elderly hybrid threw away a cigarette and came over to meet them: thin and dark and shifty eyed.

"Here are the papers," Jack said, waving them while he spoke in the Italian that was their common language; it was easier than any of the other Western tongues for a Romanian speaker to acquire. "And here are three thousand euros in advance. You get the container to Istanbul and you get twenty more."

"*Sì, sì,*" the man said, smiling like a lamprey. "I know this is an important cargo, me. Very important, very *valuable*, eh?"

Beneath the growing physical misery, Guha felt a little comfort; you didn't have to have the old blood to be a bastard. Ordinary humans could manage that quite well on their own. Jack took a stride closer and his hand moved. From the mercenary driver's sudden *guukkk!* and wide-eyed stillness Guha knew what the other Brotherhood agent had grabbed.

"And, Shandor, if it *doesn't* get there, or if *anyone* opens that container, I will hunt you down and kill you. Slowly, with lots of cutting and burning and peeling and taking your teeth out one at a time, so you beg to die first. Believe me, the teeth hurt even worse than the balls. *I know.*"

Shandor tried to smile ingratiatingly, and Jack squeezed harder while staring into the man's eyes and smiling in a completely different way. She knew that look; nobody with any experience would doubt that Jack meant exactly what he said, or that he could do it. A faint scream and a very quick nod came together. The Brotherhood agent stepped back, and the driver quickly scrubbed a hand across his face to wipe away gelid sweat.

"Here's an extra thousand because I like the swift and decisive way you accept the reality principle," Jack said, extending a sheaf of bills, which was half snatched. "Don't fuck up."

Guha felt herself swaying as her partner came back, but she managed to remain upright until the truck pulled away towards the access ramp. Then she let herself lean against him as he helped her into the room they'd rented. Then she stumbled and half collapsed to fall face-down on the bed, shivering. The pain seemed to be *throughout* her, as if it were following her veins, or her nerves where they ran through the flesh.

Dimly she was conscious of hands undressing her, getting her into the bed, the sting of an injection. The pain was still there, but it ceased to matter quite so much as peace flowed out from the spot on her arm. Water and broth were held to her lips.

"So *hungry*, Jack," she said. "So *hungry*."

"It'll be all right," he said, holding her awkwardly against his shoulder. "It'll be all right. Don't worry. We're going to get them all."

Three days later she looked at the text. *"California?"*

Jack shrugged. "Looks like it."

"What about the bloody *bomb*?"

"It may actually be safer if we don't go near it," he said. "*We* might draw the attention of a Shadowspawn adept. By itself—"

"It stands out like a bloody fireworks!"

"Yeah, again. That's why we're holding it in Istanbul for now. Harvey

307

says he's working a way to disguise it, something new and radical. Plenty of time before Tbilisi."

She blew out her lips. "This is bad tradecraft."

"Yeah . . . I seem to say that a lot, you know? And now we'll be working with the Boy Wonder again." He grimaced at her frown. "Okay, I know he saved you. Hell, we'd all have died in that shitty motel if he hadn't shown up. So I'm grateful, right, but I don't *like* him."

"Or anyone else, Jack."

He sighed. "At least with him picking up the tab we don't have to fly coach."

"Magnificent, Great-grandfather," Adrienne said sincerely. "Merely an amusement, simply duck with figs and olives, but magnificent. Even better than the lemon-cured baby scallops."

"You eat with all the enjoyment of one back from the dead," Étienne said. "And I should know, since I *am* dead."

"Only the least important part of you," Adrienne replied graciously.

They were dining on one of the outdoor terraces of the Villa Leopolda, looking down over the acres of cypress and olive trees that studded the gardens and the moonlit waters of the Côte d'Azur far below. The villa was a Belle Epoque fantasy of tile and terra cotta and marble, originally built on a whim financed by colonial plunder over a century ago, like some Edwardian dream of ancient Rome. The mild warmth of the air was full of the scents of roses and lady-of-the-night jasmine; bougainvillea frothed down from the balconies overlooking them; below was a tumble of jeweled lights and gardens and the running lights of the yachts in the basins below.

"Such a pity that King Leopold did not transition to postcorporeal successfully," Seraphine said.

She was wearing the body she'd been born with, or the etheric equivalent: tall for a nineteenth-century Frenchwoman, and chestnut haired.

"Have I ever told you of the wonderful tour of his Congo Free State that we took in 'aught-three? The Force Publique officers were such good company, charming rogues. And their Batanga mercenaries were like frisky puppies, with their filed teeth and simple, earthy, substantial cuisine. A true example of the civilizing mission, a veritable utopia in the jungle."

Servants whose minds were a careful wash of no-thought whisked away the dishes, and brought out the entrée: a tiny suckling pig, its crisp skin delicately scented with lavender. Along with it came the first mountain mushrooms of the season, sautéed with onion and a little garlic, a dash of white wine, fresh tomatoes and tarragon, with just a touch of lemon juice and sea salt.

You have told me of your Congolese tour only seventeen thousand, three hundred and forty-two times, ma chere bisaïeul, Adrienne thought. *Beginning when I was about six. Though it sounds like a great deal of fun, if one enjoys the tropics; severed hands as currency, what a droll idea.*

"Yes," Étienne said. "Of course, a golden haze of nostalgia is only to be expected; in Europe in those days a certain discretion was required, whereas we could be quite free in the Free State, if you will pardon the pun. Poor Leopold. One would have thought him a natural, and his father was of a Black Dawn lodge, though of course that was before the breeding program really got under way on scientific principles. He could night-walk, a little, though his manifestation was weak. . . . It *did* take several minutes for his matrix to disintegrate after his body died, and it was rather interesting to witness."

"How we all laughed!" Seraphine said reminiscently, with a tinkling chuckle. "Seldom have I felt such utter despair. Subjectively his death must have lasted a thousand years."

"To hope for immortality and then have it snatched away . . . that would be exquisite," Adrienne admitted. "My, but this suckling pig is exquisite as well!"

"Of the season," Seraphine said. "But in spring, ah, the *Carré d'agneau a la Provençale* is superb here! We get ours from this shepherd in the mountains."

"Only here in the south does one experience lamb as it truly should be prepared," Étienne agreed. "Not only the herbs with which it is cooked, but the herbs on which its mother feeds in life up in the mountains and passes on to the lamb as it nurses."

Adrienne nodded and took a sip of her wine: a local vintage of no great fame, but more than adequate. The pork was indeed meltingly tender but firm enough for texture, and the kiss of the scallions and garlic in the oil that had been brushed on its surface complemented it completely. Not a complex dish, but one requiring real skill.

I must remember that satiety is a trap lurking before the feet of eternity, she thought. *Keep the capacity to enjoy the simple things, or life might well become a burden.*

The warm apricot tart with a dash of brandy went with the meal beautifully beneath the pale stars.

"Nice has grown too large," she said, sipping at the after-dinner pastis. "Does this not illustrate my point? At this stage of a dinner al fresco, one wishes to see the stars."

"True, true," her great-grandfather said indulgently. "You have convinced me, my descendant." A glimpse of something feral: "It would be well not to become tiresome, like your brother and his ludicrous earnestness."

"Oh, but it is in a much better cause, Étienne," Seraphine said soothingly. "And the dear girl has a point. I remember what this place was like when dear Leopold first built it. The night sky was truly lovely."

"True," Étienne said, mollified. "And at least the lad still shows good taste. That 'wife' of his . . . worthy of draining to the last drop, slowly, over years."

"*Oh*, yes," Adrienne said, lost in thought for an instant; when she blinked all three of the Shadowspawn were wearing identical smiles.

"Despite his convincing repentance, I still think he might have some sort of childish disruption planned for the Council meeting," Étienne grumbled. "That would make me truly displeased."

"Oh, I think we can manage to keep him from playing any reprehensible pranks," Adrienne said warmly.

They chatted idly for a while; the upcoming meeting in Tbilisi was the main topic, usually with an undertone of malicious gossip.

"And now for the true dessert," Seraphine said happily, and waved her hand.

The four chained to the fretted bronze poles began to scream as their vocal cords obeyed them once more. The Shadowspawn listened appreciatively.

"The children of the night, what music they make," Adrienne said, and all three laughed.

Then the victims stopped, panting and sobbing and transfixed as the lambent yellow eyes rested on them, speaking to instincts older than the age of polished stone. Adrienne had to admit it was a piquant group: a handsome French couple in athletic and well-kept middle age, and their teenage son and daughter, the beginning and end of the prime feeding years. The relationships offered so many interesting variations on emotional pain and degradation, as well as straightforward physical torment.

Their minds were a roil of terrified speculation already; being kidnapped and then left naked and unable to utter a sound during the meal was an excellent preliminary. So were the toys and cushions and implements scattered ready across the marble terrace between the terracotta jars with their trailing flowers, the little glowing brazier, and the expressionless servants standing by with hot, scented damp towels and fluffy dry ones.

Seraphine rose and let her clothes fall away as she did, falling through the momentarily impalpable substance of her body; then she transformed to a statuesque blonde.

"I've always favored this form for energetic amusements," she said. "A real strapping Danish Valkyrie."

She went to the mother of the family and gently touched her face, picking up a tear on one fingertip and then tasting it.

"Who . . . who are you?" the woman said. "Oh, God, you *changed*."

"We are the purpose of your being, *ma petite*," Seraphine said. "All your lives you have been walking towards this moment, this service of a purpose beyond your comprehension. Now it has come, for you and these whom you love so much. This night is all that you have left; be wholly present in what you are about to experience! It will be so *intense*."

She began to scream again as the sense of the words sank home and Étienne transformed, stalking forward stiff legged, with the wolf's great head held low. Seraphine flicked the chains open with her mind and threw the woman to the cushions.

Adrienne rose and sauntered over to the husband.

"And soon we will do this to the whole world," she murmured, stroking him as Seraphine fed and then lifted her face to the stars, blood running from the corners of her mouth, and her sulfur yellow eyes slitted in joy. "To literalize the metaphor."

CHAPTER SEVENTEEN

A drian Brézé stuck his hands in their thin leather gloves into the pockets of his jacket and closed his eyes, blanking the flow of his interior monologue until his mind was still and quiet and wary. Awareness of his surroundings swelled, until he was one with the cool fall day. Somewhere a dog grew aware of him, whined and went quiet; a cat on the other side of the street blinked from a windowsill, radiating an idle curiosity. The little house off Airport Road still had the yellow police tape across its doors, but he didn't think anyone was watching.

Sink in, sink in. . . .

Nothing. A few people in the other houses in the subdivision, young children and their mothers mostly; one adult peeking through the windows at his Ferrari for a moment, then shrugging aside a vague wonder. The suburb was solidly lower-middle-class and composed of flat-roofed frame houses making a feeble imitation of the haute-fake imitation adobe downtown, just the sort of place you'd expect a policeman to live in Santa Fe's high-cost, low-wage economy. He opened his eyes again and gave Ellen a quick slight nod where she sat behind the wheel of the low-slung sports car, felt her mind acknowledge it. She was wearing a scarf around her hair, and sunglasses, both absolutely unexceptional on a bright Wednesday afternoon. He was in jeans and ankle boots and a T-shirt, equally normal; the jacket was credible with the temperature in the mid-sixties, though he was actually wearing it to conceal the Glock and long curved knife the harness held on either flank.

There was a goat-stick fence beside the garage, five-foot unpeeled piñon sticks. He took three quick strides and vaulted over it, a hand lightly touching one of the poles, and came down silently on the balls of his feet. The backyard was similarly fenced all the way 'round; he wasn't hidden, exactly, but it was better than a wire barrier would have been. There was a weedy-looking Russian olive tree, a half-dead lilac, and plenty of genuine weeds, including the ferocious local goat's head, which dropped a little three-pointed seed that could cripple the barefoot or puncture tires. He thought of those as nature's caltrops. The rest was bare dirt, though his nose detected the recent presence of a dog. A bachelor's yard, one owned by a man without the time or interest to spend on appearances, right down to the battered barbecue grill that had gone a long time between cleanings.

He wrinkled his nose; there were drawbacks to the acute Shadowspawn senses. And beneath the old scorched meat and dog feces, a strong trace of rotting blood that made his lips start to draw up in a hunter's snarl. Adrian went to the glass sliding doors that gave onto a stretch of cracked concrete patio and produced a thin, slightly curved piece of steel. A moment's fiddling, a quick strong jerk, and something went *click* inside. He could have done the same with the Power, but he'd long ago decided to save that for purposes where nothing else would do.

Once he was inside the scent of old blood was much stronger; even a normal human would have found it unpleasant. Even decayed, it bore the traces of unbearable pain and raw terror; when fresh it would have been maddeningly appetizing. He followed it towards the single bedroom. Something else tickled at the senses there, the esoteric ones that came with his degree of the Power. Another Shadowspawn had been here, a powerful adept, either postcorporeal or night-walking. The traces were faint, too faint to identify an individual, but unmistakable. Gluttonous satisfaction as well, the killing frenzy and repletion. There was no need to go nearer to the outlines still painted on the floor or marked in tape on the tumbled, black-stained sheets. Instead he went to one knee and looked at the floor, bracing himself with a forearm on his thigh.

Black and rusty-brown, flaking away in the dry high-desert air, but the outlines of shoes were still visible, if you knew how to look. Someone had come in the front door and stood looking into the room with his feet in the pooling blood. Then he'd kicked off the shoes, stepped back out of the blood and turned. . . .

He followed the tracks. The place they led had been a bedroom on the original plans, redone as a study-den–entertainment center. One wall held a fairly big flat-screen, a Chinese-made early 3D model half a decade out-of-date. There were a couple of—rather bad—pictures of local landscapes, bookshelves that held a mixture of popular fiction and well-read volumes on police methods and forensics, law books and a desktop computer. The unknown had come in, sat in the office chair and used it.

Adrian extended a hand over the machine and concentrated.

Interesting, he thought. *The hard drive hasn't been pulled or wiped. Whoever was in charge here didn't do a real investigation; they just went through enough of the motions to fool outsiders. As I suspected, the Tōkairin had someone sit on it. And someone—Michiko at a guess, the traces feel a little female—came out to tie up the loose ends. But whoever sat here at the computer took something from it. . . .*

He switched it on, pulled a data stick from his pocket and snapped it into the serial port. Electronic pseudothoughts tickled at him as he waited for it to suck the larger machine dry.

Yes, a file copied just before the machine was shut down. I think Shadowspawn technophobia is about to give me a lead, he thought. *So much for the* Progressive *faction.*

This time he did let himself snarl. The low, guttural sound filled the house of death.

"Oh, my," Ellen said as they walked through the door. "Doesn't *this* bring back memories."

Adrian's house west of Santa Fe was large but not a palace, a low-slung, sprawling single-story thing built of genuine adobe as well as concrete and steel, in a style that mixed the area's traditions with a restrained modernism. The door was tall and sheathed with copper, facing the drive along the ridgeway that led to this point where cliffs fell from steep to sheer on three sides. She looked at the door. . . .

"Silver underneath?" she said. "Plus a little something for people rude enough to use explosive door knockers? I noted the fields of fire outside this time! And the cliff protects the other side."

"Silver, but of course." He grinned at her; she could tell he was enjoying both her wit and her pleasure in it. "And ceramic-steel composite sandwiched in between."

Damn, but I'm lucky to get a man who doesn't feel threatened by smart women. Of course, he's also a blood-drinking shape-shifter . . . but that's a feature, not a bug. It's not like cigarettes, after all. As long as we keep it to what my bone marrow can supply, there's no downside for either of us.

"In fact," he went on, "this hill is mostly silver ore. Not very rich silver, there was an attempt at a mine once but it did not pay, not enough precious metal spread through far too much very hard rock. Still, it is . . . was . . . why I picked *this* spot."

"And I thought it was the view," she said dryly. "Your being-high-up fetish."

"This from one with a tie-me-up-and-whip-me fetish?" he said, and ducked as she swiped at him.

Then he threw the bags through the door and swept her up to cross it; they were kissing and laughing as he bore her into the hallway beneath the vaulted exposed-metal roof. She leaned into his shoulder, enjoying the steel-cord strength of his embrace; then his arms locked hard around her and there was a nip at the base of her throat, and a hard suction. She shivered as warmth seemed to flow out from the bite, like scented soap suds in a bath of hot water sliding over her skin, leaving her whole body warm and flushed in an almost unbearable relaxation.

"Ah," she said a moment later, shuddering. "Now, *that* was what I call a welcome home."

"Welcome home, then," he said, striding through into the living room.

That had a glass wall overlooking the vast blue distance northwestward. That fell away to the high plain below in a tumble of boulders and canyons, juniper and piñon, home to eagles and deer and coyote. The room was spotless—Adrian's housekeeping service—but had the slightly lifeless feel to its air that came of long vacancy, with only a very faint scent of satchets and pine ash from the hearth.

God, it's nearly a full year since I stormed out and Adrienne caught me! she thought. *Not that I actually ever* lived *here, unless you count the odd overnight.*

"Well, put me down and we'll get unpacked," she said.

"Not quite yet," he said, setting her on her feet in front of him; the arms stayed around her, but now the hands roved.

"Mmm, nice . . . but we do need to get unpack— *Yeeek!*"

He pulled the dress up over her head, then down again behind her with a single strong jerk that pinned her arms tightly. Another two, and the bra and panties went flying in silken wisps; she had a moment's pang as she remembered the Parisian shopping expedition they'd managed to squeeze in, when she'd gone berserk in the lingerie section of a boutique on the rue Saint-Honoré.

"Adrian . . . God, that feels good. . . . Adrian, the *door's* still open! And we're in front of a *picture window!*"

"Fresh air and sunlight are good for you, wench."

A push between the shoulder blades sent her staggering forward; the arm of a couch struck her across the thighs, and she pitched forward with her toes just touching the slate flags of the floor. Goose bumps rose in the chilly air, and at the touch of the leather cushions on her belly and breasts.

"Ooof!" Then she wiggled. "Like the view, masterful Shadowspawn, sir? *Ow!*"

That at a stinging smack across one buttock, before he gripped her hips with a power just short of real pain, or perhaps slightly across the border.

Sometime later she stretched and giggled; she could hear Adrian's heart thudding against her back, but the weight was going from fun to not.

"Okay, playtime's over, let me up."

He rose, sighing, and she laughed again; she had a beautiful view of part of a sunset, if she craned her head up until her neck hurt. The way she was positioned she also couldn't rise, unless she was willing to roll onto the floor and run around with everything swaying and/or exposed.

"Get me back on my feet, would you, honey?"

"Oh, perhaps I should leave you like that while I make dinner. You look quite fetching that way, *ma belle.*"

Ellen laughed again. "Another time, when I don't need to pee. Earwax! Earwax!"

"Ah, before the omnipotent power of the mighty safe word, the evil sorcerer has no choice save obedience."

"You betcha, lover. *I'm* in charge here, and don't you forget it!"

"Never, my sweet."

It was hard to sound authoritative with your stern high in the air like this and a cold breeze on intimate places, but Ellen thought she'd managed it. Adrian helped her up with gentle force and freed her from the macramé of clothing. She stretched and they exchanged a long, slow kiss.

"Now let's have a shower, and then I shall lounge about in a fluffy robe drinking hot cocoa before the fire while my adoring Paris-trained love slave makes me dinner and lights the candles and opens the wine," she said.

His yellow-flecked eyes shared hers for a moment, then went a little cool.

He shrugged. "Sorry. I was just thinking how good it would be if we were really coming home here now, with nothing to do but live our lives."

"I have every intention of living our lives regardless," she said. "Besides, I was raised to do things. Gentlewoman of leisure will be fine later; there's a world that needs saving . . . and I really do have to pee now."

"Oh, God," Ellen said, waving her wineglass at the polished cocobolo wood that lined the big elevator. "A secret elevator in the back of the *bedroom closet* leading to the *underground lair*? Shouldn't this be in a volcano on a tropical island, or something? Either that or give onto a wilderness with a lamppost and a talking lion."

Adrian grinned at her, lounging back against the wall with his arms crossed; the ventilation system was so good that she didn't even mind the fact that he was smoking, much.

"So, where's the button?"

"There's a minor Wreaking in the control circuits. Unless someone more of an adept than I comes along, the door will not open and the elevator will not operate except for those whom I, mmmm, put on the list."

"So how do *I* do it."

"You are on the list. Just think *open* or *down*."

He blew smoke at the ceiling; she schooled her thoughts, concentrating on *down. . . .*

"Eh, voilà," he said, as the sinking feeling began, gesturing with the cigarette.

She had to admit it did give a nice period touch to the retro glamour of his black turtleneck and pants tucked into ankle boots. So did the sheathed knife and automatic, but she knew now that he was almost never willingly unarmed; it must have been a real effort to conceal the fact when they were first dating. She *had* known that he owned guns and went to a range, and mildly disapproved.

You aren't Granola Girl anymore, she thought. Then something occurred to her.

"Honey?"

"Mmmm?"

"Feeding means you really want to make out, and vice versa, right?"

"Yes. The drives are powerfully linked. Harvey has some interesting speculations on the evolutionary pathways."

She snorted and shook her head; yellow hair still slightly damp from a shower and long soak flew around her shoulders.

"Harvey can keep his big Texan nose out of my love life. The reason I asked was . . . well, when we made love before, when I didn't know . . . wasn't that sort of hard on you? I mean, you must have wanted to bite me *really* badly."

"Yes," he said, his voice bleak.

"God, Adrian, you must have willpower like a titanium steel forging!"

He shrugged eloquently. "If I did not, I would be a very bad man. Very bad indeed."

"Yeah, I got some idea of that with Adrienne. But it sort of makes me feel guilty. I never had much respect for cock teasers, and there I was being an involuntary *vein* teaser."

He winced. "Now *you* are inflicting pain, my love," he said. "There is nothing I would change about you, except possibly the occasional pun. It is a low taste. I would expect better out of someone with your education."

She grinned. "What can I say? You can take the girl out of Swoyersville, but you can't take the Swoyersville out of the girl."

The lift came to a halt and the doors slid open silently. Ellen whistled quietly.

"How deep are we?"

"Several hundred feet below the level of the house, and rather more in from any surface, except for the escape tunnels."

Her imagination poised the weight of hard rock over her head. The corridor before them gave no hint of it, except for the lack of windows. The ceiling was smooth groin-vaulted plasterwork, and easily fifteen feet high; the walls were stucco, except for a strip of Mexican mosaic tile along both sides. The floor was pale streaked marble, with a rug down the center that felt hard under her slippered feet; gaily dyed sisal, with an African look. The recessed lighting brightened automatically as they entered, and the air was a perfect seventy degrees with just enough humidity to be comfortable.

Which is more than you can say about most of New Mexico; I've spent a fortune on skin moisturizers since I moved out here.

Ellen smiled a little at Adrian's boyish pride in his ingenuity as he showed her around. The living quarters were bigger than the house above; if you included some shutdown chambers rigged dormitory style, several dozen people could live here in moderate comfort. There were kitchens, storerooms with supplies sufficient for years, workshops, an armory that even now made her mind stutter a little with the illegality of it all, but which included bows and swords and an array of knives, garrotes and assorted implements of preindustrial mayhem.

"The Power," he explained.

"Right, the more complicated, the worse," she said, and touched a rocket launcher. "I suppose guidance systems are dead easy?"

"Even Harvey or his friends . . ."

"Jack Farmer and Guha?"

"Them, or hundreds of others . . . could make them do loop-the-loops. Still, they are useful in some situations, particularly for a first strike if you can take the target by surprise."

There was even a swimming pool, doubling as a multithousand-gallon water reservoir. That was perfectly sanitary, with the right filtration system. The understated elegance of polished stone that surrounded it was just a *bonne bouche*, she supposed.

On the way back to the library-den she spoke:

"Hate to have the lights go out."

"Industrial-type stack fuel cells," he said, pointing over one shoulder. "The natural gas comes from beneath us, a trickle but good for a century or two, and there's a backup diesel system."

"Ah-hmm," she said, nodding her head and pursing her full lips. "*Definitely* ought to be in a volcano. And you should have a Nehru jacket and be stroking a white Persian cat."

At his look Ellen made a disgusted sound. "You are the least genre-savvy man in history!" Then she caught his grin. "Or the most deceitful."

"In fact, I *helped* build a base in a volcano, for the Brotherhood; helped with the Wreakings for concealment and protection. That was in a remote part of Ecuador, mountain jungle east of the Andes. The local tribes were headhunters not long ago. It even had a monorail."

"Go *on!*"

"Yes . . . no, I lie about the monorail. But it was in a volcano; for the geothermal energy." His face sobered. "Like this, it was a preparation for . . . something like Operation Trimback. That is why it is a Faraday cage, as well as having lab-level air filters. Proof against anything but a direct hit with a nuclear bunker buster."

"Ouch."

He cleared his throat. "Come, let us return to the surface. The *ragoût* will be ready soon, there is just enough time for me to do the asparagus. But we may well be sleeping down here for the next few days."

"Why?" she said. "It's comfy, but just a teensy bit . . . psychologically stuffy."

"The silver, my love. If Michiko is really attending to the matter of these detectives herself, it will be very good concealment; she will be expecting the Wreakings I set and will not pay much attention to them. And according to that so-valuable file I lifted from the dead man's computer, his partner intended to come and have a look around here, and it would appeal to Michiko to kill him on my ground; but this underground section has many sheltered exits, some of which give excellent overwatch positions on the house, which we could reach without being detected. I am afraid we are using Salvador as a tethered goat to lure in the tiger."

"Michiko prefers a snow leopard when she's night-walking," Ellen said. "She's a Gucci were-whatever. Has to be maximum *pretty* for the atrocity party."

Adrian nodded. "Another weakness. I suspect he will not mind being the goat, if things go badly for the beast. And he could be useful to us. You and I, together, with her distracted, might well put an end to her."

"Ah," Ellen said. A hot flush ran over her skin. "Oh, I would *so* like to meet Michiko again under . . . different circumstances and show her that the fun-to-kill-you thing works both ways."

Adrian made a *tsk* sound. "You have been associating with me too much, my sweet."

"Nope. It was associating with *her* that gave me the motivation. You've just shown me *how.* Lead on to the *ragoût.*"

"I shall. And . . . I have a good feeling about this."

"That's reassuring."

"Unless Michiko is having one too. We shall have to see who grasps the world-lines with the Power more strongly."

"You mean we have to make our own luck."

His grin was slow and savage, and she answered it in kind.

"Literally," he said. "Quite literally."

The road to Adrian Brézé's house was ten miles north on the I-25 and then west. The empty highway stretched through the night, cool air flowing in through the open windows as the tires hummed. Eric Salvador knew he was going to his death—but maybe he'd learn *something.* Maybe the world would make sense again.

Since when has it made sense anyway? I'm thirty-two years old, no wife, no kids, and my best friend died because I couldn't figure out what was going on. The only thing I've ever been any good at was killing people and frightening them. Cesar had twice my brains and now he's dead and his girl's dead and I can't make myself think about what I think . . . I know really did it.

And maybe they're dead because I wouldn't say it, because I was afraid of being called a nut. Or actually being a nut . . . am I crazy? Or is the world?

West, and then north again on a dirt road. The Sangres low on the horizon in the light of the three-quarter moon. That and the stars were the only light as the last gas station fell away.

He hesitated for a moment, and then snapped off the car lights himself. That was a commitment, acknowledging to himself that the extra danger was justified by the value of surprise. Something at the back of his brain wanted to reach up and pull down the night-sight goggles on the helmet he wasn't wearing.

Only a few distant earthbound stars marked houses. The road turned winding in the pitch-dark night, and then there was a steep drop to his left, a hundred near-vertical feet; this was the edge of the plateau. He forced himself to stop when the wheels skidded and a spray of gravel fanned out and out of sight.

He clenched his hands on the wheel and made his breathing slow, smelling the sourness of his own sweat, tobacco and booze. Then he held one hand before his face until the trembling stopped. He was in shitty shape, not enough sleep or exercise and too many smokes and drinks.

"Am I trying to kill myself?" he murmured. Then: "No. Not yet. I've got to find out what this all *means.* I just wish I was in better condition for a fight. Not twenty anymore, got to work harder at it."

He did the next hundred yards with the engine off, rolling downhill dead slowly. After that, driving was too dangerous without lights. Instead he got out and walked down the last stretch of road, taking his time and placing his feet carefully, thanking his father and uncles for taking him hunting, and the corps for making him even more familiar with moving quietly through unlighted countryside after sunset. The night scents were strong, the sweaty leather of chamise, the strong resin of the bleeding pines. An owl went by overhead with a *woot-woot-woot*, and something that might be a coyote or just a big rabbit scrambled through the scrub downslope. Gravel crunched under his feet—it was nearly a year since Adrian Brézé had vanished, and the housekeeper came in only once a month to clean, but there were a few more ruts than that would account for.

Someone's coming here. Just lately.

The house itself was built right into the edge of the cliff; the final dip in the road left him looking down on its fieldstone-and-adobe walls. It seemed to squat, as menacing as those huddles of cubes you saw in the 'stans, with a distant family resemblance to a pueblo. Then his experienced eye took in the dispositions.

Hey, whoever built this had a firefight in mind. You can't tell until you're up close, but it's a fucking fort. No big windows this side, no ground-level holes in the wall big enough to get through, the other's right above a sheer cliff. Great, now I expect an MG to open up from a bunker.

He took his gun in his hand. That hadn't done Cesar any good at all, but it made him feel a little better down below logic. Closer, closer . . . it didn't *feel* as empty as it should. He got out his illegal forced-entry kit, kept for those rare unspoken occasions when you said, *Fuck the rules*; then something made him reach out a hand and push. The high copper-surfaced door swung open to his touch, and a few soft lights came on under the high metal ceiling. The floor was trendy polished concrete in a mottled beige color, with colorful Navajo rugs.

Yeah, about what I expected, he thought, tucking away the leather folder of tools and blinking as his dark-adapted eyes adjusted. *Hombre, this is the OK Corral.*

The whole of the opposite wall was glass, right at the edge of the cliff;

very clear glass, and now that he thought about it, probably the laminated, bullet-resistant type. The land fell in crags and gullies washed pale by the moon, until the rolling surface of the semidesert stretched eastward to the edge of sight. There were a couple of pictures on the walls, ancient and beautiful even to an untrained eye. He drifted through the house, feeling like a ghost in its well-kept emptiness, and then took up a position by the big wall-size stone hearth opposite the windows, where he had maximum situational awareness.

"Why did I think I could find something here?" he said aloud, just barely moving his lips, as he waited and anticipation turned a little sour. "Besides learning that the rich don't live like the rest of us. I have got to get my groove back. I wouldn't have lasted a week on the rock pile like this. But I was so sure—"

"Maybe a little bird told you."

The voice seemed to come from behind him. He wheeled. Nothing. Back again . . . and the woman was there. A spurt of dreadful joy filled him. This wasn't a dream, or pixels. That was an actual person in front of him. Granted, she was naked and where nobody should be. . . .

He raised the Glock in the regulation grip, left hand under right.

Crack. Crack.

The ten-millimeter bullets punched into her belly and she folded backwards.

Crack.

Two in the center of mass, one in the head; the last snapped her head around in a whirling of long black hair and a spray of blood and the bullet starred through the glass behind her. He felt his teeth begin to show as he walked towards her. The gold-flecked eyes were already beginning to glaze.

Then her head came up. "Oooooh, that *hurt*," she said. "That can be sort of hot, you know? For starters. Then I get to hurt you. You like that, lover?"

Salvador leapt backwards, almost fell as he half sprawled against a malachite-surfaced table of rough-cast glass, then wrenched himself into a crouched firing position.

Crack. Crack. Crack—

Ten shots. Five hit. Five more punched the great window behind, starring it, then collapsing it out in a shatter of milky fragments. Even then the part of his mind that was mostly training thought that was odd if it was the laminate he thought it was.

"Oooooh, oooooh, you're so *rough*," the thing crooned as it advanced on him, laughing.

A hand reached out towards his neck. Then jerked back as she hissed:

"We really have to do something about those silver chains. Maybe we could make people think they cause cancer?"

She dabbed at the blood on the side of her head and stuck the fingers in her mouth for a moment, tongue curling around them.

"Mmmmm, tasty!" But you want to take that stupid chain off, don't you . . . that's right. . . ."

The eyes grew, the yellow flecks drawing together like drops of molten gold, running into two lakes of fire. Depth, depth, drawing him into a whirling—

She screamed, pain and rage. The great ten-foot wings beat behind her as the talons slammed home and the hooked beak drove into her neck. The snow leopard rolled over and over—

—*leopard?*—

—its paws striking in a blur of speed and claws amid a saw-edged screeching. The eagle dropped out of the air into a huge tawny *something* and the big cats rolled over and over, shrieking and striking and lunging for each other's throats and racking their hind feet to rip bellies as furniture smashed and broken glass crunched under their weight.

Then the man was standing with his back to Salvador, every muscle in his lean body standing out like static waves as his thumbs dug into her throat. She was making the same bestial snarling sound as she reared back with a knee braced against his chest and her hands driving up between his forearms, and the world seemed to *twist* between them, things flickering in and out of existence, nightmare glimpses of possibilities that ought not to exist. Salvador doggedly began to drag himself to his feet, looking around for something to throw. Something to hit with.

Crack!

Much louder this time. The double splash of impact and her skull started to deform under the huge kinetic energy, and then a sparkle, and she was gone. Blood fell to the floor, a sharp, sour, iron-salt smell, and stomach contents; he recognized the acidic not-quite-vomit fecal stink. The man went to one knee for a second, panting, then rose and turned.

"You're Adrian Brézé," Salvador said, trying to make his mind function again.

The gun came up, almost of its own volition. The slim dark man pointed a finger at him.

"Don't. Just *don't*. It's been a long day. And you need silver bullets for it to work."

"Silver bullets?" Salvador snarled. "Silver fucking *bullets*—"

Adrian Brézé cast a glance over his shoulder; the first paling of the night sky showed that dawn was coming, and he winced a little.

"It becomes late for night-walking; I'd better go corporeal. Right back, Detective Salvador, when I've fetched my real body."

Silver bullets. I don't think I want to be in a world where silver bullets work and people just . . . stop being there.

Salvador looked down at the pistol. *Why the hell not?* he thought, and began to bring it up towards his mouth. *That's safer. Only amateurs try to shoot themselves in the head. . . .*

"I wouldn't do that if I were you."

"Why don't you kill me? Why don't you kill me?" he screamed. *"Why don't you just fucking kill me?"*

"That's 'why don't *they* fucking kill you,'" the man said. "I can tell you, if you want to know."

"You're one of them."

Brézé was slight but built like a lynx or a gymnast, a bit below medium height, pale olive skin and dark hair and gold-flecked brown eyes . . .

"You're *Adrian Brézé*!"

"Yes."

Salvador drew breath in, held it, let it out. "Okay, I get it: I'm supposed to believe you're a *good* monster."

"Oh, he's not just good, he's a *great* monster, believe me. But all mine, mine, mine."

Salvador jerked at the other voice, looked down at the pistol, then ejected the magazine, worked the slide to take the last round out of the chamber, and dropped it to the table he was sitting on. A worked-copper-and-turquoise box had spilled open, full of slim cigarettes. He took one out and lit it; some distant part of himself was proud of the fact that his hand didn't shake. The second voice belonged to a woman.

Tall, blond, legs up to there, hourglass figure, dressed in dark outdoor clothes and boots, with a knit cap over her head and a rifle cradled in her arms—he recognized it, a big Brit sniper job he'd seen SAS types use, long scope, aircraft-alloy body. This one looked as if it had been tweaked a bit in ways he didn't recognize. Her face was a little thinner and a lot harder than the pictures, not so much of the wounded-fawn look; he recognized part of what waited in the blue eyes, from his mirror.

"You're . . . Ellen Tarnowski."

"Technically, Ellen Brézé, now. No, I'm not one of them. You can't catch it from getting bitten, it's hereditary." A sudden charming smile. "And believe me, I know the biting part! Not contagious at all, even if you're married to one and use the same toothbrush occasionally."

"I get the feeling you've changed."

"I had to . . . ah . . . take a couple of levels in badass, let's say."

"You killed her."

His eyes went back to the puddle of blood; there wasn't a body. A pretty disgusting mess, but no body.

"*Oh*, yes." Her eyes were large and turquoise blue; for a moment they held a hot satisfaction. "There's a body, probably a long way away, but it's empty now, and in a little while it'll just stop breathing. Nobody home anymore. I put a bullet through *that* part of the bitch."

"That . . . that wasn't his sister, was it?"

"No. That was Michiko. She's a friend of his sister's, Adrienne. Sort of a wannabe Mistress of Ultimate Darkness. Incidentally I jammed a hypo full of very bad stuff into Adrienne's foot, and I had a *lot* of very good reasons to do that. And she came down with a case of dead from it."

Salvador laughed; it was a bit shaky, but genuine. "I think you *have* changed, lady."

Brézé was back. Now he was dressed, in the same sort of clothes; a light jacket covered a shoulder rig with a knife worn hilt-down on one flank and a Glock on the other.

His real body. Oooooo-kay.

"All right," Salvador said, taking a pull on the cigarette. "Fill me in. I know I'm really somewhere locked up, under heavy meds, howling at the moon, right? Or totally catatonic. I lost it in Kandahar and I'm in a padded cell at some VA warehouse and the whole last ten years are a whack-job dream."

For some reason that made Adrian Brézé smile. "I'm a Shadow-spawn. . . . That's what we call ourselves, mostly. But . . . well, I *try* not to be a monster. It's complicated."

"Like the past year has been so simple? I want answers."

"Think carefully about that, Detective. You can choose to learn, or you can choose to forget. . . . I can do that, with your cooperation. If you forget, you can make yourself a new life. If you learn, it'll probably kill you—but at least you'll know why you're fighting, *mon ami.*"

"If you offer me a blue pill and a red pill I'll fucking kill *you*!"

The couple laughed. "It's actually two file cards with Mhabrogast glyphs, but otherwise yes, life imitates old film. Take your pick," the man said.

He produced two squares of light pasteboard, sat, and began to draw on them with a black Sharpie, the movements fluid and sure. Spiky-looking symbols grew on both pieces of paper; something made him look away slightly, as if seeing them produced an itch four inches behind his eyes.

Then he held up one: "Knowledge—and you can try being the guer-rilla." The other: "Ignorance—and long life. Longer, probably, at least."

Salvador looked at the butt of the cigarette. Then he tossed it accurately into the blood; it hissed into extinction.

"Like that's really a *choice?*"

"Yes, very much so," Brézé said. "You could probably choose to forget, and be . . . not safe. Not in any more danger than the rest of the human race, at least."

"Okay."

He took a deep breath. Just having all this go away was a little tempting . . . until he remembered that he'd still be swimming with sharks.

Only I wouldn't know they're there. Not until they bite my ass off.

"I have got a *lot* of payback coming and I need to know how to get to the people who owe me. Right, I embrace the suck, it isn't the first time. Let's start with some explanations."

There was a subdued *clack-snack-snick* as the blonde cleared her rifle and put it down on the stone ledge before the empty fireplace.

"No," she said. "*You* guys start by sweeping up the glass and mopping that blood. Then we go . . . downstairs to the dungeon, and we talk."

CHAPTER EIGHTEEN

"**J**esus, this place feels weird," Salvador muttered to himself. "Completely Rando."

He sipped at his latte and watched the people go by the curbside restaurant, enjoying the mild Californian coastal warmth. He was feeling pretty good physically, too, and he looked down at his gut with considerable approval, and the definition of his arms where the biceps swelled at the T-shirt. Not as ripped as he'd been when he was humping an MG-240 through mouj country, but he wasn't in his twenties anymore, and a lot of that had been sheer nervous energy burning stuff off anyway, or just having nothing to do with his spare time but pump iron, under the no-booze, no-cooze rules of engagement in theater.

The mellow afternoon sun was like silk, and there was a scent of eucalyptus and earth and good cooking and flowers in the air. Apart from the risk of imminent death, life was good, and he was working towards revenge for Cesar and a whole lot of others.

This place feels as weird as a lot of my days as a Helmand Province tourist, and I don't like fancy coffee. Got to fit in, though. I'm not the guy with sensors on my helmet and an Apache gunship and GPS-guided artillery shells and all the good shit on call here. If the other side can find *me they can squash me like a cockroach . . . if I'm lucky. Scuttle through the cracks, don't attract attention until you have to. And they can walk through walls. And read minds.*

Adrian had warned him that the wards and blocks in his brain wouldn't stand up under close examination, and that a strong adept could break them, and him, by main force. The process of implanting them had been unpleasant, but he welcomed any protection he could get, and they were supposed to make people more likely to open up to him somehow, at least for a day or so.

Like the man said, I'm the guerrilla now, and I need every trick I can get. It sucks . . . so embrace the suck, Eric, embrace the suck. But it's creepy here, not just dangerous.

Rancho Sangre Sagrado was far too *pretty*, just for starters. Virtually all of it was built in one style, a Californian try at looking high-toned Mexican-Spanish that had been very popular back towards the beginning of the last century, and influential since. All arches and whitewashed walls or colored stucco, red barrel-tiled roofs, colored mosaic tile accents on corners or walls, glimpses through wrought-iron gates into spectacular courtyard gardens, the occasional square or round tower on a store or public building with those odd outswelling things called machicolations.

It wasn't that he didn't *like* the style; in fact, he thought it was rather handsome, and it certainly suited the landscape and climate; plus it was less obviously made-up than Santa Fe's flat roofs. The only reason his early Spanish ancestors had built Santa Fe the way they did and lived in flat-roofed Pueblo-style buildings was that they couldn't afford what they really wanted, which would have looked a lot more like *this*. New Mexico had been the ass-end Siberia of Spain's empire, isolated by poverty and deserts and Apaches, the place you sent Cousin Diego after the embarrassing thing with the nun.

But there were was nothing else here, not even on the outskirts, not a single fifties-sixties public washroom–style heap of stained concrete and buckled aluminum, nothing more recent, like a funhouse mirror twisty-fancy with mirrored glass, not even any of the usual standard suburban frame.

There wasn't even a church; and while he wasn't religious except when talking to his heavily Catholic grandmother to keep her happy, it added a note of oddness. There was a building that looked like it *had* been a church, white and fancifully carved like some he'd seen in Mexico, but it was apparently some sort of community theater now.

And I have my suspicions about the sort of shows they put on there, too.

The whole place felt vaguely un-American, in the strict sense; it felt like someone had settled on a way it should look and then just enforced it for better than a hundred years, with new construction strictly because there were more people, and that in the same style. It reminded him of Santa Barbara, which he'd visited on leave from Camp Pendleton years ago, but more so; or of the heavily conserved parts of Santa Fe, for another, but with more consistent application of a thick layer of folding green to tidy up the edges. As far as he could see there was no equivalent of his hometown's Cerrillos Road, a strip of ticky-tack and motels and

RV parks with the best view of the Sangres in town. Everything looked like it was washed and scrubbed and repainted and the flowers given a quick swipe with a cloth every morning.

Idly, he punched *New Urbanist* into his tablet; he was simply waiting for evening now, and picking up a little intel by listening in on people. Ellen had used the term about the place in his briefing. A quick flick through the articles confirmed that she'd been right.

A lot like Celebration, Florida, only not built all at the same time.

Even the three-tiered fountain in the brick circle at the middle of the intersection in front of him was like the one in the picture, three terra-cotta basins of diminishing size. It made him wonder whom the architects had been getting their directions from . . . but then, in the month since meeting Mr. and Ms. Brézé, so had a lot of things. Even the loopiest conspiracy theories looked tame compared to the truth, and now whenever he looked around it was like he could see things bulging and squirming beneath the surface—even people's faces. Who knew, who knew . . .

"Your pastries, sir," the waitress said.

She set down a plate with fragrant-smelling muffins in a cute little basket.

"Thanks."

He glanced over automatically at her cleavage, which was a pleasant sight, and chatted for a moment; she was in her late teens or early twenties, red haired and freckled and fresh faced . . . and dangling between those creamy jiggling-firm cheerleader titties was a tiny pendant. A jagged trident across a black-rayed sun on a chain. The Brézé house badge, and the symbol of the Council of Shadows and the Order of the Black Dawn. The oldest and most senior of all the Shadowspawn houses, the ones who'd spread their genetic knowledge of the Power to the secret clans worldwide, and the lords of Rancho Sangre. Nearly everyone he'd seen here wore one, around the neck or on a bangle or a key chain or whatever.

It meant she was a renfield. That she knew who and what ran this place, and had been *initiated*. A collaborator.

He astonished himself with the wave of violent hatred that swept through him: a blast like stomach acid at the back of his throat, a vision of a bomb scything through the crowd around him in fragments of nails and bolts and furniture and leaving wreckage and flames.

Whoa, he thought. *Watch it! The kid can't help where she was born. She might be an okay person.*

"Another latte, please," he said, and read her name badge. "Tiffany."

Instead of letting the images cycle through his head he ate another apricot-walnut muffin: very good indeed, and even the butter had real taste. The menu said, *All local, all organic,* right under the classic Art Deco Sunkist label cover from the nineteen twenties, and had a little small-print, *Brézé Enterprises*, down in the lower left corner.

Ellen had also said the place was like a rich man's show-ranch, only with people instead of palomino horses. Everyone in it was a renfield, except for stoop labor trucked in for the day from elsewhere. And occasional travelers, not all of whom made it out alive.

When the waitress returned to fill his cup he let his wrist bangle show; it had the *mon* symbol of the Tōkairin clan on it.

"Oh!" the waitress said. "Hi! You're one of the faithful too! We don't get all that many outsiders here, not faithful. Meat sacks don't count, of course."

"Of course."

He decided that making allowances for Tiffany's upbringing was futile. These people were, for all practical purposes, devil worshipers from long lines of devil worshipers.

Faithful and meat sacks. Well, that's one way of looking at it, he thought. *One thing about being a detective, you get used to talking to skanks like this little* puta *without letting your feelings show. And yeah, the briefing said it's hard even to* find *this place if you're not in the know. Brigadoon from Hell, not on the maps, the computers don't reference it, Google Earth can't find it.*

"Yeah," he said easily. "Down here from the bay to do some purchase orders at the fruit co-op. I'm part of the acquisition team for the clan's town houses. They insist on the best, and now that the Tōkairin and the Brézés are buddies again, you're it here."

Rancho Sangre was surrounded by farms, mostly in orchards and vineyards; they rolled away to the varied green of the Coast Range just west of town.

"You don't look like a produce buyer," she said, smiling. "You look more like you work on the muscle side, a house soldier or something. Kind of rough, not a cubicle dweeb."

A thrill of alarm shot through him; the problem was that he *did* look like that. Not just his build, but the scars on his arms and face, and the way he held himself. He hadn't expected a waitress to pick up on it, though.

Goddammit, I'm not a spook! I wasn't an undercover cop, either. Everyone in Santa Fe knows who all the cops are!

"I used to be on that side of things," he said. "But I'm retired from ops now. We get old, eh? Even if people your age can't believe it."

"Oh, you don't look *old*, just *scary*. The Gurkhas here are too, I suppose, but they really keep to themselves and they're too different. And there usually isn't anything for them to do but run through the woods and train. You look like you really did stuff; I suppose up in the big city they need a lot of guys like you."

Well, that's flattering.

"You're born here, obviously."

"Third generation. My dad works for the co-op," she went on pleasantly, nodding. "Supervisor in the packing plant, that's really hard when you don't use any preservatives, it has to be just right. Mom's a guidance counselor at the high school."

"I'm glad to be here. It's quiet in San Francisco with all the daimyo out of town, and this makes a change of pace. Not that I'm sorry to have missed that big ruckus last year."

"Oh, God, yeah, that party and the fight and everything!" she said. "And it was so much fun up until then before it all got spoiled, all the new people and the celebrations. I was working up at the *casa grande* for the party, Theresa the manager tapped me, and it was a complete blast. Lucky I was in the infirmary and tranked out of my mind when the bad stuff came down, so I only heard about it later. Couple of people nearly got *killed*, and there was that horrible thing with *Doña* Adrienne."

"You were sick?" he asked. "How'd that happen?"

She sat down to talk; business was slow, and this was a small town, only a few thousand people and no tourist trade.

And, of course, we're both faithful.

"Oh, not sick, just banged up and low on blood. They had a lot of extra staff in to help with the guests, you know, Theresa had the sheriff go around and pick us out at school. Mainly I was sort of a temporary lucy, you know, 'cause I'm pretty, which *sure* beat cleaning the rooms or the kitchen. Even if it was more twenty-four/seven."

"You certainly are pretty enough for anyone, even the Masters," he said gallantly.

"Thanks." Another giggle. "There were two of the Tōkairin Shadowspawn tag-teaming me, some sort of security guys from things they said. . . . God, I was sore all over for a week, I didn't know there were that many ways *to* get screwed! They had those funny tattoos all over, too, and I mean *all* over."

"Ah . . . not too scary, I hope."

"No. Well, yes, but usually hot-scary, not just plain scary. I knew they probably wouldn't really kill or cripple me, you know how it is with us, and they had the refreshments the Brézés brought in for that. I saw them go at a couple of those meat sacks and it reeeeeally got gross, I nearly barfed. But they're just meat sacks, after all."

"Nothing too bad, eh?"

"Not once I got into it. It just got sort of blurry for me when they were turning into animals and stuff and fucking with my head with the Power, so I can't be sure what they actually did to me after that, except I'm not pregnant, of course, and all the bite marks and bruises and stuff healed up. I mean, I *thought* they'd bitten parts of me off and eaten them while I watched, but obviously they didn't. Wild!"

"They wouldn't want to insult the Brézés by killing a renfield without permission," Salvador observed.

"Right. And I got bled enough to get a bit of the addiction, which made coming down a complete bummer, like a mixed-drink hangover for days, even with the transfusions. But fun while it lasted, I was really starting to enjoy them feeding on me, it's better than grass any day after the first couple of times. My sister Jill was too young, and boy, did she get sniffy and whine about missing the party. You know how sixteen-year-olds are about acting like adults."

"I've got a couple of younger brothers and sisters too," Salvador said sympathetically.

And she's what, nineteen? Christ.

"Yeah." A malicious smile came over the perky face, a moment's leer. "Then her initiation came up a couple of months later, and with *Doña* Adrienne gone and *Don* Jules and *Doña* Julia back here they handled it, really old-school."

"Old-school?"

"Yeah, at mine *Doña* Adrienne just bit me on the neck and gave me a kiss; the bite didn't even sting much, and that was it, 'Here's a Band-Aid for the hickey, here's your funky black robe, here's your pendant, worship the Shadowspawn faithfully and you'll be one of the masters over the cattle, the meat sacks, yada, yada; now go back to studying for the SATs like a good girl.' But Jilly, they went at her the way my mom says they did with *her* and my dad back forever ago. It was sort of fun to watch her wiggling and hear her yell. First *Don* Jules stuck his—"

Salvador didn't consider himself a particularly squeamish man; he hadn't been as a marine, and years as a cop gave you a plumber's-helper view from society's toilet bowl. He still blinked a little at the blow-by-blow description of what had happened to this Jilly on an altar in front of a crowd of family and neighbors chanting the equivalent of *amen* while swaying back and forth, holding candles and clad in black robes.

"So she howled herself hoarse and got all weepy about it afterwards for a couple of weeks, even when we told her to shut up about it, which tells you how well she'd have done up at the *casa grande*, and Dr. Duggan had to trank her for a while, which was a relief, 'cause my room's right next to hers and she kept waking me up with the nightmares. But she's been a lot less of an annoying little snot since she stopped that, which means she's growing up, I suppose."

"Glad to hear it," Eric said. "*Don* Jules and *Doña* Julia are here now? I should send a message up to the *casa grande* if they are. The word is that Tōkairin renfields should show complete respect now, not just be polite."

"Oh, no, they cleared out a couple of days ago, with all their baggage and lucies and servants, for a long trip. Even Monica's gone—my mom plays tennis with her, and she was complaining about how it was going to disrupt the tournament schedule. Some sort of big Shadowspawn do, somewhere *way* far away. Isn't it exciting?"

"It's important, I hear."

Tiffany leaned closer, her eyes glittering. "Totally! I hear"—she dropped her voice—"that they're going to come out in the open somehow, the Shadowspawn are, that is. Real soon! On TV and everything, you know, the president kneeling and them chopping off his head and raping his daughter or whatever. But that last part may just be someone blowing smoke. Though it would be funny."

"Right, I'd heard the rumors. Big changes, sure enough."

She nodded enthusiastically, her silky hair bobbing around her shoulders.

"They'll be gods again then, with temples and sacrifices. And we from the faithful families will all be lords over the meat sacks, like it was always promised. No more of these crap waiting-table jobs for summer money 'cause they need to keep everything hidden!"

"Yeah, I understand there will be leadership positions going begging."

"High priests and secret police and CEOs! We'll all have like big houses and sports cars and . . . and stuff . . . and absolutely hordes of slaves and we can do anything we want with the meat sacks."

"Sounds like fun."

"Totally toga party! I'd like to kill a couple, just to see if it's as big a spiff in the quiff as everyone says it is, and have them grovel and beg and cry and everything. I mean, I could see the Shadowspawn really got off on that when *I* was doing it. And we won't have to stay in town all the time or watch what we say in front of meat sacks, and I can go to concerts and raves and all that like the people on TV and the Web. Or maybe spring break in Puerto Vallarta."

"It's certainly got the Masters completely focused," Salvador said. "Hardly any of them left in the bay area. Usually there are a couple of dozen, at least."

Tiffany nodded. "There aren't any Masters left in town here at all, well, there are *Doña* Adrienne's kids, I suppose. I've seen them a couple of times. Just kids, if you don't know better. Sometimes the servants bring them down into town, or they have playdates and things."

Bingo, third confirmation and that's the charm, he thought, disguising a hunter's satisfaction with a bite of muffin. *Definitely out of town, kids still definitely here. Plenty of nannies and such, I should think, and the security detail, but the living . . . well, active . . . monsters gone.*

"Didn't your *Doña* Adrienne have another lucy? I think I heard someone mention that."

"Oh, Jose. No, he's retired . . . well, you know, retired from being a lucy. Out of town now, his aunt's got this business he helps with. The Villegas are sort of stuck up 'cause they've been here forever, but he's nice."

A sigh from the girl, as she propped her chin on a fist. "I'd like to travel. What's San Francisco like? There's this great place for clothes my mom got to go to once and she's still talking about it."

It struck Eric suddenly that quite possibly this Tiffany Meachum had never been more than a few miles from the town where she'd been born.

Man, I'm never going to read 'Salem's Lot *again,* he thought as he did riffs on the backstory of his supposed identity; the Brotherhood had a good system for producing them and he'd studied hard. *Isolated small towns with horrible secrets just aren't going to be any fun even to imagine. I wonder what's in the cellars and attics here?*

"So," she said a little later. "I get off at six. My place or yours?"

Salvador choked slightly. "Ah . . ."

"Well, you *do* want to fuck me, don't you?"

He answered with a wordless grunt, and she gave him a winning smile.

"I can probably get Jilly in on it too if you'd like that. Bet you've never had sisters at the same time! Rough stuff's fine, either way, I like pitching and catching. Your hotel might be better, 'cause my folks are, like, ancient and yell and pound on the door if I get too loud, and I really like to do that. Or you could gag me."

"Ah, sorry. Can't."

For a moment he felt a horrible temptation; it had been a long time since his dates had included anyone but Ms. Rosy Palm. Then he mentally recoiled at his mind's prompting vision of what he'd feel like afterwards.

You are too old to be thinking with the little head, Salvador. Also you have to look at yourself every day in the mirror.

"Oh, don't be all unfun!" she said, sensing his recoil. "I could get Don, my boyfriend, too," she added, with a considering glance. "If that's your thing."

"No offense, but I'm really busy. Another time."

"Oh, well, it was fun talking, Miguel. Have a nice day. Hail to the, ah, the Black Eternal Dawn . . . Eternal Black Dawn, and, uh, and whatever!"

"Jesus," he whispered softly to himself.

Lucy Lane was extremely quiet, a curving row of neo-Spanish houses deeply embowered in big trees, with lovely gardens out front and even better behind, from the glimpses he got. The narrow street made it almost drenched in sweet, heavy flower scent; the roundabout at the end gave onto the hills behind the town, and to the left was the high stucco-and-tile wall around the *casa grande*. Its roofs showed over the top, and the tips of trees. The brooding presence was never really gone anywhere in town, but here it was overwhelming.

Right, peones down here, hacendados up there. Ms. Cortines must feel right at home, not. I was right about this place being un-American, unless you count maybe Alabama.

From what he'd heard—the briefings had been brief, limited to the essentials—the Brézés had been aristos back in the old country, as well as satanists and magicians using powers they didn't understand until the nineteenth century. The sort who, back when, had hunted peasants for sport with horses and dogs, before what Adrian had called *Madame la Guillotine* taught them a few limits. Only, the Brézés hadn't wanted any limits. They'd apparently brought their conception of how things should be organized along when they came here, as well. This wasn't exactly a castle on a crag somewhere in the Auvergne with a village huddled at its feet, but it wasn't exactly not like that either.

Right, Salvador said to himself. *According to Ellen, the one called Jabar got killed before she left, Peter Boase escaped, Monica's not here, and it doesn't look like there's anyone home anywhere but Cheba. Good news about this Jose guy being off the lane, that'll simplify things.*

He felt hideously conspicuous, even though it was getting dark; California weather could make you forget what season it was, but the sun went down at the right time, anyway. The streetlights were picturesque, frosted globes on wrought-iron stands, but not the most efficient outdoor lighting he'd ever seen. Of course, the people who controlled the process could see in the dark anyway.

He didn't like to think what would happen if the local cops caught him loitering with intent on the street that was, essentially, the local Brézé drive-by buffet. He'd also been warned that his cover story wouldn't hold up if someone actually contacted the Tōkairin for a background check. Not even normal Shadowspawn sloppiness got *that* bad, and even a large clan didn't have so many close servants that they had to rely entirely on computerized lists.

Plus I don't think the local police are much into the Miranda rights thing, somehow.

The outside light came on at number five, and four people came out.

Right, Monica's kids. Boy eleven, girl ten. Older woman—probably their grandmother. And Eusebia Cortines, formerly of Coetzala and Tlacotalpan.

His professional instincts stuttered a little when she hit his eye. She was about seventeen, and *not* your typical girl from a little *ejido* village. For one thing she looked to have a strong dash of African in there with the predominant *india* and some Spaniard, to judge from the cinnamon-coffee color of her skin and the way her blue-black hair was loosely curled, as well as her full lips. Slim, straight figure, but a high, full bust—also not typical, peasant girls tended to stocky builds and breasts at best of the perky persuasion.

Okay, stop snorting and pawing the ground, let's hope she's not as mentally fucked-up as the last pretty girl you saw.

She hadn't been, from what the others said, but she'd also been here a year as a lucy. A pretty traumatic situation to begin with, and Shadowspawn could do things to your head. He'd experienced a little of that with Adrian putting in the blocks and wards; his cover identity would account for that, if he'd been a Tōkairin *soldato* once. They used their renfield mercenaries against one another in their squabbles and didn't want them to be too utterly vulnerable. But that had been clinical, not whatever the local monsters had been doing with her on a whim in this theme park for demons.

These village girls are tough, though. He'd had enough experience with wetbacks to know that. *And Adrian said she looked mentally resilient to him. Now for the risky part.*

If she yelled for the cops he was dead, or much much worse. Shadowspawn had ways of torturing you that didn't have to end with death. Just plain didn't have to *end.*

He waited until the older woman and the kids had driven off, then walked through the gate and up the brick pathway. The risers of the steps leading to the arched front door were mosaic tile, and there was a colorful surround in the arch above. It was a nice house, carefully maintained but lived-in; number one was the only other that did, and it had a couple of bicycles out front in racks, kids' models.

It wasn't the first time he'd knocked on a door that might have someone unhappy to see him behind it. Policemen saw a lot of that. He drew a breath and rapped; it was more personal than ringing the bell.

"Yes?" she said, when the door opened; Salvador had been pretty sure that she spent an instant looking at him through the peephole.

"My name is Eric Salvador, Señorita Cortines. I come from a certain man you met, who was not as he seemed."

"Oh, fuck," said Salvador; he'd never met Adrienne Brézé, and from the impact she'd had on other people he had no desire to do so. "She's *alive?*"

"Yes. Everyone else is not to know, you understand? So I can't say so, the witch makes sure of that. Only to you I can, I don't know why, my head doesn't start buzzing."

That must be the Wreakings that Adrian had implanted.

No wonder they're sloppy about security! They can just reach into people's minds directly!

Salvador stared at her. The Mexican girl seemed extremely self-possessed, if a little pale and moving carefully. She was leaning back on a pale, elegant sofa, her hands busy with some sort of lacework, dressed in a silk blouse, braided belt, elegant slacks and tooled leather sandals, an orange cat curled up beside her. There were a few paintings on the wall; those would have been Ellen's while she was here.

But the bookcase held a slew of school primers and language guides and some illustrated books on crafts; and he suspected the color scheme, heavy reds and navy blues with highlights of orange and crimson and green, was the current tenant's idea. A plate of sugar cookies had been put out, and a pot of strong black coffee.

"You're . . . sure?" he said. "Sure she's not dead?"

She rolled her eyes; he had to acknowledge that it was a stupid question.

"*¡Ai!* The things the evil bitch does to me every couple of days, I'm very sure, me."

Well, here's some crucial information. Christ! Well, no battle plan survives contact with the enemy.

"But she's gone?"

"Yes. She, her parents, Monica. Only the children left. They've all gone to get ready for this big meeting."

She grimaced and took a small case out of a pocket and tossed a little white pill into her mouth and swallowed.

"She drank a lot of my blood just before she left, but already it hurts; and she made me help with Jose, so I'd know what was coming to me. This medicine from the doctor helps a little. She laughed about how I would beg her to beat me and take me in the worst ways when she came back. Damn her to hell!"

They were speaking in Spanish; it wasn't Salvador's first language, hadn't been in his family since his grandmother's time, but he was fully fluent and had been as long as he could remember. Though the dialect he'd learned from his grandmother's generation was quite a bit different from hers; there had already been more English words mixed in, for starters. Her English was reasonably good, but still heavily accented, and sometimes a little too much like a literal word-for-word translation for fine detail to come through to anyone who wasn't bilingual already.

He suspected she'd spoken a lot of Nahuatl before moving to the big-city ambience of Tlacotalpan. Coetzala must really be in the boonies.

"She *nearly* died, she was very sick," Cheba added. Clinically: "That would have been bad. I would have been killed myself, sacrificed. They do that, I hear, like the days of the old gods, sending the servants along with the master. Also—"

There was a disturbing glint in her big dark eyes, a flicker like a kiss of flame.

"—also I want to kill her myself. See her die. See her *die*! If that blond gringa can *nearly* kill her I can finish the job."

Okay, no Stockholm syndrome here.

"Then you will help us?"

Cheba put her lacework down. "Maybe."

"Maybe," she said again. "*¿El brujo quiere mi ayuda? ¡Le costará!* If the sorcerer wants my help, it will cost him!"

"Well . . . he's offering a way to escape."

"Like he did last time? And so I escape, what am I going to do? I have no papers, no money, I don't speak the language really well yet."

"This is a bad place."

She shrugged, her eyes hard. "I grew up selling baskets on the streets in Tlacotalpan. What do you think that's like for an *india* with no money? It's a bad place! I'm getting ready here, me, learning things. What happens to me—" Another shrug. "That bastard son of a whore Paco, the coyote who smuggled us across the border and sold us to the witch as *snacks*, he and his friends did things to me too. I saw him die, I'll see *her* die. Meanwhile I have a nice house and enough to eat, and I learn and I prepare. Revenge is like *mole*, you have to cook it slow for the best taste."

Salvador hid an admiring grin, but he thought she caught a bit of it. She was smarter than most, but otherwise she reminded him of others he'd met, the ones not simply beaten down and numbed by misery. She had a lynx-eyed grasp of the main chance, and wasn't going to let any-thing get in the way. It was annoying, but she had never had enough to indulge in luxuries like sentimentality.

"Okay, what do you want?" he said.

"What do *you* want, you and your boss?"

"He wants the witch's children."

"He's the father, right? She boasted to me about that, once. That she tricked him or something." A sniff. "As if men needed to be tricked into *that*."

"Ah . . . yes."

"I have helped look after them a little. They are not bad children, but very strange. Now, here is what *I* want. I will help this man you work for to fight the *brujos*. I want a chance to kill Adrienne. Also I want papers, not a green card but citizen's papers, and I want enough money to open my own shop."

She touched the lacework beside her on the sofa, gently nudging the cat's interest away.

"I have learned enough of what they like here. Some I can make, some buy from the south, I know where to go and I can bargain. What city for the shop, I am not sure. A safe place. Give me that and I will help."

Eric Salvador grinned openly this time. "You are a lady who knows her own mind," he said.

"I am one who has no time for foolishness," she said.

"This is no time for foolishness!" Cheba said.

Adrian shook his head. The Brotherhood commandos were gathered in the safe house, a disused warehouse in Paso Robles they'd used before, a dim expanse smelling of old motor oil and olives. Adrian, Farmer and Guha, Ellen, and Eric Salvador; their backup and exit groups were elsewhere, waiting. The only ones without a look of shocked astonishment on their faces were Cheba and Salvador, who'd delivered the news. Adrian himself felt as if he'd been punched in the gut; Ellen had gone gray and staggered backwards to sit on an old fruit crate. Farmer and Guha had their heads together and were whispering frantically.

"I killed her," Ellen whispered. "I swear to God I got her right in the foot with the hypo and pressed the plunger."

"You did," Cheba said. "But one of the other guests, the woman Michiko, cut off her foot almost instantly, before much of the poison got into her. Then she was very sick for months. The foot *grew back*. Like a bud on a plant."

She shuddered. Adrian nodded; he didn't know if the original Shadowspawn had had that ability, but the Council's eugenics program had established it among the purebreds a few generations earlier. Probably in normal humans switching off that particular suppressive gene would have meant death by cancer, but his breed didn't have that sort of bad luck. Or perhaps the cells that went wrong had extremely bad luck themselves.

"We are very hard to kill," he said, feeling himself gathering strength. "Very hard indeed. Things . . . fall out well for us."

"I killed Michiko, though," Ellen said, taking deep breaths.

"How do you know?" Cheba asked.

Ellen glared at her. "I shot her in the head with a silver bullet from a rifle!"

"Oh. Good for you, gringa!" Then briskly to Adrian: "So. This man here agreed to my terms. You will keep this promise."

Adrian bowed gracefully, amused and impressed. "I authorized him to bargain for me," he said. "The citizenship and the money are"—he waved his hand—"easy enough."

"Easy enough for you!"

"Precisely. Easy enough for me," he said, with a hard smile.

This was not a woman who would respect anyone who could be pushed, Power or no.

"You could have asked for more."

"I asked for what I wanted. More I can make for myself. What I asked for, you owe me. It is justice, not charity."

"Very well. As to Adrienne . . . I will kill her the moment I can. So will any of us here."

Ellen nodded vigorously, and so did Guha and Salvador.

"*Shit*, yeah," Farmer added. "Get a number and stand in line, señorita."

Adrian amplified: "I certainly don't object to your killing her if you get a chance. Be my guest; you have ample cause. But nobody will let her live an instant longer than they must. She is too dangerous, too tricky, too likely to seize any opportunity to wiggle out of a trap."

Cheba scowled ferociously for a moment—Adrian thought there was even the hint of a pout—then reluctantly nodded.

"*Bueno*. I see that this is necessary."

"Living well while your enemy does not is the best revenge," Adrian said.

"A head cut off and put on a stick is the best revenge," Cheba said with enormous sincerity. "Still, you are right, she must be killed."

"As to protection, no place will be safe while the Shadowspawn rule. The *world* is not safe; they plan soon to kill on a scale that the worst conquerors of the past could see only in nightmares. I will do my best; but I guarantee nothing and I wash my hands of you if you do not follow my orders in matters of your safety from them. Agreed?"

She looked at him for a long moment. "Agreed. You are a man who does not promise more than he can do, I think."

"You're right," Ellen said unexpectedly. "Adrian . . . are we still going through with this plan?"

"Yes," he said decisively. "That Adrienne is alive makes everything that has happened in the past year . . . acquire a different meaning."

"No *shit*," Farmer snarled.

He put his hands to his head. "Nothing on precog . . . Anni?"

"Nothing," she said. "But with Adrienne, it would be like trying to see a match against a bonfire."

Adrian nodded. "We must look at each event through a different lens."

Guha and Farmer looked at each other; the man shook his head, and she shrugged slightly.

"But this plan is still good. Dead or gone, she is not *there*, and neither are my parents, so there is no adept at Rancho Sangre. Even better, if we have the children, we have a lever over her."

Ellen looked at him, surprised and a little shocked.

"You wouldn't *hurt* them?"

"No." A hard smile. "You know that. Adrienne will suspect it . . . but she will not be sure, and she will be restrained by that uncertainty. Also it will injure her prestige with other Shadowspawn, which can only be good. Whatever she plans, whatever her cunning, she cannot simply sweep them aside. If we can prevent Trimback One, the Brotherhood is in a position to thwart her plans for the parasmallpox plague."

He looked around; the others remained silent. "Then let us do as we planned. With one modification."

Except for Cheba, the others were already in tough dark clothing and boots, gear that would be practical in a fight without screaming *military* or *terrorist* to a casual observer. Light flexible body armor of the latest nanotube variety didn't bulk them out unduly, and for once the Power wouldn't be with the other side. The weapons were Tavors, Israeli machine carbines with a full suite of sensor sights, and grenade launchers; the silver-inlaid and warded knives were a backup this time. Ellen had her sniper rifle, and they all wore comm headsets.

Salvador grinned as he slapped a magazine into his stubby assault rifle. "Like old times," he said.

Adrian shook his head. "We are still at a disadvantage in a straight-up fight. In and out without violence is best."

"How?" Cheba said skeptically. "The *brujos* are gone, but there are many guards with guns. The lesser servants are like machines that walk, but some of the others are cunning and watchful. And . . . what do you call them . . . Wreakings in the ground, the walls, the air. I can feel them sometimes, like great hungry beasts, like giant rats scuttling between the walls of the world."

"So," Adrian said, and walked up the ramp into the truck. The vehicle *looked* unexceptional. Inside the ordinary commercial shell was ceramic armor. The padded container within was just big enough for him and his gear. He lay down in it and swung the lid closed, dogging it firmly from the inside. Velvet blackness pressed down on his eyes, impenetrable even to Shadowspawn sight, though not to the Power. He crossed his hands on his chest, hand to opposite shoulder, and cleared his mind of all but the glyphs he sought.

"Amss-aui-ock!"

All of the humans bristled a little as he sat up through the lid and carefully came erect and walked down the ramp. A night-walker spoke to fears far below knowledge. Salvador was sweating a little; he was newer to this than the others . . . except Cheba, who jumped back a little.

"So?" she said. "How will this help?"

"I was going to go into the *casa grande* like *this*," he said.

And changed. Then she was looking at herself, naked. She spat something in a language that was not Spanish, and forced herself not to back away as he/she approached.

"You have changed a little," he said, studying her with vision and the Power. "You are in better condition . . . several teeth capped, no need to imitate that . . . no calluses on your hands. . . ."

He closed his eyes and sought inward. The DNA template simply gave you the adult form of the organism at maturity, with optimum development; modifying it to mimic somatic changes caused by an individual's life history was considerably more difficult. Even a little clumsiness could kill the pseudobody, which meant you had to start over . . . and subjectively experience death, as well, even if only for an instant, and a chance of the Final Death if you were really careless. The others stared as the hair grew shorter and the face a little thinner.

"There," he said, and opened his eyes. "I could pass for you. But now I have a better option, with your news, señorita."

He smiled grimly and *changed* once more. This was the easiest of all; the body was a Shadowspawn one, and related to him as closely as possible except for a clone or identical twin. Cheba did give a little jump backwards, as Adrienne Brézé grinned at her. Then she closed her eyes for an instant, lips moving.

"Is this correct, Cheba? Our lives may depend on it!"

She moistened her lips and forced herself to concentrate. "The . . . the hair is shorter. It fell out when she was sick and had to grow back. And . . . just a little thinner."

Another careful look as he changed. "Yes, yes, that is right."

"Good." He looked at Guha. "I'll need some of your street clothes; they'll be the right size. Jeans and a T-shirt and a jacket, yes. A Glock and a wrought knife, too. And my Ferrari is something she might have picked up."

Ellen brought him the clothes, and he dressed quickly. The way the body moved was odd, in a way less natural than a beast's, but it wasn't the first time he'd transformed so.

"How do I look?" he said.

Ellen studied him critically. "Tuck the shirt in. And you need some lipstick, just a touch. . . . Here, I'll do it."

"Now?" he said, when her light, deft hands were done.

His voice sounded a little odd to him as a soprano as well.

"Gorgeous, lover!" she said, and gave him a long kiss.

He grinned again as it finished. "I fear you are shocking our recruits," he said.

Ellen cocked a brow at Salvador. "Hey, don't knock it. All the advantages of polyamory and monogamy rolled into one!" Fiercely, to Adrian: "We're going to pull this off."

Adrian nodded. To Cheba: "It is credible that she would bring you in the front door?"

"Yes. Sometimes she takes me places, dates, she calls it. To humiliate me, I think. I don't let it, I just learn how to act in fancy places or wear the clothes. Someday I will have these things of my own."

"She is not a nice person. Let that return to bite her."

"Yes!"

The brooding presence of the *casa grande* grew as the sports car rumbled through the streets of Rancho Sangre. The scent of time, of Power, of generations of blood and terror and unclean death.

"You drive like her," Cheba said, startling him a little. "Very fast, stupidly fast. But very well."

Adrian shrugged. "We are related." A wry smile. "We are mirror images, in a way. Similar, but . . . reversed. Each seeks to destroy the other, because each of us sees what we might have been."

The great wrought-iron gates with their gilded designs of tridents and blackened bronze suns opened automatically. The Gurkha mercenaries snapped to attention, presenting their assault rifles. Adrian nodded at their noncom and followed the winding brick-paved road, with stars showing in flickers through the live oaks arching overhead. Scents of cypress and cut grass and oleander came to them, and wind fluttered their long hair beneath the head scarves.

A servant in a braided white jacket and black trousers hurried out to open the car door.

"Leave it here," Adrian said, with a lordly nod. "Come, my sweet little nibblesome *bizcocho*," he went on, and walked in with an arm around Cheba's waist, feeling the stiff disdain in her body language.

She was supposed to be acting as she would with Adrienne, which he suspected wasn't easy.

Tall doors and the great entry hall went by. He fought down his excitement and his dread, struggling for focus; that was always just a touch harder when he wore a female form, but he was considerably more aware of detail, more able to track multiple lines of thought and action at the same time.

"Assistant household manager," Cheba whispered in his ear as they reached the top of the stairs and the beginning of the corridor that led to the private wing. "Thomas Kenworth. He is the one who really runs the *house*, while Theresa does the bigger things."

A middle-aged man, cadaverous, with very cold blue eyes. Adrian could sense his blank surprise, and beneath it a very thin thread of suspicion. Not yet conscious, manifesting only as a feeling of unease, and anyone who wasn't uneasy around Adrienne wouldn't last long. And this one had some sensitivity; not trained, but he *felt* as if he were a little over twenty on the Alberman, nearly as strong as Harvey. Adrian's night-walking manifestation was very strong; there were times when he forgot he was not embodied in this state himself. But there were ways to detect it, if you knew how.

"*Doña,*" the man said, bowing. "This is unexpected!"

"Predictability is so *boring*," Adrian said. "Of course, it wouldn't do for *you* to go off on tangents, Thomas, but that's another matter, eh?"

A flash of fear. "How may I serve you?"

"I decided that my nights would be too lonely without athletic little Cheba here, so I ducked back to fetch her. And the children; they should be present at the historic moment. Send someone to pack their things, immediately."

"But, *Doña*—"

A touch of ice, and a painful tug at the man's mind. "Is there a problem with *immediately*, Thomas? I'll go through to the nursery, and I would appreciate it if I didn't have to wait. You know how waiting upsets me."

The man hastened off, pulling his phone from his belt as he did.

Adrian suppressed an impulse to blow out a sigh of relief and wipe his brow. He didn't hurry either, instead strolling along and remembering to sway slightly.

"That was as she would do it," Cheba murmured. "But she did not threaten so very often. Sometimes she would just kill instead. Mostly she would smile, and order, and they all obeyed very quickly."

Adrian nodded jerkily. *I must remember that my Adrienne is* my *vision. Not untrue, but not all the truth of another being.*

They turned down the long corridor . . . and Adrian flung himself backwards, his arms outstretched. Cheba turned to him, her face puzzled as his gaze went to the tile surround that outlined the arch, and down to the floor. The way was closed by two doors of gilded bronze fretwork, but that was not the problem; they were light and not locked.

"What is the problem?" she said. "The children's quarters are beyond here."

Adrian hissed as the hint of pain ran along his nerves. One step farther . . . His stomach lurched a little as he read the twisting paths grouped around the portal. He had felt something like this at Ellen's apartment, over a year ago, when his sister had left a trap for him. A probability cascade, an avalanche of *might-be*s, each more disastrous and deadly than the last. He relaxed the focus of his eyes, his hands moving in small, precise gestures, murmuring Mhabrogast beneath his breath, *Seeing*.

But that had been an improvisation. This was something that had taken days or weeks, great skill, and several lives. It was so complex that it was almost sentient, alive in its own way, a thing like an eternal scream, ready to lock you in its arms and spiral down the slope of entropy on a journey that would never end.

"What?" Cheba said again, sharply.

"You said that you could feel the Wreakings sometimes?" She nodded quickly, her dark eyes going wide. "Well, they are here. Very strong, and some of them new. Like rats in the walls of the world, indeed, and aimed at me—or at my kind, at least. If I had walked beneath that arch with the Power active and hostile intent, neither of us would have left here alive."

"What do we do?"

"You fetch the children; it is not keyed to normal humans, and I think it *is* keyed pass to you specifically. I will wait here. Quickly now!"

Cheba walked through the familiar rooms with their cheery, horrible murals. Past one where the Little Mermaid dragged the Prince beneath the waves with strong cold arms and a contented little smile, and into the big play chamber. Shrill voices sounded, and one of the nannies was there reading a magazine.

"Hi, Cheba!" she said. "The little devils are hard at it." She yawned. "I do wish they slept at the same times as the rest of us. They'll be going strong after midnight."

Cheba nodded and made herself smile, not daring to speak. The danger was like a snake coiled in her stomach, making her skin flush hot and cold. Hate drove her, the memory of laughter and unendurable pain and loathsome pleasure that was even worse eating at her soul.

The playroom was big, nearly as big as her whole house, and that was huge compared to anywhere she'd ever lived before. There was a great complex dollhouse, and a jungle gym and trampoline and who knew what else. A small form caromed into her and threw her arms around her waist.

"Caught you!" Leila said. "Hi, Cheba! Now I eat your brains!"

"We're playing Zombie Apocalypse, Cheba!" Leon called happily, lumbering with his arms outstretched. *"Braaaiiins!"*

A deep breath and she smiled. "You cannot eat my brains tonight, *mi reinita*," she said to Leila, rubbing her head. "Your mother is here to fetch you and Leon. She has decided that you should go on her trip with her after all, and me too."

"Why are you so scared, Cheba?" Leila asked innocently. "You feel all fizzy and scared."

"Your mama scared me," she replied; which was entirely plausible; they knew about that, if not the details.

"Oh. I hope you taste good when she bites you; you need to be bitten, I can feel it. C'mon, Leon. It's *Maman!*"

"Oh, good!" Leon said. Then, curiously: "Is it about our dad?"

Cheba froze, then cleared her throat. "Why do you think that, *patroncito?*"

"Because I asked *Maman*, and she said that we might see our father sometime soon. I'd like that."

"Perhaps you will," she said, and he nodded solemnly; she was unpleasantly conscious that he could probably read the truth in her statement.

But he cannot read my thoughts. That does not come to them while they are children. Feelings yes, thoughts no.

"Come! Your mother is impatient."

"The children's luggage is ready and has been loaded into your car, *Doña*," the man Thomas said; he looked as if he were slightly out of breath.

Then he blurted out: "Why are you here, *Doña?*"

His eyes lifted to the archway. Then they went wide; Adrian could feel the logic chains shifting in his mind. His mouth had just begun to open when the Shadowspawn drew and fired.

Crack!

A small blue hole appeared in the man's forehead; bone fragments and pinkish gray brain, blood and hair spattered on the pale surface of the wall behind him. The ricochet peened away from the stone, flicking a divot of plaster and revealing the limestone block beneath as it keened down the passageway.

Killing him with the Power would have been quieter, but it might have activated the guardian Wreakings . . . and he would need all his reserves before they got away, probably. Cheba stumbled to a halt with a boy and girl on either side of her, her hands resting on their shoulders. Adrian's heart lurched for an instant at the sight of their faces; then control clamped down steely cold.

"You're not my *maman*—" the girl began, as the boy gazed gape-mouthed at the dead man.

"*Tzi-ci-satza,*" Adrian snarled, and made a gesture with his left hand. Push *with the mind . . .*

The children's eyes rolled up in their heads, and their minds plummeted down into something *almost* like natural sleep. He'd expected that, hoped for it; Shadowspawn children were often prekeyed for that, with Wreakings laid on in earliest toddlerhood. He had been, and Adrienne as well; removing it had been part of their training when they neared puberty. Cheba gave a cry of dismay and clutched at the small forms, cushioning their fall to the carpet.

"They're all right," Adrian snapped. "Asleep, merely. You carry the girl. Hurry, an alarm has gone off!"

"But—"

"They will not shoot and endanger Adrienne's children, they know she would flay them by inches for the rest of eternity. *Go!*"

A seven-year-old was more of a burden than he'd anticipated; Adrienne's body was very strong for her size, but that size was a fifth less than his. The utter limpness helped; his heart started to turn again, as the boy's face drooped into the curve of his neck.

No time, no time . . .

They took the distance at a quick walk. Adrian could feel the electronic nerves of the security system shrilling; he split off part of his mind to *push—*

Wires melted, arcs sprang between conduits. Redundant systems came online as the lights flickered, but some of those failed too. Cheba gasped but toiled along behind him. Servants fled his shout of, "Get out of my way!"

The guards at the front door hesitated just a moment too long, caught between the impossibility of firing and the knowledge of what would *also* happen if they let their mistress' children be abducted.

Crack! Crack!

Both flipped backwards and slumped to the ground; at ten yards he could manage head shots. He dropped the Glock and scooped up the Steyr assault rifle in one hand as they stumble-ran down the long steps.

"Alert! Alert! Intruder is not *Doña* Adrienne! The *Doña's* children have been captured! Alert! Aleeeiaeoughtg—"

The loudspeakers exploded in cascades of flame. Adrian staggered; he was using the Power with reckless abandon. They dropped the children into the Ferrari's narrow backseat.

"I will hold them!" Cheba snapped, and scrambled in to kneel facing backwards, her arms bracing the small forms.

Adrian vaulted into the driver's bucket seat of the sports car, his foot stamping on the accelerator. The turbocharged engine screamed like a horse in agony, and the rear wheels spun black smoke into the night. Lights were snapping on all across the estate grounds as the acceleration punched him back into the padding; he could hear Cheba grunt as she threw herself forward to pin the children safely in place against inertia.

He took the curving approach with insane daring, mind like a needle point of diamond as he pushed at the probabilities even as his body switched wrists on the wheel and worked the shift-stick. The last stretch was level . . . right to the firmly closed and locked gates. The covers on the stone gate pillars had flipped up, and the tele-operated robot guns were tracking him. He grinned like a shark and stood on the brake, turning in a skidding pinwheel that came within a hair of flipping the car as it scrubbed off velocity. The air stank of burning rubber and burning fuel oil and the sweat of terror, a scent that made the hairs stand up along his neck in a predator's bristle. Cheba was screaming now, but he could feel how she still braced herself with everything that was in her.

She is almost as brave as Ellen, some remote part of him thought.

The operators of the guns at last dared to fire one economical burst directly into the long hood of the Ferrari. The engine seized just as the nose came around to point at the gate once more. The two guards had thrown away their rifles, and they were running at him with their heavy kukris raised, the in-curved chopping blades glinting where their silver inlays caught the floodlights. Their minds were like eyes that had looked into the sun, but their training and the warrior souls within kept them moving; their reflex was to run *towards* danger.

Even as the car slowed Adrian was moving. Forward, letting his clothes fall away as he reverted to his own default form, impalpable as he passed through the windshield. Then another change in midleap, and the sabertooth gave a screaming roar; and for an instant Adrian understood in his bones how his ancestors had ruled the world for a hundred thousand years.

He landed as delicately as a house cat pouncing for a butterfly, and one plate-broad paw slammed hooked claws across a mercenary's face and throat, the dewclaw ripping half the scalp free. The man gave a bubbling shriek and spun away to die with his face swiped away like a putty mask, leaving only red bone and grinning teeth and staring eyes above a spouting tear in the throat.

"Ayo Ghorkali!" the second man shouted, and struck.

A half ton of carnivore slammed into his chest as the blade came down, and a razor edge of silver sliced into the skin over Adrian's spine. In the same instant his bear-thick forearms closed around the man, ripping at the body armor that covered his back, shredding it. The six-inch fangs stabbed down as the grip positioned the prey. Crisp popping sensations as the serrated ivory steak knives drove deep.

Blood foamed across his mouth, irresistible, wine of terror and effort. He allowed himself six long swallows, and felt new strength course through him. When he rose it was as a naked man whose face dripped a red that was almost black in the flickering light.

Two lances of fire from outside the estate wall rammed into the robot turrets and they exploded in flame and smoke-trailing fragments. Half a second later the reinforced bumper and grille of the van rammed the gates. Tortured steel snapped, and the great portals buckled enough to let a man through. It wasn't a man, though; Guha came instead, running towards the wrecked car whose hood was wreathed in fire. Adrian turned; a platoon of Gurkhas was double-timing down the roadway towards him, spread out in a rough skirmish line with their kukris raised. As he saw them they broke into a charge.

His hands went up. *"Aki, tzeeen, alalaaal!"* he screamed, the Mhabrogast tearing at his throat, turning his mind into a set of lethal razors.

Four of the Gurkhas simply dropped in their tracks; hearts locked in spasm or brains flooding from burst veins. Another two began hacking at each other madly; and two rifles exploded as the propellant in the cartridges spontaneously ignited. The others wavered for an instant, then came on still faster. Adrian staggered with the effort, wheezing suddenly as the stolen strength of the dead soldier's blood flowed out of him again. For a moment his night-walker's form flickered, and he was a pillar of mist with yellow eyes, until it steadied again.

A heavy machine gun cut loose behind him, tracers snapping by overhead; Jack Farmer was shooting from the hatch on the vehicle's roof, screaming:

"Die, you cocksucking traitors, die, motherfuckers, die, die!"

His shooting was much less frenzied than his shout, or the emotions pouring off him. Men died; the .50 caliber made nothing of infantry armor, especially at this range, blasting through and turning bodies into tumbling bags of smashed bone and flesh or ripping off limbs. Ellen was out of the van too, her sniper rifle snapping off rounds as she braced it through a gap in the gate. The .338 Lapua rounds were silver-cored, which didn't matter, and heavy and moving fast, which did. She worked the bolt methodically, swayed back a little with the recoil, set herself, picked another target through the night-vision scope, breathed out, fired.

Cheba ran past with Leila in her arms. Salvador met her at the gap in the buckled gate, snatched the child and practically hurled her through, and then into the vehicle. Guha was close behind her when one of the Gurkhas at last lost control and began shooting, a long burst that walked tracer towards her.

Adrian groped for the Power, but he was spent. Guha saw the burst coming and dropped, curling her body around Leon's small form and wrapping herself in a protective shield. Three of the light high-velocity bullets smacked into her back with sounds like fists striking meat. Little spots flecked up on her clothing, and the armor beneath was the light law-enforcement type. She sprawled, blood draining from mouth and nose.

Adrian took three paces and heaved her over his shoulder. Ellen was beside him, rifle discarded; she grabbed for his son and dragged the boy backwards out of the pool of blood, throwing him into a fireman's carry. Together they struggled through the wreckage of the gate. Adrian tossed Guha's limp form into the van, and dove after her.

Blackness.

"Had the devil of a time getting you out of that steel coffin before you smothered," Farmer grumbled, looking down at the plastic cast on his arm. "That's where I got this from a stray round, and the ricochet hit Cheba in the thigh. We weren't even sure your etheric form had made it back to the meat body. Then the black helicopter spiraled in and we piled in. . . . God, what a movie it would make."

Adrian smiled thinly. He still felt as if every inch of him had been beaten with clubs until his skin came off and then he was dipped in acid; that was what you got for overusing the Power. Even a private feeding with Ellen had made him feel only a *little* better, enough to keep down some of the Brotherhood's shanghaied Red Cross blood. The institutional beige-and-brown atmosphere of the safe-house hospital wasn't helping either.

"You need help, honey?" Ellen said. "You *could* stay in the wheelchair for this, you know."

Slowly Adrian stood. The rail of the bed rattled a bit as he put out a hand when everything swayed, and then steadied. He opened his mouth to say he could stand on his own, then smiled and let her put an arm around his waist; his went over her shoulders.

"Thank you," he said. "Thank you very much."

"You're welcome. This way. The doctor says she can't say much, but she insisted."

"She saved my son," Adrian said. "She can insist as she pleases."

The hospital was set up in orthodox fashion, until you noticed there were no exterior windows; the rooms opened off a central corridor, with two or three beds in each. Most were vacant; the next held a sullen Cheba, and Eric Salvador sitting in a chair beside her bed being politely implacable about keeping her in it. Beyond that was Guha's.

No convalescence here; it was simple flat-out borderline-fatal injury. Adrian's nose flared slightly at the smell of pain. The doctors thought the agent would live, but three pulverized ribs and a perforated lung were not something you could shrug off. Jack Farmer was speaking as they walked in:

"And you *are* going to take some time off. We never did get to go on that holiday in Mauritius you always talked about. . . . Okay, here he is."

The nurse watching the monitors gave him a warning glance as he nodded.

"Second . . . time . . . save," Guha said breathily as he bent over her.

The painkilling drugs were making her muzzy, but he could feel the effort of will she put forth into mastering it. The tubes rattled a little as she moved one arm slightly.

"Got to tell you. Harvey . . . said not. Owe you. Harvey . . . has the bomb. I . . . can feel . . . you should know. Black-path if you don't. Harvey . . . has the bomb."

"Bomb?" Adrian said softly.

There was an image in her mind. A flash of light . . .

"Used . . . plutonium from the . . . Never mind. Twenty-five kiloton. In Istanbul. To Tbilisi."

Adrian blinked. "What? You could never conceal something like that—"

"Boase. Figured it out. *Got* it. Harvey's taking it to Tbilisi."

Her eyes fluttered closed. The nurse pointed warningly out the door, and Adrian walked—stumbled—in that direction, holding himself up against the jamb. Images strobed through his mind, a wild tangle of possibilities with a dead center where the Power simply *wasn't*.

"Bomb?" Ellen said. "That redneck maniac has a *nuclear bomb*?"

"He's going to try to destroy the Council," Adrian said with soft wonder. "All the most powerful Shadowspawn adepts in one place. That hasn't happened since before Hiroshima. And with Boase's shield to keep it from being detected."

"And it's going to work!" Farmer said with quiet vehemence. "We're going to *win*."

"There are *over a million human beings in Tblisi*, you . . . you *fanatic*!" Ellen began.

Adrian held up his hand. Both of them fell silent, and he stared at the wall. Ellen's hand stole into his and he squeezed it, drawing strength.

"You don't understand," he said. "Either of you. Adrienne is alive. She's been moving behind the scenes all year, and *we didn't know* she was alive. *She must know about the bomb*. She's been playing us like a violin!"

"God," Farmer said, half a grunt, as if he'd been struck.

Ellen made a wordless sound.

"*Harvey* doesn't know she's alive. He has to be told."

Farmer backed up three steps. "He can't be."

"What do you mean?"

"He went into Istanbul and picked it up, and he was going to deliver it under deep cover. I think he was afraid the Brotherhood would change its mind. I don't know how to contact him—and with that thing of Boase's we can't even use the *Power* to trace him."

The three looked at one another. A moment later, Adrian spoke:

"What have we done?"

EPILOGUE

The dun plain of Anatolia stretched out before Harvey Ledbetter, dark and immense, rising to snowcapped mountains in the far distance as the big truck rumbled through the shadows. He whistled tunelessly in the blue glow of the control screen and sipped at a cup of tepid, acrid-strong coffee; his eyelids felt as if sand had been forced underneath, but keeping going through fatigue was the oldest of his skills. Then he began to sing along with the sound system that filled the bubble of warmth.

The tune was an old favorite, Cory Morrow:

> *This is some kind of crazy*
> *You're my favorite kind of lonesome . . .*

Behind him, the bomb was invisible to the eye of the Power. But he knew it was there.

Singing, he drove eastward through the night.

DISCARD